Praise for Marta Perry

"Abundant details turn this Amish... series launch into a... on ...eep

"Crisp writing and d... ...'s latest novel. *Where S...* ...entertaining read."

—*RT Book Reviews*

"Perry's story hooks you immediately. Her uncanny ability to seamlessly blend the mystery element with contemporary themes makes this one intriguing read."
—*RT Book Reviews* on *Home by Dark*

"Perry skillfully continues her chilling, deceptively charming romantic suspense series with a dark, puzzling mystery that features a sweet romance and a nice sprinkling of Amish culture."
—*Library Journal* on *Vanish in Plain Sight*

"*Leah's Choice*, by Marta Perry, is a knowing and careful look into Amish culture and faith. A truly enjoyable reading experience."
—Angela Hunt, *New York Times* bestselling author of *Let Darkness Come*

"*Leah's Choice* is a story of grace and servitude as well as a story of difficult choices and heartbreaking realities. It touched my heart. I think the world of Amish fiction has found a new champion."
—Lenora Worth, author of *Code of Honor*

**Also available from
Marta Perry
and HQN Books**

How Secrets Die

When Secrets Strike

Where Secrets Sleep

Abandon the Dark

Search the Dark

Home by Dark

Danger in Plain Sight

Vanish in Plain Sight

Murder in Plain Sight

MARTA PERRY

ECHO OF DANGER

HQN™

HQN™

ISBN-13: 978-0-373-78927-6

Echo of Danger

Copyright © 2017 by Martha P. Johnson

This edition published by arrangement with Harlequin Books S.A.

For questions and comments about the quality of this book,
please contact us at CustomerService@Harlequin.com.

® and TM are trademarks of Harlequin Enterprises Limited or its
corporate affiliates. Trademarks indicated with ® are registered in the
United States Patent and Trademark Office, the Canadian Intellectual
Property Office and in other countries.

www.HQNBooks.com

Printed in U.S.A.

Dear Reader,

Welcome to Echo Falls, a small Amish and English community in north-central Pennsylvania, where the isolation builds both a strong sense of community and a dangerous habit of keeping secrets. When someone or something threatens to reveal those secrets, the danger can be very real and very deadly.

I love writing about isolated communities, because that creates a sense of danger lurking around every familiar corner. In *Echo of Danger*, Deidre's daily balancing act between her devotion to her child and the task of placating her powerful father-in-law becomes horrifically complicated by the murder of a close friend—in Deidre's own house. Nothing, she finds, can be more dangerous than trusting the wrong person.

Please let me know how you feel about my story. I'd be happy to send you a signed bookmark and my brochure of Pennsylvania Dutch recipes. You can email me at marta@martaperry.com, visit me at www.Facebook.com/martaperrybooks or at www.martaperry.com, or write to me at HQN Books, 195 Broadway, 24th FL, New York, NY 10007.

Blessings,

Marta Perry

This story is dedicated to my husband, Brian,
with much love.

Death isn't the greatest loss in life.
The greatest loss is what dies inside of us while we live.
—Amish proverb

CHAPTER ONE

HER FATHER-IN-LAW SET down the coffee she'd poured for him and glanced around Deidre Morris's sunny, country-style kitchen. "I've found a buyer for your house."

The seemingly casual words, dropped into what had supposedly been an impromptu visit to see his grandson, sent ripples of alarm through Deidre. Her own cup clattered, nearly missing the saucer. "I… What did you say?"

Judge Franklin Morris gave her the look he'd give an unprepared attorney in his courtroom. "I said I've found a buyer for you. He's offering the best price you can expect for a place like this. And you'll be able to move into Ferncliff by the end of the month."

Deidre pressed suddenly cold hands against the top of the pine table that had belonged to her grandparents. She should have guessed that there was something behind this visit. Judge Morris was far too busy to drop in on anyone. And nothing he said was ever casual.

She was going to have to take a firm line, clearly, and that wasn't easy with a man who was accustomed to speaking with the force of law. *Stupid*, she lectured herself. *He can't force you to do anything you don't want to do, even if he is Kevin's grandfather.*

"I'm afraid there's some misunderstanding. I have no intention of selling this house." And certainly not of moving into the chilly mansion where every moment of the day was governed by her formidable father-in-law's wishes.

"I realize you have a sentimental attachment to your family home." He seemed to make an effort to sound patient. "But since you won't have any need of the house once you and Kevin move in with us, selling seems the sensible solution. You can invest the money for the future. However, if you prefer to rent, I suppose that can be arranged." He'd begun to use his courtroom voice by the end of his little speech.

But she was neither a plaintiff nor a defendant. And this house had been home to her family for three generations, now four. "I don't want to rent or sell. This is my home, mine and Kevin's. This is where I plan to live." Surely that was clear enough.

The judge's face stiffened, making it look very much like the portrait of him that hung in the county courthouse, marking his twenty years on the bench. The firm planes of his face, the small graying moustache, the piercing gray eyes—all seemed granted by providence to make Franklin Morris look like what he was, a county court judge.

The chink of a glass reminded her that they were not alone. Kevin sat across from her, his blue eyes huge and round above the chocolate milk that rimmed his mouth. Deidre's heart clenched. A five-year-old shouldn't be hearing this conversation.

"Kevin, why don't you run upstairs and finish the

get-well card you're making for your grandmother. That way Grandfather can take it with him when he goes." She gave him a reassuring smile, wishing someone would send reassurance her way about now.

"Yes, that's right." The judge's face softened into a smile when he regarded his grandson in a way it seldom seemed to do otherwise. Maybe he felt he had little else to smile about, with his only child dead at thirty-two and his wife constantly medicating herself with alcohol. "She'll love to have a card from you."

Kevin nodded, his chair scraping back. Without a word, he scuttled from the kitchen like a mouse escaping the cat.

Her son's expression reminded Deidre of the most important reason why they'd never be moving into Ferncliff. She wouldn't allow Kevin to grow up the way his father had, doubting himself at every turn, convinced he could never measure up to what was expected of him. She turned back to the table to be met by a stare that chilled her.

"Deidre, what is this nonsense? I could understand your reluctance to make a move in the immediate aftermath of Frank's death. But you've had nearly a year. It was always understood that you and Kevin would move in with us. We have plenty of room, and it's the sensible thing to do. With Frank gone, I'm the only father figure the boy will have."

And that was exactly what Deidre feared most. This was her own fault, she supposed. She should have stood firm when the subject had first come up, but she'd still been dazed at the suddenness of Frank's death, unable to come to terms with the thought of the screaming, shrieking crash of his treasured sports car against the bridge abutment.

She hadn't been in any condition then to mount a major battle with the judge, so she'd taken the easy way out, claiming she couldn't possibly make any more abrupt changes in their lives until they'd become accustomed to the tragedy. When both the family doctor and her minister had chimed in with their support, the judge had graciously backed down.

But now it was the day of reckoning. Taking the easy way out had only postponed the inevitable.

"I realize that you hoped to have us close, especially after Frank's death." Deidre chose her words carefully. No matter what damage she considered he'd done to Frank by the way he'd raised him, the judge had lost his only child. "But Frank and I chose to live here, and all of our plans for the future included this house as our home."

"All that has changed now." The judge brushed away the years of her marriage with a sweeping gesture of his hand. "Without my son…" He paused, and she feared his iron control was going to snap.

He'd never forgive himself or her if he showed what he'd consider weakness in front of her, and a spasm of pity caught at her throat. His only child gone, his wife an alcoholic… Small wonder he had all his hopes centered on his grandson.

The judge cleared his throat, vanquishing whatever emotion had threatened to erupt. "I'm only thinking of what's best for Kevin. We can offer him so much more than you can alone. Surely you realize that. An appropriate school, the right background… These things count for something in the world beyond Echo Falls."

Ambition, in other words. That was what he'd wanted for Frank, and he'd never let Frank forget what he'd supposedly given up by coming back to Echo Falls and marrying her instead of going out into the glittering future his father had wanted for him.

But she could hardly use that as an argument with her father-in-law. "Kevin's only five. There's plenty of time to be thinking about the right school for him. At the moment, he needs security, warmth and familiarity in his life, and that's what he has." She saw the argument shaping in his eyes and hurried on. "Please don't think I don't appreciate all that you and Sylvia do for Kevin. You're a very important part of his life and nothing can change that." She managed a smile. "After all, we're less than a mile away as it is."

Less than a mile, yes, but to her mind there was a huge difference between the comfortable family house on the edge of town, surrounded by fields, woods and Amish farms, and the cool, elegant mansion on the hill.

Her father-in-law's chair scraped back as he rose, standing rigid to look down at her for a long moment. "I'm sorry you can't see the sense of my offer, Deidre. It would be easier all around if you did."

He turned, stalking without haste from the room, down the hall and toward the front door. Deidre, hurrying after him, reached the door in time to have it close sharply in her face.

Well. Her hands were cold and trembling, and she

clasped them together, needing something to hold on to. Surely she must be imagining what seemed to be a threat in the judge's final words. Hadn't she?

"Mommy?" Kevin scurried down the stairs, waving a sheet of construction paper. "Grandfather left without the card I made."

"I'm sorry, sweetheart. I guess he forgot."

Deidre put her arm around her son to draw him close, taking comfort from his sturdy little body. She held the picture he was waving so she could see it. Kevin had drawn himself, holding a handful of flowers in all sorts of unlikely shades of crayon. He'd printed his name at the top in uncertain letters.

"But my picture…" He clouded up. "I made it especially for Grandma."

"We'll put it in an envelope and mail it to her right now, okay?"

That restored his sunny smile, and Kevin ran to the drop-front desk in the corner of the living room. "I'll get an envelope."

"Good job, Kev. I know this will make Grandma feel better."

She hoped. A report that Sylvia was ill usually meant that she'd gotten hold of something to drink. Once started, she couldn't seem to stop. Much as Deidre grieved for Sylvia, she didn't mean to expose Kevin to the difficulties inherent in living with her.

That was one more reason why the judge's plan was impossible. She just wished she could get rid of the sinking feeling that Judge Franklin Morris didn't give up on anything until he had what he wanted.

JASON GLASSMAN HAD been in Echo Falls, Pennsylvania, for less than twenty-four hours, and already he was wondering what he was doing here. He'd elected to walk the few blocks from his new apartment to the offices of Morris, Morris and Alter, Attorneys-at-Law, so he could get a close-up look at the town that was supposed to be home from now on.

Small, that was one word. He'd imagined, given that Echo Falls was the county seat, that there'd be a bit more to it. It was attractive enough, he supposed. Tree-shaded streets, buildings that had stood where they were for over a hundred years and would look good for a hundred more, a central square whose fountain was surrounded with red tulips on this May day.

He passed a bookshop and spotted the law practice sign ahead of him. Morris, Morris and Alter would, if all went as planned, be changing its name to Morris, Alter and Glassman before long. He should be grateful. He *was* grateful, given that the alternative would have been practicing storefront law in a city where everyone knew he'd escaped disbarment by the skin of his teeth and where disgrace dogged him closer than his shadow.

He didn't often let the memories flood back, keeping them away by sheer force of will. Now he let them come— a reminder of all he had left behind in Philadelphia.

He'd gone to the office unsuspecting that morning, kissing Leslie goodbye in the apartment building lobby as they headed toward their separate jobs—he at the prosecutor's office, she at a small, struggling law firm.

And he'd walked into a firestorm. The materials that had been so painfully collected as a major part of the

prosecution of George W. Whitney for insider trading
and racketeering had unaccountably been compromised.
Someone had given away their source, who was now
swearing himself blue in the face that he'd never been in
touch with Jason Glassman, that the records had been al-
tered, presumably by Glassman and that the whole case
was a put-up job designed to vilify a valuable and civic-
minded citizen.

The case lay in shreds at their feet. All the hours of
tedious work, all the manpower that had been poured
into it, were wasted. The district attorney had needed
to find someone to blame, and he hadn't gone far. Jason
had found himself out of a job and lucky to escape arrest.

Disappear, the district attorney had said. *Don't give
statements to the press, don't try to defend yourself,
and we won't pursue criminal charges or disbarment.*

A devil's agreement, he'd thought it, but he hadn't
had a choice. He'd left the office, driven around in a
daze, had a few drinks, which hadn't helped, and finally headed for home, trying to think of how to explain all this to Leslie.

But Leslie hadn't been there. All of her belongings
had vanished, and she hadn't bothered leaving a note.
Clearly she'd heard and decided it was too dangerous to
her career to continue an association with him.

He'd thought that was all it was, and that disappointment had been bad enough. It was three days before he
learned that Leslie was now an associate at Bronson and
Bronson, the very firm defending George W. Whitney.

So all those nights when he was working at home,
when she'd leaned over his shoulder looking at his prog-

ress, offering suggestions and support, had just been so much camouflage for an elaborate betrayal.

He'd been incensed. But when his first attempt to confront her had resulted in a protection-from-abuse order being filed against him, he'd had just enough sense left to cut his losses. The last he'd seen of her had been an elegant, expensively dressed back disappearing into the recesses of Bronson and Bronson while he was dragged away by security guards.

And here he was in Echo Falls, Pennsylvania.

Jase paused, hand on the door of the firm's office. Franklin Morris had made a generous offer to his son's law school classmate, especially since Jason and Frank had never been close. But Jase knew perfectly well that Judge Morris wanted something in return.

The receptionist seated behind the desk in the spotless, expensively furnished outer office was fiftyish, plumpish and looked as if she'd be more at home baking cookies than juggling the needs of a busy law practice, but the judge had said she knew more about the law than most young law school graduates. She greeted him with a smile and a nod of recognition. Word of his arrival had obviously preceded him.

"Mr. Glassman, of course. I'm Evelyn Lincoln. Welcome to Echo Falls. The judge is waiting for you." Not pausing for a reply, she led the way to a paneled oak door bearing Franklin Morris's name in gilt letters, tapped lightly and opened it. "Mr. Glassman is here, Your Honor."

He followed her in, not sure what welcome to expect.

"Jason, I'm pleased to see you again." Morris's smile

was polite but restrained, suggesting that it was up to
Jase to be sure this was indeed a pleasure. "Come in."
Without rising from behind the massive cherry desk,
he nodded to the leather client's seat.

"Thanks. And thank you, as well, for lining up the
apartment for me."

Judge Morris waved the gratitude away. "Evelyn took
care of all that. You've met her already. Trey Alter, my
associate, is out of the office today, dealing with another matter for one of our clients."

"I look forward to meeting him." He'd been wondering how Alter would react to the judge's hire.

"You'll want to take some time to move into your office and get up-to-date on the cases we have in hand,"
he continued briskly. "Trey will be relieved to have
someone to share the load, since my judicial responsibilities keep me from taking a more active role."

Jase nodded. Judge Morris couldn't be involved in
anything that might conceivably appear before his court,
but that still left plenty of work. It had been assumed
that the judge's son would take over, but his death had
changed things. There was obviously a need here.

He just wasn't convinced that he was the right man
to deal with it. He suppressed a grimace, thinking that
old sayings became clichés because they were true most
of the time. *Beggars can't be choosers.*

"I've gone over the case material Alter sent me, and
I'm ready to dive in right away." He hesitated, but it had
to be said. "As for the other matter we discussed, it's not
going to be easy to investigate your daughter-in-law in a
town this size, not without making people suspicious."

Morris's jaw tightened. "I don't expect you to mount a stakeout. Something a little subtler is required."

"I see that, but I'm not sure what you think I can do." Jason tried to keep his distaste for the strings that had been attached to the job offer from showing in his voice.

Swinging his chair around, the judge reached out to grasp a framed photo from the shelf behind him. He thrust it across the desk so that Jase could see it clearly. "My son. And my grandson." The boy was hardly more than a toddler in the picture, face still round with baby-hood curves. Frank hadn't changed much from law school, still a good-looking guy, attractive to women, but with an ominous weakness about his mouth and chin.

Judge Morris paused, emotion working behind the facade of his judicial face. "Deidre was never good for Frank, never. He had a brilliant future here, could have become the youngest county court judge we've ever had. But she didn't encourage him. From the day they married, she tried to separate Frank from his family."

Not that unusual a story, was it? In-law relationships were notoriously dicey. Jase sought for a way to deliver an unpalatable truth. "Even so, I'm afraid that's not a basis to file for custody of your grandson…"

"I do know something about the law." Morris's tone was icy. Maybe he realized it, because he shook his head quickly. "Of course not. My goal isn't to take Kevin away from Deidre. She *is* his mother, after all. But she's always been rather unstable, subject to irrational likes and dislikes, making quick decisions that end up hurting someone. If Frank were alive, he could serve as a balance to that…but he's not, and I'm determined to do what I can to protect his son."

This was becoming more unpalatable every minute. But how did he say no to someone who'd just given him his future back? "If you don't intend to sue for custody, then what?"

"Leverage." Judge Morris pronounced the word heavily. "I need leverage to convince Deidre that she and Kevin should move in with us. Once that happens, we'll be able to provide the stability and the good life the boy needs. Without a father, subject to his mother's whims… Well, I'm concerned about what will become of him."

It sounded like the kind of messy, emotional case that had sent him into specializing in financial fraud, where the only emotion involved was greed. "Naturally you're worried about your grandson. But I'm not sure what I can do."

"Deidre is having an affair with a married man." His expression was harsh with condemnation. "At least, that's what my son thought. For all I know, that might have been what sent him speeding into a concrete wall. Find me proof, and I'll know what to do with it."

"If you're sure of your facts…" he began.

Judge Morris stood abruptly, the framed photo in his hands. He stood at the window, staring down at the photo and then setting it back on its shelf, centering it carefully.

"In my position, I have to be careful. It wouldn't do for a county court judge to be seen as collecting evidence against his own daughter-in-law. I don't expect you to shadow her or sneak around taking photographs. You're close to Deidre in age, living right next door. It shouldn't be hard to gain her confidence and keep an eye on the situation."

He caught Jase's expression and gave a thin smile. "It wasn't a coincidence that Evelyn rented the apartment in the old Moyer house for you. Deidre's family home is the white colonial to the left as you face the house."

"The place with the swing set in the backyard." He could hardly help noticing it. His bedroom windows overlooked the property. Obviously the judge's staff work was excellent. "There's no guarantee that I can find anything to help you," he warned.

Judge Morris gave a curt nod. "I accept that. Don't imagine that your position here is conditional on success." A muscle in his jaw worked. "Deidre is a manipulative woman who betrayed my son. I have to keep her from damaging my grandson."

Manipulative. Betrayed. Did Judge Morris know that those words would strike fire in him? Maybe, maybe not, but it didn't really matter. He already knew what his answer had to be.

"All right. I'll do my best." Now his jaw clenched. He didn't have a very good track record when it came to outwitting a manipulative woman. But this time, at least, he was forewarned.

DRESSED FOR HER evening meeting, Deidre peeked into Kevin's room. He'd been determined to stay awake until the arrival of Dixie, her neighbor, who'd offered to babysit tonight. But he was already sound asleep. She tiptoed to the sleigh bed that had been hers as a little girl and bent to kiss his smooth, rounded forehead. Kev slept with abandon, as always, one arm thrown over his head and his expression concentrated.

"Sweet dreams," she whispered.

She'd told him that the bed, with its curved headboard and footboard like an old-fashioned sleigh, had always brought her good dreams. Maybe it worked for Kevin, too. Although he sometimes woke up in the middle of the night, he never seemed frightened, going back to sleep as quickly as he'd wakened.

Leaving the door ajar so Dixie would hear him if he called out, Deidre hurried downstairs, glancing at her watch. This first meeting of the Echo Falls Bicentennial Committee would probably be a fractious one, with representatives of every segment of town life in attendance. She'd promised to arrive early at the library and start the coffee—one of the inevitable chores falling to the only person on the library board who was under seventy.

A tap on the front door heralded Dixie's arrival, and she came in without waiting for Deidre to answer. "Am I late?"

She slung her jean jacket over the nearest chair and pushed her black hair over her shoulders with a characteristic gesture. She eyed Deidre's tan slacks, blue shirt and camel sweater with disappointment. "You look as if you expect this meeting to be boring. Why don't you spice things up a little?"

Dixie herself wore a scarlet tank top that clung to every curve of her body. Her voluptuous body, Deidre amended. When they'd been kids together, and every other twelve-year-old girl had been straight as a board, Dixie had seemed to mature overnight into someone who'd befuddled the boys in their class and even drawn covert looks from a few male teachers.

Even though Dixie had returned after years away, divorced and apparently ready to start over, some things hadn't changed. She still attracted males like a magnet. After all, single women their age were a rarity in Echo Falls.

"I'm representing the library board, remember? Besides, I don't have the figure to wear something like that outfit." She nodded to Dixie's bright top and formfitting jeans.

Dixie tossed her hair back, laughing. "Sure you do. And I'd like to see the expressions on the old girls' faces if you turned up in this."

One thing about Dixie...she never apologized for anything she wore, said or did. It must be nice to feel that confident. Deidre never had, and she'd settled for an updated version of her mother's style, typically small town, middle-class and designed not to raise a single eyebrow.

"I'm almost ready, and Kev is sleeping. I promised him you'd come in and kiss him good-night, but I didn't promise you'd wake him up." She retrieved her cell phone and tucked it into her bag.

"Okay, will do." Dixie picked up the television remote but didn't switch the set on, a sign she had something to say. "Did you see the new tenant next door yet?"

"Someone moved into the second-floor flat at last?" The old Moyer place had been converted into three apartments, with Dixie renting the top floor. "I hope they're not going to be noisy."

"Not they, he. Thirtyish, single and sexy. Just what we need in the neighborhood."

Deidre gave her a look. "Had a long chat with him, did you?"

Dixie grinned. "We barely exchanged two words. But believe me, I didn't need conversation to make up my mind about him. Lean, dark and tough-looking. He's the brooding, dangerous type, and that suits me fine."

She could only hope Dixie didn't intend to launch herself headlong into a new romance. Her past was strewn with the guys she'd been convinced were the real thing. Needless to say, they hadn't been.

"Who is this paragon? And what brings him to Echo Falls? Maybe you'd better be sure he's going to hang around before you make a dead set at him."

"That's the thing." For a moment Dixie looked uncertain, an unusual expression for her. "I hear he's actually the new lawyer in your sainted father-in-law's firm." Dixie gave her a sidelong look. "You hadn't heard?"

No, she hadn't heard. Silly, to be bothered by the news that someone was taking Frank's place. After all, it had been almost a year, and the firm was constantly busy.

"I knew they needed someone, but didn't know they'd made a decision. Funny that the judge didn't mention it when he was here today."

She didn't think her expression had changed at the mention of that visit, but Dixie knew her well.

"What's he up to now?" She held up a hand to stop

Deidre's protest. "Don't bother denying it. The judge is always up to something, isn't he?"

Deidre shrugged. It would be a relief to vent to someone, and she and Dixie had been friends long enough for her to know Dixie was safe. "The same conversation we had before. I thought it was settled, but apparently not. He wants us to move in with him and Sylvia." A chill slid down her spine at the thought.

Dixie abandoned her lounging posture on the sofa to sit bolt upright, anger flashing in her dark eyes. "You can't be considering it. Move into that mausoleum? I'd rather be dead."

"No, of course I'm not considering it. If I wouldn't move in there when Frank was alive, I'm certainly not going to do it now. I couldn't raise Kevin in that..." She couldn't find a suitable word that was compatible with her sense of politeness.

"Mausoleum," Dixie repeated. "Good. Don't you even think of giving in to him."

"I'm not," she protested. "But you know what the judge is like."

"He's a boa constrictor." Dixie spat out the words with more than her usual emphasis. "Get caught in his coils, and the next thing you know you'll be digested, just like that poor wife of his."

"Sylvia has other problems. I'm not sure her husband can do much for her."

"He's probably the one who drove her to alcohol to begin with," Dixie muttered. "And you know how he treated Frank when he was growing up. You can't let him get his hands on Kev."

"I'm not going to." She didn't know when she'd seen Dixie so passionate. "All I have to do is keep saying no. He can't force me. Honestly, Dixie, there's no need to get so upset about it."

"You're too trusting, you know that? You think everyone's as nice as you are. They're not."

Dixie's reaction was fueling her own, and she had to look at this sensibly. "I've got to get going. Again, thanks so much for staying with Kev. And don't worry about the judge. I'm not. Really."

Deidre reminded herself of those brave words as she drove to the public library, just off the square in Echo Falls, and pulled into the parking lot behind the building. No worrying. Obsessing about Judge Morris's plans wouldn't do any good.

She shifted her focus firmly to the upcoming meeting. At least she wasn't the first arrival. The lights were already on, a welcome given the fine mist that was forming.

She picked up the tote bag with the coffee and doughnuts and ducked through the mist to the back door, hurrying inside. In the flurry of greeting people and getting the refreshments ready, she managed to shove Judge Morris firmly to the back of her mind. Like Scarlett, she'd worry about that tomorrow.

The meeting was being held in what was normally a quiet reading area in front of the fireplace. Folding chairs had appeared to supplement the sofa and love seat donated by some library patron who'd probably been redecorating. Concentrating on refilling the doughnut tray, Deidre didn't notice that someone was coming toward her until he spoke.

"Hard at work as always, I see." Adam Bennett, the pastor of Grace Church, was mature enough to be aware of the status his collar gave him and young enough to be made a bit uncomfortable by it. He flushed now, as he often seemed to when he spoke to her.

"Not very," she said, smiling. "Will you have a doughnut?"

"No, no, thank you." He shied away as if his wife had lectured him about the dangers of fatty foods. "I wanted to introduce someone to you. Deidre, this is Jason Glassman, the new associate in Judge Morris's office."

For an instant Deidre could only stare at the man who'd come up behind Adam. Brooding and dangerous-looking indeed, as Dixie had said. His tailored suit and tie would be more at home in a big-city office, and his lean face gave one the impression of a man stripped down to the essentials and ready for action. There was nothing casual about the assessing look he turned on her, and she was suddenly aware of the sticky icing on her fingers.

When in doubt, take refuge in good manners, her mother always advised. Deidre wiped her hand on a napkin before extending it.

"Mr. Glassman, it's a pleasure to meet you. I'm sure my father-in-law is relieved to have someone to…" She'd started to say *assist*, but this man didn't look as if he'd ever been an assistant to anyone. "To take over the extra caseload. I know the office has been very busy."

"Please, call me Jason." His deep voice held nothing more than conventional courtesy, but the clasp of his hand lingered a bit too long, and his dark eyes studied and probed, as if to warn he'd know everything about her before he was finished. "I'm just getting settled in. I understand we're neighbors, as well."

"We're all neighbors here in Echo Falls." Adam glanced from one to the other as Deidre pulled her hand away, his voice uncertain. "I was just telling Jason how happy we'll be to have his help with planning the celebration."

"Not planning, just listening. I understand no one else was available tonight, and the judge thought the office should be represented. I'm just holding a watching brief." The way his eyes held hers made it sound as if she were the one he was watching.

Deidre gave herself a mental shake and took a step back behind the protection of the coffee urn. Jason Glassman would have better luck turning his measuring look on Dixie. She'd know just how to respond.

"I see the chairwoman is ready to begin." She nodded toward the fireplace, where Enid Longenberger was shuffling through her notes. "Maybe we'd better take our seats." Busying herself with the arrangement of trays, Deidre gave the two men plenty of time to find chairs before she slipped into one as far away from Glassman's disturbing presence as possible.

What had the judge been thinking? Surely he couldn't picture this man settling into a quiet career in Echo Falls. He looked as if he'd be bored to death in a week. Certainly he did nothing to dismiss that opinion as he sat, eyes half-closed, through the inevitable suggestions, ranging from the mundane to pie-in-the-sky ideas that would only happen if a benevolent billionaire decided to lend a hand.

The meeting dragged on even longer than she'd expected, with Enid obviously determined to give everyone a chance to offer an opinion. Deidre found herself taking surreptitious glances at her watch. Dixie claimed to enjoy staying with Kevin, and she'd never let Deidre pay her, so she made a special effort not to keep Dixie out too late.

Finally, the subcommittees had been assigned, a general outline of ideas approved and the last grumbler had been satisfied. Enid banged down her gavel with an air of decision, and people started filing out the doors, some lingering to rehash the meeting with their friends, as they often did. Deidre kept herself busy clearing up the coffee service as the room slowly emptied. She didn't think Jason Glassman would approach her again, and she didn't want to give him any excuse to do so. Something about the man set her nerves on edge, and she didn't think it was the attractiveness and underlying masculine sexuality that Dixie had obviously noted.

When she went outside, locking the back door behind her, Deidre realized she had dallied almost too long. The lot behind the library was empty except for her sedan, and darker than it usually seemed—or maybe that was just her mood.

The streetlamp in front of the building was blocked by the roof of the library, and the closest one in the other direction didn't extend its light this far. The massive brick block of the bank building on the other side of the lot effectively hid it from view of anyone passing on Main Street, giving it an isolated feeling.

Deidre walked quickly to the car, heels echoing on the concrete, fingers clasped around her keys. She'd never felt unsafe in Echo Falls after dark, and she wasn't going to let an odd case of nerves make her start now. Unlocking the car, she slid in and slammed the door, feeling like a rabbit darting into its hole.

She turned the key in the ignition, listening for the comforting purr of the motor. The engine gave a sputter, a grinding sound and then stopped. Nothing. She tried again. She couldn't have stalled it. But there was still nothing. The engine was dead.

It was pointless to keep turning the key. Fumbling for her cell phone, she tried to come up with the most sensible course of action. If she called the auto club, they'd undoubtedly send someone out from Williamsport, a good thirty miles away, and she'd be stuck here for an hour. She could try one of the people who'd been at the meeting, but they wouldn't be home yet, and she suspected none of them were entered on her cell phone. If Dixie weren't babysitting—

A sharp rap on the window next to her sent her heart jolting into overdrive. She turned to see Jason Glassman peering in at her, his strong-featured face an ominous mask in the dim light.

"Trouble?" He raised an eyebrow, giving his face a hint of caricature, and she was swept with a feeling that trouble was exactly what the man represented.

CHAPTER TWO

JASON TILTED HIS face to the available light, making sure the Morris woman recognized him. With a slight nod, Deidre lowered the window manually, apparently deciding he was trustworthy.

She was wrong. Her car wasn't starting because he'd made sure it wouldn't. Nothing serious. A mechanic would spot the loose connection in thirty seconds, but he was banking on Deidre not even looking under the hood.

"My car is dead." She glanced at her watch. "I can't imagine what's wrong."

He shrugged. "I'm not much of a mechanic, but I'll be glad to wait with you while you call your garage. Or my car is here, and I can easily take you home."

Now she managed a smile. "The garage will have closed at five, and nothing short of a three-car pileup would get George Frazer away from his television at this hour. If you're sure you don't mind…" Deidre was already opening the door.

"Not at all. We're neighbors, aren't we?" So easy. She didn't suspect a thing. Too bad the drive was so short, but at least he'd have some chance of talking with her. "I'm parked out front."

They walked together along the alley toward the street, their footsteps echoing on the concrete. Shadows lay around the building, and it surprised him that Deidre didn't seem warier. Maybe small-town living deadened the instincts.

"I appreciate the offer. It's certainly time I relieved my babysitter."

"Teenagers always have the meter ticking, I suppose," he said lightly, wondering who watched the judge's grandson when she wasn't there.

"It's not that. A friend of mine is staying with my son. I hate to call a teenage sitter on a school night, especially when I think a meeting might be lengthy."

They'd reached his car, and he opened the passenger-side door so she could slide in, then went around quickly to get in and start the car. "It wasn't my imagination then. It did go on and on."

"And on," she said, amusement in her voice. "I'm afraid it wasn't a very good introduction for you. But typical. Everyone has to have their say."

"Even if someone else has already said it." He slanted a smile at her.

"Especially if someone has already said it. No one wants somebody else claiming credit for his or her good idea. I have a theory that the amount of work that gets done is in inverse proportion to the number of people on the committee."

He had to laugh at Deidre's dry tone.

"I shouldn't laugh at them," she said, shaking her head. "They all mean well. I just hate keeping Dixie out late, even though she insists she doesn't mind."

"Dixie?" The name rang a bell. "I think there's a Dixie in my building."

"The same one. Dixie James. We've been friends since kindergarten, although she just moved back to Echo Falls a couple of years ago. Speaking of which, I hope you're settling in all right." She sounded like a good hostess, checking on a guest's comfort.

All in all, he was beginning to wonder if Deidre Morris, with her honey-colored hair and candid blue eyes, wasn't just a little too good to be true.

He suspected a show of candor on his part would win her sympathy. "I don't know if I should bring it up, but I hope...well, I hope it doesn't bother you that I seem to be taking your late husband's position in the firm."

Jase didn't think he imagined a hesitation before she spoke.

"Not at all. I know the firm needed another person. Trey Alter's been overworked, especially during the times when court is in session and the judge is unavailable."

That last bit sounded a tad formal. He should have asked the judge what his current relationship was with his daughter-in-law. If they were in a state of open warfare, he'd have to step cautiously.

He'd been wondering if he should mention her husband or play dumb. But anyone might let it slip that they'd been in law school together. Better play it safe.

"I was sorry to hear about Frank's death. I noticed it in the alumni newsletter. Guess I should have sent a card, but...well, you wouldn't have known who I was."

She turned in the seat to look at him. "Were you a friend of Frank's?" So that had caught her attention.

"A classmate. I was working too hard to have much time to socialize. But he was a nice guy."

"Yes, he was." She didn't sound overtly mournful, but it had been about a year, and she was probably used to dealing with condolences by now. "When you see our son, Kevin, I think you'll notice the resemblance." She was smiling now, maybe at the thought of the kid. "At least, I always thought he looked like Frank, although Frank didn't agree."

"Frank thought he looked like you, did he?"

"He claimed Kev was Pennsylvania Dutch through and through. That's my side of the family, the Wagners. You'll have to get used to all the German-sounding names in an area like this, especially with the number of Amish we have."

She was talking more easily now. He'd made some progress, despite the fact that they were pulling up to the house already. She'd feel as if she owed him a favor, and that would make it easier to pursue an acquaintanceship that the judge seemed to feel would pay off.

Jase drove past his own driveway and turned into hers. "I'll drop you right at the house. No point in walking across the lawn in the dark."

"You don't need…" Deidre stopped, staring.

He followed the direction of her gaze, and his nerves went on alert. The front door of her house stood open. That couldn't be normal.

Deidre grabbed for the door handle, and his hand shot across to arrest the movement.

"Stay here. Call the police. I'll check it out." He slid out of the car, not looking back to see if she'd obeyed him. Something was wrong, and there was a defenseless child in that house.

It took him seconds to reach the porch. Deidre was right behind him, and he didn't waste his breath telling her to stay back. They hit the doorway at the same time, and he grabbed her arm, stopping her from plunging inside.

His gut clenched. A woman lay on the area rug in front of a sofa, blood from a head wound soaking into the fibers. Dixie, he supposed. The child—

Deidre gave an anguished cry that sounded barely human. She yanked free of his restraining hand, running toward the stairway at the back of the room. Then he saw what she had. That small bundle on the bottom step, tangled in a blanket, had to be her son.

DEIDRE STUMBLED TO her knees next to Kevin, reaching for him. Some rational part of her mind shouted for her to be careful, not to move him suddenly.

She had to hold him—had to know he was breathing. Sliding her arms around him, she managed to cradle him against her. His lips were slightly parted, and a gentle breath moved against her cheek. Relief flooded through her.

Please, God. Please, God, let him be all right...

Deidre's fingers found a fluttering pulse. But he was pale...so pale that the faint blue shadows under his eyes looked like bruises.

"Kevin, baby, can you hear me?"

Nothing, but she could see the vein pulsing at his temple.

Someone knelt beside her, and she realized it was Jason. "Careful. Don't move him."

"No. His head…"

Jason bent over her son, seeming to trace the swelling behind Kevin's ear with his gaze. "EMTs are on the way. They'll be here soon. Two ambulances, I told them."

"Dixie…" She hadn't been able to take her eyes off Kevin long enough to look. And now, when she tried, Jason's solid body blocked her view.

"Head injury," he said briefly. "It looks…bad."

Deidre's sluggish wits started to move again at that moment. Kevin must have fallen, but Dixie… How could she have gotten a head injury sitting on the sofa?

"What…what happened to her?" Ridiculous to think that he would know any more than she did.

"Someone hit her. She couldn't have done that much damage falling."

Amazing that he could sound so calm. Dixie had been attacked. How could that be true? That meant that someone had come into her house and done this.

Jason had turned, surveying the room. Looking for evidence? Deidre cradled Kevin closer, trying to control the trembling that had seized her. She had to be strong. She had to be there for Kevin. She couldn't fall apart now. Frank was gone, and she was all Kevin had.

Jason's hand came down on her shoulder, his firm grip steadying her. "It'll be all right."

He didn't sound as if he believed the words. She

didn't. How could anything be all right again when the unthinkable had happened?

Sirens wailed. Jason stood up. "I'll go signal them. Hold on."

Deidre managed to nod. She'd hold on because she had to. She couldn't lose Kevin.

In what seemed a moment, her small living room was filled with people. They'd obviously called out both of Echo Falls's paramedic teams. One surrounded Dixie while the other moved swiftly into place around Kevin.

"You'll need to move back just a little." It was a female voice. "I'm just going to slide your arms out from under him, okay? You don't need to worry. Joe has him."

She must have made some sound as hands pulled her away, because the woman patted her. "Just ease back a bit. You can put your hand on his foot, okay? That way he'll know you're still here."

Her throat was too tight to allow for speech. All she could do was close her fingers around Kev's bare foot, sticking out of the blanket. The superhero pajamas he'd insisted on wearing were getting too small for him. She should get him a new pair. Clinging to the thought was holding her to normalcy for a moment. She held on to a world in which the biggest threat to a small boy was outgrowing his favorite pj's.

The paramedics talked to each other in low tones, and then the woman put her arm around Deidre. "We're going to transport Kevin to the hospital in the ambulance. You can ride with him, okay?"

Deidre nodded, unable to think beyond the moment

and the clasp of her hand around Kevin's foot. Voices murmured in the background, people giving orders, asking questions, making arrangements. All she could do was move when they told her to, watch Kevin being lifted onto a stretcher and maintain a tenuous hold on the feeling that assured her he was still alive.

As they made their way toward the door, someone moved in front of her. A police officer, saying something she couldn't take in, focused as she was on Kevin. Then Jason was deflecting him, drawing him away.

"I was with Mrs. Morris. I'll answer your questions."

Good, because she wasn't going to stop, wasn't going to let anything or anyone separate her from her son.

Lights flashed in the dark outside, turning the trees odd colors. Someone helped her into the back of the ambulance. She slid to a position as close to Kevin as she could get, all her attention focused on him, shutting out everything else. The paramedics murmured to each other, but her mind couldn't seem to sort out the words.

They slid out of the driveway, making the turn toward town and the hospital. The siren wailed, and they sped along. People would be looking out windows, wondering who and what.

Kneeling in the ambulance next to Kevin, Deidre was barely aware of the journey until they came to a smooth stop. She glanced up to see the lights of the emergency room, and then they blurred in a flow of smooth, controlled activity as the doors opened and the ER staff moved to join the paramedics. Kevin was so small—there hardly seemed to be enough space for everyone to work on him.

In seconds they were out on the pavement. As Deidre followed the gurney carrying Kevin inside, another ambulance wailed into the drive behind her. Dixie. She breathed a silent prayer. But Dixie of all people would understand that she had to stay with Kevin.

HALF AN HOUR LATER, she stood alone in the small room set aside for families waiting for news of their loved ones. With its neutral-toned upholstered furniture and muted landscape prints, it had been designed to convey a balance between hope and comfort. She should know—she'd been on the hospital auxiliary committee that decorated it. A discreet plaque on the wall informed anyone who noticed that the lounge had been given through the generosity of Franklin and Sylvia Morris.

She clenched her hands, trying not to give way to fear, to panic. The door opened, and her breath caught. But it wasn't one of the doctors. It was Judith Yoder, her neighbor, her friend. Deidre's control broke, and she stumbled into Judith's outstretched arms.

"Hush, hush." Judith patted her as if Deidre were one of her children. "Don't cry. You must be strong for Kevin. You can be, I know. Let the *gut* Lord help you."

Judith's Amish faith might seem simple to an outsider, but it was bedrock strong and would carry her through anything. It seemed to bolster Deidre's own faltering strength.

Deidre choked back a sob and straightened. She managed to nod. "How did you know?"

"Eli saw the flashing lights from the bedroom window. He could tell it was at your house."

She knew it hadn't been as simple as that. Eli, being a volunteer firefighter, had probably run to the phone shanty to call dispatch and find out what had happened. Then he'd have called an *Englisch* neighbor to drive Judith to the hospital. But nothing would be too much trouble for either of them when a friend needed help.

Judith sat beside her on the sofa, clasping her hands as Deidre spilled out everything that had happened in a probably incoherent stream.

"They took Kevin for tests. I heard someone say to have an operating room ready. I haven't heard anything about Dixie. I don't know what's happening." That was the worst thing—not knowing.

"When someone said a woman had been seriously hurt, I thought it was you." Judith's previously calm voice trembled.

Deidre closed her eyes for an instant, seeing Dixie lying on the rug in her living room. "If I'd been home…" She struggled for breath. "Dixie was only there because she was doing something kind for me."

Judith's grasp of her hands tightened. "Ach, Deidre, you must not start blaming yourself. This is the fault of the person who did it, no one else."

She tried to accept the words, but guilt dug claws into her heart. She hadn't been there. Kevin had been in danger, and she hadn't been there.

Judith seemed to understand all the things she didn't say—the fear, the panic just barely under control. She talked, a soft murmur of words that flowed around Deidre in a comforting stream even when she didn't fully listen.

The door opened and closed as others began to arrive—the judge, gray-faced and controlled, demanding answers no one had; the minister, looking young and uncertain; even Jason, who surely realized he didn't need to be here at all but seemed unwilling to leave.

Deidre roused herself to speak to Jason. "Thank you for your help. I'm sure you'd prefer to go home."

It was her father-in-law who answered. "I've asked Jason to stay, for a time, at least. He can deal with the police and any reporters who show up." His tone implied that any reporter unwise enough to attempt to speak to them wouldn't have a job for long.

One of the aides carried in a tray with coffee and tea. Deidre shook her head, but Judith insisted on fixing her a mug of hot tea with plenty of sugar.

"It will make you feel better. Drink it up, now."

It was easier to obey than to argue. And Judith was right. The hot liquid eased the tight muscles in her throat and warmed her cold hands.

The judge paced. Jason leaned against the wall, solid and apparently immovable. After what seemed an eternity, Kevin's pediatrician, Elizabeth Donnelly, came in, accompanied by a tired-looking older man.

"Deidre." Liz came quickly to clasp her hands. "Kevin's in good hands, and it looks hopeful. This is Dr. Jamison, who worked on Kevin from the moment he came in, and he can explain what's happening…"

"Is the boy going to recover? Is he awake? Does he know what happened?" Judge Franklin rushed into speech, demanding the attention of everyone in the room.

"As Dr. Donnelly said, it looks hopeful." The older

doctor seemed unfazed by the rapid-fire questions. "Kevin has what I would consider a fairly severe head injury, but nothing that we feel requires surgery at the moment. We're monitoring him closely, and we plan to keep him in a medically induced coma for a day or two to help minimize any damage. If the brain should swell, we might need to go in to alleviate the pressure, but if not, we could see a fairly rapid recovery."

Deidre's thoughts had hung up on one word. *Damage.* "Do you mean— Will Kevin have brain damage?"

Liz squeezed her hand. "We just don't know yet. The next twenty-four hours will tell us a lot. Hang in there."

"Thank you." The words were automatic. "Can I see him?"

The two doctors exchanged looks. "For a few minutes, at least," Liz said.

"I'm coming, as well." The judge grasped Deidre's arm, and she thought it was the first time in a year that he'd voluntarily touched her.

She glanced at him, and then looked away. The pain in his face made it indecent to stare.

They followed the doctors down the hallway, and it seemed to Deidre that she was moving as awkwardly as a robot. She had to concentrate on putting one foot in front of the other, and she longed for Frank's presence beside her. But Frank was gone, and he had never seemed so far away.

Then a door opened, and she saw her son. Despite the machines and wires that formed a mechanical cocoon around his bed, Kevin looked as if he were sleeping, his head turned slightly to one side as it always was in slumber. She slipped forward, able to move now that she could see him.

She folded her fingers over his hand. He was alive. Whatever happened, she would deal with it, but Kevin was alive.

Liz moved a chair up to the bed and nudged her into it. "Just sit here with him for a few minutes. Don't attempt to wake him. The nurse may have to ask you to leave at some point. I know I can count on you to cooperate."

Don't make a fuss, in other words. But she wasn't the type to fuss, was she?

Liz turned away, and Deidre reached out to catch her hand. "My friend, the one who was with Kevin, do you know how she's doing?"

Liz's eyes clouded. "I'm sorry. I've been told that Dixie James died without regaining consciousness."

JASE SLIPPED OUT of the waiting room and watched as Deidre and her father-in-law trailed the doctors down the hall. They disappeared from sight into the boy's room. An unaccustomed emotion wrenched at his heart. Poor little guy. Still, things did sound hopeful regarding his recovery.

He'd really been pitchforked into trouble when he'd set out to meet Deidre Morris tonight. There was a bright side to his actions in sabotaging her car—at least she hadn't been alone when she'd made that grisly discovery.

So why did the memory of his actions bring with it a wave of guilt?

Jase glanced back at the waiting room, but he was
too restless to sit in there. He had to talk to the judge as
soon as possible. Given what had happened, he'd surely
want to delay any action against his daughter-in-law,
and Jase would be relieved to be out from under the
burden of that task. Whatever Deidre's other failings,
there'd been no mistaking her anguish over her son.
He didn't doubt that she'd have changed places with
the boy in an instant.

Kevin's injury had been bad enough, but at least it
had looked like an accident. But the woman—that had
been deliberate. He was no expert, but he'd be surprised
if anyone could have survived that blow to the head.
What on earth was going on in this supposedly peace-
ful small town?

The hall was as quiet as a hospital ever was, the
lights slightly dimmed and most of the patient room
doors closed. Two nurses were having a conversation
about their weekend plans at the nurses' station, their
voices as cheerful as if it was the middle of the afternoon.

He moved toward Kevin's room, making little sound
on the tile floor. A talk with the judge was definitely
in order. He'd done his best to answer the cop's questions, automatically not volunteering anything extra.
But the police would have to question Deidre sooner
or later, and if he was meant to represent her, that had
to be clarified.

Pausing, he watched the door, reluctant to make a
move. It swung open, and he had a brief glimpse of the
child on the high, narrow bed, with Deidre sitting next

to him, her eyes intent on his face. Then the door closed as the judge, still gray-faced, approached him.

"Can we have a word?" Jase kept his voice low.

Judge Morris glanced around, nodded and led the way to the window at the end of the corridor, safely out of earshot of the nurses' station.

"How is the boy?" He sounded awkward. Not surprising, since he felt awkward. Dealing with emotion had never come easy to him.

"You heard what the doctor said, so you know as much as I do. It's a matter of waiting." Judge Morris looked as if the concept was completely unfamiliar to him.

"I'm sorry." Jase hesitated. "Under the circumstances, I take it you won't want me to proceed with any further investigation."

Morris's face froze. "Then you take it wrong. It's more important than ever now."

"But with your grandson in the hospital..."

"That's the point," Morris snapped. "Why is he here? Was he injured because something Deidre did put him in danger? I have to know, or how can I protect him?"

Jase got where he was coming from, but at the moment there seemed nothing to tie Deidre to the attack on the woman. "It's possible it was an attempted burglary that turned violent. Nothing to do with either Mrs. Morris or Ms. James."

The judge shook his head impatiently. "A burglar would have seen the lights and known someone was home."

"True, but even so, the violence was directed at Dixie

James." It seemed to him more likely that, if it wasn't a burglary or a random attack, someone had either followed Dixie or had known she was babysitting that night.

"We have too little information to speculate, I suppose." The judge glanced around, as if expecting that information to materialize because he wanted it.

"Deidre is unlikely to do anything to raise questions about her behavior while her son is in the hospital," Jase pointed out, trying to be the voice of common sense.

"I suppose not, but I still want you to represent her with the police. And help her deal with any reporters." The judge turned away, and then turned back as if struck by a second thought. "I'll have a word with the chief of police to make sure he keeps you abreast of what's happening in the investigation. It's best to be prepared."

Being prepared to the judge obviously meant pulling as many strings as necessary to ensure that he took care of his grandchild. Jason couldn't fault his goal, whatever he thought of his methods. In any event, he didn't have much choice.

"All right." Movement down the hall caught his eye. "Looks as if the cops are here." Two officers, one young enough to look as if he were growing into his uniform and the other a silver-haired older man, had just emerged from the elevator.

The judge looked at them and stiffened still more. "Under no circumstances are they to attempt to question my grandson. I won't have his recovery jeopardized by an overeager policeman. See to it."

Jason nodded, privately thinking that not much effort would be necessary. The doctors would no doubt do that job for him. "They'll be wanting to speak to your daughter-in-law tonight. They do have an assault to solve."

"Murder," Morris corrected. "The doctor told us the woman didn't survive. I'll have a word with them on my way out, and I'm relying on you to make sure their questioning is as brief as possible."

Jase nodded. He suspected that would be an easy matter after the judge spoke to them. Judge Morris clearly carried a lot of clout in this town, and the police would be more aware of that than anyone.

He watched as the judge approached the two, spoke for a moment and then gestured to Jase. Obeying the summons, he approached to find himself being surveyed coolly by the older man.

"Chief Carmichaels, Jason Glassman. Glassman is the new associate at the firm. He'll be handling anything necessary for my daughter-in-law."

With a curt nod, the judge stalked to the elevator and pushed the button. Even the elevator obeyed him, opening promptly.

By what seemed to be common consent, the three of them waited until the doors had closed before turning to business. "I hear the boy's in a bad way." Chief Carmichaels's expression softened. "Poor little guy."

"I understand the doctors are hopeful that he'll recover. But they're keeping him in a medically induced coma for the next few days." He trusted he didn't have to spell it out for the man.

Carmichaels nodded. "Meaning we won't know what, if anything, he saw until he comes out of it."

"Maybe not even then," Jase pointed out. "People sometimes have no memory of the events leading up to a head injury. And I doubt you can expect much from a five-year-old, anyway."

"We have to try." Carmichaels's tone was mild, but Jase didn't miss the steel in his eyes. This was a man who would do his job, no matter what anyone said. Still, he'd probably try to do it without antagonizing anyone, which would help.

"As for Mrs. Morris…" Jase began.

"Now, Mr. Glassman, I'm sure a big-city prosecutor like yourself knows we have to talk to her, no matter how inconvenient it might be. This is now a murder case."

In other words, his reputation had preceded him. It would have been foolish to think otherwise.

"She's sitting with her son at the moment." If the chief's words had been a challenge, he wouldn't take it up. "I'm willing to ask her to come out for a few minutes, providing you keep it brief. I was with Mrs. Morris the entire time and probably better able to observe the situation, since I wasn't personally involved."

"I understand you drove her home from a meeting at the library. You went together, did you?" The chief's silver eyebrows lifted slightly, as if it seemed unlikely to him.

"No, I just met Mrs. Morris for the first time at the meeting. Afterward, I noticed she was having trouble getting her car started, so I offered her a lift home."

"And you went into the house with her," Carmichaels added.

"Only because I noticed the door standing open. We city-dwellers are always on alert for signs of a break-in, as you can imagine."

The chief nodded, as if satisfied with that explanation. "If you'll ask Mrs. Morris to give us a few minutes, then we'll get out of the way."

Jason frowned as a thought occurred. "Are you leaving someone on duty here?"

"I don't have a big enough force to spare a man, but I can ask the security guard to check in often. You have a reason to think the child is in danger?" There was an edge to the cop's voice.

"I've only been in town two days. I know next to nothing about the situation, but if the child might be a witness to murder…" He let that trail off, satisfied that he'd made his point.

"We'll make sure he's never left alone." He glanced toward the door meaningfully, and Jase took the hint. He wanted to see Deidre, and he didn't appreciate being told his business by an outsider. Nobody did, but maybe an outsider saw more by virtue of the fact that everything was unfamiliar.

He slipped into the room, pausing for a moment to be sure he wasn't startling Deidre or the boy. But Kevin was deeply asleep, his chest barely rising and falling as he slept, and Deidre looked up immediately at the change in light when the door opened.

"Sorry to interrupt," he murmured. "Chief Carmichaels needs to ask you a few questions. If you'll just come out for a minute or two…" He could see her instinctive response.

"I can't leave Kevin. What if something happens?"

"I'll get someone to stay with him." But even as he spoke, a male nurse, identification plainly displayed, entered the room.

"I'll be here with Kevin for a few minutes." He gave Deidre a reassuring smile. "I'd have to ask you to step out, anyway. And I won't leave until you come back, okay?"

Seeing she had no choice, Deidre removed her hand slowly from her son. She bent over and whispered something to him before coming to Jase.

"It's all right," he said quickly, putting a hand on her elbow. If she got any paler, she'd be whiter than the sheets. "I'll make sure the cops don't overstay their welcome."

She looked up at him then, meeting his gaze with a look of surprise and gratitude that startled him. "You shouldn't have gotten involved in this at all. If you hadn't been so kind as to give me a lift, you could have been safely home by now."

Kind. There was her child lying in a coma, and she thanked him for being kind when he was the one who'd sabotaged her car. He couldn't feel any lower if he tried.

CHAPTER THREE

"*Komm*, now, you must eat." Deidre's cousin, Anna Wagner, pressed a container of hot chicken soup into her hands. "Mamm made it this morning just for you. She didn't want you eating hospital food."

Deidre could imagine the disdain with which her aunt had said those words. Amish mothers had a profound distrust of institutional food of any sort.

She didn't feel like eating, but Deidre obediently put a spoonful in her mouth. To her surprise, her tight throat seemed to relax at the warmth, and she discovered she was hungry, after all. No wonder they called it comfort food.

"It's great. Thank your *mamm* for me."

Anna's normally cheerful young face sobered as she looked at Kevin. "We're all praying. And he looks a little better, ain't so? His color is most natural."

"I think so." Maybe it was the effect of the chicken soup, but Deidre dared to look ahead, just for a moment, to the day when a normal Kevin would be clattering down the stairs and sliding across the hall.

She couldn't imagine getting through this without being surrounded by people who loved and cared about her and Kevin. Anna was getting up, obviously ready to leave, but there'd be someone else in the waiting room, ready to come in and join her silent vigil… Relatives or friends, they'd be here.

Someone tapped softly and pushed the door open a few inches. Jason Glassman hesitated. "May I come in?"

Anna snatched up her bag and kissed Deidre. "*Ja*, it's fine. I'm just going." Cheerful, outgoing Anna gave him a smile that was accompanied by a speculative gaze before she slipped out.

"My cousin," Deidre said. Realizing the container was empty, she set it down as he approached.

"He looks better," he said, as everyone did who came in. Some of them were just trying to be encouraging, but Jason had seen Kevin at the worst, and that meant something.

"I think so. But I'd like to hear it from the doctor."

"I'm sure." He glanced toward the door. "You have an Amish cousin?"

"I have thirty-four Amish cousins, to be exact. That's not counting their children." She took pity on his baffled look. "My father grew up Amish, but he left the church when he was a teenager. He maintained a good relationship with his parents and siblings, and so they've always seen me as one of their own."

"Someone mentioned that you have a business selling Amish crafts. Do you do that with your Amish relatives?" Jason took the chair next to her where Anna had been sitting.

Had he been asking about her? Natural enough, under the circumstances, she supposed.

"Not exactly, although some of them do participate.

I do a web-based business that allows Amish craftspeople to sell their products online. My partner is Judith Yoder, my neighbor. Although our family trees probably interconnect if you go back far enough."

Jason looked from Kevin to her. "I guess this isn't the best time for small talk, is it? Have the police been back?"

"No, thank goodness." She edged her chair a little closer to the bed, needing to be able to reach out and touch Kevin.

"They will be." Jason sounded certain, making her frown.

"What's the point? I can't tell them anything more." Everything she had seen, he had, as well.

"They're waiting for Kevin to wake up." He sounded as if that should be obvious. "They're hoping he saw what happened to Dixie."

"No." The word was wrenched from her as her heart cramped. "If he saw that..." She put her hand over Kevin's as if that would protect him. "No child should have to bear that."

"I'm sorry. I guess I put that badly. If he saw anything at all when he came down the stairs, it could help the police find the person who attacked your friend."

She pressed her free hand to her temple, wishing she could push the thought out of her mind. Dixie, laughing, generous Dixie, was gone forever. She'd never hear her caustic comments or feel Dixie's rare, warm hug. Deidre's heart clenched painfully.

And Kevin might have seen something. Must have, surely, to cause him to fall. She didn't want to consider it, but it had to be faced, and by bringing it up now, Jason was helping her to prepare. That had probably been his aim. An attorney had to think of that sort of thing for a client.

"I see that they have to find out. But they can't do anything to endanger his recovery. He'll need love and assurance, not questions."

"I know. Believe me, I'll do everything I can to hold them off. I can ensure that we're present for any conversation the cops have with him. And it will only take place when his doctor says he's well enough." He leaned toward her, his eyes dark and intent. "That's the best you can expect."

Deidre managed to nod. He was trying to help, she knew. And at least she wasn't having this conversation with her father-in-law. "All right. I guess it sounds as if I'm not even thinking of Dixie, but I am. She was a good friend, and…" Her throat tightened, and she couldn't go on. The image of Dixie lying there was too vivid, stabbing at her heart.

"You told the police that you'd locked the door when you left the house. Are you sure?" He was probably trying to get the conversation back to a less emotional level, not that anything could.

"Positive. I remember doing it." She shrugged. "When I was growing up, I don't think my parents ever locked the doors. But things are different now, even in a town like Echo Falls. I locked it and double-checked, as I always do."

"There was no sign of a break-in. That means either they had a key or your friend let the person in."

She was already shaking her head. "The only person I can think of who has a key is my partner, Judith. If we're away, she comes in to deal with things for the business and to water my plants."

She was tempted to ask him why he was so intent about this. He'd have some sense of responsibility simply because he'd been with her, but it would surely be more natural for him to want to walk away afterward.

Of course, the judge had asked him to represent her. No doubt he saw it as part of his job.

Jason frowned, his lean face taut. "So Dixie probably let him in, whoever he is."

"I suppose so." She hadn't even thought of it, and she tried to focus, but her mind kept straying back to her son. Surely the doctor would come in soon. "But I can't see her letting someone in when she was staying with Kevin. Dixie was…" She hesitated, trying to think of how to explain Dixie to someone who hadn't known her. "She gave the impression of being interested in having a good time and nothing else, but at heart she was so warm and giving. She loved Kevin, and she was very careful with him. She…"

Her voice broke, the memories overwhelming her. Dixie and Kevin laughing together over some silly knock-knock joke. Dixie giving up her afternoon off to take him to a children's movie…

"Sorry." He must have regretted opening the subject, but he didn't seem inclined to back off. "Does Kevin often get up at night?"

"No." It was another thing she hadn't spared the time to ponder. "If he were frightened or ill, he'd call out to me or come to my room, but he ordinarily sleeps through the night."

But not with the intensity and stillness he displayed now. Her fingers squeezed his.

"Would he be likely to wake up if he heard voices downstairs?"

Jason was far more demanding than the police had been. Deidre reminded herself again that he probably thought it was his duty. "He might, but…" The thought struck her. "He knew Dixie was coming, and he'd tried to stay awake to see her. I guess if he heard her voice, he might have had the idea of going down to talk to her."

She could picture him heading for the stairs, trailing the blue blanket that he still liked to have when he went to sleep. She gasped and fought for control, closing her eyes.

Jason's hand closed strongly over hers. "What is it?"

"Nothing. It… I just pictured it too clearly."

"I'm sorry." His voice seemed to deepen, as if he understood.

How could he? He barely knew her. Deidre took a steadying breath. "Kev didn't necessarily see anything. He could have tripped on the blanket."

"Possible." Jason drew back, letting go of her hand. "But the police have to find out. Whoever killed your friend is still out there. He has to be found, both for her sake and your son's."

Fear jagged through her. "You mean Kevin might be in danger if that person thinks he knows something."

"I mean the sooner the police know everything he

knows, the better," he said bluntly. "Then he can't be a danger to anyone."

That made sense, but somehow it didn't offer a lot of comfort. Would the person who attacked Dixie reason that way?

"I just don't understand it. If someone broke in, intending to rob the house... But they'd hardly do that when someone was there, would they?"

"The police couldn't find any signs of a break-in." His flat tone seemed to eliminate that possibility. "You'll want to check, but there was no obvious indication that someone was trying to rob you."

Deidre rubbed her temples. "Surely no one would have come there to deliberately hurt Dixie. How would they even know she was there? And if they thought I was home..." She didn't finish the sentence. It made even less sense that way.

"That's a good question. You'd expect, if someone was targeting her, they'd do it at her apartment, not at your house."

"I can't imagine anyone hating Dixie that much. She had some rough edges, but she hadn't had an easy life. And she was so good-hearted. She'd have done anything for Kevin."

"She was divorced, I gather. Any problems with the ex-husband?"

She ventured a glance at him. His face was stern, maybe judgmental. "Not anything recent. I don't think she'd been in contact with him at all since she came back to Echo Falls. His name is Mike Hanlon. I don't know where he lives."

The police would look into that, of course. Didn't they say that the spouse was often responsible in a murder?

"Would she have let a boyfriend in while she was there with Kevin?"

"No!" Her temper, already frayed, unraveled at that. "Dixie dated, but there wasn't anyone serious, and even if there had been, she wouldn't have invited him to my house. She wasn't a teenager."

Skepticism showed in his narrowed eyes. "You can't be sure of that."

"Yes. I can."

She glared at him, knowing what was happening. He'd heard rumors linking Dixie with one man or another. He'd added that together with the way she dressed and the fact that she worked at a bar, and he'd come up with an answer—categorizing her.

Jason looked ready to snap back at her. But the door swung open, and Liz Donnelly came in, a chart in one hand. Deidre started from her chair, everything else dismissed by her need to know what Liz and the other medical personnel thought. She couldn't seem to find words to ask the question.

Liz smiled. "It's good news, really it is. All the tests we've done so far show little or no brain swelling, and his brain function looks normal."

Deidre sagged against the bed. She'd been so braced to face whatever came that the relief was overpowering.

Liz patted her shoulder and then moved to the bed, taking a look at Kevin while she gave Deidre time to compose herself. "Everything here seems fine. Blood pressure right where it should be. Temperature normal. Breathing fine."

"He's going to be all right." She had to hold back the tears.

But Liz seemed reluctant to go that far. "We can't say positively what effects the injury might have until he's awake, but if all continues to go well, we'll wake him up slowly tomorrow morning."

And when Kev woke up, they'd know. They'd know if he'd seen the attack on Dixie, and she'd have to find a way to help him through the consequences, no matter what.

STILL THINKING ABOUT the situation with Deidre and her son, Jason walked the few blocks from the hospital to the office. One thing he had to say about Echo Falls—nothing was very far. The town stretched along the valley floor, making Echo Falls narrow and long as it followed the contours of the land.

The ridges on either side were heavily forested, increasing his sense of isolation. Not the sort of place he'd ever imagined himself settling down. How long was he going to be able to take it?

For the moment, he didn't have much of a choice. If he could hang on here for a few years, rehabilitate his reputation, have something positive on his résumé, he'd stand a chance of making a fresh start in a city more to his liking. Until then, he was stuck.

Just like he was stuck in this tangled situation between the judge and his daughter-in-law.

How much of Morris's dislike was based on fact and

how much on unfair prejudice against his son's wife? He couldn't tell. His job at the moment was to protect the kid, nothing more. But the more he saw of the situation, the less he liked it. He was torn between the judge's opinion of who Deidre was and the woman who sat in agony waiting for the doctor's verdict on her son.

And what did he do with the lingering thought that the tragic circumstances had brought him into just the sort of relationship with Deidre that the judge had suggested.

Jase walked into the reception area of the office to find a guy about his own age perched on Evelyn's desk, apparently joking with her, to judge by their smiles. Since he was wearing a coat and tie, Jason deduced that this must be the partner he hadn't met yet.

They both turned toward him at his entrance, Mrs. Lincoln adjusting her smile subtly. The man slid off the desk and held out his hand. "You must be the new guy. I'm Trey Alter. Welcome."

Jase had a quick impression of something a little guarded behind the welcoming smile, accompanied by the kind of self-assurance that only came to those born to the position they occupied.

"Jase Glassman." He shook Alter's hand, revising his estimate of the man's age. He was probably a few years older than Jase, fit and solid with an easy smile.

"Sorry I wasn't around when you got in. I had a case that went to the federal court in Williamsport. I hear you've had quite an introduction to our little town."

Obviously he'd heard all about it. Probably everyone in town had by now.

"Not what I expected, I admit. I'm just glad I happened to be around so that Mrs. Morris didn't walk into the situation on her own."

"A lucky coincidence." Trey's voice was dry. "I understand the judge asked you to act for Deidre...Mrs. Morris."

Was he thinking that it should have been him? Most likely he was another person who'd known Deidre Morris her entire life. But he couldn't have any idea of exactly why the judge had pushed Jase into this position.

"I was on the spot," he said, careful not to sound defensive to someone who obviously belonged here.

Before Alter could respond, the outside door opened. Chief Carmichaels came in, nodded all around and zeroed in on Jase. "I'd like a word or two, Mr. Glassman."

"Of course." He wasn't sorry to be interrupted. "Come through to my office."

He led the way, reflecting on the fact that it hadn't been his office long enough to feel a sense of possession. The wall of bookshelves wasn't full yet, although it probably would be by the time he unpacked the cartons sitting in front of the shelves. He'd been a lot busier than he'd anticipated.

"Have a seat, won't you?" Jase gestured to the client's seat and sat back in the leather desk chair that still seemed molded to its previous occupant's shape.

But Carmichaels paced to the window instead, staring out for a moment at what he probably considered *his* town. "This used to be Frank's office." His voice was neutral, but Jason wondered if there was implied criticism in the words.

"I know." What else was there to say? "Frank was a classmate of mine at Dickinson Law."

Carmichaels grunted, turning to face him. "I figured there had to be some connection. So…you're representing Deidre Morris's interests, right?"

Jason nodded. The chief was taking his time getting to the point of this visit. "She doesn't need an attorney, but the judge wants me to shield her and the boy as much as possible. So far we haven't had any problems with reporters, but…"

"If you do, you let me know. I'll give them a quick boot on their way." The chief came down heavily on Deidre's side at the mention of the press.

"Good."

Carmichaels walked to the desk, frowning. The silver hair and slightly thickened body made him look older, but he probably wasn't much more than in his early fifties. He gave the impression of shrewd intelligence hidden behind a stoic facade.

"So I tried to sound out Kevin's doctor today. She referred me to you."

Jase leaned back in the chair. "You didn't really expect her to tell you anything, did you?"

They seemed to cross swords for an instant, but then Carmichaels gave a shrug and a half smile. "It was worth a try. Look, Judge Morris asked me to cooperate. That's all very well, but this is murder. I'll cooperate with you, but not at the cost of my investigation."

The judge's power to control events might not be as

strong as he apparently thought it was. But Jase still had a client to represent.

"Relax, Chief. I've already prepared Mrs. Morris for the fact that you'll have to talk to Kevin. She understands, but she insists it can't be until his doctor says so. And not at the cost of the boy's well-being." He deliberately echoed Carmichaels's words.

Apparently deciding he meant it, the chief gave a short nod. "Okay. You'll let me know as soon as I can question the boy." It wasn't a request.

Now it was Jason's turn to want something. Time to see how far this cooperation extended. "Any progress on the case?"

Chief Carmichaels gave him a long look. "I'd think it a burglary gone wrong, but no one broke in. No evidence of ransacking, everything in perfect order except for the woman lying on the floor. You saw."

"Was there any evidence that she fought back? You'd expect that, wouldn't you?"

"None," he said flatly. "From all we can see, it looks as if the woman was sitting there quietly when someone walked up and hit her. Used the heavy base of the lamp from the end table."

"So deliberate." Jase tried to think through what that meant. "No one who got that close could have mistaken Dixie James for Deidre."

"No. Whoever did this knew who he or she was attacking. I can't make it fit any other way. But finding out who and proving it are two different things. You know that."

Was that intended as a barb? Maybe not, since the man was already continuing.

"Dixie James had a bit of a reputation as a partier since she got back to town. There were plenty of boy-friends, and the most likely scenario is that one of them came to the house that night. She let him in, things got out of hand, turned sour." He shrugged. "If so, we'll get him."

"Mrs. Morris says that Dixie would never have let someone into her house when she was babysitting." He wanted to hear the chief's reaction.

Carmichaels didn't speak at once. "I've known Deidre Wagner…well, Morris…since she was a kid. A good person. Honest, kindhearted, just like her folks were. Now, with her father gone and her mother remarried and living clear out in Arizona, she doesn't have any-one to rely on."

"I didn't realize she was so alone." He probably should have, but the subject had never come up.

"She has all her Amish kinfolk. Like them, she doesn't easily recognize dishonesty in others." He paused. "That's a good quality, but it's dangerous, too." He focused on Jase, and his expression seemed to hold a warning. "I'd be upset if anyone hurt her."

Was that warning intended for him? Or was the ref-erence aimed at Dixie James? Carmichaels couldn't know about the judge's plans, or the extent of Jase's involvement in those plans.

"As her attorney, I feel the same," he said, carefully expressionless.

But he was going over what Carmichaels had said

about Deidre in his mind. The man's opinion of her was as far from Judge Morris's as possible. Maybe he was right, maybe not.

But one thing he'd said Jason couldn't buy. In his experience, honest women weren't just rare—they were an endangered species. And he didn't suppose he'd found one in Deidre Morris.

DEIDRE HAD RUSHED home early the next morning to shower and change, leaving Judith with Kevin. She wouldn't have left without being sure there was someone there he loved, just in case he woke up.

She'd nearly forgotten that she'd left her car at the library, but Jason had brought it back, running again, and handed her the keys. He had waved off her insisting on paying the garage bill, saying it had just been a loose connection.

Now she willed the elevator to get to Kevin's floor more quickly. Even knowing someone would call her cell if there'd been any change, she had to see for herself.

Nothing had changed in the quiet room. Judith smiled at her from the chair beside the bed. "It's been perfectly calm and quiet while you were gone, but I'm certain sure Kevin's color is better today."

"Has the doctor been in?" She drew up a chair next to Judith and put her hand over Kevin's, needing the skin-to-skin connection.

"Not yet." Judith touched her arm comfortingly. "Soon, I'm sure."

Now that she'd seen for herself that Kevin was safe,

Deidre could manage to widen her thoughts to include someone other than her son. "I'm really sorry to drag you out at this time of the morning. How will Eli manage getting the children fed and off to school?"

Judith chuckled. "He probably gave them cold cereal out of a box, but that's all right for once. It'll make him appreciate me more, ain't so?"

Since they both knew Eli and Judith had the happiest of marriages, Deidre didn't think Eli needed any prompting. "You be sure he knows how much I appreciate it. Do you have a ride home? I could ask…"

"It's all settled. One of the ladies from your church offered to drive me. I hear they've all been standing by to take turns doing whatever needs done."

Deidre nodded, and the tears she hadn't allowed herself to shed for Kevin filled her eyes at the kindness. "So many people have helped me since this happened. I don't know how I'll be able to thank them all."

"Seeing Kevin well is all the thanks anyone needs." Judith glanced at the clock that was mounted above a mirror on the far wall. "I should probably go down. I don't want her to have to drive around waiting for me." She studied Deidre's face. "If you want me to stay…"

"No, no, I'll be fine. I'm just eager to talk to the doctor. She said they'd probably let Kevin wake up today if all continued to go well." Her heart lurched at the thought of seeing his eyes open, of knowing he recognized her. "Please, go on home. I'm fine now."

Judith embraced her. "We are all praying," she whispered. And then she was leaving, passing Pastor Adam in the doorway.

"I don't want to intrude, but I had to see how Kevin's doing." He gave her a tentative smile. "Better?"

"I think so. The doctor should be in soon, so…"

Adam nodded. "I understand. I'll leave you." But he didn't. He stood there awkwardly for a moment, and then he came closer and put his hand on her shoulder. "You know how much I…we all care. If there's anything, anything at all, just…"

He sounded so eager to help that Deidre wished she could think of something for him to do. "I'll call you, of course. Thank you, Adam."

He nodded, patted her shoulder. "I'll go now. Be sure you call me."

Finally he was gone. Alone with her son, Deidre wrapped Kevin's hand in both of hers. "You're going to wake up soon." She kept her voice soft. "All the boys and girls from your kindergarten class have made cards for you. When you open your eyes, you can look at them, okay?"

She heard the door and stopped, but Liz Donnelly just smiled and nodded. "It's okay to talk to him. But right now Dr. Jamison and I want to have a few words with you."

Jamison followed Liz into the room. He stood silent for a moment, studying a chart he carried, and Deidre's heart began to thud. At last he looked up and focused on her.

"As we explained to you earlier, the reason for the sedation was to allow the brain time to rest and recover by reducing swelling."

He seemed to expect a response, so she nodded.

"All of the tests we've run are looking good, so we've ordered to stop the sedation. Once your boy wakes up, we'll be able to assess the situation in a different way."

"Does that mean you'll be able to tell if there's been any permanent damage?" Her throat tightened as she said the words, and her hands felt clammy.

Jamison looked at Liz, as if passing the question off to her. Liz came and sat down knee to knee with Deidre.

"We just don't know. Once Kevin is awake, we'll want to see if there are any overt signs of damage. But signs can be very subtle, and there's also the fact that he might demonstrate some impairment at first and then have that completely disappear as his brain continues to heal." She patted Deidre's hand. "It's a game of wait and see at this point, but we're agreed that we don't see any indication of trouble now."

Deidre managed to nod. What it boiled down to was that they really didn't know. But when she looked at Kevin, his cheeks rosy as they always were when he slept, she found it impossible to believe he wouldn't simply be himself when he woke.

"When do you think he'll wake up?"

Liz glanced at her watch. "Anytime in the next hour or so. You can talk to him the way you were, but don't make any other effort to rouse him. It's better to just let him come out of it gradually on his own."

Again Deidre nodded, but with a flicker of irritation. What did they think she was going to do—try to shake him awake?

"Good." Liz rose, and Dr. Jamison was already halfway out of the room. "We'll leave you with him, then.

When he starts responding to you, just ring for the nurse and have her page me. I expect to be here in the hospital."

"All right." Much as she liked Liz, she was ready to have her go. Talking about the possibilities of difficulties with Kevin's brain made them uncomfortably real.

But apparently she wasn't destined to be alone with Kevin, because no sooner had the doctors left than Jason came in. "You haven't been left by yourself, have you?" He seemed to echo her thoughts.

She managed a smile. "You just missed Pastor Bennett. And Judith was here before that."

"Good." Apparently he, like everyone else, thought she needed company. He looked at Kevin and nodded, as if pleased with his appearance. "What's the verdict? Are they waking him up today?"

"Yes." There was a world of relief in the word, but it was tinged with anxiety.

Jason seemed to pick up on what she didn't say. He studied her face and then came to sit next to her. "What's wrong?"

"Nothing." She shook her head, trying to deny the longing to spill out her worries and fears.

"There must be something, or you wouldn't look that way."

She couldn't help smiling at his words. "You've only known me a few days. You can't possibly know what my expressions mean."

"Granted, it hasn't been long, but they've been eventful days. You get to know a lot about people when you see them in a crisis." Jason's face tightened, making her wonder what had induced that grim look.

"Kevin's going to wake up soon." She squeezed the small hand that lay in hers. "When he does, we'll have an idea of whether there's any permanent damage. And we'll know what he remembers."

That was on everyone's mind, it seemed. The police, of course, but maybe also the person who'd attacked Dixie. Was he still here in Echo Falls, waiting? Or had he fled? Surely that was what he'd have done.

"Whatever happens when he wakes up, at least you'll have him back again." He put a hand on the back of her chair rather than on her shoulder, as Adam had done.

She blinked back sudden tears. "Yes. Maybe I'll be able to take him home soon. I won't know what to do when we get back to real life." She gestured to their surroundings. "This…all of it…doesn't seem real."

Jason seemed to consider her words. "It's not normal, anyway. Well, today is the first step back. By the way, Judge Morris sends his apologies. He wanted to be here this morning, but he had to be in court."

So that was why Jason had come. It wasn't anything personal. Surely she wasn't disappointed. She couldn't be relying on the man. She barely knew him.

"I'm sure. I'll call and give Sylvia the latest news once Kevin is awake."

Sylvia hadn't come to the hospital to see Kevin, and Deidre had been glad for that. It wasn't that Sylvia didn't care; it was that she was too fragile emotionally to be helpful.

Kevin's hand stirred in hers—just a butterfly touch at first, then a definite movement.

"Kevin." She leaned over him. "Baby, are you awake?" She sensed, rather than saw, Jason snap to attention next to her. "Kevin?"

Nothing happened for a minute that seemed to last forever. Then Kevin moved, wiggling a little as he did when she woke him for Sunday school. His forehead wrinkled.

"Wake up, baby," she said, keeping her voice gentle. "It's time to get up now." They were the same words she said every morning.

And, just like all those other mornings, Kevin blinked and opened his eyes. At first he stared, seeming puzzled, at the ceiling. Then he focused on her face. His blue eyes widened and he smiled. "Mommy."

She'd never heard anything better in her life. It took a giant effort to keep her voice calm, her manner casual. "You awake, baby?"

"Sure." He started to get up, then stared at the tube leading into his arm. "Mommy?" His voice shook. "What's happening, Mommy? What's that thing?"

"It's okay." She eased him back on the pillow, putting her arms around him. "You had a little accident and had to come to the hospital. But you're getting better now."

"Oh." He settled down but still looked troubled. She thought he was trying to remember. "Did I fall out of the tree? That's what happened, right? You told me not to climb so high, but I wanted to see."

"Climbing the apple tree, you mean?" At a movement from Jason, she glanced at him. "That morning," she said quietly. "Is that what you remember, Kev?"

He frowned. "I remember climbing up high in the tree. That's all."

Kevin was making up his own story about what had happened. It was a story that probably seemed normal and comforting to him.

Comforting because he didn't know how he got hurt. Here was the answer everyone had been waiting for. Kevin didn't remember anything about the attack on Dixie. However the police might feel about it, Deidre couldn't help but be relieved.

CHAPTER FOUR

FROM WHAT JASON had seen during the time he'd spent at the hospital, Kevin awake was going to be quite a handful. It would try everyone's patience keeping a lively kid like that quiet. But it was a lot better than watching him lie in the hospital bed unconscious.

Sitting unobtrusively while Deidre talked to the doctor, Jason had come away with an answer that troubled him. From what the pediatrician had said, she hadn't been at all surprised that Kevin didn't remember what had happened in the hours prior to his injury. Apparently that occurred often with head injuries. So for the moment, Kevin could be of no help at all to the police. Chief Carmichaels would be disappointed.

But there was also the possibility that the memory would come back as the child's brain healed from the trauma. And if it did, what then?

Deidre had wanted to reject that result. Her fear had been palpable. But he couldn't entirely dismiss the judge's comment that something Deidre had done had put Kevin in danger.

Not intentionally, he was sure. He'd seen enough of her devotion to the boy to know that. But what did he really know about her?

For that matter, what did he really know about the judge? This situation was becoming more uncomfortable by the moment. He'd been desperate enough and raw enough emotionally to grab at the lifeline the judge had offered him. But the strings attached to that offer were pretty ugly when viewed impartially, and right at the moment, he didn't see a clear way out of the position he was in.

He'd nearly reached the edge of town, where the row of graceful old Victorian houses petered out and farmland took over. He'd offered to pick up some toys to keep Kevin occupied, so he had a legitimate reason for going into Deidre's house alone. He had the key she'd lent him so that he could complete his errand.

Pulling into Deidre's driveway, he parked and slid out. The front door was locked, of course, but it responded readily to the key.

His fingers closed over the key as he stepped inside. Would the judge expect him to take advantage of the situation to have a copy made? Possibly. But even though his values had taken quite a battering during the events of the past six months, he wasn't willing to compromise them that much.

He spared a flickering thought for Leslie, who hadn't had any such compunction, and then dismissed her. Maybe it was a good sign that he'd been too busy to think of her more than once since he'd arrived in Echo Falls.

Jason came to a halt in the living room and had a cautious look around. The previous time he'd been here, he'd been focused on the emergency and the need to act.

He'd barely been aware of the surroundings. He looked first at the spot where Dixie James had lain, on an area rug in front of the sofa. That rug was gone now, maybe to the police lab or maybe disposed of, and in its place was an oval braided rug, whose mellow colors blended with the blue upholstery on the sofa and chairs.

The room seemed furnished for comfort rather than style, as if a family had acquired pieces they liked over a couple of generations. A child's toy airplane nosed against a framed photo of an older couple on an end table, and several magazines had slid to the floor from an overburdened rack. It wasn't messy, just lived-in, he supposed.

He could imagine it annoying the judge, though. He'd already noticed that everything in the office had to be exactly the way the judge liked it, down to the way the pens were arranged on Evelyn's desk.

He moved through the adjoining dining room, where tulips drooped in a vase, dropping their petals onto the polished surface of the table, and on into the kitchen. Deidre had apparently resisted the current urge toward steel appliances and granite. The cabinets were painted wood, and geraniums bloomed in a pot on one window-sill, while what were probably herbs grew on the other.

Beyond the kitchen he found what must be the head-quarters of Deidre's business. On one side, shelves and racks held packing supplies, while two walls were covered with shelves holding a variety of handcrafted items—everything from placemats to quilts to wooden toys and more. He zeroed in on the computer at one end of a long wooden table.

He switched it on. Deidre apparently hadn't seen the need to password protect it, and he easily accessed the files. The computer seemed devoted to the business, though, with sales records, addresses, sample newsletters and photographs of items offered for sale.

Searching her email was similarly nonproductive—it contained only correspondence related to the business. If Deidre had personal emails, she obviously kept them elsewhere.

Glancing at his watch, he retraced his steps and started upstairs. He couldn't take too long completing his errand, or Deidre might become suspicious. Still, he might not have another chance to prowl around her house undetected.

The police would have gone over the stairs with meticulous care, but as far as he knew, there had been no indication that Kevin's injury had been anything other than accidental. He'd started down the stairs, tripped and fallen. Whether he'd tripped in shock from what he'd seen was an open question.

Four rooms upstairs. Which one was Kevin's was obvious—typical little boy's bedroom, decorated with train wallpaper and bright curtains to match. The items he'd come to fetch would be there, but for the moment, he wanted to see the rest of the upstairs. There was a guest room and next to it what might have been a study for Frank, furnished with bookshelves and a desk. He considered taking the time to search the desk, but if Deidre were hiding anything about an affair, it was unlikely to be there.

Her bedroom was the likeliest place. He moved into

the room, feeling like an intruder. But that was part of the job, wasn't it? Like the living room, this room had an air of permanence, as if the furniture had stood where it was for a lot of years and was comfortable there.

Jason dismissed the thought. This was no time to get nostalgic for a permanence he'd never experienced. He went quickly to the dresser, a massive affair of highly polished maple, and pulled open a drawer. Moving quickly, he felt under clothes, looking for any crinkle of paper or odd shape.

In the third drawer he found it—a sheaf of something under the drawer liner. He drew out the bundle. Cards, greeting cards, stretching back over the years, it seemed. A birthday card signed "Mommy and Daddy," a graduation card, several Valentine cards. He opened one that read: "I don't know what I did to deserve someone like you. You are my strength." It was from Frank.

Feeling like a Peeping Tom, he shuffled through the rest and came up with nothing. As he put them back into place, he felt something else, something tucked back into the corner under the paper. He was reaching for it when he heard footsteps on the stairs.

Closing the drawer as quietly as he could, he managed to be in the center of the room when Judith Yoder appeared in the doorway. She didn't look surprised, but then she'd have seen his car in the driveway. But she did look suspicious.

When she didn't speak, he hurried into speech. "I'm glad you're here. Maybe you can help me. Deidre asked me to pick up a few things for Kevin, and I haven't been able to spot the first one on the list. Do you know where his handheld electronic game might be?"

The suspicion in Judith face wasn't allayed. "Not in Deidre's bedroom." She jerked a nod toward the next room. "*Komm*. It'll be in here."

He was very aware of her covert glances as she took the list from his hand and began collecting the items. A couple of small toy train pieces, a few books, a pack of crayons, the electronic game.

"Thanks. I'm afraid I'm not up on little boys' toys."

Judith tucked everything into a bright tote bag. "Please tell Deidre I'll be in later this afternoon." She handed him the bag. "Let me see you out."

He'd gotten the bum's rush a few times in his life, but never with so much politeness. Judith closed the door firmly behind him, and he headed to his car.

So she'd be seeing Deidre this afternoon, would she? What exactly would she have to say about this little episode? It seemed to him that his relationship with Deidre Morris might be ending sooner than either he or the judge had expected.

A FEW DAYS LATER, juggling a backpack and a shopping bag provided by the hospital, Deidre ushered Kevin into the house at last. It had seemed like forever, and she wondered how long it had felt to Kevin. She kept a close eye on him as they walked into the living room. Would being home bring back memories?

But Kevin seemed perfectly normal. He spotted Judith coming out of the kitchen with Benjamin and rushed over to them.

"Hey, Benjy, did you know I was in the hospital? I had my own room and a television, too."

Benjamin grinned. He wasn't too fluent in English yet, but the two of them chattered together in a scrambled mixture of English and Pennsylvania Dutch. "Me and Mamm brought whoopie pies."

"Wow!" Obviously that was far more important than the hospital stay. "Can we have one now, Mommy? Can we?"

Deidre glanced at Judith and got a smile and a nod in response.

"Okay, you two. One each. Kevin, don't run."

Heedless, the two boys raced to the kitchen. Judith chuckled. "I wonder how many times you'll say that in the next few days."

"I might as well save my breath, but I have to try. The doctor said to keep him quiet."

"Does the doctor have a five-year-old boy?" Judith asked innocently. "Might as well try to stop the wind from blowing."

"True." Dropping the bags, she gave Judith a hug. "Thanks for the treat. Maybe we'd better see if there's any milk for them before they choke on mouthfuls of chocolate."

"No need. I already poured it. And made sure you have what you need in the refrigerator. I knew you wouldn't want to run to the store first thing. Your cousin Anna dropped off chicken potpie for your supper, so all you have to do is heat it up."

Deidre had a ridiculous urge to cry. "I don't know what I'd do without you. Everyone has been so kind, coming to sit with Kev, cleaning the house, running errands…"

"Everyone wants to help." Judith hesitated, and her serene oval face actually looked troubled. "That makes me think of something I must tell you."

"Something bad?" She was instantly apprehensive.

Judith considered. "Maybe not. It bothered me, is all. The other day when I came over I found somebody here. That Mr. Glassman. He said you'd asked him to pick up some things for Kevin."

Deidre's tension slid away. "Actually he offered, but it was really helpful. Kevin was just about bouncing out of the bed, and I needed something to entertain him. It's okay that he was here. I had lent him my key."

"*Ja*, that's what he said. But I found him upstairs in your bedroom."

"In my room?" Odd, but she could easily see reasons why that would be. "Maybe he was just trying to find the things on the list. And he hadn't ever been upstairs before."

"Maybe." Judith didn't sound convinced. "But I'd think he'd have seen that Kevin's toys were in his room, not yours." She hesitated a moment. "He is a stranger."

He was. She kept forgetting that. Natural enough, since he'd been with her through one of the most traumatic experiences of her life. But how much did she know about him?

"You're right to tell me. Thank you, Judith. *Denke*." She used the Pennsylvania Dutch word for thanks automatically.

"What will you do?"

"I'm not sure, but I'll have to decide soon." She glanced at her watch. "He's coming over so he can be here when Chief Carmichaels talks to Kevin this afternoon."

"*Ach*, that man and his questions." Judith looked exasperated. "He even talked to Benjamin, and what could Benjy tell him? Benjamin was in bed and asleep, and he hadn't even seen Kevin since the morning."

"I guess if they didn't ask questions, they wouldn't be able to find out what happened." She tried to be fair, although her sympathies were with Judith. She glanced at the boys, sitting at the kitchen table and chattering around mouthfuls of chocolate and cream filling. "But I hope it doesn't upset Kevin to have them asking him about that night. Maybe it's wrong of me, but I hope he never does remember."

They stood for a moment, watching their sons. Even though their lives were different in so many ways, she and Judith valued the same things: home, family, tradition. Judith would say that she was content in the place God had put her. It was a good place, despite what had happened to Dixie.

"We should go, since you're expecting people." She swept into the kitchen. "*Ach*, look at the two of you. Such dirty faces. Let's get clean, and then Benjamin and I must get home." She smiled at the expected outcry. "Benjamin can visit tomorrow, if your *mamm* says it's okay."

While Judith supervised the cleanup, Deidre put the milk away, noting that the refrigerator was filled with dishes she hadn't put there. Obviously the neighbors were intent on seeing they didn't go hungry.

By the time the front doorbell rang, Judith and Benjamin had already gone out the back. "Somebody's here!" Kevin started to run to the door, but Deidre was close enough to grab him.

"You're not supposed to run, remember? Just for a few days."

Kevin nodded. "I know. But it's hard to remember."

"Try," she said. "Okay, let's answer the door."

Jason had arrived before Chief Carmichaels was due, as they'd arranged. At first the judge had insisted that he be personally present for this interview, and he hadn't taken kindly to her obvious negative reaction. Imagining the tension that could so easily develop any time her father-in-law was present, she'd been relieved when he'd given in to Jason's reminder that he was representing her and Kevin. It had been hard enough running interference between the judge and the doctors, let alone trying to referee between him and the chief.

Jason came in, giving Kevin a friendly smile. "So, you're home at last. Bet it feels good."

Kevin nodded, instantly at ease. After a couple of visits with Jason at the hospital, Kevin had decided, apparently for reasons that made sense to a five-year-old, that Jason was an okay guy. "The hospital wasn't bad. But being home is better."

"Right." He sent a questioning glance to Deidre. "Did you tell him about Chief Carmichaels yet?"

"No, I was just about to." She reminded herself that she ought to ask him about what Judith had said. But not now. She touched Kevin's shoulder. "Kev, Chief Car-michaels is coming over in a few minutes. He wants to ask you about your accident."

"You mean when I fell out of the tree?"

Obviously she should have cleared that up for him before this, but she'd wanted to let him hold on to his comfortable story for as long as possible.

"You didn't fall out of the tree, sweetie. It was later when you fell. During the evening. You fell down the stairs."

His small face crinkled, and he shook his head. "But the tree…"

"You've forgotten some things from that day. That happens sometimes when a person gets a bad bump on the head."

Kevin seemed to digest that. "Okay. I remember Chief Carmichaels from when he came to kindergarten to talk to us about safety. He let me wear his hat. Remember, Mommy?"

"Yes, I remember." Kevin had been so proud, stand-ing there in the cap that was way too big for him.

"But why does he want to know about me falling?"

"Well…" How did she explain that without getting into the thing she didn't want to say?

Jason squatted down to Kevin's level. "See, Kev, it's this way. Sometimes the police look into accidents to see what caused them. Like if anyone was to blame."

"Oh." He nodded. "Okay."

Jason rose, opening the attaché case he'd carried in with him. "I hear you like trains, and I thought maybe you'd like this one." He held out a new locomotive for Kevin's train set.

"Wow." Kevin's eyes widened. "Wow. It's for me?"

"For you. In honor of coming home from the hospital." Jason grinned. "Think it'll work?"

"It's great." Seizing the train, he raced for the stairs. "I have to put it on the track."

"Don't run," Deidre cried as he reached the stairs.

"I'm not," he protested, scrambling up them.

Deidre's breath caught, her chest tightening as he scooted past the place where he must have tripped.

"It won't always be this bad." Jason's voice was low and infused with more than simple empathy. "Even the worst memories fade with time."

She looked into his face, but it didn't tell her anything. He was too good at hiding his feelings.

"That sounds like personal experience talking."

He shrugged. "I guess we all have bad things we don't want to remember." He turned, glancing out the front window at the sound of a vehicle. "Looks like Carmichaels is here. Are you ready?"

"I guess I'll have to be, won't I?" Deidre straightened her shoulders and tried to summon up some courage. Whether Judith was right or wrong in her opinion of Jason, at the moment Deidre was glad he was with her.

JASON DIDN'T KNOW where that need to reassure Deidre had come from, but he'd better get back to a more professional stance with her in a hurry. It was not part of his assignment to get that involved with her. All he wanted was evidence, one way or the other, to either prove or disprove the judge's opinion of her.

Carmichaels entered, greeting Deidre with an avuncular hug. "Bet you're glad to have that boy of yours home. How's he doing?"

"Fairly well, so far." She glanced at Jason as if asking him something, and he nodded.

"Before you talk to Kevin, I think Mrs. Morris wants to set up some guidelines."

Carmichaels's gaze went from Jason to Deidre, speculative. "Now, Deidre, you know me well enough to know I'm not going to bully the boy."

"Of course, but I'm still concerned." She seemed unconscious of the fact that her hands were clasped tightly. "He doesn't remember anything about most of that day. He won't be able to help you."

"We won't know that until I talk to him, will we?" Carmichaels glanced around. "Where's the best place for us to talk?"

"Sorry." Deidre's fair skin flushed. "Come and sit down." She looked at the sofa and seemed to change her mind, leading the way into the dining room instead. "We'll sit here at the table, all right?"

Carmichaels might have preferred the scene of the attack, but he didn't argue, just pulled out a chair and sat down, planting his elbows on the table. "How about calling Kevin, and we'll get this over with."

"Not yet," Deidre said quickly, gesturing Jason to a chair. She glanced at the stairs, as if afraid Kevin would appear too soon. "Since Kevin imagines he fell earlier in the day, he doesn't remember Dixie was here. So he doesn't know that she's... That she died."

"Deidre, you don't believe you can keep it from him, do you? Kevin could hear about it from almost anyone. Lord knows the whole town's been talking about nothing else." Carmichaels looked disapproving, and Jason had to agree with him on this one. What was she thinking?

"I know he has to be told." Deidre's color was high, and there was a stubborn look to the way her chin was set. "But I thought it was best if he heard it in his own home. I'll tell him soon, but you'll have to respect my decision as to when and how."

That was Jason's cue to do his job. "If we don't have your assurance that you won't mention the James woman's death in the boy's presence, then I'm afraid I can't allow you to question him."

"Sounds like you've got it all worked out." Carmichaels shrugged heavy shoulders. "Okay, I won't say anything about her death. But he's a smart kid. He's going to figure it out soon enough."

"All right, then." Deidre seemed ready to accept the chief's word. "I'll get him." She walked to the bottom of the steps and clutched the newel post. "Kevin, come down for a minute, please."

It said something about the way she'd brought up her son that he didn't embark on a shouted argument. Instead, he appeared at the top of the steps.

"Don't run," she said quickly, and he suspected that the words had become a kind of talisman for her. If she could keep him from running, she could keep him safe.

Deidre wouldn't believe that rationally, but the instinct was still there.

"Okay, Mommy." Kevin put his hand on the railing, sliding it down all the way to the bottom.

"Remember, I told you Chief Carmichaels wanted to ask you a few questions about your accident, Kev." She led him to the table, one hand on his shoulder.

Kevin didn't look upset at the prospect, but when Deidre sat down and held out her arms, he climbed into her lap and leaned against her.

"This won't take long, Kevin. Then you can go back and play, okay?" Carmichaels was clearly making an effort to keep it low-key.

Kevin nodded, his expression wary.

"Well, now, what can you tell me about your accident? Just say anything you remember."

Kevin leaned against his mother, turning his head to look up into her face. She nodded in encouragement. "It's all right. Just tell the chief what you remember."

"I remember climbing in the apple tree," he said promptly.

At Carmichaels's baffled look, Deidre explained, "That happened earlier in the day. It seems to be the last thing he remembers."

"You don't remember being on the steps in your pajamas?"

Kevin shook his head. Again he looked up at his mother. "Is that where I fell?"

"That's it. You must have tripped on your blanket and tumbled down." She kept her voice even, but Jason could see that it was a struggle.

"Let's go back a little bit," Carmichaels said. "What did you have for supper?"

Clearly Kevin didn't like not knowing the answer. His face scrunched up. "I don't know."

"Do you remember that Dixie was coming to stay with you?"

Jason thought Deidre stiffened at the mention of Dixie, but she didn't interrupt.

"No." He twisted to look up at his mother again. "Did Dixie watch me that night, Mommy?"

She stroked his hair. "Yes, sweetie, she did."

"That's easy, then." Kevin's face relaxed in a smile. "You just ask Dixie what happened. She'll tell you."

Before Carmichaels could speak, Jason rose. "I think that's enough, Chief. Kevin can't help you."

"Maybe if we talked a little more…"

"No." Deidre put both arms around her son as if shielding him. "No more."

"That's it." Jase defied the man to argue. Deidre was within her rights. "The doctor who tended Kevin will tell you that he shouldn't be pushed to remember."

Carmichaels planted his hands on the table and pushed himself to his feet. "Okay. You've made your point. Thanks for talking to me, Kevin."

The boy nodded, but then he burrowed his head against his mother's chest. Her arms tightened around him.

"I'll show you out." Jason conducted Carmichaels to the door. In a way, he sympathized with the man's frustration. He had a murder to solve, and the only potential witness couldn't remember. But Jason had to protect his client, even if it threw a roadblock in the way of the investigation.

When he'd closed the door behind the police chief, Jason turned back into the room. He was just in time to hear Kevin's voice, trembling a little. "Mommy, why did everyone look so funny when I said to ask Dixie? She'd know what happened. Why don't you ask her?"

Tears shone in Deidre's eyes, but she managed to maintain her calm. "I'm afraid we can't. You see, Dixie got hurt that night, too."

He looked up at her, frowning a little as if he struggled to understand. "Did she go to the hospital, like me?"

"Yes. She went in an ambulance, like you did. But she was hurt a lot worse than you were, Kev." She stroked his head, and Jason could see her fingers shaking. "I'm afraid Dixie didn't make it. She died."

Kevin didn't move for a moment. Then his lips began to tremble, and tears welled in his eyes. "Like…like Daddy?"

A spasm of pain crossed Deidre's face. "Yes. Like Daddy."

Kevin began to cry…huge, wrenching sobs that shook his whole body. He buried his face against his mother's chest, clinging to her.

Deidre held him close, rocking back and forth. Above her son's head, Deidre's gaze met his, and Jason saw the anguish there. It ripped at his own heart, too.

ONCE KEVIN WAS tucked up in bed that evening, Deidre found it impossible just to kiss him good-night and leave the room. Usually he was the one who tried to prolong bedtime. Now it was she who suggested another story, another song.

But when he drifted off in the middle of a favorite book, she knew she had to let him rest. If she curled up on the bed next to him, as she very much wanted to do, she'd be telling him there was something to be afraid of. She couldn't plant that idea in his mind.

Bending down, Deidre kissed Kevin's soft cheek. He snuggled into the pillow, and his breath came slow and even. She forced herself to slip out of the room.

Stopping in the hallway, Deidre glanced down the stairs, seeming for an instant to see it the way Kevin must have that night, stretching out endlessly, with only the glow of the table lamp to dispel the darkness.

She ought to go down to the workroom and catch up on orders, but for the first time it seemed very far away. Finally, she went to the linen closet. It took her a couple of minutes to unearth the baby monitor she'd stowed on the top shelf ages ago. Setting the base just outside Kevin's door, she carried the wireless receiver down with her. Kevin would be humiliated at the idea, but he need never know, and at least she'd hear him if he woke up.

Even with the precaution of the monitor, Deidre found it hard to concentrate when she reached the computer. There were several orders waiting for confirmation, and a few inquiries about special orders—mostly people who wanted an item made with a particular design or color. Focus eluded her. If she wasn't thinking about Kevin, she was reliving the events of the afternoon.

She still hadn't managed to talk to Jason about what Judith had said. But it had hardly been the time when he was so helpful in dealing with Chief Carmichaels, and so sympathetic while she told Kevin about Dixie.

It seemed unfair. Kevin had experienced too much loss in his young life. Not that losing Dixie compared to his father's death, but he had loved her, too.

And she had loved Dixie, too. Their friendship had been different from hers with Judith, of course, even though she'd known them both as children. But where Judith shared her values, Dixie had been much more of a free spirit.

In her own way, Dixie had helped her through the painful time after Frank's death. Dixie's core of solid warmth was as dependable as it was surprising to people who judged her only on her exterior. Now she was gone, and tears clogged Deidre's throat at the thought.

Deidre pushed away from the computer and rubbed her temples. Life would even out again. She knew that. But right at the moment, it was difficult to believe.

The telephone rang. Deidre frowned at the displayed number for a moment. It wasn't one she recognized, and she answered cautiously.

"Deidre? Is that you, Deidre? It's Lillian James."

Dixie's mother. Deidre's throat tightened. She should have called her. "Lillian, I'm so sorry. So very sorry about Dixie."

"Letting me get that call from the police... I'd think the least you could have done was call me yourself."

Deidre stiffened. She'd forgotten what a negative person Dixie's mother was. She'd always had something to complain about. But in this case…

"I'm sorry, Lillian, but the police insisted they had to be the ones to give you the news. I know what a shock it must have been."

"You don't know what it was like, hearing news like that in the middle of the night." Lillian's tone sharpened. "Terrible, and I didn't have a soul there with me to help. You just don't know."

Actually she did, but there was little point in saying so.

"Poor Dixie. My poor little girl." Her voice quavered. "It's not right. Why haven't the police done something about it?"

Deidre rubbed her forehead again. "I'm sure they're doing their best to find the person responsible."

"Heartless, that's what they are," Lillian continued, as if she hadn't spoken. "They were on the phone again today asking me what arrangements I'd made. As if I could be thinking of that when I was flat out with shock."

"It's hard on you, I know." She tried to remember where Dixie had said her mother was living now. Somewhere near Pittsburgh, she thought. "Would you like me to refer you to a funeral director here? I'm sure they…"

"I can't!" Lillian's voice rose to a wail. "Nobody can expect me to do that. I'm too shaken up to even think about it."

"But Dixie is your daughter. Surely you want to do this last thing for her." Maybe that was a stupid thing to say, but she couldn't come up with anything else.

"I can't. I just can't. That's why I called you. You were Dixie's closest friend. You'll do it, won't you?"

Unable to sit still any longer, Deidre paced across the room, the phone pressed to her ear. "I really don't think that's possible. Kevin just came home from the hospital, and…"

"Poor little lamb. He loved Dixie, too. I'm sure he'd want you to do it."

Deidre clamped her lips together to hold back a sharp retort. She stopped in her pacing at the side window, staring out blankly as she tried to think of the proper response. Unfortunately, she knew what it would come to in the end. She wasn't capable of refusing.

Dixie had never minced any words about her relationship with her mother. *She's a manipulator.* Dixie's voice seemed to ring in her mind. *She goes through life using people. Well, I'm done letting her do that to me anymore.*

Maybe Dixie could have managed that, but Deidre didn't have her toughness. She glanced idly toward the building next door, toward the darkened windows of Dixie's apartment, letting Lillian's complaints flow on unheeded.

Averting her eyes from the windows, she noticed the clump of rhododendron at the corner of her property nearest the street. Its immense purple blossoms nearly hid the car that was parked at the curb.

No, not parked. Someone was sitting in it, though all she could make out was a man-size shadow. Her nerves seemed to snap to attention. What was he doing there?

"Deidre, did you hear me?" Lillian's voice was sharp

in her ear. Deidre dropped the curtain she'd pulled back and moved away from the window. She was jumping at shadows.

"What did you say?" She forced herself to concentrate on Dixie's mother.

Lillian sighed. "I said you're the logical person to make the arrangements for Dixie. After all, you were her best friend. And she died in your house."

Deidre realized she was rubbing her forehead again. She'd give it until she'd finished this phone call. If the man was still there, she'd call the police and tell them someone was watching the house.

"I suppose you want me to clear out her apartment, too." There was a certain amount of sarcasm in her tone, and she pulled herself up short. No matter how they'd gotten along, Lillian had lost her only child.

"Sure, that would be great," Lillian said quickly. "I don't want the stuff. You can sell it and just send me the money."

"What about the funeral costs?" Deidre moved close to the window again, but this time she just pulled the edge of the curtain back an inch or two so she could see out.

The car was still there, and it seemed to her that the man was leaning forward, peering intently at her house. She dropped the curtain back into place, her hand closing into a fist. If Frank were here, he'd laugh at her for being afraid of the dark. This was the time of day she missed him the most. The house felt empty without him.

"Funeral costs?" Lillian contrived to sound as if she'd never heard the phrase. "I thought you'd want to take care of that. Seeing as how you were such good friends and all."

Deidre found she was clenching her teeth so tightly that her head throbbed. Somehow she didn't think anything she said was going to force Lillian to take on this responsibility, but Deidre would be darned if she was going to pay all the costs, as well.

"I'll deal with everything," she said, suddenly eager to escape the call, "once I receive written authorization from you allowing me power of attorney. And any money in Dixie's account or realized from selling her personal belongings will go toward the funeral expenses."

She was surprised at her own temerity. Something about the thought that she was being spied on seemed to bring out the nerve Dixie had always said she didn't have.

"Well, I'd have thought..." The whine trailed off. "All right, then." The final words were snapped, and the call ended.

Fingers trembling a little, Deidre clutched the phone as she went to the window. If the car still sat there, she'd call the police.

The instant she pulled the curtain back again, the car began to move. It glided down the street and out of her field of vision.

She couldn't very well call the police and tell them that the vehicle had been there and now was gone. But the incident left an indefinable apprehension prickling along her skin.

CHAPTER FIVE

By THE NEXT AFTERNOON, the previous night's fears struck Deidre as foolish. She hadn't escaped the thoughts entirely, but they'd been superseded by her pleasure that Kevin seemed almost back to normal again.

Deidre couldn't as easily get rid of her dread regarding making the funeral arrangements for Dixie, and she knew perfectly well why. It had been only a year since she'd done that for Frank. This new grief seemed to have renewed her pain over his loss. Seeing the funeral director again, choosing the casket and the flowers, arranging the service—how did she do all of that without reliving the worst days of her life?

She had to, that was all. So she would do it, one step at a time.

She moved to the window of the workroom for a quick look. Kevin and Benjamin were playing an unskilled version of baseball in the backyard while she and Judith packed orders for shipment.

"I did just take a look at the boys," Judith reminded her, voice gentle.

"I know, I know." She turned away from the sight of Kevin hurling a plastic ball toward Benjamin. At least, that was where it was intended to go. It landed in the middle of the flower bed instead. "I don't know why the ball always has to land in the middle of that clump of irises. They'll never bloom at the rate at which Kevin is stepping on them."

"Irises are sturdy. They'll straighten up in no time, just like Kevin is doing." Judith whipped a strip of packaging tape around the box she held with a practiced hand.

"He is better today." Her spirits rose at the fact. "'Have him take it easy for a few days,' the doctor said. You'd think she'd never met Kev."

"Five-year-old boys have only two speeds. Asleep and running full tilt." Judith chuckled. "Men aren't much better. Remember when Eli had that bad flu last winter? The minute his fever broke, I caught him trying to head out to the barn for the milking. I practically had to sit on him to keep him in."

Deidre nodded, smiling. She remembered how worried Judith had been, too. She and Eli were two halves of a whole, and having him so sick had shaken her. Deidre picked up a pair of wooden birds and began wrapping them in Bubble Wrap. She and Frank had been a pair, too. If he'd been in the house last night, she wouldn't have noticed half a dozen cars parked out front.

The memory disrupted the even rhythm of the packing, and Judith gave her a sharp look. "Is something wrong? Something more, I mean."

Deidre avoided her eyes. Somehow she didn't want to talk about that car or the person in it who'd sped away when she'd looked out. Talking about it might make it seem more threatening than it was.

"Now that we're home, I'm finding it hard not to be reminded of what happened here."

Judith gave that her usual grave consideration. "*Ja*, I see how that would be. Still, this house has seen a lot in all the years since your grandfather built it. Sorrow, but happiness, as well. Much more happiness, ain't so?"

As usual, Judith's perspective steadied her. In the long history of this home, it *had* seen plenty of love and joy. Maybe that was strong enough to counteract the taint of murder. Deidre managed a smile. "I don't know if houses can have feelings, but that's a good thought."

"I've always thought a home takes on the character of the people who live in it, ain't so?" Judith affixed the last label to a package. "Your house has a feeling of *wilkom*. Of hospitality. One bad happening can't change it."

Deidre hoped she was right. "I know that, right now, with the sun streaming in the windows and the boys yelling outside. But at night, when I've put Kevin to bed, he seems…well, too far away. I guess I'll get over it, but right now I'm behaving like a new mother, tiptoeing into the bedroom to be sure the baby is still breathing."

"*Ach*, I did that, too." Judith studied her for a moment. "Would you want me to come and spend the night for a couple of nights? Eli can manage fine, and I'd be glad to."

Deidre clasped her hand for a moment in gratitude for the offer. But of course she couldn't accept. "No, I don't want you leaving your family to fend for themselves so you can babysit me. The last thing I want is to make Kevin feel as though there's something to be afraid of."

Before Judith could argue, the pop of the plastic bat hitting the ball caught Deidre's attention. "Don't tell me one of them finally managed to connect with the ball." She headed for the window, but Judith reached it first.

"Not on their own," she said. "They have company."

Deidre pushed the curtain back to look out. She might have known. There was a certain persistence about Jason that was difficult to deflect.

She stood watching him for a moment. His face was relaxed and smiling as he showed Benjamin something about holding the bat, his big hands covering the boy's small ones. His expression wasn't remotely like the look he generally turned on her, which came more under the heading of wary and suspicious. Come to think of it, that made his determination to be involved in their lives even more of a puzzle than it already was.

"It's wonderfully kind of him to take so much trouble with the boys." Judith reached for her bonnet. "I'd best be getting home to put supper on. I'll *komm* tomorrow."

"I'll walk out with you." She knew only too well that Kevin, who had not yet mastered discretion, was only too likely to blurt out something she'd rather not have anyone hear. "Why not let Benjy stay for another half hour? I'll watch him walk home across the field." Watching him would be impossible in late summer, when corn turned the field into an impenetrable forest of stalks, but now she'd be able to see the boy all the way to the farmhouse door.

"Sounds *gut*." They went out together, and Kevin came running to her.

"I hit the ball, Mommy!"

She caught him, mindful of the urge to sweep him safely into her arms. "No running, Kevin. Remember? Not until the doctor says it's okay."

"I'll remember. But did you see me hit the ball?"

"That's great. And I think Benjamin did, too, right?" She smiled at Benjy, who gave her a gap-toothed grin. His fair skin had already picked up a smattering of freckles.

"They're pretty good, both of them." Jason smiled from one boy to the other. "Does Echo Falls have a baseball team?"

"Not one that takes five-year-olds." A fact for which she was very thankful. She'd heard from friends who had older children about the endless games their kids played.

"We can get really good before we're old enough to try out." Kevin was the eternal optimist. "Right, Benjy?"

Benjy, whose English was a bit spotty, just grinned, and she wasn't sure he'd understood. In any event, although the Amish kids played ball, they seldom joined actual leagues.

"I must be going." Judith bent to give Benjamin a rapid string of instructions in Pennsylvania Dutch, most of which Deidre could follow. Then, with a wave, she set off toward home.

"Did you understand all that?" Jason's eyebrows had lifted. "Pennsylvania Dutch, was it?"

She nodded. "Most of it. I've been hearing it all my life, after all. Kevin knows a fair amount, and with what English Benjy knows, they manage to communicate pretty well."

"I've noticed." The boys had devised a game of walking around and around the bat that they held upright in between them. "They do a nice job of entertaining themselves."

Deidre wondered whether there was an implied criticism in the words. "I curtail the electronics as much as possible. I'd like Kev to have the kind of childhood his father and I had here in Echo Falls. Isn't that natural?"

Jason shrugged. "Maybe so. Most parents I've run into seem to want their kids to be up on all the latest. Prepares them for the world they'll live in, I'd think."

She was tempted to make a retort about his obviously childless life, but restrained herself. Like most people not possessed of children, he thought he knew it all. He'd lose that belief after a few short weeks of parenthood.

"I'm not worried about Kevin being left behind," she said, her voice cool.

"No, I guess not. He's a sharp kid." His voice changed a little. "Did you realize the police were in your friend's apartment today?"

Deidre shook her head. "I suppose they have to go through her things. I wasn't able to tell them where her ex-husband is, but she probably had his address written down somewhere."

"I imagine it's more than that on their minds. They'd be looking for any indication of who she might have been involved with."

The idea made her feel as if something crawled on

her skin. Poor Dixie, to have her private life dragged out into public. The newspaper stories were bad enough with their speculation. Everyone in town would be talking about it, wondering who could have done it. Her preoccupation with Kevin had insulated her from much of the gossip, but it had to be flying.

Jason glanced at the boys, still occupied by their game and surely getting very dizzy by now. "I've been meaning to ask you about something that has me puzzled."

"Yes?" She prepared to rebuff any further comments about her parenting.

"Why on earth is the town called Echo Falls?" He sounded aggrieved. "I haven't seen anything resembling a waterfall since I've been here."

Deidre let the smile spread across her face. "You have. You just haven't noticed it." She called to her son. "Kev, Jason wants to know where Echo Falls is."

Kevin abandoned the game, letting the bat fall. "It's right there. Can't you see it?" He pointed toward the ridge that soared upward from the valley floor.

Shielding his gaze with his hand, Jason peered toward the ridge. "Where?"

Deidre pointed. "Do you see that little dip in the line of the ridge? It's actually a cleft separating two ridges. Just drop your gaze down from there and look for the glint of something bright. Now that the trees are leafing out, it's harder to spot."

"Well, I see something, but it can't be much of a falls. What is it…three feet high?"

"Actually it's close to ninety feet." Deidre was enjoying herself. "Not terribly wide, but very powerful."

"It's huge," Kev said, making an exaggerated gesture. "Wait till you get up close. It's loud, too. You'll see."

Jason seemed to be measuring the distance with his eye. "I'm not sure I'd want to hike all that way."

"But you have to!" Kev wailed. "Everyone goes to the falls."

"Of course you have to see the falls, especially if you're going to be living here." Deidre took a slightly malicious pleasure in needling him. "After all, you can't very well claim you're a resident of Echo Falls if you haven't."

"We'll go for our hike and picnic pretty soon, won't we, Mommy? We do that as soon as the weather gets warm enough. We see the falls, and we take our lunch in knapsacks, and sometimes we eat at the old mill." His expression lit up. "I know! You can come with us. I'll show you everything. He can, can't he, Mommy?"

She'd always loved Kevin's open nature and his friendliness, but at the moment she could do with a little restraint.

Jason was eyeing her, and his smile told her that he was very aware of her discomfort. She'd certainly fallen into her own trap, hadn't she? She had no intention of taking Jason on a family outing, but she couldn't very well say so. Not with Kevin right there, looking at her appealingly.

"Mommy, can't he?" Kev clearly expected her to jump right in with an invitation. And Jason... What did Jason expect, giving her that sardonic look?

"If he wants to, of course he's welcome, Kev. But Mr. Glassman might have something else to do. And anyway, we haven't decided when we're going yet." She darted a look at Jason, knowing he was enjoying the entire fiasco. "I'll let you know when we decide," she added.

But she was sure of one thing: she'd pick a time when it would be impossible for Jason to go with them on their family trek to the falls.

JASON WATCHED DEIDRE'S expressive face. Did she realize that her thoughts were written there so clearly? She obviously didn't want to ask him along on the proposed picnic, but her old-fashioned manners wouldn't let her come right out with it. Well, she didn't need to worry. Hiking through bug-infested woods to look at a waterfall, no matter how high, wasn't on his agenda.

With one of those quicksilver movements of his, Kevin darted off toward the swing set, with Benjamin following at a steady trot. They made an interesting pair—Kevin fast, agile and talkative, and the Amish boy steady, solid and silent. But the silent part might be because Jason was a stranger, he supposed.

Jason half expected Deidre to make an equally quick departure, but she glanced at him, frowning a little.

"Do you know anything about when Dixie…Dixie's body, that is, will be released for burial?"

The question wasn't one he'd even considered. "No, but I'm sure I can find out for you. Why?"

"I'd like to know before I start making arrangements with the funeral home."

Now he was the one frowning. "You? Why are you making the arrangements? Her family…"

Deidre was shaking her head before he finished. "There's only her mother, and she doesn't live in the area. When I spoke with her, she asked me to take care of things here."

He studied her face, sensing her reluctance. "Is that some unwritten rule of small-town life that I don't know about? Someone gets herself killed in your house, so you become responsible for the funeral?"

"And clearing her apartment. And dealing with disposing Dixie's belongings." Deidre looked frustrated at the thought. "But her mother insists she can't handle it, so she passed the job on to me."

"I'd say pass it right back again." Ridiculous to be feeling protective of Deidre—to be thinking that she'd been through so much herself that she shouldn't have to take on this burden, as well.

"Easier said than done. You don't know Lillian." Deidre brushed back a strand of silky hair that the breeze had tossed in her face. "Anyway, I was Dixie's closest friend here. I'll handle it. I did tell Lillian she'd have to grant me power of attorney. That's right, isn't it?"

He nodded. "Limited power of attorney will allow you to do what needs to be done. If you're set on it, I'll have a word with the coroner's office and let you know what I find out."

"Good. Be sure to chalk up the billable hours." She smiled at his surprised look. "That's what Frank used to say when people would come up to him at parties expecting free legal advice."

"Anything I can do for you comes under the heading of professional courtesy." The knowledge that he was acting for the judge behind her back made it difficult to sound light. "Does it bother you…that I seem to have taken over Frank's place at the office?"

"Not really." Her clear blue eyes didn't show any regret. "The office wasn't as important as it might have been to Frank if it had been his own practice."

He thought he could interpret that without much trouble. The past few days had shown him how much the judge liked to run even the smallest things. He could imagine that he'd have had high standards where Frank was concerned. The Frank he remembered had seemed to relish the freedom law school had offered. He'd talked about breaking free of the family firm, about heading for the city, the way so many classmates had done. But he'd chosen to come back to Echo Falls instead. Because of Deidre? Maybe so.

Before he could say something that would probably not sit well with Deidre, a vehicle pulled into the driveway and came to a sputtering halt by the detached garage. *Vehicle*—he guessed that was the right word. It was an elderly pickup, the color of which was difficult to determine, since there was evidence of repeated attempts to repaint. The primary component was rust.

The individual who ambled toward them was about as odd-looking as the truck—fairly short and stocky, with dirty-blond hair straggling to his shoulders, he wore a pair of stained bib overalls with what was probably someone's discarded dress shirt. As he drew closer, Jason noticed that his round face was oddly unlined and expressionless, like that of a doll that had been freshly painted, making it impossible to guess his age.

"Billy, hi." Deidre was smiling. Kevin stopped climbing the sliding board long enough to wave.

The man came to a halt in front of them… He stared at Jason for a moment, not blinking. It was oddly unnerving.

"I didn't expect you today, Billy." Deidre drew his attention away gently. "Did you come to work on the porch steps?"

Billy shook his head. "Who's he?" He jerked a nod toward Jason.

"This is Jason Glassman. He's working in the judge's office now. Jason, this is Billy Kline. He's been helping me with some odd jobs around the house."

Billy ignored the introduction, just as he ignored the hand Jason held out. "Brought something for Kev. 'Cause he was in the hospital." He drew a small object wrapped in a faded bandanna from his pocket.

"One of your animals?" Deidre's eyes lit. "He'll love it, I know. Kev, come here," she called. "Billy has a present for you."

Kev slid off the end of the board and galloped toward them, slowing to a trot at a frowning look from his mother, with Benjy following along behind. "Hey, Billy. Did you make me something?"

Jason was beginning to get curious about the contents of the bandanna. Both Deidre and Kevin acted as if it were something special, but he… The thought went astray when Kevin pulled the bandanna away, revealing a carved wooden bird.

Not just a bird. It was a hawk, wings spread in flight.

Even though it was crudely carved, it still managed to give an impression of strength and freedom. Looking at it, he could almost imagine it taking off from the boy's palm.

"Wow, that's really something," he said. He glanced at Billy, but he was following Benjy and Kevin as they went swooping the hawk through the air, so he turned to Deidre instead. "Does he do many of those carvings?"

"Not as many as I'd like. I could sell any number of them for him, but Billy says he just makes them for people he knows. And since he doesn't know the people who might order them, he's not interested."

She didn't seem to find anything strange in that attitude. "You'd think, to look at him, that he'd be glad of the money."

Deidre shook her head, smiling a little. "Billy does all right. He couldn't hold down a regular job, but he's a good worker when he puts his mind to it."

"I take it he's somebody else you've known all your life." Was there anyone in this town who wasn't an old friend or relation of hers?

"Pretty much," she admitted. "He's about my age, and he used to hang around on the fringes of school activities even after he dropped out." Deidre's blue eyes seemed to darken with concern. "He was very fond of Dixie, and I've been worried about how he's taking her death."

Jase's attention sharpened at the words. "Was she fond of him, too?"

"I've thought sometimes..." She hesitated, as if not sure she should go on.

"You've thought what?" he prompted. Didn't she realize that someone she knew was very probably a murderer?

She shook her head. "It's nothing. Since Dixie came back to town, she'd ask him to do things for her. Nothing big—just the sort of chores I pay him for. But she..."

He got it now. She didn't want to criticize her dead friend. "She didn't pay him, is that it?"

"He wanted to help her. They were old friends."

He could hear the defensive note in her voice, even if she wasn't aware of it. Before he could press her on it, Billy came back. He focused on Deidre, once again ignoring Jase's presence.

"Do they know yet? Did they catch him?"

"Not yet." Her voice was gentle. "But I'm sure they'll find the person who hurt Dixie."

Billy shook his head, and his hands tightened into fists. Jase was uneasily aware of the muscles under the faded shirt.

"They have to!" His voice rose. "It's not right. Dixie..." Suddenly he was crying—great gasping sobs that shook his whole body.

Deidre patted his shoulder. "I know. I miss her, too. She was our good friend, right? Ever since we were kids. Remember how you gave her the pretty stone you found in the creek? She really loved it."

Something about the low, loving voice seemed to get through to Billy. He nodded, knuckling his eyes. "She did, yeah."

"We'll always have a place in our hearts for her, but I don't think she'd want to see you crying, would she?"

Billy scrubbed at his face with his hands. "She'd say only babies cried. She'd say she was too tough to cry. But she wasn't. She..."

For an instant he seemed to shudder on the brink of another outburst. But he turned and almost ran back to his truck.

"Poor Billy." Deidre watched the truck pull out, brushing against the thick clump of rhododendrons at the end of the drive. "I was afraid he'd take it hard."

Jase studied her face. "Just what kind of relationship did he have with Dixie?"

"What are you implying?" She glared at him. "They were friends since they were kids, that's all."

"Right, I know." Her naïveté irked him into saying more than he should. "You and Dixie and Billy and Frank and whoever else—all friends since you were kids. But kids grow up. Maybe it's time you took a look at who those kids turned into. Billy might have the mind of a child, but he's a grown man. You need to wake up and stop trusting everybody."

Deidre seemed to turn to ice. "I don't have any reason not to trust them."

The implication being that she knew them but she didn't know Jase. Which left him without a leg to stand on, because if she did know him, then she'd know that he was the last person in the world she should trust.

BY THE TIME Deidre was fixing supper, she'd managed to exile Jason from her thoughts at least a dozen times. Too bad he refused to stay gone.

The idea that he could think someone like Billy could possibly have harmed Dixie… It was ridiculous. She'd known him all her life—

She stopped. So what if she trusted people? Wasn't

that better than going around constantly on the alert? Echo Falls had its share of troubles, but by and large, it was a good place to live. A safe place, most of the time, despite what had happened to Dixie. She wouldn't let that tragedy make her either cynical or fearful.

Maybe Jason's life had taught him not to trust. If so, there was nothing she could do about it. Besides...

The doorbell rang, and she wiped her hands on the dish towel and hurried toward the front hall to find her mother-in-law waiting on the porch.

"Sylvia, how nice to see you."

She made an attempt to give Sylvia her usual kiss, but her mother-in-law's arms were filled with several large bags and the kiss landed somewhere short of her cheek. Still, it was close enough to catch a faint whiff of alcohol and to note the haphazard placement of blush and lipstick on Sylvia's thin face.

With her ash-blond hair carefully arranged and her casually expensive clothes, at a glance Sylvia looked younger than her years. It was her ravaged face beneath the makeup that betrayed her.

This was not one of her good days, apparently. Which made it all the more surprising that Sylvia seemed to be alone. The judge was careful about allowing her to drive.

"Did you drive yourself over?" She hoped not.

"Franklin locked the garage door on my car. He said I shouldn't be driving. Silly. It would serve him right if I broke the lock and drove off."

"You wouldn't want to cause any damage." Her

mother-in-law seemed unusually belligerent today. "How did you get here?"

"Madge brought me. She wanted to come in, and I just told her she could go right on to the pharmacy and pick up some things. Always spying on me." Sylvia's voice fell to a discontented murmur, and she seemed to lose track of what she was saying.

Madge Hepple, the family housekeeper, was rather nosy, but looking after Sylvia had to be a thankless and sometimes impossible job. The judge would undoubtedly blame Madge if Sylvia had gotten hold of something to drink.

Heart sinking, Deidre put her arm around Sylvia's waist to lead her into the living room. "It's nice to see you, anyway. Have you been shopping?" She helped Sylvia put the bags on the floor and settled her on the sofa.

"Shopping? Oh, the bags, you mean. Presents, for Kevin. Poor little Kevin." Sylvia's eyes filled with tears. "Poor baby. I wanted to come to the hospital, you know I did, but Franklin said...said it would be too upsetting. I'm sorry. I should have come anyway, I know." The tears spilled over.

"It's fine, Sylvia, really. There was nothing you could do there." She patted the thin restless hands that twisted in Sylvia's lap. It seemed to be her time for comforting the weeping. First Lillian, then Billy and now Sylvia. "It's much better for you to come now that he's feeling well again. I'll call him."

Kevin should have heard his grandmother's arrival. Going to the bottom of the stairs, she called up to him.

"Kevin? Come down, please. Grandma is here to see you."

Kevin appeared at the stop of the stairs, and at his mother's nod, he came down docilely enough. He was wary of Sylvia's moods, and Deidre couldn't blame him for hesitating. He was too young to understand the reasons for them.

He reached her, and Deidre put a reassuring hand on his shoulder. "Go and give Grandma a kiss. She brought something for you." She feared it sounded as if she were bribing him, but whatever worked to smooth the relationship was worth it.

Kevin crossed the room with a little more spring to his step. "Hi, Grandma. How are you?" he added, mindful of his manners.

"My poor little boy." Sylvia hugged him close. "Poor boy."

Kevin wiggled himself free. "I'm all better now. Honest."

Sylvia mopped her eyes. "So you are. I was so worried about you. I kept thinking what would I do if I lost—"

"Why don't you show Kevin what you brought?" Deidre interrupted ruthlessly. She wasn't going to have Sylvia planting the idea in Kevin's head that he might have died.

"Yes, of course." Sylvia rummaged through the bags. "The man at the store said these were just right for a boy Kevin's age. I hope you like them."

Kev was already pulling the elaborate building set with all its accessories from the bags, and his expression surely told her the answer to that question. His grin nearly split his face. With the parcel that had arrived this morning from her mother and stepfather, Kevin was getting as many presents as he did on his birthday.

"It's the whole set. Look, Mommy, the whole set with all the extra pieces. Wow. It's all for me?"

"All for you, sweet boy." Sylvia patted his cheek, obviously gratified by his reaction. "You deserve it after everything you went through."

"He's fine now," Deidre pointed out. "It's best not to dwell on it, don't you think?"

That seemed to get through to Sylvia. "Of course, of course. I know just what you mean. I won't say another word about it."

Deidre knew better than to rely on that, but at least for the moment she could smile.

Kevin was already ripping the box open, intent on getting at the pieces as fast as possible, and bits of cellophane and cardboard fluttered across the floor like confetti, with each new piece that was unearthed being greeted with shouts of happiness.

Deidre didn't miss the way Sylvia pressed her fingers to her forehead. She couldn't tolerate much in the way of boyish enthusiasm. That fact was among the many things the judge seemed to ignore in his determination to have her and Kevin move in with them. Or maybe Kevin wasn't supposed to be a normal little boy in that house.

"Kev, take those into the dining room and set it up there, okay? We need to be able to walk in here."

She countered his mulish look with a firm one of

her own, and he began trundling the pieces into the next room. Deidre usually discouraged building sets anywhere but in his room, but it seemed only fair to let Sylvia see his enjoyment at a safe distance.

But even with the toys at a distance, Sylvia still seemed distracted. She picked up a sofa pillow, hugging it against her and pulling at the fringe. Her lips worked a little, as if there was something she wanted to say.

"You're a good mother." She blurted the words out, then pressed her fingers to her lips.

"That's nice of you to say." Deidre uttered the conventional response while wondering how much longer Sylvia was going to hold herself together. "Would you like a cup of coffee? Or tea?" She couldn't think of anything else that might help. How long would Madge take at the pharmacy?

Sylvia didn't seem to hear the offer. She shook her head, the ready tears forming again. "I wasn't a good mother to Frank. I can't deny it. You know, don't you? I wasn't a good mother."

Sylvia had spent too many of Frank's formative years in and out of rehab, but all that was in the past. Right now, Deidre would settle for averting the sort of scene she didn't want Kevin to see.

"You loved him." She clasped one of Sylvia's twitching hands again. "That was most important. Frank always knew that you loved him."

But Sylvia shook her head, tears beginning to flow. "You're a good mother," she said again, as if she was arguing with someone. "A boy should be with his mother."

"Well, of course, but if a mother can't…"

"I keep telling him." Sylvia's voice broke on a sob. "I keep telling him a boy belongs with his mother. She knows what's best. But he won't listen."

Something cold seemed to touch the back of Deidre's neck. "Are you talking about Frank?"

Sylvia managed to focus on her for a moment. "Kevin. Kevin belongs with his mother. With you."

Deidre tried to push away the dread that pressed on her. "Of course Kevin belongs with me. No one can take him away from me." She glanced quickly at Kev, but he was totally wrapped up in the pieces he was putting together. "Sylvia, what are you talking about?"

Sylvia's eyes were wide. Frightened. "Franklin," she whispered.

Her obvious fear was infectious. The world spun around and settled back into place as the doorbell rang.

Sylvia gasped, shooting a look toward the door. "Madge. Don't tell. Don't tell."

"I won't tell anyone." Deidre grasped both her hands in a firm grip. "But first you have to tell me what you're talking about. What does Franklin want to do?"

The doorbell rang again. Sylvia cast it an agonized look. "I can't. I can't."

She had to steel herself. Had to voice the thought she could hardly bear to let into her mind. "What does Franklin think he can do to us?"

"He says Kevin should be living in our house. He says it's not safe for him here. He's going to make it happen."

Deidre stood, feeling as if every separate muscle had

to be told to work. She moved toward the door. She had to open it, had to appear normal to Madge.

Since the judge hadn't repeated his intentions to move them into Ferncliff, she'd been assuming that he had accepted her answer. She'd thought that Kevin's accident would push all of that out of his mind.

It seemed she'd been wrong. Instead, it had made him more determined to take away their freedom to live their lives the way she and Frank had planned.

Sylvia probably feared he could somehow force Deidre into agreeing, but she was wrong. And if the judge thought that, he was in for the fight of his life. She was, as well, and it was a fight she couldn't possibly lose.

CHAPTER SIX

DESPITE THE JUDGE'S assurance that the police would cooperate with him, Jason entered the chief's office the next day with less than his usual confidence. Chief Carmichaels had struck him as a guy who would walk a careful line where the integrity of his office was concerned.

Still, ostensibly his inquiry was a perfectly legitimate one—to find out when Dixie James's body would be released for burial. The fact that he'd also like to know what progress the cops were making in the case lay at the back of his mind like a weight. There was no reason to believe Deidre and her son were in danger from the killer, but he couldn't entirely dismiss the possibility from his mind. Even Chief Carmichaels's firm statement to the press that Kevin didn't remember anything might mean nothing to a frightened, desperate killer.

Carmichaels rose from behind a desk that was littered with papers, holding out his hand. "Morning, Counselor. What can we do for you?" He waved Jason to a chair.

"Mrs. Morris wanted me to find out when she could make funeral arrangements for the deceased. It seems the woman's mother asked her to take care of things here."

He thought he'd kept any personal judgments out of his words, but Carmichaels grimaced slightly. "That sounds like Lillian James."

"You know her, then?" He leaned back, prepared to talk about anything that might lead to a discussion of the case.

"Knew her," he corrected, hands relaxing on the desktop. "Years ago, I guess. They must have left Echo Falls when Dixie was maybe thirteen or so."

"What took them away from here?" That was something no one had ever explained, the same way no one had explained why Dixie had come back.

Carmichaels's heavy face settled into a frown. "Seemed like Dixie kind of went off the rails when she got into her teens. Started getting rebellious, getting into trouble with older kids."

"Her parents didn't do anything about it?" He didn't find uncaring parents surprising, but he figured people around here might.

"The father was never in the picture, not that I can remember. And Lillian wasn't what you'd call an attentive mother. After a few close calls that might have ended up with Social Services taking notice, they cleared out. Just gone with no notice to anybody."

"Seems surprising that Dixie would come back here."

The chief shrugged. "Way I hear it, she wanted a fresh start after a divorce. She probably thought there were folks here who'd help her out for old time's sake."

People like Deidre, Jason supposed, who seemed to

have a weakness for helping lame ducks across busy highways. Harmless enough normally, but with Dixie, it had inadvertently led to endangering her son.

Carmichaels seemed to recall the reason for Jason's visit. "As for releasing the body, I've got the final report from the coroner's office here." He shuffled through papers and came up with a file, opening it with what almost seemed like deliberate slowness. "Looks like the coroner's satisfied with the cause of death—severe blow to the head that crushed the skull."

"Isn't it surprising there were no wounds that indicated she had tried to defend herself?"

Carmichaels lifted an eyebrow. "Thought you dealt with white-collar crime."

Now it was Jason's turn to shrug. "Like plenty of young attorneys without a family firm to step into, I started out with the public prosecutor's office as an assistant DA, doing anything that came along."

"Figures." The chief seemed satisfied. "Yeah, you'd expect to find some indication that she'd put up an arm or hand to shield herself, but there was no sign of it. Looks like the assailant caught her completely off guard."

Jason came to the obvious conclusion. "So either she didn't hear him coming, or he was someone she didn't think she had reason to fear."

"Even if she had the television on, with the boy asleep upstairs it wouldn't have been loud enough to cover the sound of somebody entering." Carmichaels had obviously thought it through. "Besides, you said the door was open when you got there. If it had been locked when Deidre left, Dixie had to have let the person in."

"A boyfriend?" Deidre had said Dixie wouldn't have done so, but Deidre had a way of taking a rosy view of people that might not have been justified in Dixie's case.

"Seems the most likely idea. And we're looking for the ex-husband, just in case you were wondering."

Jason was surprised into a smile. "I guess I was, at that. You haven't laid hands on him yet?"

"We will. Or somebody will. We started inquiries at the last place Dixie lived before coming back." Carmichaels leaned back in his desk chair, which creaked in protest. "Any more ideas you wanted to share?"

Since he seemed to have thawed, Jason decided to bring up Billy. Deidre wouldn't like it, of course.

"A guy stopped by the house yesterday who was pretty emotional about Dixie. Just wondered if you'd looked into him. Billy Kline, his name is."

"Billy?" The chief said the name sharply, and then repeated it more thoughtfully. "Billy Kline. What would his interest be in Dixie James?"

"From what Mrs. Morris let drop, I gather he was one of the old friends Dixie found helpful when she came back to Echo Falls. Other than that, I don't know what their relationship was." He hesitated. "Look, you probably know better than I do what his mental state is. But when he burst out crying..."

Carmichaels seemed to relax. "If that's all, it's nothing. Billy does that when he gets upset or frustrated. There's no harm in him. Everybody knows that."

"Maybe so. But speaking as an outsider, it seemed

to me he was carrying a lot of anger around with him. And he's strong enough."

"Even then…" Obviously Carmichaels found it just as hard as Deidre had to imagine anything violent about Billy. "Well, I'll have a talk with him. If he'd seen something of Dixie since she came back, he might be helpful."

Carmichaels seemed to consider that the end of the conversation, because he stood. "If there's anything else, you be sure to tell me."

He'd like to press about the results of their search of the woman's apartment, but he didn't want to push his luck. "So I can tell Mrs. Morris to have the funeral home get in touch with the coroner about pickup?"

Carmichaels nodded. "If she's determined to take it on, I guess she can get on with it."

"You sound as if you don't quite buy Lillian James's excuses for not handling the funeral herself."

"People don't change." He grimaced. "Lillian James never accepted any responsibility that she could get someone else to handle, including her kid. So now she's latched on to Deidre. And knowing Deidre, she couldn't say no. Her folks were the same way. Anybody needing help or a handout could be sure of getting it from them. Unlike Frank's folks."

"The judge and his wife aren't charitable?" It wasn't his business, but something told him the interrelationships of people in this town counted for a lot.

"Charity, yes." Carmichaels walked to the door with him. "So long as it's something that puts up a plaque with the donors' names on it. That's not the same as putting yourself out to give somebody a helping hand."

"Still valuable, I guess." No, he couldn't see Judge Franklin Morris "putting himself out" to help anyone other than his family, as the chief had phrased it.

"Guess so." Carmichaels stopped with his hand on the doorknob. "Seeing as you're new in town, maybe you ought to get to know people before you line up too firmly with one side or another."

"I didn't know there were sides to pick." Not true, was it? There was definitely a side to choose between Deidre and her formidable father-in-law.

"Maybe. Maybe not." Carmichaels didn't seem to want to commit himself further. "I'll be seeing you, I guess."

Nodding his thanks, Jason walked through the door and onto the street. The sun had been shining when he'd come in, but now a light rain was slanting across the pavement. Spring weather was changeable.

Like his attitude. He'd been fully prepared to do what the judge wanted him to do in regard to Deidre. But that had been before he'd gotten to know her.

If she hasn't done anything wrong, then she has nothing to fear.

Somehow that rationalization wasn't carrying a whole lot of weight with him right now.

"So I've called the funeral home, and Gary Wilson is stopping by later to talk over the arrangements." She was relieved that it was Gary she'd reached, rather than his father, who'd handled Frank's funeral. Gary was a friend. He'd known Dixie, and Deidre could talk easily with him.

"I asked Adam Bennett to conduct the service," she went on. "He didn't really know Dixie at all, but I'm sure he'll do a good job." Deidre and Judith sat in the kitchen with coffee and the sticky buns Judith had brought while the rain poured down outside and the two boys played with Kevin's new building set.

"I'm certain sure of that. He seems like a *gut* man. It's a shame Dixie's *mamm* can't be here. I can't imagine…" She let that trail off. Judith would never say anything negative about someone, but her feelings were clear. "So the police will let you go ahead with it?"

Deidre nodded. "Jason Glassman spoke to the police for me. He called to tell me the funeral home people could pick up the body. So the service will be on Thursday."

"Something quiet, I guess."

Deidre nodded. "Normally I would invite people to the house afterward, but since Dixie died here…" She rubbed her forehead. "Well, I just can't. So the funeral will be at eleven, followed by a lunch at the church. The women's group offered to bring the food."

"I'll be *sehr* glad to bring something, too. I'll drop it off at the church kitchen." Bringing food in the aftermath of trouble was Judith's normal response.

"Thanks, Judith." She was on the verge of tears, not sure whether they were for Dixie, who died so horribly, or for her own fears over what Frank's father might intend.

She was suddenly aware of Judith's hand clasping hers. "There's something more wrong, ain't so?"

Deidre hesitated, words crowding her tongue. But Judith, of all people, was safe. She could say anything to her and know it would go no further. Contrary to Jason's apparent opinion, she didn't trust people indiscriminately, but she knew Judith too well to have doubts.

"It's Sylvia. She came to bring Kev that building set, and she said..." Deidre paused. A glance at the boys assured her that they couldn't possibly hear. "She seems to have gotten the idea that Franklin is trying to force us to move in with them."

Judith's fingers tightened on hers, but she didn't make the mistake of overreacting. "Did she actually say that?"

"She hinted at it." Deidre tried to reconstruct the conversation in her mind. "When I asked if that was what she meant, she nodded."

Her oval face solemn, Judith considered. "Do you think she really knew what she was talking about? Everyone knows she's had to go for treatment plenty of times."

"I know. That's why I'm not sure what to do about it." Deidre rubbed her forehead, feeling the effects of a sleepless night spent worrying. "She could be imagining things, or possibly she's misinterpreting something the judge said. I'd like to believe that. But if it's true, what will I do?"

"I think you should get a lawyer."

Deidre blinked. She hadn't expected an answer to the question, and to hear Judith suggesting an attorney... The Amish almost never went to the law to settle problems, preferring to let the wisdom and judgment of the church deal with their issues.

"I don't know if it's really a matter for an attorney. I mean, logically there's nothing the judge can do other than put pressure on me to agree."

"I don't know much about the law regarding such things," Judith admitted. "But everyone knows the judge has a lot of power. Influence. I think you should ask someone for help."

"Who?" That was really the question. "Who would I get who'd be willing to stand up against Judge Franklin Morris?"

"Jason has been helpful, ain't so?" But Judith looked troubled.

"Helpful because the judge asked him to be," she said.

Judith smiled. "I think he has other reasons than that. But he works for the judge, so I guess he couldn't go up against him."

"And any other attorney in town would feel the same way, even if they don't work for him. After all, they try most of their cases in front of him."

Human nature being what it was, they couldn't help but be influenced by the judge's position. Jason might think she wore rose-colored glasses, but on that she could see clearly.

"You will have to get someone from out of town, that's all," Judith said with finality. "But first…"

"I know. First I should make sure it's true and not Sylvia's imagination." She rubbed her temples again, feeling as if she were caught in a nightmare.

"You could come right out and ask him," Judith said.

"He'd ask where I got that idea." She could hear him in her mind. "He'd be bound to know it came from Sylvia, and I had to promise her I wouldn't tell. You know how she is. She'd shatter under the least bit of pressure. I can't do that to her."

"I guess not." Judith patted Deidre's hand. "I will think on it and pray about it. But in the meantime..." She was looking toward the front of the house. "You have to decide something, because the judge is coming up your front walk right now."

Deidre felt her stomach clench just as the doorbell sounded its peal. Striving to look normal despite the emotions that were rampaging inside her, she went to the door and pulled it open to face the judge.

"I'd like to talk to you, Deidre."

No polite preliminaries and a forbidding frown told her that the judge's thoughts were not pleasant just now. Her mind raced. Had he found out that Sylvia had told her something? Was he here to deny it or to accuse her of pumping her ailing mother-in-law for information?

"Of course. Come in." She was proud of how calm she managed to sound.

Her father-in-law's glance took in the two boys playing noisily in the dining room and Judith, standing in the kitchen door watching them. Kevin looked up.

"Hi, Grandfather." He was obviously torn between his grandfather's arrival and the lure of his new toys.

The judge's face relaxed in a smile. "I see you're having fun with your new building set."

"It's the best toy ever," Kevin said, giving an extravagant gesture. "Come and see it."

"Another time, all right?"

Before she could wipe the smile from her face, the judge turned back to her. "We'll need to talk in private. This isn't for Kevin's ears."

He could hardly expect her to send Judith and the two boys out in the rain.

"Why don't we talk on the porch? It is a little noisy inside. Kevin is certainly enjoying the building set Sylvia brought him."

Without replying, the judge stepped back out onto the porch and waited for her to follow him. She did so, closing the door.

The rain had cooled the air, and she ran her hands along her arms to warm them. Although given the coolness of the judge's stare, that might equally well be the cause of her chill.

"Is something wrong?" She wouldn't precipitate matters by plunging into questions about what Sylvia might have let slip to him. If that was why he'd come, he'd have to bring it up himself.

"I heard something about you that I find very upsetting."

She held her breath, mind searching for possible responses that would satisfy him.

Then he went on. "Jason Glassman mentioned that you are making yourself responsible for the funeral for Dixie James. In the church, no less. I couldn't believe he had it right, but he seemed sure."

For an instant Deidre was so relieved that this wasn't

about Sylvia that she didn't actually respond. And then the meaning of his words penetrated.

"What is so surprising about that? Dixie was a friend, and she has no family here. Her mother asked me to handle the arrangements."

"You should have had sense enough to tell her no. Why on earth would you agree to such a thing?"

The biting tone of his question had her crossing her arms over her chest as if to protect herself. "I told you. She was my friend." Surely he could understand that.

Her father-in-law's responding look was wintry. "Not a very suitable friend. Surely you know how she encouraged men to chase after her. It was bad enough that she was murdered in your house. Now you want to connect yourself to her still further. Don't you know how people will talk?"

Shaken by his vehemence, she bit back a hasty response and tempered her tone. "Franklin, I'm sure you're overreacting. People won't think anything except that I'm doing a kindness for Dixie's mother, who wasn't able to make the trip."

His jaw worked, and she thought he was struggling to regain control of himself. She'd never seen him lose his temper—that wasn't his way. He could tear a defendant's excuses to ribbons with a cool, judicious judgment, but he prided himself on fairness. Surely he'd see that he was being unreasonable.

"I suppose it's too late now to change things," he conceded finally. He stared out at the slanting rain instead of looking at her. "Perhaps I was a bit hasty, but I don't like to see you subjecting yourself to more talk."

"I know you meant it for the best." Relief that he'd returned to normal made her a little giddy. "Dixie's death has generated a lot of talk, but I'm sure it will fade. As soon as the police arrest someone, things will return to normal."

"Perhaps," he conceded grudgingly. "As to an arrest, Carmichaels doesn't seem to be any closer to a suspect. Unless Kevin remembers something…" He let that trail off.

"He hasn't, and I don't think that's likely. And even if he does eventually remember the events of that night, he may still not have seen enough to identify the man."

"In my opinion, we'll probably never know," he said abruptly.

That was apparently his final word. With a quick nod, he unfurled his black umbrella and headed for his car.

Deidre stood for a moment, not ready to go back inside and let Kevin see her face. That had been the most distasteful conversation she'd ever had with her father-in-law. He'd always had concern for appearances, but why he'd think the funeral would make matters worse, she couldn't imagine. And she still didn't have any idea whether Sylvia's warning had been an alcoholic dream or a solid fact.

A SURPRISING NUMBER of people filed into the church sanctuary for Dixie's funeral. Deidre, turning slightly from the front pew, took a quick survey and hoped the women's group had provided enough food. A foolish thought—there was always enough and some to spare for these events.

Was it curiosity, kindness, or both that prompted so many people to leave their work or their homes this morning? Maybe a little of each. Dixie would undoubtedly have been sarcastic about it, had she known. A smile at the thought eased the tension that had been gripping her throat.

Odd. There was Trey Alter, with Jason Glassman right behind him. Well, not odd that Trey would be present. He'd been a couple of years older, but he'd have known Dixie when they were kids, and he was well enough established with the firm that he wouldn't be swayed by Judge Morris's disapproval.

But she hadn't expected to see Jason. She hadn't forgotten how caustic he'd been about her trust in Dixie the last time she'd spoken to him. Was he here as the judge's surrogate? Surely not, given her father-in-law's attitude toward the whole idea of the funeral.

She'd decided that this would be too much for Kevin, so he was enjoying himself following Eli around the farm this afternoon with Benjy. He hadn't asked any further questions about Dixie, and she hadn't been sure whether to bring up the subject or let it alone.

The organist came to the end of the piece she'd been playing while people were entering, and Adam stepped forward to the pulpit. She suspected he was nervous about conducting such a high-profile funeral, but he was hiding it well. He announced an opening hymn, and the service was underway.

Deidre tried to concentrate on the familiar words

of the service and not let her mind wander to other funerals, other losses. Sometimes focusing fiercely on the words was the only thing that kept the tears at bay.

She had chosen not to have people share their memories of Dixie, given the circumstances, so the service moved on quickly. But that didn't keep her from recalling her own memories of Dixie…the time they'd slept in an improvised tent in the backyard and clung together each time they heard a noise; their efforts to convince her mother to let them start a dog-washing business one summer; the hikes up to the falls, where they scared each other by repeating all the legends that had grown up around the spot.

Jason wondered how she could have such trust in Dixie, but how could she not, when they'd shared so much of their childhoods? With Dixie gone, a part of her childhood was vanished, as well. No one else shared those particular memories, and Dixie's passing had left a hole in her life.

By the time the funeral drew to its close, Deidre was holding back tears only by an enormous effort. Maybe that was one of the functions of a funeral, to push you to experience those emotions and deal with them.

People began to move, most following Adam's directions and going out the door that would lead them to the lunch prepared in the fellowship room.

She slid the hymnal into its rack and noticed Jason coming toward her. But before he reached her, Gary Wilson was there, taking her arm.

"Hang in there. If you want to slip out, we'll keep things moving along here." His professional solemnity vanished for a moment when he smiled, reminding her of the kid he'd been, always in trouble for talking back. "I can guess what Dixie would say about all this ceremony, can't you?"

"Pretty well." She couldn't believe he'd managed to amuse her, but that was Gary's gift. "Thanks, but I'll stay."

"Good for you. I'll check back later to see if you need anything."

As Gary slipped away, Jason moved up beside her. "Another one of your childhood friends?" he asked, and she couldn't tell whether he was being sarcastic.

"Yes, I'm afraid it's impossible to get away from them. Gary wanted to know how I was holding up."

"Looked like he said something funny."

"He wondered what Dixie would have said to all this. She'd have found it funny, I think." At the thought of Dixie, her eyes suddenly filled with tears and her throat closed.

"I'm sorry." His voice went low, and his hand closed warmly over her arm. "Take it easy."

She blotted tears away. "Give me a second, and I'll be good as new."

Jason nodded and stood where he was, his tall frame effectively shielding her from the people who moved past the pew. It was hard to remember that she was annoyed with him when he was being so kind. Deidre touched her nose with the tissue. Some women might be able to weep attractively, but she doubted she was one of them.

She slid the tissue into her bag and gave him a genuine smile. "There, all better. Won't you come over to lunch?"

"The funeral baked meats?" He raised an eyebrow. "I don't think I qualify. I didn't even know her."

"You're here. That's what counts." She gave him a nudge toward the door. "Come on. The food will be good. The women of the church always go all out for a funeral."

Ahead of them, elderly Grace Fleming glanced back, obviously overhearing the remark. "It's the last thing we can do for someone, so it ought to be the best food we can manage. How are you, Deidre? And who is this young man?"

Jason blinked, apparently not used to being called a "young man," but in comparison to Miss Grace's ninety-some years, anyone under fifty was young.

"This is Jason Glassman, Miss Grace. He's the new attorney in the judge's office. Jason, this is Miss Grace Fleming. She ran the only nursery school in town for a number of years, along with being the only person who could ever keep order in the junior high Sunday school class."

Jason took the fragile hand that was extended to him, bending down to the diminutive figure. Miss Grace never disappointed. She wore her usual navy blue sprigged dress that she'd worn to every funeral in town for as long as anyone could remember.

"It's an honor to meet you, Miss Fleming. I'm sorry it's under such sad circumstances." To do him credit, he sounded genuine.

Miss Grace sighed. "Sad indeed. Dixie was such a

promising child. It's too bad there was so much trouble when she got into her teen years. I've always thought a different home environment would have made all the difference for her." She shook her head and began moving toward the hallway. "Poor child," she murmured. "Poor, lost child."

Jason fell into step with Deidre, apparently accepting her lunch invitation. "Chief Carmichaels mentioned that Dixie went off the rails when she hit her teens. Is that how you remember it?"

"I suppose so." She frowned. "It's funny how things change as kids start to mature. Suddenly Dixie didn't seem to be remotely interested in the things that the rest of the girls liked. All she could talk about was makeup and boys. It was as if she'd grown up overnight."

"So you grew apart," he concluded.

Deidre remembered why she was annoyed with him. "I suppose you think that's a reason why I shouldn't have trusted her with my son."

The line had spread out as people entered the large room where lunch was being served, with some heading straight for the buffet line while others sought out friends or staked a claim on a table. Jason stepped to the side, away from the nearest cluster of people, drawing her with him with his hand at her elbow. He stood looking down at her quizzically.

"Is that a cue that I should be apologizing for what I said about your trusting nature?"

"You might take it that way." Deidre looked up at him. Was that warmth in his eyes?

"That presents me with a problem, you see." His

tone was light, but there was something she couldn't identify running underneath the lightness. "It really does worry me that you trust people so easily. I know, I know. You're going to tell me that you know all these people inside and out."

"I'm not as naive as all that." She tried to keep her tone light in return, but it was suddenly hard to concentrate. She was too aware of how close he was. His hand moved to the sensitive skin on the inside of her arm, sliding down toward her hand very slowly. "I mean, I...I know that people have some secrets they keep. Everyone does, even if it's something perfectly harmless."

"What's your secret, Deidre?" His voice was so low that the words reached her in a whisper.

The movement of his fingers against her skin was setting up a ripple of heat. Disconcerting. She hadn't felt this in...well, she didn't know when she'd felt this. All the more reason to be cautious.

"If I told you, it wouldn't be a secret, would it?" To her annoyance, her voice came out in a whisper, as well. People would be looking at them, wondering... "Besides, you haven't told me yours."

He released her arm, and her skin was cold where an instant ago it had been alive with warmth. "Too many to name," he said. He glanced toward the table. "Are you getting in line?"

"No, I...I'd better make the rounds and greet people." She stepped away from him. What was wrong with her?

Jason nodded, his lean face expressionless. "I'll talk to you later, then."

Deidre tried to concentrate on the people she spoke

with, but even with the length of the room between them, she was still too intensely aware of Jason's presence. It was as if there were a live wire connecting them, running across the room, making her aware of his every movement.

Carrying a laden plate, he'd made his way to the table where Trey was sitting. They exchanged a word or two, and then Jason sat down next to him.

"Deidre, I don't think you heard a word I said." Enid Longenberger, president of the library board, gave her a sharp glance. "You're looking pale. What's wrong?"

"Nothing, nothing. I'm so sorry. I just wanted to be sure I'd thanked everyone who came. Dixie would have been so pleased."

Actually, Dixie would have had some tart words, but Enid didn't need to hear that.

"You take my advice and get something to eat yourself. You need to keep up your strength with all the worry you've been through." Enid gave her a little push. "Go on, now. I was going to ask your advice about the annual book sale, but that can wait. Now scoot."

She wasn't sure lunch would help what ailed her at the moment, but she certainly didn't want to start talking about the library book sale just now. Deidre moved toward the serving table, carefully not looking to see if there was an empty seat at Jason's table.

A movement by the door caught her eye. The heavyset man who stood there wasn't anyone she'd ever seen before. Odd. She'd have said she knew every soul who was likely to attend Dixie's funeral, but she didn't know him.

She ought to speak to him…but before she could

move in his direction, the man seemed to notice her staring. He turned, shoved open the door and vanished in the direction of the street.

Odd, she thought again. Dixie'd undoubtedly had friends where she'd lived before coming back to Echo Falls, and it was conceivable that some of them would come to the funeral. But why had the man left so quickly when he saw her watching him?

CHAPTER SEVEN

WHEN JASON ARRIVED back at the office after the funeral, he was greeted by Evelyn with the message that the judge wanted to see him as soon as he returned. To complain because he'd left the office to attend the funeral of a woman he didn't even know?

It shouldn't be that. After all, the judge's interests were supposedly being served by Jase sticking close to Deidre.

Close. He paused with his hand on the door. If the judge could have read his mind in those minutes he'd stood holding on to Deidre and feeling her skin warm under his hand... *Don't think about it*, he ordered himself. Especially not while he was talking to the judge.

Franklin Morris was standing at the window, staring out, when Jason entered the room. He didn't turn when he spoke.

"Did anything untoward happen at the funeral?"

The question startled Jase. What did the judge imagine could have happened in such a setting? "Nothing that I'm aware of. The minister led a short service, and then everyone adjourned to the church hall for lunch."

"All their tongues clacking away, I suppose." Frowning, Judge Morris took his seat behind the desk.

"I suppose so." The judge had made it clear that he hadn't liked Deidre's participation in the funeral. Was that why? A fear of gossip? Jase would think someone in the judge's position would be immune to such concerns.

The judge looked at him from under lowering brows. "Have you learned anything?"

Anything negative about Deidre, in other words. Something in him rebelled. "Nothing," he said flatly. "In my opinion, there's nothing to find. There's no indication she's remotely interested in any man." He seemed to feel the warmth of her skin again, to see the blue of her eyes darkening as she looked at him.

"If the man is married, as my son suspected, they would be careful."

If the judge was determined to go on a wild-goose chase, he'd rather not be dragged along. "So careful no one in this town suspects?" Jase let the skepticism show in his voice. "I get the impression Echo Falls is a hotbed of gossip. If they're not talking about Deidre in connection with a man, chances are there isn't a man. The only men I've seen around the house are the handyman, Billy Kline, and that minister of hers."

The judge stared at him. Then, seeming to have made a decision, he pulled out a key ring, selected a small key and fitted it into the lower drawer of his desk. He pulled out a manila folder, flipped it open and handed it to Jason without a word.

Jason stared at the paper. Ordinary copy paper, computer-generated type, he noted automatically. Nothing to give a clue where it had come from. Innocent-looking, but for the poisonous message it contained.

*That daughter-in-law of yours isn't the angel she
pretends to be. Ask her why the minister comes to
see her so often, why don't you? There's nothing
innocent about the way they look at each other,
and everybody knows it.*

He made an effort to keep his face and his voice expressionless. "Where did this come from? And when?"

"Arrived in the office mail. Marked personal, so at
least Evelyn didn't open it."

The judge's face wore an expression of fastidious distaste. Obviously he didn't want his office tainted by a
hint of scandal. "I don't remember just when, probably
a few months before my son died. About the time Frank
told me about his suspicions. I pressed Frank about it,
but he wasn't willing to say more."

"Do you have any idea who sent it?"

"Some well-wisher, I suppose." His tone was acid.
"As you said yourself, there are plenty of people ready
to pass on any dirt they uncover."

Jason's eyebrows lifted. "Are you saying you consider this genuine? The minister, of all people? Surely
he wouldn't take a risk like that, even if she were interested in him. And as far as I can see, she treats him the
way you'd expect her to treat her minister."

"I have no idea whether it's true or not, but the fact
is that people are suspicious."

"One person."

It seemed odd, this business of sending the letter to
the judge. Why would anyone? It would be more logical
to send it to Frank and the minister's wife if someone

wanted to cause trouble. Of course, it might have been sent to them, as well. And that might have been what roused Frank's suspicions.

"Where there's one, there will be more." Judge Morris took the folder back from him and busied himself locking it away again. Then he looked back at Jason. "I don't want to believe it of Deidre. But for my grandson's sake I have to be sure."

Actually, Jason was beginning to think the judge would be delighted to believe it, since it would give him the leverage he needed to get his way. At least something—maybe his judicial temperament—insisted on the truth, which he expected Jason to provide.

The judge's gaze was still on him. Waiting for a response to the question he hadn't asked.

If Jason refused to be involved, what would happen then, aside from his finding himself without a position? The judge might well recruit someone else to dig up information about Deidre, and that someone might be even less scrupulous than he was.

So what choice did he have? None, that was what.

"All right. I won't give up yet."

THE NEXT AFTERNOON, with Kevin safely at kindergarten, Deidre decided she should make a start on clearing Dixie's apartment. Otherwise, the thought of it would hang over her head all the longer. She'd do a preliminary look around, just to see what things should be sold, donated and what personal items Dixie's mother might want to have.

That thought gave her pause. Would Lillian be interested in anything? She seemed remarkably unsentimental. She should have asked, Deidre supposed. Still, it might make more sense to do that after she'd had a look around.

Deidre hesitated on her own front porch, eyeing the house next door. It was still known locally as the Moyer house, although it had been a long time since anyone named Moyer lived there. The Victorian had been built to last, and the present owner kept it in good shape. The gingerbread trim had been repainted just last fall in a chocolate color that stood out against the white frame. Something colorful would have been more in keeping with the era, she'd thought at the time, but it wasn't her business, even though she had to look at it.

She was stalling, and she knew it. Mostly because it felt so intrusive to go into Dixie's apartment without her, but at least in part because of the second-floor resident.

Jason wouldn't be there, she assured herself. His car wasn't in the driveway, and why would he come home in the middle of the afternoon? She'd be finished long before he returned. She started across the lawn and slipped through the gap in the hedge that separated the two properties.

Feeling for Dixie's key ring, she mounted the steps to the porch, where the wicker furniture rested in lonely display. People didn't seem to sit on front porches these days, not as they once had. She remembered her parents sitting on their front porch on long summer evenings, talking softly while she curled up on the swing and let the sound flow over her in a comforting wave.

The stairwell inside, which had once stood open to the downstairs, had been walled in so that the inhabitants of the flats had privacy. It was eerily silent. The McIntyres, who rented the first floor, had gone south for the winter and not yet returned, and of course there was no sound from the second or third floors.

Hand on the polished rail, Deidre made her way upstairs. She paused for a moment on the second floor, staring at the uncommunicative door to Jason's apartment. Why was she letting the man unsettle her so? He was a stranger, and if not for the chance that had placed him with her the night Dixie died, she would have no more than a nodding acquaintance with him.

She'd never particularly believed in fate. And as for the attraction that had flared between them so awkwardly…it was best to ignore that. Actually, she'd prefer to believe that Jason hadn't even noticed. Whatever she'd felt was undoubtedly due to the stress she'd been under.

Satisfying herself with that explanation, Deidre headed up the last flight of stairs and unlocked the door to Dixie's apartment. She stepped inside and felt her breath catch. The police had finished their searching, according to Chief Carmichaels, and she could feel free to do what she needed to. They'd left the place looking just the way Dixie left it when she hurried out to come to Deidre's that night. That day's newspaper was spread out on the coffee table, and a lightweight jacket hung over the back of the sofa.

Tears stung Deidre's eyes, and she blinked them away. It wasn't the first time she'd had to clear up after a death, and the only way of handling it was to keep her mind on the task. Getting out the notebook and pen she'd brought, she began making an inventory of the apartment's contents, refusing to let herself dwell on the memories they roused of Dixie.

By the time Deidre had finished the living room and kitchen, she still had nearly an hour left before she had to pick up Kevin from kindergarten. She may as well make a start, at least, on the bedroom.

Dixie's bedroom spoke of her more clearly than the rest of the rooms put together. Her scent still clung to the air, and the waitress uniform she'd taken off when she got home from work was slung over the only chair. After glancing at the dresser drawers, Deidre caught a glimpse of herself in the mirror and tried to rub away the furrows between her brows. Yes, this was difficult, but that was all the more reason to get it done as quickly as possible.

The top drawer of the dresser contained lingerie, and she sifted through it quickly. Most of it could go to the clothing drive. Her fingers touched something hard under a pile of bras, and she drew it out, frowning a little.

Tissue paper, wrapped around a small object that felt like jewelry. She unwrapped it slowly, wondering why it wasn't in the jewelry box. The paper fell away, and she knew in an instant why it had been hidden.

This was not a piece of the bright, chunky costume jewelry that had suited Dixie so well. It was an antique gold pendant, thickly encrusted with diamonds. It was genuine. And it belonged to Sylvia Morris.

Deidre sat down abruptly on the side of the bed, staring at the necklace. There was no mistake. She'd seen the piece often enough to recognize it. She'd even worn it once, at Sylvia's insistence, for a Chamber of Commerce party. Sylvia had talked of giving it to her, saying it would be hers one day anyway, but Deidre had felt uncomfortable at the idea and dissuaded her. The necklace had been a gift from the judge to his wife, and she felt convinced he wouldn't like the idea of Sylvia giving it to her.

But all that was beside the point. What was it doing in Dixie's dresser drawer?

Deidre tried to think it through logically, but her logic seemed to have fled. As far as she knew, Dixie had never even met Sylvia, and she'd certainly never been invited to the judge's home.

Had someone stolen it and given it to Dixie? Deidre tried to envision a scenario where that was likely. She couldn't.

An insidious thought crept into her mind. Frank would have had access to the pendant. For that matter, Sylvia might have given it to him to give to Deidre. None of which explained why Dixie had it.

Her hands were suddenly very cold, and the chill seeped into her body. Frank had disapproved of Deidre's friendship with Dixie, and she'd never really understood why. When Dixie first returned to town, he'd seemed happy to see her, but that had changed after a month or two.

Deidre's thoughts skirted around a possibility, not

wanting to touch the dark shape that was forming in her brain. If Frank had given the necklace to Dixie...

Her stomach lurched, and she pressed her hand to her lips. He couldn't have. They couldn't have. Not her husband and one of her closest friends.

It's not true. Deidre found herself saying the words out loud. "It's not true." There must be a hundred other explanations. She was imagining things. She should be ashamed of even thinking that.

Fingers closing around the necklace, she walked back into the living room, unable to stand still and unable to get back to the job at hand. What was she going to do about this?

If, through some quirk of fate, the necklace had actually belonged to Dixie, then she had an obligation to turn it over to Dixie's mother. But how could she know?

A sound yanked her out of a fruitless line of thought. Something had creaked beyond the apartment door. The stairs, maybe? She held her breath. The police? But Chief Carmichaels had said she could start clearing Dixie's belongings.

She listened, but the noise, whatever it was, had stopped. Just as Deidre started to turn away, she caught something—some movement—from the corner of her eye. A flicker of reflected light, as if the brass doorknob had turned.

It wasn't turning now. And she wouldn't let herself give in to irrational thoughts. She'd prove to herself no one was there. Dropping the necklace in her bag, she stalked across the room, grabbed the knob and yanked the door open. Her breath caught, and she couldn't speak.

Luckily the man on the other side of the door looked as startled at seeing her as she was at seeing him. Big, burly, dressed in a black T-shirt, leather jacket and faded jeans, he looked as if he'd be at home on a motorcycle. He recovered from his surprise, moving as if he'd come inside.

"I'm sorry to stare. You startled me." Deidre stepped into the hall as she spoke and pulled the door closed. Whoever he was, she wasn't letting him in without a good reason.

Black eyebrows drew together in a frown. "This is Dixie James's place, right? Who're you?"

Deidre straightened at the rudeness, giving him a cold stare. "I'm a friend of hers. What do you want with Dixie's apartment?" She'd seen him before, she realized belatedly. "You were at the funeral, weren't you? You left before I had a chance to talk with you."

Her change in tone seemed to throw him off balance. He stood glowering for a moment and then jerked a nod.

"Yeah, I was there."

He wasn't making this conversation easy. "You could have stayed for the lunch, you know. Any friends of Dixie's were welcome."

His only answer was a shrug.

She tried again. "You aren't local, are you? How did you hear about it?"

"Buddy of mine told me. Thought I should know." He paused. "Mike Hanlon. I was married to Dixie."

Deidre's mind scurried through the mentions Dixie

had made of her ex-husband. Nothing positive, that was certain. Still, he'd cared enough to come to the funeral.

"I'm so sorry for your loss. I'm Deidre Morris. Dixie and I were friends since we were children." Maybe the situation required a little more explanation. "Dixie's mother wasn't well enough to come, so she asked me to take care of things here."

"Figures," he muttered. He jerked a nod toward the door behind her. "So this is Dixie's place, right?"

"Yes." She felt behind her to be sure the door was closed. Closed, but not locked.

"I want in. There's some things I have a right to." His tone edged toward belligerent.

Deidre was uncomfortably aware of how isolated they were. Not another soul was in the building, and the whole neighborhood seemed to doze in the spring sunshine.

"I'm sorry, but you'll understand I can't let anyone inside."

His big hands clenched into fists, and it struck her forcibly that one of Dixie's comments had been that her ex was a bit too ready to strike out when things didn't go his way.

"You were in there."

"I have power of attorney from the next of kin to handle the property Dixie left." She tried to make it sound impressive. The power of the law was all very well, but it needed something or someone to back it up.

"I gotta right," he growled. He took another step closer to her, blocking out the light from the window. "Get out of the way."

"What's going on?" The crisp, authoritative voice cut through her fear like a knife. Jason. Relief swept through her. She'd never been so glad to hear his voice.

In a few quick steps he reached them. Hanlon backed up, and she could breathe again.

"Deidre, are you all right?" He asked the question without moving his gaze from Hanlon, and she had the sense that Jason held the man immobile with that stare.

"I'm fine." She made an effort to get a firm grasp on normalcy. "Mr. Hanlon wanted access to Dixie's apartment, and I was just explaining to him why that was impossible."

Hanlon transferred his glowering look to Jason. "I was her husband. I gotta right."

"Ex-husband," Deidre pointed out. Ridiculous to feel as if Jason had rescued her. She could have handled the situation.

"Then you have no rights here." Jason could sound just as threatening, and beneath that urbane exterior there was a hint of something darker in the way he looked at Hanlon.

The man seemed to size him up for a moment and reconsider his response. "Look, you don't understand." Hanlon took another step back. "All I want is something to remember her by. She had some pictures of the two of us. Nobody else is going to want those, right? So what's the harm in letting me take a look for them?"

"Mrs. Morris is the only one authorized to go through the apartment, other than the police." Jason raised an eyebrow. "You can speak to Chief Carmichaels if you like."

"No need to bring the police into it." He turned to Deidre, maybe thinking her more likely to be influenced by emotion. "I just want something to remember her by, like I said."

"I'll keep an eye out for any photographs as I sort through Dixie's belongings," she said. "If there are any pictures of the two of you, I'll see that you get them. Just leave your address with me."

But Hanlon was already turning away. He stalked down the stairs and out of sight.

Baffled, Deidre looked at Jason. "So does he want the photos, or doesn't he?"

Jason, frowning, clasped her wrist. "Are you sure you're all right? He scared you, didn't he?"

Deidre made an effort to smile. "I'm all right." She couldn't help the shiver that moved across her skin. "Let's go inside if we're going to talk about it." She opened the apartment door as she spoke.

"So your ban on anyone entering doesn't extend to me?" he asked, following her in.

"I'm assuming my role of power of attorney includes my lawyer. If it doesn't, it should." She gestured to the contents of the room. "What do you suppose he really wanted?"

Jason shrugged. "At a guess, anything portable and valuable. He didn't strike me as the sentimental sort."

Deidre felt as if the diamond necklace was clamoring to proclaim its existence from inside her bag. "He and Dixie weren't on good terms, from the little she said about him."

"What did she say?" Jason prowled restlessly around

the room, touching nothing but seeming to see everything. A good thing she'd put that necklace out of sight. She wouldn't want to try explaining it to Jason.

"That he drank." She frowned, determined to keep any tremor out of her voice. "That he was quick with his fists when he was thwarted."

He stopped prowling and swung to face her. "So you thought it was a good idea to have a confrontation with him in an otherwise empty building. Not smart, Deidre."

"I didn't pick the place." Her temper rose. "What would you have me do? Step out of his way and let him ransack Dixie's apartment?"

"I'd expect you not to open the door to him." A couple of quick, impatient strides brought him close to her. "Do I have to say it again? You're too trusting."

"I'd rather be too trusting than too cynical," she shot back, uncomfortably aware of how near he was. Near enough that she seemed to feel the frustration surging in his body. "Anyway, that's not how it was. I thought I heard something, and I opened the door to see what it was."

That didn't seem to pacify him. He frowned down at her. "I don't like it."

She blinked. "What?"

"The whole situation. Especially your involvement. It seems to me your friend Dixie let you in for a lot of trouble in return for your friendship."

"What now? Are you blaming Dixie for being killed? She's the victim, remember?" Deidre clung to the enmity between them, because it was a protection against any other feelings.

"It's not that, and you should know it." He gave her the look a teacher might give to a not-quite-prepared student. "Dixie was involved in something that made someone angry enough to kill her." He paused, seeming to think about his own words. "Angry, or jealous, or frightened. Whatever it was, it was extreme enough to lead to violence."

What he said made sense, but she didn't quite see where he was going. "I suppose that's true, but it doesn't mean she brought it on herself."

"No, but she did manage to put your son in danger."

She winced at the truth of that. "Dixie loved him. She'd never have put him at risk intentionally."

"Play with fire, and you're likely to get burned. Sometimes that extends to the people close to you."

Deidre hated the cynicism of the remark, but she could see some sense in it. "I would think whatever it was, Dixie didn't see it as a physical threat." She frowned a little. "She was always very sure of herself. As an adult I mean, not as a child. She thought she could handle anything."

"Clearly she couldn't. And now she's brought this ex-husband into the picture, threatening you."

"He didn't exactly threaten," she protested. "And Dixie couldn't have guessed I'd ever even meet the man. She thought he was out of her life for good."

"Well, he's not. He's right here in Echo Falls, and he knows who you are."

She looked up at him to find his brown eyes dark and serious. "That really worries you."

"Let's say I take it seriously enough that I think the police have to be told."

"But surely…" She wasn't sure why she held back from that response. "He didn't actually do anything."

"If the police are involved, we can hope he won't be able to do anything. Besides, you don't know that he's just arrived. You're assuming he came to town for the funeral."

"Well, yes." Her breath caught. "You think he could have been here sooner? You think he might be the one who attacked her?"

"An ex-spouse is usually a prime suspect," Jason said. "The police have to be told. I'll do it, if you prefer not to."

Deidre let out a long breath. Just when she thought the worst of this was over, it had gotten a lot more complicated. And Jason didn't even know about the necklace and the problem it introduced. What was she going to do with it?

"Well?" Jason didn't seem to have a big store of patience. "What will it be? Will you tell Carmichaels, or shall I?"

Deidre glanced at her watch. "I have to pick up Kevin from kindergarten in less than twenty minutes. I don't have time to get into a complicated explanation now. I'll call him after I get home."

"You're not just fobbing me off, are you?" Jason grasped her wrists, compelling her to look at him. "You promise you'll tell Carmichaels?"

"I'll tell him today. I promise." She shook her head. "You're really a worrier, you know that?"

That seemed to surprise him. "Not usually. You seem to bring that out in me."

His gaze warmed her skin, and she couldn't find any words. If she tried to talk, she suspected she'd babble. "I…I guess you feel responsible for your clients."

"Not all of them." He seemed to enjoy her discomfort. There was a smile at the back of his eyes. "You are the exception, Deidre. In a lot of ways."

"I don't know…" She met his gaze fully and immediately knew she was lost. His lips closed on hers before she could speak.

Jason's arms went around her, holding her against the solid planes of his body. She couldn't seem to keep herself from responding, sliding her hands up until she grasped his shoulders while the kiss sent her senses reeling off into space.

It had been so long—too long—since she had been anything other than a mother, a daughter, a friend. With Jason's mouth on hers, his hands moving possessively on her back, she was something more—a woman, a woman who could ignite passion, could feel it…

With a gasp she came back to herself. She couldn't do this. Except that she'd already done it.

At her first slight withdrawal, the pressure of Jason's kiss ebbed, his arms relaxed. He drew back, his gaze searching her face.

Deidre took a quick step out of his arms, feeling the color flooding her face. She wasn't ready to be involved with someone else. She still felt like Frank's wife, and letting another man kiss her was a betrayal of their love.

Maybe someday, but not with someone like Jason—a stranger about whom she knew almost nothing.

Jason was the one who ought to be embarrassed, she told herself. He'd started it. But he looked pleased with himself instead.

She wanted nothing so much as to run out of the apartment, but she could hardly do that when she held the keys, to say nothing of the responsibility for Dixie's belongings.

"I think you'd better go," she managed finally.

Jason nodded as if that kiss had been the most natural thing in the world. "I'll talk to you later."

When the door closed behind him, she could finally breathe. She pressed both palms against her burning cheeks. What had she done?

CHAPTER EIGHT

STARING AT THE necklace didn't seem to be getting her anywhere. Deidre put the pendant down on the desk in her workroom and glanced out the window at the dark clouds massed over the ridge. If only she'd never seen the necklace...

No. This wouldn't go away just because she didn't want to face it. If Frank had given it to Dixie, then everything she'd thought she knew about both of them was a lie.

It couldn't be true. Oh, she and Frank had their disagreements, like any married couple, usually because he was willing to give in to his father, no matter the cost to them. But their relationship had been solid, based on a lifetime of knowing each other. If he'd been involved with Dixie, that would mean she hadn't known him at all.

Deidre rubbed the back of her neck, feeling the tension that had taken up residence there. The necklace had to be dealt with, and to do so, she had to know how it had come into Dixie's possession.

Which seemed impossible. Here she was at a dead end again. Maybe if she talked the whole thing over with someone, she could see her way more clearly. But who? Echo Falls was filled with people she'd known all her life, people she trusted, people related by blood or long friendship. But when she thought of confiding in any of them about the necklace, she cringed.

Jason's lean, frowning face inserted itself into her thoughts. She had begun to trust him, even to rely on him. But then he kissed her. Even worse, she'd kissed him back, and she was no longer sure of her footing.

She could imagine what Dixie would say to her qualms. She was single. Jason was single. There was no reason why they shouldn't be attracted to each other. Or, Dixie would say, to act on it.

But Deidre's view of life was seldom as clear-cut as Dixie's had been. She barely knew Jason. Worse, he worked for the judge, and she still didn't know whether Sylvia's dark suspicions were true.

Something clattered against the window, and she jumped before realizing it was the wind, rattling the branches of the forsythia bush against the pane. The wind meant rain was coming, and she did a quick mental inventory of the west-facing windows. No, none had been left open.

Judith's advice about getting an attorney to represent her had seemed logical, and Deidre had gone so far as to make a short list of people in Williamsport who might be possibilities. Although someone from even farther afield might be better, given the judge's influence.

The truth was, no matter how many lists she made up, no attorney could do anything for her unless and until she was sure the judge intended to do something more than ask her to move in. Doing anything before that point would be like an open declaration of war between them.

The windowpane rattled again, setting Deidre's nerves on edge like nails on a chalkboard. She ought to get Billy to cut that bush back.

Something sounded from the front of the house, and she shot out of her chair in alarm. And then laughed at herself. It was someone knocking at the door, that was all. She was letting her imagination run away with her.

She went quickly through to the front of the house, taking a glance up the stairs as she passed. Sometimes a storm woke Kevin, but he was more likely to sleep right through it. Reaching the door, she drew aside the curtain on one of the narrow side windows and looked out.

Nothing. She ought to be able to see a person standing there. Maybe the wind had knocked something over on the porch. Flipping the dead bolt, she opened the door and took a half step out. The porch furniture was undisturbed, and the pots of geraniums on either side of the steps sat out of the prevailing wind. It must have been a branch she'd heard.

Closing the door, Deidre locked the dead bolt again, shivering a little from the cool breeze. Of course she was under stress, but that was no reason to give in to fear. Maybe a cup of herbal tea would soothe her. Her mother always swore by mint tea to settle the nerves.

Deidre was headed for the stove when she heard a knock again, this time at the back door. Her nerves jumped in response, and she shook her head. This might require something stronger than herbal tea. Obviously she'd taken so long to get to the front door that whoever it was had seen the lights in the back of the house and come around to the back door.

Reaching the door, she flipped the switch to the back door light. Nothing happened. Maybe the bulb had burned out. Skirting the refrigerator, she leaned over to peer out the closest window. Thanks to the storm, it was far too dark to make out anything but a dark shadow.

A chill slid down her spine. She wouldn't be so foolish as to open the door without knowing who was there. But she couldn't ignore it. If something had happened to one of Judith's children, if they needed a car to get to the hospital…

Beset by differing fears, she put one hand on the door. "Who's there?"

There was no answer but the wind. She tried again, louder. "Who's there?"

Nothing. But below where her hand rested on the door, the knob started to turn.

Deidre snatched her hand away as if she'd touched flame. For an instant she stood there, mesmerized, as the knob turned first one way, then the other. It was locked. Thank heaven it was locked.

She bolted for the wall phone, snatched it from the cradle and punched in 911. Pressing the phone to her ear, she sent a quick glance toward the window. Nothing, but if the intruder looked in, she was as visible as if she stood on a lighted stage. Backing up to the door, she flipped off the kitchen light as she stammered out her address to the dispatcher.

"Someone's trying to get into the house. Please, hurry."

The dispatcher was murmuring something soothing,

telling her to stay on the line, saying the police would be right there. Barely listening, Deidre slipped out of the kitchen.

Kevin. Nothing must happen to Kevin. She ran to the stairs, then forced herself to stop at the bottom. She had to stay here, where she could open to the police when they came. But if Kevin woke...

She settled for sinking onto the bottom step. His door was ajar. If he called out, she'd hear him, or hear the monitor she still set up every night. Clutching the cordless phone, she stared at the front window, willing the police car to appear.

It felt like forever, huddled there, ears straining for any sound from the back door. How hard would it be for anyone to break in? Probably not very, but surely he must realize she'd called the police. Even as she thought it, she caught the gleam of the lights atop the police car as it pulled into her driveway.

Thankful they hadn't come with sirens screaming, she hurried to the door, opening it the instant the officer identified himself. It was Sam Jacobson, looking so young it seemed he must be dressed up in costume as a police officer. But even the badge was enough to chase her fear away.

"What happened, Mrs. Morris?" He was looking past her, eyeing the spot where Dixie's body had lain. "Did someone break in?"

"They didn't get in." A gust of rain blew in the open door, and she caught his arm and pulled him inside so she could close it. "I heard someone at the front door, but by the time I answered, no one was there. Then I heard a knock at the back. I couldn't get the light to come on, and when I called out, no one answered." She paused for breath. "Then I saw the knob turning. He was trying to get in, so I called 911."

"That was the right thing to do." He stood up a little straighter. "Now, did you hear any glass breaking, anything like that?"

She shook her head. "I'm sure he didn't get in."

"Okay, I'll just have a look around outside. You keep the door locked until I come back, all right?"

She nodded. No chance she'd forget that. She watched from the window as he cast the beam of a powerful flashlight around the bushes in front of the house. The rain had stopped as suddenly as it'd started, but the wet leaves glistened in the light.

The flashlight was now moving quickly along the side of the house. Still, she didn't suppose anyone could hide under the low shrubs.

Deidre moved to the back windows, turning on lights as she went. She held her breath as young Jacobson flashed his light around the backyard. But of course the intruder, whoever he was, wouldn't be hanging around.

Realizing she was still connected to the dispatcher, Deidre thanked her and snapped the button to end the call. Before she could return the phone to its cradle, it rang again.

It was Jason, sounding alarmed. "Are you all right? What's happening?"

"We're okay, really. Someone…someone tried to get into the house. The police are looking around now, but I'm sure he's gone."

"I'm coming over."

Before she could tell him not to, he'd hung up.

WHAT THE DEVIL was going on? Jason ran down the stairs and out the door. Even if someone feared that Kevin could identify him, surely Chief Carmichaels's statement that Kevin didn't remember anything would allay those fears. Why would anyone make a serious attempt at a break-in at this relatively early hour? They'd have to know that Deidre would still be up.

He was jogging across the lawn toward the house when the beam of a flashlight stabbed him in the eyes. He stopped, raising a hand to shield them.

"Police. Who're you?" The voice sounded very young and a little nervous.

"Jason Glassman. I live next door. Mrs. Morris asked me to come over." A slight exaggeration, but she probably wouldn't deny it.

The light lowered. "You see anybody around here tonight? Like maybe lurking on the property?"

"No, but I was busy with some work, and I didn't look out this way until I saw your lights. Mrs. Morris says someone tried to get in. Did you find anything?"

Now that his eyes had grown accustomed to the dark, Jason could make out a young, serious face. The boy shrugged.

"No sign of anyone now. I was just going to tell Mrs. Morris."

"I'll go with you." They walked together to the front door, with Jason wondering just how thorough his search had been. It couldn't have been ten minutes, if that, since he'd seen the police flashers. His adrenaline pumping, he wanted to charge ahead and satisfy himself that Deidre was okay, but suspected she wouldn't appreciate that.

And she'd be telling herself she hadn't appreciated that kiss this afternoon, either, but that would be a lie. Her response had given her away. She'd been just as eager as he had, whether she wanted to admit it or not.

Ridiculous to be congratulating himself when that was the last thing he should have done. He'd let his instincts run away with him, and look where it had gotten him. He was supposed to be investigating Deidre Morris, not falling for her.

He backed away from that phrase in a hurry. Just because he found her attractive, that didn't translate to falling for her. He was past that stage in his romantic life. Leslie had cured him completely, and he wouldn't be making that mistake again, even if he hadn't been hiding a secret the size of Mount Rushmore from Deidre.

Deidre opened the door as they approached. She looked pale, standing under the porch light with the darkness pressing close. She glanced from the patrolman to him.

"You didn't need to come," she said, predictably. "I'm sure the officer has things in hand." She turned to the kid. "Did you find anything, Sam?"

"No, ma'am. You can rest easy. There's no one anywhere on your property who shouldn't be."

"Any signs of the intruder?" Jason interrupted with a query of his own.

"Nothing that I could see." His gaze seemed to land

on his feet. "Sure it wasn't just the wind knocking things around, Mrs. Morris? It was plenty fierce there for a bit."

Deidre stiffened visibly. "I know it was, but that wouldn't make the doorknob turn, would it?"

He cleared his throat. "You sure about that, are you? I mean, maybe it was like a trick of the light or something."

"I'm sure." Deidre clamped her lips together as if to keep herself from saying more. "Thank you for checking."

Off the hook, he gave a sigh of relief. "No trouble, ma'am. That's my job. Don't you hesitate to call if anything worries you."

Touching his cap, he spun and marched to the waiting police car.

Deidre looked after him, frustration written plainly on her face. "Now it'll be all over town by tomorrow that I'm imagining things." She shifted her gaze to him. "I suppose you think so, too."

"No, I don't." The certainty he felt surprised him, but even if he hadn't been aware of the circumstances, he wouldn't have thought Deidre was a woman likely to panic at a sudden storm and a few odd noises.

She blew out a long breath. "Sorry. I shouldn't take it out on you." She hesitated, then gestured to the doorway. "Would you like to come in?"

He suspected the stiffness in her manner was caused by her memory of that kiss. "I'd like to hear what happened from you, but first, can you let me have a flashlight?"

"A flashlight? But the officer just looked around and didn't find anything."

"Call me stubborn. I'd like to see for myself."

Deidre moved to the small cabinet under a mirror in the entry and took a flashlight from the drawer. "Here you are. Just knock when you're done. The doorbell might wake Kevin."

He nodded, switching on the light. Satisfied that it emitted a strong beam, he backed off the porch, sweeping it along the porch floor, the steps and the shrubs on either side. There was nothing to be seen here except some dry twigs that had probably been blown from the trees by the wind.

Why should there be? The intruder could easily have kept to the walk, avoiding leaving any marks on the damp ground.

Still sweeping the area with the torch, he moved around the house, taking careful note of the mulched flower beds along the foundation. He didn't hit pay dirt until he reached the back of the house. There, under a window that looked in on the office at the back of the house he'd seen earlier, the mulch was scuffed and disturbed.

Jason squatted, holding the beam steady on the marks. Thanks to the rain, most likely, the ground was too scuffed to show an identifiable print, but it seemed obvious that someone had stood there, looking in the window. Had Deidre been sitting in the room? Judging by the fact that the chair was pushed out and the computer on, he'd guess she had been. Revulsion swamped him for a moment at the image of an unidentifiable figure spying on her.

The white clapboards didn't show any marks, nor the windowsill. Jason stood, frowning for a moment. It seemed unlikely that Chief Carmichaels would make any further investigation, although he might if pushed. So it was up to him.

Juggling the flashlight by clamping it between his arm and his side, he snapped a couple of quick photos of the disturbed ground with his cell phone. Not professional, by any means, but better than nothing.

Jason moved along the back of the house without finding anything else. When he got to the back porch, he found that by reaching up he could easily touch the lightbulb. It felt loose in his hand. He gave it a twist, and the light came on.

Unsatisfactory. The bulb could have worked its way loose on its own, he supposed, but it was way too easy for someone to get at it…someone who didn't want to be seen.

He finished his circuit of the house without finding anything and tapped softly on the front door. Deidre opened it immediately and motioned him in.

"Did you find anything?"

Jason set the flashlight down. He didn't like to alarm her, but Deidre needed to know where she stood, both for her sake and the boy's. "It looks to me as if someone stood by the back window that looks in on the room where your computer is."

Her eyes widened. "Stood by the window… You mean someone was watching me?"

"Looks that way. Is that where you were before you heard the knock on the door?"

Nodding, Deidre spun on her heel and went quickly toward the back room. He followed. Apparently she needed to see for herself.

She stood at the window for a moment, looking out at the dark. Then she grasped the shade and pulled it all the way down. When she turned to face him, she was forcing a smile.

"I guess I won't sit in here after dark without taking precautions. Thank you, Jason."

Her earlier stiffness with him was gone, and he was irrationally relieved.

"There's another precaution I think is necessary. That back porch light is too easy for someone to get at. It wasn't on because it was loose in the socket."

"Deliberately loosened?" She caught the implication.

He shrugged. "Hard to say. But what you need is a motion-sensor light with a protective screen over it. I'll pick one up tomorrow and install it for you."

He half expected an argument, but she seemed too disturbed by the thought of someone tampering with the light to dispute who would replace it.

"I never thought of that." She sat down abruptly and gestured him to the other chair. "When I was growing up, we never even locked the house unless we were going to be away overnight."

"Times have changed." Not wanting to destroy the momentary peace between them, he didn't bring up her too-trusting nature. "And given what happened here, it's only sensible to take precautions."

Deidre paled. "You think this was someone after Kevin?"

"No. No, I don't think so." He didn't, did he? "If Dixie's attacker was afraid Kevin might be able to describe him, he must know by now that isn't so. Even if he didn't trust the police statement, he'd realize that if Kevin knew anything, the police would also know it. What would be the point of putting himself in more jeopardy by going after the boy now? But I am wondering about that ex-husband of Dixie's."

Some of the strain went out of her face. "I guess it's possible, but why would he want to play tricks like that? It's not as if he made a serious attempt to get in."

"Resentment toward you for not allowing him access to Dixie's apartment, maybe? Just plain meanness? I don't know, but I think Chief Carmichaels should be reminded that he might have been here tonight. You did tell him about Hanlon trying to get into the apartment, didn't you?"

"Yes, of course."

"In any event, he'll want to talk to Hanlon, and suspicion of prowling will give him a bit more ammunition, maybe a reason to throw a scare into him, if nothing else."

She nodded. "I'll call him in the morning." Her smile looked a bit more genuine this time. "I'd really set people talking if I called him at home at this hour."

"You've got plenty of reason to be upset. I'm sure people realize that." If they didn't, they should.

But Deidre had stopped listening to him. Instead, she was intent on a small white receiver that sat on the corner of her desk. A baby monitor, he realized after a moment. A rustling sound came from it, and then a sleepy voice.

"Mommy?"

Deidre was out of her chair in an instant. "I'll just settle him down again." The words were tossed over her shoulder as she hurried toward the stairs.

He eyed the monitor. At a guess, Deidre had started using it again after she brought Kevin home from the hospital. He heard Kevin call to her once more and then the sound of her footsteps came through the device.

"Okay, Kev, I'm here." Her tone was soft, soothing. "Did something wake you up?"

Kevin murmured something, maybe only half awake. "…dream. Bad dream."

"Only a dream." The bed creaked as she sat down on it. "Dreams can't hurt you."

Jason knew how concerned she had to be about her child, given everything that had happened. He had to admire the strength that allowed her to stay calm and reassuring with her son.

"We'll just tuck you in again, right? And put Bear on one side and Doggie on the other. They'll chase away the bad dreams."

Kevin gave a murmured assent, already sliding back into sleep, he suspected. Deidre hummed something—a tune he couldn't immediately identify, though he found it soothing.

That was what mothers did—at least, the kind of mothers who lived in houses like this and didn't rely on alcohol or drugs or men to make it to the next day.

Jase ran a hand through his hair and tried to rub the tension away from the back of his neck. Keeping silent got harder every day, but telling her that the judge had him investigating her wouldn't help. It would bring things to an open breach, with no telling what the results would be.

If he proved the judge wrong about Deidre, she'd never need to know. She wouldn't have to live with the idea that her husband hadn't trusted her. That was a comforting rationalization, but tonight's happenings had thrown a different light on things.

If you wanted to know what had been intended, you had to look at the results.

And the results of tonight's prowling, whatever else happened, could be a rumor going around that Deidre was unstable, imagining things.

How much might that benefit the judge in his mission to control his grandson's future? Common sense wouldn't allow Jase to picture Judge Franklin Morris creeping around in the dark and knocking on doors. It was ludicrous to think that, wasn't it?

Deidre came back in, glancing at the monitor as if to assure herself that Kevin had gone back to sleep.

"All's well?" he asked lightly.

"I think so." A frown formed as she sat down again. "He hasn't had any bad dreams since…well, I don't remember when."

"He's been through a lot of upset lately." He didn't know much about kids, but that made sense. Since that hadn't reduced her frown, he added, "You're a good mother, Deidre."

She looked a little startled. "Thank you. It's funny... Sylvia Morris said something like that to me the last time she was here."

"That's good, right? If your mother-in-law thinks so, it must be so."

Deidre smiled, but there seemed to be something more troubling her. For a moment he thought she was going to confide in him, but the moment passed.

"Poor Sylvia. I suspect it was more that she felt she hadn't been a very good mother to Frank. Because..."

She let that trail off, but he knew the rest of it. Everyone in town seemed to know that Sylvia Morris had alcohol problems. He could sympathize with Frank on that score.

"I know. Her problems have been going on for a long time, have they?"

Deidre nodded. "I remember a birthday party for Frank... He must have been only about six or seven. She burst into the middle of it, singing and acting silly. I didn't have any idea then what caused it. I just remember feeling so embarrassed for Frank."

"It's not easy for a kid. Your mother's supposed to be the rock who's always there for you."

She was looking at him as if seeing more than the words. He very nearly spoke, nearly told her things about his childhood he didn't tell anyone.

The phone rang, saving him from making a fool of himself. With an apologetic grimace, Deidre picked up.

"Adam?" She sounded surprised, glancing at the clock as if wondering why her minister was calling this late.

And Jason wondered, as well. He saw again that anonymous letter, and his jaw tightened. He couldn't hear what the man was saying. He could only judge by her responses.

"We're fine, really. The police stopped by because I thought I heard a prowler."

She paused, obviously listening. He could actually catch an agitated flow of sound, though he couldn't distinguish any words. Pastor Adam was clearly disturbed.

"No, that's not necessary. I appreciate it, but it's not needed."

Another crackle of sound from the phone, still high and fast.

"But I'm not alone." Deidre's voice had firmed. "I have a friend with me, and there's nothing you can do here. Thanks for calling, I do appreciate it."

A few more exchanges, and she finally hung up.

"Adam Bennett. Someone apparently saw the police car in front of the house and called him. You see what I mean about how fast news gets around?"

At the moment, Jason was more interested in Adam's assumption that he should race to the rescue.

"Maybe you should have let him come over. He obviously wants to help you." He wanted to see her reaction… to look for any sign that her relationship with the minister was anything other than what it appeared.

Deidre's eyebrows lifted. "But I don't need him. I didn't want to hurt his feelings, but it would be foolish for him to come rushing over."

"Maybe he feels responsible for you." He paused. "As your minister, of course."

"I suppose he feels responsible for all his congregation. He's young enough to think he can solve everyone's problems." She sounded indulgent, as if she spoke of a younger brother.

"Mothering him, are you?" He didn't know what put that edge in his voice. He couldn't be jealous.

She stiffened. "Why would I do that?"

"That seems to be your pattern. Mothering him the way you mothered Frank."

He'd gone too far—way too far. What had happened to his control?

Deidre rose, her posture stiff. When she spoke her words could have formed icicles. "You don't know anything about my relationship with my husband. If you…" She stopped, seeming to struggle for control, and turned away from him.

"Thank you for coming over," she said finally. "I think you'd better leave now."

He thought so, too. He'd already done enough damage for one night.

CHAPTER NINE

"THANKS SO MUCH for coming with me, Judith." Deidre paused from packing clothes from Dixie's closet to send a glance of appreciation at her friend. "I hated the thought of doing this on my own."

Not only the doing, but just being alone in Dixie's apartment after what had happened the last time she was here. She wasn't afraid, exactly. Just nervy about the memory of seeing the doorknob turn and confronting Dixie's ex-husband.

"I'm happy to help. Sorting the things folks leave behind can be difficult." She straightened, her arms full of the stack of jeans she'd taken from the bottom drawer of the dresser. "Sometimes, especially if it was an older person, you can enjoy reminiscing while you do it, ain't so?"

"I suppose. It's a little more difficult when you think of Dixie's life cut short the way it was." Deidre folded a sundress, hands smoothing the bright tropical flowers. "Dixie just bought this a few weeks ago. She couldn't wait for the weather to be hot enough to wear it." Deidre quickly put it in the box designated for the clothing drive, trying not to think of how well the bright print would have suited Dixie.

Judith pulled open another drawer and stopped, frowning a little. "There are some folders here with what look like forms and bills. What should I do with those?"

"We'll have to start another box with things to take back to my place." She'd never realized how difficult the simplest things could become in the event of a sudden death without a surviving spouse. "Not that Dixie owned that much, but all the paperwork has to be gone through, and most companies won't let me deal with her accounts unless I produce a copy of the death certificate and my authorization." This experience had been quite an education in bureaucracy.

"*Ach*, it's simpler just to deal in cash and keep your money under the mattress, I think." Judith's eyes twinkled.

"As if you could make me believe you carry on that way. I know perfectly well you and Eli have an account at the bank."

Judith shrugged, putting files into one of the boxes they'd carried over. "Even the Amish have to keep up with the times in some ways."

Having finished with the clothes that had hung in the closet, Deidre reached up to the shelf and began pulling things down. For a few minutes they were each absorbed in what they were doing, and Deidre found her thoughts straying to what had happened the previous night. She could hardly forget it, when she'd had a visit from Chief Carmichaels first thing this morning.

At least he had seemed to believe her, and like Jason, he'd frowned over the scuffed earth beneath her windows and advised a motion-sensor light. If he'd had any thoughts as to who might have been tormenting her, he'd kept them to himself, but his face had been grave when he left. And she suspected the young patrolman's ears were going to be burning shortly over the fact that he'd missed what Jason had found so readily.

Jason. She'd been trying to avoid thinking of him, but that didn't seem to be working too well. He had been a tower of strength when he'd rushed over to help. And when they'd sat and talked for a few minutes, she'd felt that they were beginning to know one another.

Then Adam Bennett called, and everything had changed. Now that she thought about it, Jason had been a bit short about the minister's attentions once before. He almost seemed to have something against the man, and she found it hard to believe anyone could take an instant dislike to someone as innocuous as Adam.

She finished putting sun hats and handbags into a box for the church rummage sale and pulled the lid from a box that had been stored at the back of the closet shelf. It was filled with what seemed a miscellaneous collection of things—a few books, some trinkets, a group of what looked like figurines wrapped in tissue paper and who knew what else.

"I think this box will have to go back to the house for sorting." She put the lid back on it. "How are you coming along?"

"I've finished the dresser. Shall I start on the kitchen?"

Deidre glanced at her watch and shook her head. "Kevin will be getting home from school soon. Ruth Blair said she'd pick him up and walk him home. We'd

better stop where we are." She looked around at the bags
and boxes. "We made good progress today. Thanks to
you, it's not going to take as long as I feared."

"Many hands make light work," Judith said. "That's
why we call it a work frolic when we get together to
do a chore."

"Well, I appreciated this work frolic." Deidre picked
up the box, shoving the closet door closed with her foot.
"Can you manage that one?"

"For sure." Judith hefted the other box. "I'm ready."

They went out, and Deidre paused in the hall long
enough to double-check the door. She'd be glad when
this job was finished so she could stop feeling responsible for the apartment and its contents.

As for the rest of the situation…well, she needed to
see Dixie's murderer apprehended. It wouldn't ease her
grief, she knew that. But at least then she'd know. When
Frank died, she'd obsessed for months about why he'd
lost control of the car. She'd finally pushed it out of her
conscious thoughts, putting it in the category of things
she might one day understand.

But Dixie's death was deliberate murder. Until they
knew, how could anyone feel entirely safe?

Deidre led the way out the walk instead of brushing through the gap in the hedge as she usually did.
The boxes they carried weren't heavy, but they were
awkward.

"Did you set up for the auction house to take care of
the furniture?" One of Judith's numerous cousins was
an auctioneer, so naturally she took an interest.

"Yes, they'll come and pick it up as soon as I'm

ready. And I have someone with a truck to get the things for the rummage sale and the clothing drive to the church. I just have to finish sorting."

"You'll be glad to be done, ain't so?"

Deidre didn't reply at once, her gaze caught by a car that slowed down as it neared them. Frowning, she tried to make out the face of the man behind the wheel, but the sun reflected off the windshield.

"Deidre?" Judith's voice was questioning. "Is something wrong?"

"I thought for a minute it was that ex-husband of Dixie's coming back again. But I must have been wrong, because he didn't stop." She remembered Jason's speculation that Mike Hanlon could have been her prowler last night and felt uneasy. "Let's get on inside with these things."

They carried the boxes straight through to the workroom, since that seemed the best place for sorting. Judith slid hers under the table, so that it would be out of the way.

"I should get home, but I nearly forgot to tell you that your cousin Lovina is going to let us sell some of the wall hangings she's been making." Judith smiled. "Surprising, ain't so?"

"Astounding. What did you do to convince her?" Lovina was actually a second or third cousin of Deidre's, and she'd steadfastly refused to allow them to sell any of her wonderful quilted creations online. She didn't want to get involved with the internet, she'd insisted, and she didn't care if the bishop said it was all right.

"Nothing," Judith said, laughing. "I had to listen to

a long scolding about not getting too worldly, but in the end, I think she just wanted to do something to help you. You are family, even if you are *Englisch*, and you've had trouble."

"I wouldn't have believed it." Cousin Lovina was crotchety, as her daughters said, but she was the most gifted quilter Deidre had ever seen. "Well, we'll have to be careful to tell her all about the buyers, and maybe that will make her feel better." She sobered. "People have been so kind. I can never repay it."

"No one wants you to. You just let folks help you, for once. It's good for them." Her lips quirked. "Especially that lawyer. He strikes me as someone who doesn't often go out of his way for strangers, but he has for you, ain't so?"

Deidre felt the mix of emotions that the mere mention of Jason's name engendered. "He has, and I'm not sure why. He can be so helpful one minute and then turn around and act as if he doesn't approve of me the next."

Judith's dimples showed as she gave Deidre a squeeze. "That just means you're keeping the man off balance because he has his eye on you. It's probably good for him."

"He's not interested…" she began, and then stopped. How did she know that? He'd kissed her, after all. And she still hadn't figured out what that had meant.

She noticed that the light was blinking on the answering machine, and that made for a good excuse to stop talking about a subject that made her increasingly uncomfortable.

But after she pressed the button, she realized this wasn't going to be much of a distraction. It was her father-in-law, and he was clearly annoyed that she wasn't there to receive his call.

"I've heard about your prowler scare last night. It's all over town by now, but I should have heard it from you."

Deidre made a face, since he couldn't see her. She hadn't wanted to listen to a lecture—that's why she hadn't called.

"I understand that the patrolman didn't find anyone on the property, but surely this will convince you that I'm right. If you and Kevin had moved into Ferncliff by now, that would never have happened. We have the security to make it impossible, and for the sake of Kevin's safety and well-being, I should think you'd recognize that fact."

He'd stopped abruptly, as if maybe wondering if he'd gone too far. Then he began again, seeming to make an effort to sound conciliatory.

"Both Sylvia and I urge you to move in with us. We have plenty of room, and we certainly don't intend to interfere in your life. We just want our grandson to have the security he deserves. Think about it."

The message ended there.

Judith had come over to stand next to her during the last part of the recording, putting a comforting arm around Deidre's waist. Now she gave her a little squeeze.

"You see? That man isn't one to give up easily on what he wants. That's why I think you should get a lawyer of your own for advice." She paused, shaking her head. "*Ach*, listen to me. I'm telling you what to do just like that father-in-law of yours does. You'll be thinking I'm no more worth listening to than he is."

"No, I won't. I know you really do have my best interests at heart. After all, we've been friends forever." She managed a weak smile. "You know what my earliest memory is?"

Judith shook her head.

"It's wading in the creek together, and your mother laughing at us and trying to get us to catch minnows."

"I remember that, too. Your *mamm* brought a pail down for us to keep them in, but we couldn't bear to take them out of the creek."

Now her smile was a genuine one. There was nothing like a happy memory to chase away the blues. Unfortunately, the chill imposed by her father-in-law's words still lingered. He'd sounded so…implacable.

How far was he willing to go to get his way?

JASON CHANGED CLOTHES quickly after work, grabbed the bag holding the lighting fixture he'd bought and headed across the lawn toward Deidre's house. A busy day at work had been fairly successful in keeping his mind off her, but it would be too much to hope he could keep thoughts of Deidre at bay indefinitely.

He walked around the house, approaching the back door. How Deidre would receive him was anyone's guess. He'd made a mistake—a big one. It had been no part of the judge's plan that he should alienate Deidre by criticizing her relationship with her husband. On the other hand, he didn't seem to be operating according to Judge Morris's plan any longer.

What had possessed him to snipe at her after that phone call from Adam Bennett? He should have taken comfort from the fact that she hadn't appeared to nourish any tender feelings for the man.

The truth was, he couldn't be impartial about Deidre any longer. It mattered to him whether she was the devoted mother and honest woman she appeared to be or a manipulative deceiver who might put her child in jeopardy, as the judge seemed to believe.

He tapped at the back door, half wishing he could accomplish this task without seeing Deidre. He couldn't. He had to have access to the circuit breaker, and…

Deidre opened the door, obviously surprised to see him. She gave a quick self-conscious push to the strand of blond hair that had fallen from the band at the nape of her neck. She wore faded jeans, sneakers, an oversize shirt and had a streak of dust on her cheek. She looked adorable.

"Jason. I wasn't expecting you." Her tone was cool. So she hadn't forgotten how they'd parted.

He held up the package. "I have the motion-detecting light fixture to install for you." If he kept it businesslike, maybe she wouldn't tell him to get lost. "Where is your circuit box?"

She blinked, surprised. "You don't need…"

Before she could finish, Kevin had run into the kitchen and was grinning at Jason.

"Hi. What are you going to do? Can I help?"

"Sure you can." Without waiting for Deidre to interfere, he turned to the switch by the back door. "Is this the switch for the porch light?"

She nodded, her jaw setting. She was thinking he'd taken unfair advantage. Maybe he had.

Jase flipped the switch, and the light came on. He put a hand on Kevin's shoulder and nodded toward the porch light. "I'm going to try to turn it off from the power box. I need you to watch it and give a shout when the light goes out, okay? That way I'll know I have the right one."

Kevin nodded, small face serious. "I can do that. I'll yell real loud."

He turned to Deidre. "The circuit panel?"

"In the basement." She spun, her sneakers squeaking on the tile floor, and led the way.

Once she'd opened the cellar door and switched on the light, she preceded him down the stairs. "Watch your head," she said.

He put up a hand to make sure he didn't crack his head on the rough-hewn beam above the steps.

"I didn't realize how old this house is." He tapped the beam. "Wooden pegs?"

Distracted from her distaste for him, Deidre nodded. "You can see the original beams here and in the attic, and they're pegged together. The house dates to about the 1850s, when the town was settled. My dad always liked to show the beams to visitors." She grinned. "Most of them either didn't notice, didn't care, or didn't know what it meant. It was built by his great-grandfather, if I'm counting the generations right."

"History isn't just in documents and monuments. It's in the way ordinary people lived." He shook his head. "You shouldn't get me started. If I hadn't been an attorney, I'd have been a history teacher. It always fascinated me in school, maybe because I had a teacher who made it come alive."

"Maybe you'd have enjoyed teaching more," she suggested, seeming genuinely interested.

"Maybe." He shrugged. "But the law pays a lot better."

"Money isn't everything." A flicker of disapproval crossed her face.

"Easy to say when you've always had enough."

The words came out too quickly, and he wished them back. He didn't go around betraying his origins to people. Either they felt sorry for him or they assumed a sort of false heartiness as if to say it didn't matter what he'd come from, when all the time they were thinking that it did.

"Where's the circuit box?" he said before she could respond.

"Here." Seeming to accept the fact that he wasn't inviting her into private territory, she gestured to the wall. The gray metal box looked incongruous against the stone of the foundation.

He opened the box and turned to shout toward the door at the top of the stairs. "Ready, Kevin?"

"I'm ready!"

The childish treble sounded eager. Too bad this wasn't going to be more exciting for him.

As usual, there was a chart on the box's door of which breaker was for which outlet. Also as usual, it was so faded it was impossible to read.

Deidre leaned closer, a wisp of her hair brushing his cheek. "I guess I should do something about the list, shouldn't I? But I think all the outside lights are on the last few circuits."

He considered prolonging the process, just to enjoy having her so close. He snapped the bottom breaker to the off position. "Is the light still on, Kev?" he shouted.

"Still on," he called back.

Jase returned that one to the on position. "I owe you an apology," he said, flicking the next switch. "How about now?" he shouted.

She didn't speak, and he knew it would take more. Kevin hollered, "No!" He juggled the switches, moving to the next.

"Look, no excuses. Your relationship with Frank is none of my business, okay? I'm sorry for what I said."

He flipped the switch. Before he could call out, he heard an excited squeal from upstairs.

"That's it! That's it!"

"Good job, Kev." He closed the panel and turned to Deidre. "Are we okay?"

She seemed to struggle for a moment, but then she nodded. "Okay." She turned and went quickly back up the stairs.

He followed her, wondering if she meant it. But at least she wasn't inviting him to leave, so maybe he'd redeemed himself for his hasty words.

They went out together to the small back porch. He could reach the fixture easily enough, but he'd need a bit more height to work comfortably. "Do you have a step stool I can use?"

"Yes, of course."

Deidre disappeared into the kitchen and was back a

moment later, carrying a small folding step stool. She started to flip it open at the same time he reached for it, and their hands were entangled. She stepped back, letting him take it, and he was sure he didn't imagine the faint flush that deepened her fair skin.

"What can I do?" Kevin danced around him as he mounted the step stool, while Deidre retreated.

"Suppose you hold the tools and hand them to me when I need them, okay?"

He'd taken the precaution of bringing a screwdriver and pair of pliers with him, along with a roll of electrical tape. He hadn't wanted to give Deidre any excuses for turning him away.

Nodding, Kevin picked up the tools, and Jase began unscrewing the fixture. It was a simple matter, something he'd learned working nights on a maintenance crew while he'd scrimped his way through college. He'd bluffed his way into the job, but he'd learned a lot. Enough, at least, to sound like an authority as he explained to Kevin what he was doing.

"Remember how we made sure the light was off before we started? That was so we could be sure not to get hurt. You can get burned or shocked by an outlet if you're not careful."

Kevin nodded solemnly. "Billy always says you have to be careful with tools."

"You help Billy when he comes over, do you?"

"He says I'm a big help. He's been around lots. We're getting the spring chores done."

So Billy had been here a lot recently. Deidre had disappeared back into the kitchen, leaving them alone, so he couldn't ask her about it. Maybe that was just as well, since he didn't want to antagonize.

"We're almost there." He'd just set the last screw in place. "You want to screw this one in?"

"Can I?" Kevin dropped the tape in his excitement. "How do I do it?"

"Simple." He put the screwdriver in the boy's hand and lifted him up. "Just fit the end in that little slot in the screw and turn it."

He put his hand over Kevin's and helped him to tighten the final screw. "There, all done. We just have to turn the circuit back on, and it's all ready."

They exchanged high fives, with Kevin grinning widely. It had been oddly satisfying to be showing the boy how to do something. He didn't know that he'd ever done such a thing before.

"Mommy, we did it! We're done!"

Deidre came out, smiling. "That's wonderful. Were you a help?"

"I couldn't have done it without him," Jase said. "Okay, now we have to set the angle of the sensor down a bit, so we know it will come on when anything moves out here." He did so as he spoke.

Kevin nodded, but his forehead wrinkled a little. "Why do we need a light that shows us when something moves?"

Jase decided the wise move was to let Deidre answer that.

She looked startled for an instant. "Well, that way, we don't waste electricity by having the light on all the time. It just comes on when someone's coming to the door, so they can see the steps."

Jase grinned. "It'll also tell you when a stray dog, cat or raccoon comes close to the house, but that's okay, isn't it?"

Kevin nodded vigorously. "I'd like to see a raccoon. Hey, Mommy, do you think we'll see a raccoon when we go to the falls on Saturday?"

So their picnic at the falls was planned. And Deidre hadn't mentioned it to him.

A faint color filled Deidre's cheeks, and she carefully didn't look at him. "You usually just see raccoons at night, Kev. So I don't think so. But we might see squirrels and chipmunks. Maybe even a deer."

"That'd be cool. We can keep a list of how many animals we see, right, Jason?"

"Well, I…"

"Please do come with us," Deidre said quickly. "If you don't have something else to do, that is."

Was she hoping he would come? Funny—before he'd told himself a hike in the woods wasn't his thing. Now he didn't want to miss it.

"Sounds great. What time do we leave?"

Her smile looked just a bit stiff. "We'll set off at about ten. We can drive up one of the back roads and then hike from there. A backpack would be a good idea."

"Will do." Maybe, by the time they came back, she'd have gotten over being annoyed with him.

A metallic rattle announced the arrival of the battered old pickup Billy drove. He got out, stood looking at them for a minute and then pulled a long pair of garden clippers from the truck bed.

Kevin, who seemed to be everyone's friend, went running to meet him. "Hey, Billy. Guess what we did. We put up a new light on the back porch."

Billy's gaze went from the boy to Deidre to Jason. "What'd you need a new light for? The old one broke?"

"This is a special light," Kevin announced. "If anything moves by the back porch, the light comes on. Cool, isn't it?"

His eyes shifted again. "Yeah, I guess." He brandished the clippers. "Gonna work on the hedge, okay?"

Deidre nodded. "That's great, Billy. It's been looking a bit shaggy since the rain."

She stood for a minute, watching him get started, frowning a little.

"Something wrong?"

Deidre shrugged. "No, I guess not. I didn't expect him to be here today, but that's Billy for you. He doesn't keep to a schedule."

Billy was clipping vigorously, with Kevin trotting along behind him and attempting to gather the clippings. "Has Billy said anything more to you about Dixie?"

Had Chief Carmichaels even bothered to question him?

"No." Her blue eyes followed his movements, and a worried frown gathered between her brows. "I tried. I know he's upset about it, but he doesn't seem to want to talk."

Did she worry about everyone she knew? "Maybe

that's how he deals with pain. Some people can't bear to discuss it." Which pretty much described him, too.

"I guess," she admitted. "The thing is, I have something that he'd made for Dixie—one of his figures. It was in a box of mementoes I brought home to sort. I thought he might want to have it back, but I don't want to upset him."

He couldn't help thinking that he'd like to see Billy's reaction, whether it upset him or not.

"I'd offer it to him, at least. He doesn't have to take it if he doesn't want the reminder."

Apparently that tipped the balance for her. Deidre nodded and went into the house. Through the windows, he could see her walking into the workroom, where she lifted a box onto the table.

He was reminded of the watcher, standing by the window, and his hands clenched. She was remembering to close the shades and curtains once it got dark, wasn't she? Even then, a pane of glass wasn't much to have between her and someone who wished her ill.

You don't know that, he reminded himself. The intruder might have been an ordinary Peeping Tom, a teen intent on vandalism or someone who thought it was funny to play tricks outside a house where a murder had occurred.

He didn't seem to be convincing himself.

Deidre reappeared, holding a small wooden figure in her hand. "Look." She held it out to him. "He really has a gift for this sort of thing."

The figure was a doe, this carving showing more delicacy than the one he'd done for Kevin. There was a grace and beauty about it that couldn't be denied, and he suspected it spoke of the feelings Billy had had for Dixie.

"Has he always done carvings?" He turned it over in his hands.

"Ever since I can remember. When we were kids and a gang of us used to go exploring in the woods, he'd always have a jackknife and a piece of wood with him. Whenever we sat down to rest, he'd pull it out and start whittling."

He tried to picture a group of kids allowed to run loose in the woods and failed. "Do you let Kevin do that?"

"Not yet. He's not old enough. I trust him and Benjy to go back and forth to the farm. And I'm sure they run all over the farm property when he's there."

He glanced up at the ridge, looming over them. "Will you let him when he's older?"

Deidre looked at him as if he were from another planet. "Of course. All the kids do. In a group, of course. I wouldn't want to see even an adult go off alone and risk getting lost." She smiled. "You're thinking that's careless parenting, and it would be in some places. But that's an advantage of living in a place like this. Kids learn a lot from each other when they don't have adults directing their every move."

He considered the young professionals he'd known in the city. Their children's lives had been carefully designed, with lessons and playgroups and organized sports filling up their free time. They wouldn't agree with Deidre's philosophy.

FREE Merchandise is 'in the Cards' for you!

Dear Reader,

We're giving away FREE MERCHANDISE!

Seriously, we'd like to reward you for reading this novel by giving you **FREE MERCHANDISE** worth over **$20** retail. And no purchase is necessary!

You see the Jack of Hearts sticker above? Paste that sticker in the box on the Free Merchandise Voucher inside. Return the Voucher today... and we'll send you Free Merchandise!

Thanks again for reading one of our novels—and enjoy your Free Merchandise with our compliments!

Pam Powers

Pam Powers

P.S. Look inside to see what Free Merchandise is **"in the cards"** for you!

W

e'd like to send you two free books like the one you are enjoying now. Your two books have a combined cover price of over $10 retail, but they are yours to keep absolutely FREE! We'll even send you 2 wonderful surprise gifts. You can't lose!

"A COMPELLING STORY...
INTRICATE AND FASCINATING."
—TAMI HOAG,
NEW YORK TIMES
BESTSELLING AUTHOR
ON DARK ROAD HOME

NEW YORK TIMES BESTSELLING AUTHOR
KAREN HARPER
FALLING DARKNESS
A SOUTH SHORES NOVEL

MARTA PERRY
ECHO OF DANGER

REMEMBER: Your Free Merchandise, consisting of **2 Free Books** and **2 Free Gifts**, is worth over $20 retail! No purchase is necessary, so please send for your Free Merchandise today.

Get TWO FREE GIFTS!

We'll also send you 2 wonderful FREE GIFTS (worth about $10 retail), in addition to your 2 Free books!

Visit us at:
www.ReaderService.com

Books received may not be as shown.

YOUR FREE MERCHANDISE INCLUDES...

2 FREE Books **AND** 2 FREE Mystery Gifts

FREE MERCHANDISE VOUCHER

Please send my Free Merchandise, consisting of
2 Free Books and **2 Free Mystery Gifts**.
I understand that I am under no obligation to buy
anything, as explained on the back of this card.

191/391 MDL GLTQ

Please Print

FIRST NAME

LAST NAME

ADDRESS

APT.#   CITY

STATE/PROV.   ZIP/POSTAL CODE

NO PURCHASE NECESSARY!

SUS-517-FM17

Seeming to consider the conversation closed, Deidre took the wooden deer back from his hand. "I'd better get this over with. If he's upset, I'm blaming you," she added lightly.

As well she should. He followed her as she walked across the grass, wanting to see for himself how Billy took it.

"That's looking nice and even," Deidre said once they were within earshot.

"I'm helping," Kevin said. "But I think I'm thirsty. Can I get a drink, Mommy?"

She nodded. "Get a juice box from the fridge. And see if Billy wants one."

"Do you, Billy? We have lemonade or apple."

Billy stopped clipping to consider. "What're you having?"

"Lemonade. That's my favorite."

"Okay. Get me one, too." They might have been the same age based on the way they were talking.

Deidre waited until Kev had run to the house before she held out the wooden carving. "I thought you might want to have this, since you made it for Dixie."

Billy snatched it out of her hand. "What're you doing with it?" Jase took a step closer to Deidre.

"You remember, Billy." Her voice was gentle. "Dixie's mother asked me to clean out her apartment."

"Yeah, I guess." He stared down at the deer, turning it over and over in his hands. "You weren't gonna throw it out, were you?"

"No, of course not. I'm sure Dixie treasured it." She paused, as if considering whether that was correct, but

Billy didn't seem to notice. "Anyway, I brought some things over to decide what to do with, and I thought you might like to have this back."

He ran his finger along the neck of the doe. "She did like it," he said, oddly insistent. "I know she did."

"Of course she did." Deidre was trying to be comforting, but obviously she wasn't sure what was behind his words. "It probably reminded her of those hikes we used to go on in the woods, remember?"

Billy looked up, his face twisted. "She liked to do that, didn't she? Until…" He shook his head, lips pressing together as if to hold back something.

Jase was uneasily reminded of how he'd burst into tears that last time they'd talked. He wasn't going to do that again, was he?

Billy sniffed a time or two. Then he wrapped the deer in a faded red bandanna and stowed it in a pocket. "I'll keep it. Dixie would want me to. I was her friend. Her good friend," he said again, emphasizing the words. "Better than anyone."

His voice broke. He grabbed the clippers and took off in a shambling run for the truck.

Picking up a small branch that had gone flying, Jason eyed Deidre. What was she thinking? "I guess the trimming is done for today."

Deidre stared after Billy, rubbing her forehead. "Maybe I shouldn't have given it to him. It's hard to know how he'll react. Still, I think eventually he'll be glad to have it."

"I think so," he murmured. Billy was upset, but he hadn't given much clue as to why, other than his sorrow over losing his friend. What had he meant by his insistence that he'd been Dixie's best friend? It was odd, but he had a feeling it might be important.

CHAPTER TEN

CARRYING A BACKPACK loaded with lunch and drinks, Deidre headed out to the car on Saturday with Kevin dancing around her, eager to get started. He carried his own small backpack and bubbled over with excitement.

"Will there be a lot of water coming over the falls? Do you think we'll see any deer? I want to find some wildflowers. Will there be any?" He tugged at her navy Windbreaker. "Mommy, answer me!"

"Which question do you want me to answer, sweetheart?" She grinned at him. "You have to give me a chance."

"All of them." He gave an extravagant gesture. "Hey, there's Jase." He started to bolt toward Jason, but she grabbed him by his backpack.

"Did he tell you it was okay to call him that?" Teaching manners was a constant effort.

"Yeah, he said so." Kev wiggled. "Let me go, Mommy."

She released him and watched as he raced to Jason. His lips were already moving a mile a minute. Good. Let Jason try to answer his questions. He was the one who'd wished himself onto them today.

She had to put up with Jason's presence, for Kevin's sake, but that didn't mean she was letting him get too close. She'd found his kiss too disturbing to her equilibrium. It had been days ago now, but still she couldn't quite get it out of her mind.

"Morning. Everybody ready to go?" Jason looked cheerful. He had on a pair of well-worn jeans, hiking boots and a dark red T-shirt that emphasized the breadth of his shoulders. It was enough to make any woman steal a second glance.

"Good morning." That sounded rather frosty, but she couldn't help it. "Let's toss our bags in the back, and we'll head out."

"Right." He took hers before she could put it in, hefted it and shook his head. "What do you have in here, rocks?"

"Water and juice boxes. You'll get thirsty hiking, even though it's not too hot."

"I don't doubt it, but there's no reason I can see that you should carry them all." Without asking, he unzipped her bag and transferred the water bottles to his. Then he put them both in the back, grinning at Kevin.

"I think I saw lunch in there, Kev. You hungry yet?"

He shook his head, clambering into the back and grabbing his seat belt. "I'll work up a really good appetite walking. We always have our lunch where we can look at the falls."

"Well, we wouldn't want to break tradition." Jason switched his gaze to her, and Deidre went quickly to the driver's seat, prepared to rebuff any suggestion that he should drive.

But he slid into the passenger side without comment, and she had the ridiculous notion that he knew just what she'd been thinking. Worse, that he might be laughing at her.

She glanced at him, found his dark eyes studying her, and hurriedly focused on the mirror as she backed out of the driveway. The trouble was that Jason was the first man she'd gotten close to since Frank died. That was it. Everyone in town still thought of her as Frank's wife, and there hadn't been anything remotely sexual in any of her relationships.

But Jason had seemed to look at her from the beginning as an attractive, available woman, not as someone's wife. It had been a long time since she'd encountered that. Maybe she'd just forgotten how to handle it.

She pictured Frank's face in her mind and discovered, to her panic, that she was remembering a static photo, not the living, breathing, fallible human being. Was he slipping away into the past? But he never could, not when she had Kevin.

A short distance down the road, she turned onto the dirt lane that would take them as far as they could go in the car. "This lane skirts the Yoder farm." She glanced at him. "Judith, my partner."

Jason nodded. "I know. That's where Kevin's buddy Benjamin lives."

He seemed to be gazing at the herd of Holsteins moving slowly across the pasture. She noticed Judith already had a clothesline full of clothes flapping in the light breeze, the bright solids of the dresses contrasting with the somber black pants.

"Look at the colors of the women's and little girls' dresses," she pointed out. "Those will soon show up in Judith's quilts. She has a real gift for combining the solid colors in her quilt designs."

He nodded politely, though she doubted he was much interested in quilts. "You and Judith seem to enjoy being in business together."

"Of course." She hit a rut in the lane with a tooth-rattling jolt. She'd better keep her eyes on the road. "We were part of each other's lives from the time we were very small." Her gesture took in the fields and the wooded hillside. "This was our playground. We loved to pretend we were the first ones to explore the land." She risked a sideways glance at him. "You probably did the same, didn't you?"

She was startled to see Jason's face tighten.

"Not many places to explore where I grew up. We were too busy staying off gang turf to go wandering."

He glanced toward Kevin in the backseat and clamped his lips together, leaving her wondering and a little shaken.

She'd assumed, if she'd thought of it at all, that he'd come from the same kind of upper-middle-class background as Frank and most of his classmates. Apparently she'd been wrong. And he didn't appear to be very forthcoming about it.

Jason seemed to make a determined effort to shake off his mood. He gestured to the surrounding woods. "Is this all private land?"

"A mix of private and government owned. Judith and Eli's farm ended back at the fence line. From there up to the top of the hill is State Game Lands, but over on the right, it's all private."

He nodded to a gravel lane going off to the right. "Does that lead to a farm, then?"

"Hunting cabins," she said briefly, concentrating on avoiding the ruts washed out by the spring rain. "Sometimes people come in the summer, but generally the cabins are used once or twice a year for hunting trips, and they sit empty the rest of the time."

The lane petered out into a wide spot where they'd leave the car.

"Here we are," she announced. "We walk from here, so grab your backpacks. Kev, you need some insect repellent before you head into the woods."

"Do I have to?" Kevin's response was always the same. "It smells yucky."

"Yes, you have to." She sprayed it onto her palm and then rubbed it onto Kevin's face before spraying his clothes. Then she handed it to Jason.

"Do I have to?" he said, grinning.

"Unless you want to risk taking a deer tick home as a souvenir, you do. I always think they're worse this time of the year."

Apparently he took her seriously, because he anointed himself thoroughly. "Not going to do my face for me?"

She avoided his eyes. "I think you can manage." She did her own spraying, and by that time Kevin had put on his backpack and was waiting at the trailhead.

"Let's go," he said impatiently.

They headed after him. "He'll slow down after a bit as he gets tired," she said. "It's mostly uphill."

"Good." He fell into step with her where the path

was wide enough for two. "I'd be ashamed to admit I can't keep up with a five-year-old."

"More likely we'll have to carry him on the way back. I will, I mean," she corrected hastily.

"I think I can manage that without getting too close to you, can't I?" The laughing note had left his voice.

"I...I don't know what you mean." That didn't sound convincing even to her.

"Don't you, Deidre?" He shrugged. "Okay. Well, take it however you want." He lengthened his stride. "Hey, Kevin, wait for me."

Left behind, she struggled with the meaning of his words. So he knew she was trying to keep him at a distance, which also must mean he knew she was attracted to him.

But that didn't mean she was going to act on that attraction. And to do him justice, he hadn't attempted anything since that one kiss. Maybe he wanted a relationship between them as little as she did. That should be reassuring, but...was it? Or had her emotions gotten the better of her plans?

She'd told herself, when she'd begun to recover from the shock of Frank's death, that it only made sense to take the possibility of a serious relationship off the table. Kevin was the most important person in her life. She wouldn't subject him to anything that might make him feel less secure, including the idea of another man taking his father's place. Besides, at that point she hadn't been able to imagine feeling for anyone else what she'd felt for Frank.

She still couldn't, could she?

The trail led through an area thick with hemlocks and maples. The maples were just leafing out, making the woods less dense than they would be later in the summer.

"Kevin, look here," she called out. She stopped, waiting until the two of them came back to her. Then she knelt, drawing her son down with her. "See these plants, like little umbrellas?"

Kevin touched one gently. "It's like an elf's umbrella," he exclaimed.

"Right." She smiled. "Look underneath it."

Kevin bent over to peek and came up smiling. "It's a flower. A little white flower. Look, Jason."

Jason squatted beside him and looked in turn. "You're right, buddy." He glanced at her. "What is it?"

"That's called a May apple. If you look at it later in the summer, you'll find what looks like an apple where the flower is now. But you can't eat it," Deidre added hastily. "It's not a real apple."

"May apple," Kevin repeated. "I'll remember."

He was on his feet in an instant and moving again, but Jason lingered, giving her a questioning look. "Is there anything about this place you don't know?"

"I grew up here, remember? Some things you learn sort of by osmosis, I think. My father loved to teach me the names of plants and how to identify the different trees. And constellations. He'd sneak me out of the house on summer nights to look at the stars."

She smiled at the memory, grieving because Kevin wouldn't have that with his grandfather. Her dad had died too early to know him.

They started moving again, but this time Jason stayed close by her. "I guess there's a lot to be said for a childhood like yours. Not everyone's so lucky."

She hesitated, but he was the one who'd brought it up, which seemed to invite a question. "I take it that you grew up in a…a difficult environment?"

"Yeah, if you can call spending a lot of my time on the streets difficult." She couldn't miss the edge to his voice.

"Your family?" she ventured.

"I never knew my father. My mother was…" His face tightened with remembered pain. "She looked for refuge in a bottle. She didn't find it."

"I'm sorry." Her mind was spinning. This was so far from what she'd imagined that she could hardly grasp it. "But how did you…" She stopped, thinking she was on the verge of being tactless.

"How did I get out?" His tone steadied, and his face no longer betrayed him. "I was lucky. I had a teacher who saw possibilities in me and steered me in the right direction. And a coach who pushed me to dream big." He shook his head. "I still can't quite believe where I've ended up. It could so easily have gone the other way."

"I'm glad you found people who believed in you, but I'm sure you deserve a lot of the credit yourself. You did the hard work to get where you are."

He shrugged, staring ahead at Kevin trudging along the path. "I have to keep my guard up. I've seen how easily it can all slip away."

Deidre watched him, wishing she was wise enough

to say the right thing. "If you keep your guard up all the time, it can be hard to let people know you."

He flashed a look at her. "That's the idea."

"But you let me in," she ventured.

"Maybe you caught me at a weak moment." He quickened his steps. "Kevin, what's the rush?"

"We're almost there." Kevin hurried back to them and grabbed Jason's hand, tugging it. "Come on, hurry up. I want to show you the falls."

Giving in to his excitement, they hurried around another bend in the path. They could hear the falls now, sending out their constant roaring. Then the falls came into view, rushing down the rocky cliff face and sending up the spray that cloaked the surroundings in a magical mist.

Jason's face was everything Kevin could have wanted. He looked dumbfounded. "But…that must be close to a hundred feet high."

"Not quite," she said. As they grew nearer, the roar of the water made it necessary to pitch her voice a little louder. "Ninetysomething, I believe. It is awesome, isn't it?"

He nodded, not taking his eyes off the water. "I wouldn't have imagined it." He ruffled Kevin's hair. "Thanks, Kev. I'm glad you convinced me to come. I wouldn't have missed it for anything."

Kevin grinned, gratified. "Mommy knows all about the falls. You can ask her anything."

"Well, not anything," she said. "My father loved natural history, and every excursion turned into a lesson."

"You've got a captive audience, so go ahead and

teach us." He grabbed Kevin's hand. "Sit down on this rock, Kev. Your mother's going to tell us all about it."

She had to laugh as the two of them seated themselves on a long, flat rock and looked at her expectantly. "Okay, I'll tell you what my dad told me. This is actually the break between the Allegheny Plateau and the valleys." Kevin seemed confused, so she sat down next to him. "See, the land north of us is all high ground. But where we live is in the valley, and there are lots of other ridges and valleys all along this part of Pennsylvania. So the water had to get from that higher ground up there to the valleys below, and that makes a waterfall." She might have simplified it a little too much, but Kevin would have plenty of other chances to learn about his world.

"It's a very impressive waterfall." A breeze sent a spray of water across Jason's face, beading it with moisture. "Is this privately owned land?"

"Not anymore. The Morris family used to own a big chunk of it, but when the State Game Lands took over the area, Kevin's great-grandfather deeded most of his land to them, as well. That way the falls were protected."

"Tell the story, Mommy," Kevin said. "Tell the story about the Native American girl."

"Legends?" Jason lifted his eyebrows quizzically.

"There are always legends about waterfalls, I think." She lifted her face to feel the spray. "I can understand why."

"Tell it, Mommy." Kevin nudged her. "We want to hear."

"That's right," Jason added. "We're ready to hear a story." Kevin leaned against him, and Jason put his arm around her son as naturally as if he did it all the time. The sight did something funny to her heart.

She cleared her throat. "Well, it's just a legend," she said. "But the story goes that long, long ago, two tribes were at war. A young woman had ventured out in search of food when she was spotted by the enemy. She tried to lose them, so she could get back to where her family was hiding, but she couldn't. They were getting closer and closer, and she could hear their cries. She'd reached the top of the falls when she knew they were too near. She couldn't get away, and she wouldn't lead them to the people she loved. So she jumped from the top of the falls."

She got caught up in the story, telling it the way she'd first heard it years ago. "They say sometimes you can still hear her voice whispering in the voice of the falls, telling her family she loved them." Unexpectedly her throat tightened, and her eyes stung.

Silly. It was probably a made-up story anyway, like most stories people told about the falls. But still, what woman wouldn't sacrifice herself to save those she loved?

They sat silently, letting the magic of the place seep into them. Even Kevin seemed struck into speechlessness for the moment.

Jason's hand closed warmly over hers where it lay on the rock. Almost without volition, she turned it so that they were palm to palm.

Without looking at each other, with nothing touch-

ing save their hands, a flood of communion rippled
between them, carrying a message of caring, of longing, of the faintest whisper of hope. She needn't have
worried about how she would keep Jason at a distance
today. It was already far too late for that.

JASON DREW AWAY from Deidre slowly, a fraction of an
inch at a time. He'd never experienced this mix of emotions before—longing and desire, yes, but never over-
laid with this need to protect her from anything and
everything.

Not even for Leslie—well, certainly not for Leslie.
Leslie had proved herself well able to take care of herself, even at the cost of his future.

He had to be careful. If he let this feeling have its
way, there'd be no backing out.

Kevin grabbed his hand and tugged. "Come on. Let's
explore."

"Okay. Where should we explore?" He glanced at the
falls. He could see a steep trail that led up along them
and hoped nobody thought it would be a good idea to
try to climb to the top.

"We'll walk down the stream," Deidre said, swinging her backpack onto her shoulders. "See what treasures you can find, Kev."

"Treasures?" Jase shouldered his own pack, prepared
to follow her.

"Of course." She looked surprised. "If you're not
looking, how will you find something special?" She
waved her hand at their surroundings. "I want Kev to
grow up appreciating the natural world."

"What do you think he'll find?"

No sooner had the question come out of his mouth than Kevin was calling them, excitement filling his voice.

"Look! Look what I found!"

"I hope it's not an animal, or it'll be in the next county by now." Deidre, smiling, hurried to join her son.

But Kevin was squatting in a shady patch of gravel near the stream. "Look," he said in a whisper this time.

Another flower, its perfectly shaped green leaves seeming to curl protectively around the single flower stalk in the center.

"Remember what it is, Kevin?" Deidre prompted.

"Jack-in-the-pulpit," he declared. "Did you ever see one before, Jase?"

Jason shook his head. "Never did. Why is it called that?"

"I guess because the flower stands up so proudly above the leaves," Deidre said. "We don't often see them. You have to be in the woods at just the right time."

"See, I told you this would be a good day, Mommy." Kevin touched the plant lightly, but made no effort to pick it. Jase shot a glance at Deidre. "No picking?"

Kev answered. "Leave nothing but footprints. Take nothing but a memory. That's what Mommy says."

Deidre flushed. "Mommy's an old Girl Scout," she said lightly.

Jase pulled out his cell phone. "How about a picture? Can we take that back with us?"

Laughing, she nodded.

"Put your face real close to the flower, Kev, and I'll get you and Jack."

Squatting, he zeroed in with his camera phone, the boy's innocent rounded face above the perfection of the flower. "Great," he said, snapping it.

Kevin jumped to his feet as if he was on springs. "You don't know very much about the woods," he said, giving Jason a disapproving look.

"I never had a chance to learn."

"That's good, because Kevin can be your guide," she intervened quickly.

Kevin brightened. "Sure I can. I know lots."

He darted along the stream, probably looking for his next discovery.

"And he's humble, too," Deidre said ruefully.

"He can't know less than I do. I think I've lost face with him just a little."

"You'll regain it quickly enough." Her gaze was on her son as he teetered on a rock on the edge of the stream. "I hadn't realized how much he'd missed having a man around." That betraying color came up again. "I didn't mean…"

"I know what you meant," he said. "It's okay." Intent on distracting her, he said, "He's going to have wet feet before long."

"It's inevitable." She seemed resigned. "Little boys always make messes."

Big boys do that, too, Jason thought. Right now, he had to figure out how to get out of the mess he was in.

They rounded a curve in the stream where the banks

grew narrower and the water rushed, hurrying toward what lay ahead. He stared. "Is that a mill?"

"It was," she said. "Some early Morris got the idea of putting a gristmill here. Lots of water pressure, of course, but he didn't figure on how difficult it would be for the farmers to get their grain up here. It's been abandoned for years, although the judge had converted it to a cottage and used to make an effort to keep it in shape. Frank talked about coming here more often, but we never did. We thought we'd have plenty of time."

Jason grasped a tree branch to give him something to hold on to as he leaned out to have a better look. "The water wheel is still there." It leaned rather drunkenly to one side, but it turned sporadically as the current hit it.

"The grist stones are still inside," Deidre said. "Kevin, do you want to show Jason the millstones?"

But Kevin had stopped dead, staring at the mill. He didn't answer.

"Kev," she said again, questioning.

"No." He stepped backward until he bumped into Jason. Jason put a hand on his shoulder and felt him tremble.

"But, Kev, you always want…"

Jason shook his head.

Her eyes widening at his silent message, Deidre bent over her son. "Is something wrong, sweetheart?"

Kevin shook his head violently, his eyes fixed and staring at the mill. "I don't want to."

She exchanged glances with Jason, and he saw that this had taken her by surprise.

What had brought on that response? He supposed the old mill did look creepy in a way, but if Kevin was familiar with it, it was hard to understand his reaction.

"Why don't we walk back to where we can see the falls and find a place for our picnic," he suggested.

Kevin nodded vigorously. He clutched Jason's hand like a lifeline and pulled him back the way they'd come.

The feel of that small hand affected Jason in a way he'd never experienced. When had someone ever relied on him—trusted him to keep them safe? Deidre and her son had given him a whole new set of challenges. He hoped he could live up to them.

Kevin clung to him until the mill was out of sight. Then he seemed to throw off a weight and scampered ahead. "I know a good picnic place."

Deidre still looked troubled.

"Do you have any idea what brought that on?" he asked.

She made a small gesture of negation. "It's always been a favorite place of his. I don't understand it. He was fine when we were up here last fall."

"Maybe it reminded him of something scary."

"That's probably it." She looked relieved at the explanation. "I try not to expose him to anything beyond his ability to cope with, but sometimes even the kids' movies get scary. The other day I left him watching a harmless cartoon while I was getting supper and came back in to find the station was advertising a very inappropriate movie. Luckily it seemed to go right over his head."

Kevin was protected from some things by his innocence. But not from the danger that had struck Dixie down. The thought lodged in his mind, pricking at him.

Kevin, sure enough, had chosen a spot for their picnic and was waiting for them, bouncing impatiently. "Right here, okay? I'm hungry."

"That's good, because I don't want to carry all this food home." Deidre swung her pack to the ground in the spot Kevin had found—a smooth, even space a few feet back from the stream, where the trees formed a canopy over them and they could see the falls.

Deidre started pulling things from her pack, and Jase helped her spread out a cloth. Her idea of picnic fare was what a kid would like—cold fried chicken, a container of carrot and celery sticks, another of cut-up fruit and snack bags of chips and pretzels. Remembering he carried the beverages, he got them out and they settled down on the cloth.

Kevin seized a drumstick, then hesitated. "You don't want the drumstick, do you, Jase?"

He was obviously struggling between his desire to be polite to a guest and his longing for the drumstick, and Jason had to suppress a smile.

"No, I have my eye on this nice meaty piece." He picked up a thigh. "What about your mother?"

"She never eats the drumsticks," Kevin said. "I guess she doesn't like them."

He found himself loving the smile that lurked in her eyes at that. "I'm sure that's it," he said gravely.

He was hungrier than he'd realized, and apparently

that was true of the others, too, since no one talked much until the food had been eaten.

Then Kevin lay back on the cloth. "The trees look funny from here. Like they're upside-down."

"Maybe you're upside-down." Amused, Jason lay back, propped on his elbows, and looked across the boy's small form at Deidre. She sat relaxed, hands braced behind her. She'd shed the Windbreaker she'd had on earlier, and the clear blue of her T-shirt echoed the clear blue of her eyes.

He was enjoying looking at her entirely too much. He'd better focus on something else before he did something foolish.

He lay back beside Kevin. "What do you see up there?"

"Lots of leaves." Kevin pointed, but his voice sounded drowsy. "They're just starting to come out. They're baby leaves."

"I guess they are," he agreed. "I see clouds moving. They're sailing along like ships."

"Yeah, I see that. There's one, and another one…" He subsided, and his eyes drifted shut midcount.

Jason didn't move for a few minutes, afraid of disturbing him. But as the boy's breathing deepened and grew even, Jase sat up.

Deidre smiled. "I had a feeling he'd want a rest about now," she said softly. "He's not really quite up to speed after being in the hospital."

"Seems pretty speedy to me. He even sleeps intently." It was true. Kevin's brows were drawn together a little, as if he was focused on his sleep.

"He always did that when he was tiny," she said. "I

never realized a baby could sleep with such concentration. It should have given me a clue as to his personality."

She was studying her son's face as she spoke, and her expression induced a reaction in him. He saw love in her eyes, yes, but anxiety, as well. Something troubled her.

"What are you worrying about?" He asked the question before thinking that it might be intrusive.

But she didn't seem to take it that way. She gave Kevin's face a featherlight touch. "He always seems so vulnerable when he's sleeping. It makes me feel even more strongly the need to keep him safe from every threat."

He felt a similar need to defend her, but never mind that now. "There's something specific, isn't there? If you're still thinking that the person who attacked Dixie will come back…"

She shook her head. "No. Well, I'm concerned, yes. I want to see him caught and put away. But Sylvia…"

Sylvia. The judge's wife. What had she done to put that fear in Deidre's face?

"What? What did she do?"

"Nothing." She took a breath, and he saw that she was struggling to hold something back. Something she didn't want to put voice to.

Suddenly it seemed too much for her. "She said…she thinks the judge is going to try to force me and Kevin to move in with them." Once that was out, the words seemed to come more quickly. "I knew he wanted us to do so, but I'd already told him no. I thought he understood that I meant it."

"He can't force you to do something you don't want to, can he?" It was a wonder she couldn't read the guilt on his face. "How did she think he could force you?"

"She didn't make a lot of sense. I keep telling myself she's imagining things. But she seemed so convinced. And afraid. I can't help thinking... I can't stop thinking he might have some plan to force me into it."

He took a firm grip on his control. "Fear can be contagious. That's understandable. But do you logically think there's any reason the judge can push you into obeying?"

"N-no. I guess not. I've just seen so much of him trying to bend Frank to his will that it makes me nervous." Her voice shook, and she pressed her fingers against her lips. She looked at him, and her eyes seemed to plead for him to deny her fears.

How could he? Judge Morris was already doing exactly what she feared—conspiring to force her and Kevin to move in with him. And he was implicated in that conspiracy. But that didn't mean he had to continue to be.

Deidre needed reassurance, not more problems, he told himself. "That's not going to happen," he said firmly. "And I'll tell you why. Because you'll have the toughest lawyer you ever met on your side. Believe me. I learned street fighting from the best. I won't let it happen." He touched her cheek, his fingertips carrying sensation right through him. "I promise." His voice was husky.

He leaned toward her, over Kevin. Slowly, as if compelled, she swayed forward to meet him. Their lips touched, held, and the world seemed to spin away.

Nothing touching except their lips, his dazed mind noted. Nothing else, but it was enough. Whatever doubts he might have had about Deidre burned away to nothing.

He was going to protect her. He'd save her if he had to tear that town apart with his bare hands.

CHAPTER ELEVEN

DEIDRE PULLED THE car up to the back door, not quite able to believe how things had changed in the course of a few hours. She'd left home annoyed with Jason and determined to keep him at arm's length. Now...

Now, even though very little had been said between them, everything had changed. They had crossed a chasm in their relationship, and neither of them could pretend it hadn't changed. Whatever happened from this point, things were now different.

They got out of the car, and Kevin, having gotten a second wind, immediately started badgering Jason to play ball with him.

"Enough, Kev. Jason will think you have no manners at all. Thank him for coming with us, and then you can help carry things inside."

Abashed, Kev picked up his backpack. "Thank you for coming. But you had a good time, didn't you? I'm glad you came. Aren't you glad?"

"Very glad." Jason ruffled her son's hair affectionately, and the look he gave Deidre brought the heat rushing to her face. "Now let's help clean up, okay?"

Between them they grabbed all the bags, leaving her

with nothing to do but unlock the back door. She held it while they entered and then let it swing closed.

"Just put those on the kitchen counter, and I'll take care of our leftovers right away."

"Okay." Kevin scurried ahead to swing his backpack up to the counter. Jason reached over his head to deposit his backpack and hers.

Deidre unzipped her bag and started pulling out the contents. Too bad that such a perfect excursion left its supply of cleanup to be dealt with. She eyed the soggy remains of chicken bones and started emptying and rinsing iced tea bottles for recycling. Behind her, she heard Kevin return to the attack.

"Want to play ball for a bit? Hey, Mommy, can Jason stay for supper?"

"You're thinking about the next meal already?" she teased.

Jason grinned. "Your mother fixed the picnic, Kev. It's not fair to expect her to make supper, too. How about I go get a pizza?"

The idea of spending even more time in his company was nearly irresistible. "I think…" she began, and abruptly lost the thread of her words as she glanced into the workroom, fear freezing her voice.

Jason was at her side in a moment. His hand closed on her arm. "What is it?" he said softly.

His grip steadied her enough to speak with some semblance of normality. "Kevin, run out back and see if the flowers I brought home yesterday need a drink."

"I'll water them," Kev said, instantly distracted by

the idea of messing with water. The door banged behind him as he bolted out.

She met Jason's eyes, hoping she didn't look as shaken as she felt. "Someone's been in the house while we were gone."

He drew her a little closer to him. "Are you sure? How can you tell?"

Deidre nodded toward the workroom. "That box on the table—it was closed and stowed on the floor when I went out this morning. Now half the contents are strewed on the table. I'll look…"

His grip tightened, not letting her make a move toward the workroom. "Better not touch anything. Let's do this according to the book. We'll go outside and call the police."

She nodded. That was the smartest course. But…

"I don't want Kevin to know anything's wrong." She clasped Jason's hand with both of hers. "Please, Jason, you have to help me. I can't let him become afraid of his own house."

Jason nodded, already pulling his cell phone out. "Go help him water, or whatever he's doing. I'll call. Then I'll take Kevin out of the way."

Nodding, she headed for the door. She couldn't do anything else right now, but she could keep Kevin from being exposed to another police investigation.

She and Kevin were watering the row of white-and-red geraniums when Jason came out of the house, moving with a kind of suppressed energy that seemed to need an outlet.

While Kevin went to fill the watering can, they had time to exchange a few private words.

"The chief's coming himself. Quiet, no sirens. He wants you to stay so you can tell him what's missing, but he agreed I could take Kevin away for the moment."

She could see the struggle in Jason over agreeing to back away. His first instinct was obviously to take over, but it seemed he respected her enough to suppress it. Her opinion of him went up another notch.

"Good. Thank you. If you wanted to drop him at a friend's house…"

He shook his head. "You're not getting rid of me that easily. Hey, Kevin, how about if we go pick up some pizza? You and your mom can come to my house for supper."

Kevin looked at her for approval and grinned when she nodded. "Super. Can we get extra cheese?"

"Sure you don't want veggie pizza?" Jason set the watering can on the porch step and took Kevin's hand.

"Mommy likes olives and mushrooms, and I like extra cheese," Kevin informed him.

"Okay." They headed for the house next door. "We'll get one of each."

That would probably be more pizza than they could eat, but she was too stressed to call after him. It was unexpectedly lonely when they'd disappeared from view, and after fidgeting for several minutes Deidre walked to the driveway to wait for the police.

Chief Carmichaels didn't keep her waiting. His unmarked car slipped quietly into the driveway just a few minutes after Jason and Kevin had left.

Deidre realized she was clenching her hands and consciously relaxed them, forcing a pleasant expression as she moved toward the chief. Unfortunately, her thoughts were anything but pleasant. Would this nightmare ever be over?

SINCE PICKING UP a couple of pizzas was about the only way he could provide a meal a five-year-old was likely to want, Jason had figured this was the best option under the circumstances. He itched to know what Chief Carmichaels had said and done, but that would have to wait until Kevin was out of earshot.

The three of them were really pretty comfortable sitting together around his kitchen table. Kevin talked enough to fill in any gaps that occurred when Deidre glanced with anxious eyes in the direction of her home.

How long was it going to be until she felt safe and comfortable there again? If it were him, he'd probably move out, but he knew enough of Deidre to know she wouldn't desert her family home willingly. He just hoped there were enough good memories to counteract the bad ones.

Kevin had reached the point of toying with what was left of his pizza slice when Deidre reached across to pull the plate away.

"Are you finished, Kev?"

He nodded, then seemed to think more was necessary. "Thank you for supper. May I please be excused?"

"Yes, you may." Deidre looked gratified that he'd remembered his manners without prompting. "Maybe you can watch cartoons on Jason's television while we finish up."

"Sure thing," Jason said. That was a good thought. They'd be able to talk under cover of the cartoon noise.

Turned out it was more complicated than just switching on the television. Deidre was careful with what Kevin watched, as she'd said, and she checked the schedule before turning on something she considered acceptable.

But finally they were back in the kitchen. Jason started coffee and then hitched his chair close to Deidre's. "So we can talk softly," he said, responding to her raised eyebrows. "With your son in the next room, I'm forced to behave."

That did get a smile from her, but it was a feeble one.

"Okay." He wrapped his fingers around hers. "What happened with Carmichaels? What did he think?"

"I wish I knew what he thought." Her forehead crinkled. "At first he didn't seem convinced there really had been anyone there. But once he saw that only Dixie's belongings had been touched, he did take it seriously."

"Was anything missing?" That was the obvious first question.

"That's what Chief Carmichaels asked, too. The trouble is that I can't be sure." Her frown deepened. "I hadn't gone through everything yet. I'd just tossed in all the stuff that I thought should be gone through. There was a folder of bills, receipts, statements. And some of it had been in a small box in Dixie's closet— that mostly seemed to be memorabilia."

"What sort of memorabilia? Any notes or letters?"

His voice had sharpened. It was too bad Dixie hadn't kept a diary. They might be a bit further ahead in understanding why she'd been a target.

"Not that I can remember." She lifted her free hand, palm up. "Some dried flowers, a matchbook, a couple of souvenir mugs, a couple of those little figures that you get in tourist traps. You know. 'Souvenir of Ocean City.' That sort of thing. And she had a collection of china pigs. She'd started that years ago, and I could tell some of them were in the box by their shape, though I hadn't unwrapped them all."

"That doesn't sound like something her killer would be after."

A shiver went through Deidre, and he was sorry he'd said the word. Still, that's who he was assuming it was.

"We don't know that it was the killer. It could have been someone else who wanted something of Dixie's."

"What? And who? Either way, it's a criminal act. If you just wanted something to remember her by, you wouldn't break into someone's house to get it. Unless you weren't capable of coming up with other means."

"You're thinking of Billy." Deidre pulled her hand away. "I don't believe that. He wouldn't break into my house. He knows I'd probably give him whatever he wanted if he asked me."

"What about Dixie's ex? Would he think that? He wanted something from her place." The chief had supposedly been going to have a talk with Hanlon, but if he had, he hadn't confided that information to Jason.

"I suppose not, especially after I refused to let him

into her apartment." Her blue eyes widened. "He knew I had some of Dixie's things here."

"How?" Jase rasped the word, instantly alert.

"Judith and I were walking back here from the apartment, carrying boxes, when he happened to drive by. At least I think it was him. His car..." She paused. "He couldn't know exactly what was in the box, of course, but it would be logical to think we were bringing something of Dixie's here."

"Did you tell Carmichaels about that?"

She shook her head. "I didn't think of it until this minute."

"We'll have to let him know." He frowned. "But it doesn't really lead us any closer to guessing what Hanlon might be after. They'd been divorced for a while, hadn't they?"

"Close to two years, I think. You're right—it's hard to imagine what he could be wanting badly enough after that time to break into my house for it."

"We won't know that until we find out what that something might be." He hesitated, but the question had to be asked. "Is it possible Dixie was or had been involved with a married man? Someone like that might be eager to be sure there was nothing to give him away."

He expected a prompt denial, but it didn't come. Deidre seemed to withdraw into herself, as if reluctant to look at the possibility.

"Not that I know of. But if she was, she wouldn't have let me know. She knew how I felt about that sort of betrayal."

Jason reminded himself that people sometimes managed to excuse themselves for not living up to their own principles, but he didn't believed Deidre was one of them. As far as he could tell, there hadn't been any men in her life other than Frank, despite the judge and the anonymous letter writer.

"But you admit it's possible?" he pressed.

Her lips trembled for a moment, and he could read the pain in her eyes. "I don't want to believe it." Her voice had dropped to a whisper.

There was more here than just the question of what sort of woman Dixie James had been. He felt it. He grasped her hands, wanting her to face him.

"What is it? Tell me, Deidre. You can't keep things secret in a murder case. Everything comes out eventually, even stuff that has nothing to do with the killing. Tell me, so I can help you."

She held out against his request. And then suddenly she caved in, pressing her face against their clasped hands. He felt her tears.

He wanted to put his arms around her, hold her close, tell her everything was going to be all right. But he couldn't, not now. All his prosecutor's instincts told him she knew something and she had to tell.

Deidre caught a ragged breath. "I…I found it. When I was sorting Dixie's things." Another breath, as if to give her strength to go on. "A diamond pendant, very valuable. It belonged to Frank's mother."

Whatever he'd expected, it wasn't that. He grappled with the information, trying to find its meaning. "You think Dixie took it?"

"No, no. She'd never even been in that house." Her

voice gained strength. Whatever else she might believe about Dixie, she was convinced she wasn't a thief, obviously. "Someone gave it to her." Deidre raised her head and seemed to force herself to meet his eyes. "Sylvia kept telling Frank that she wanted me to have it, but I never felt comfortable with that idea. I assumed Sylvia still had the necklace, until I found it in Dixie's bureau."

He finally managed to connect the dots she was following. "You think that means that Frank gave it to her."

"How else would she get it?" Deidre's lips twisted. "Frank didn't want me to see so much of her after she came back to town. Funny, isn't it?"

It made a certain amount of sense. If Frank had been involved with Dixie, it made a lot of sense. But not enough for him to accuse Frank of infidelity.

"You're thinking they had an affair." He touched her arm gently, almost afraid she'd shatter she was so vulnerable. "There might be some other explanation. I don't know what, but if that's your only evidence…"

"I keep going over and over it in my mind," she said wearily. "You said yourself that I mothered Frank, and that's probably true. He'd been in my life forever, and I always loved him. He seemed to need me so much." Her voice broke a little. "Now…well, now I wonder if he'd started to resent that. Maybe that wasn't the best basis for marriage, but I loved him, and I was sure he loved me."

She turned toward him more fully, reaching out almost blindly, her eyes filled with tears. "I don't know what to believe anymore."

There was no way he could prevent himself from

pulling her into his arms, from holding her, comforting her, while she cried silently against his shoulder. He knew the pain of betrayal. He wanted to tell her that he understood, but that was dangerous territory, because in his own way, he was betraying her, too.

Jason pressed his cheek against her hair, longing flooding his body. She needed him. The reason the judge had brought him here stood between them like a wall. If he told her the truth, he risked having her push him away just when she needed him most.

And if he didn't... No matter how this turned out, he suspected he was going to lose. By staying in the judge's confidence, he had some chance of making sure she didn't lose Kevin. Maybe that was the only thing he would ever be able to do for her.

So he held her close, and murmured soothing, meaningless phrases, and kept the secret she was bound to consider yet another betrayal.

BY THE NEXT MORNING, Jason had hammered out an approach for himself, and he headed to the office early, hoping to catch the judge before he left. This question of the judge's intentions had to be settled, but he didn't want to give away either Deidre or her fragile mother-in-law.

But the judge had clearly told him that he only wanted leverage to persuade Deidre to move herself and Kevin in with him. The more he came to know about the judge and his wife, the less he thought of that idea. And if the judge was using him with the intention of going even beyond that, of suing for custody of Kevin, then it was time for an open break with him.

Parking at the curb, he walked toward the office, the morning sun warm on his head. Sometime this morning he also had to find out what the police were doing about Hanlon, Dixie's ex. He seemed the most likely person to have been looking for something at Deidre's place. Surely Carmichaels would at least have talked to him by now.

Impatience quickened Jase's steps. He wanted to do something, and fast. He had the sense that the situation was rocketing out of control.

Jase reached for the office doorknob, noting wryly his name in gilt under those of Franklin Morris and Trey Alter. How long would that remain once the judge realized Jason was on Deidre's side?

He turned the knob and discovered that the door was locked. Surprised, he just stared at it for a moment before reaching for his keys. No matter how early the attorneys were, Evelyn Lincoln always managed to be there first.

But even as he drew out the keys, he saw Evelyn peer out from the door into Trey's office. At the sight of him, relief washed over her face, and she practically ran to unlock the door and pull him inside.

"Oh, Mr. Glassman, I'm so glad it's you. I don't think I've ever been so frightened in my life. My heart is still pounding, and my head—I just can't think straight."

For someone who was usually in perfect control, Evelyn was definitely rattled. He grasped the hands she was waving in agitation.

"Easy, Evelyn. Just tell me what happened."

"I didn't know what to do!" She clutched his hands. "Such a thing has never happened before. Was I right to call the police?"

Jason seized his rapidly vanishing supply of patience. "I still don't know what scared you. Can you calm down enough to tell me?" He guided her to her chair behind the reception desk.

Evelyn sank into it, taking a deep breath. "Sorry. I'm acting like an idiot."

"Just start at the beginning. You got here early, like you always do."

She nodded. "I always keep the outer door locked until I see one of you or a client arrives. I was just tidying up when I heard someone at the door. He was trying to come in, and when he couldn't, he started banging at the door something fierce."

"Was it someone you knew? Someone who had an appointment?"

"No, no. A stranger. Big, kind of rough-looking." She shuddered. "I went toward the door, thinking I'd ask what he wanted, but when I got near it, he started yelling." Her face turned pink. "He was swearing at me, demanding that I let him in."

It sounded like Hanlon again. Obviously a man who used his fists before his brains. "Did he say who he wanted?"

"I don't think so. I kept saying the office was closed and nobody was here, but I don't know if he understood me." She gave him a prim look. "I wouldn't be surprised if he'd been drinking. So finally I said I was calling the police. And I went into Trey's office and locked the door and called."

"I'm sure you did the right thing." He glanced at the front window. "And here they are. You'll just need to tell them exactly what you told me."

The police were represented by the same young patrolman who'd come to Deidre's the night she'd reported a prowler. Trey Alter was close on his heels, so they both listened as Evelyn went over the whole story again with a few embellishments as far as her feelings were concerned.

While the patrolman was trying to get a more detailed description of the man, Trey moved casually over to Jason.

"Any thoughts as to who this might be?"

Jason shrugged. "No way of knowing for sure unless he decides to check for fingerprints, but I'm guessing it could have been Dixie James's ex-husband. The description, such as it is, would fit him."

Trey nodded. "If he were local, Evelyn probably would have known him, even if she couldn't put a name to him. But what would Dixie's ex want with us? We didn't represent her."

"No, but I did give Mrs. Morris advice on the legalities involved with taking over the funeral and disposing of Dixie's belongings. He came to her apartment at least once when Mrs. Morris was there, trying to get in."

Trey's lips pursed as if giving a soundless whistle. "I don't like the idea of him pestering Deidre. And that break-in at her place yesterday—are you thinking he was involved?"

"No way of knowing for sure. You heard about that already?" He was growing resigned to the way news seemed to travel around this town.

Trey nodded. "It's all over town."

Sure it was. He wished he knew whose side Trey would be on if it came to a battle between Deidre and the judge. He could be a valuable ally.

"I think Carmichaels had been looking for the ex-husband, anyway."

Trey considered, frowning at little at the young patrolman. Finally, he seemed to come to a decision. "I don't think it's much good suggesting anything to him. Sam's a nice kid, but he hasn't advanced much beyond writing tickets. Suppose I keep an eye on things here while you drop in on Carmichaels? I don't like the sound of this ex-husband, especially if the chief thinks he's got a grudge of some kind against Deidre."

"Good idea," Jase said quickly. He still couldn't guess which way the man would jump if it came to a choice, but he seemed to want to protect Deidre, and right now that was enough.

So while Evelyn was describing her feelings for the third or fourth time, Jason slipped out of the office. He'd wanted to talk to Carmichaels anyway, and now it had become a priority.

In a few minutes he was in the tiny room at the police station, describing the incident at the office to Chief Carmichaels. "I can't be sure it was Mike Hanlon," he concluded. "But it sounds like him."

Carmichaels gave a curt nod. "That's what I'm thinking, too. But what the devil is the man up to?"

"Seems to me he wants something—something he thinks Dixie had." Jason spoke slowly, reasoning it out as he did. "First he tries to get into Dixie's apartment, saying he wanted some old photos of them. I told him he should check with the police about claiming them." He looked a question at Carmichaels.

"No, he didn't say anything to us. From what I've seen and heard, I don't think that bird would voluntarily ask the cops anything."

Obviously Carmichaels would have checked up on him. "Does he have a record?"

"Drunk and disorderly, simple assault. Bar fights, mostly. It sounds like he's a mean drunk."

"Deidre said that's what Dixie told her."

Carmichaels nodded. "I don't like it. I'm not saying I think he necessarily had anything to do with her death, but I don't like him wandering around my town stirring up trouble. What does he want?" He slapped the desk by way of emphasis.

"Something he expects to find among Dixie's things, at a guess. He tries to get into the apartment openly, and he can't, because he was stopped by Deidre. Then he apparently sees Deidre carrying a box of things from Dixie's place to hers."

Carmichaels looked up alertly. "You sure of that?"

"Deidre said he drove past while she was doing it. She noticed him, so she's assuming he noticed her. And it would fit if he's the one who broke into Deidre's house and went through the box of Dixie's belongings. I thought she was going to tell you that, but maybe she hasn't had a chance."

Jase was beginning to feel comfortable working with Chief Carmichaels. He seemed to approach his job seriously and fairly, which was all he could ask.

"No word yet from the state police lab on the fingerprints we lifted. I'll try jogging them a bit." He seemed to be weighing his opinion of Jason. "While we're speculating, why would he want to talk to someone at your chambers?"

"It would be me, I suppose." Jase shrugged. "I'm the one who told him he couldn't get access to Dixie's things until the police released them, and then only with the executor's approval. He may assume I have some influence over that."

"He might at that." Carmichaels gave him a look he couldn't interpret. "Thanks, Counselor. I think we have enough to bring him in to answer some questions, anyway. We'll see where we go from there."

He seemed to think it would be a simple matter to lay hands on Hanlon. Jase hoped that was true, because it was high time they had some answers.

CHAPTER TWELVE

A FEW DAYS LATER, when Deidre reached the sidewalk outside the elementary school and glanced back, she was startled to see Kevin standing at the window of the kindergarten room. Forcing a bright smile, she waved at him, then turned and walked away resolutely.

Kevin had been clingy this morning, something that hadn't happened since the first day of nursery school last year. Normally he rushed into the kindergarten classroom, chattering away a mile a minute to anyone who would listen.

An aftereffect of his injury? It was possible, she supposed, but it would have seemed more likely to happen when he'd first come back to school. Maybe the real problem was that he was picking up on her own emotions, which often felt as if they were being beaten by her electric mixer.

She stopped to exchange smiles and waves with elderly Mrs. Greenly, who was already out watering the baskets of petunias on her front porch. That was as predictable as most things that happened in Echo Falls. It was only recently that the foundations of her ordinary, normal world had begun to rock.

If Frank had been unfaithful to her, how much of

that was her fault? It seemed so disloyal to be accusing him, even mentally, of such a thing. But she couldn't deny that finding Sylvia's necklace had opened a Pandora's box of troubling thoughts.

What she'd said to Jason was true. She and Frank had grown up together. Now, looking back on it, she could recognize that the need to protect him had started early. Somehow she'd always known that he didn't have the kind of relationship with his father that she'd had with Daddy. It had seemed inconceivable to her that he could be afraid of his own father.

She hadn't thought of him in a romantic way until the summer he came home from law school—the summer a heart attack had taken Dad with a suddenness that had shaken the foundations of her world. Frank had been so good, grieving with her as strongly as if it had been his loss, too. Somehow, over that summer, things changed between them. They weren't kids any longer, playing together, or teenagers, commiserating over each other's crushes. They were adults, ready for love, and they'd turned to each other in a way that'd seemed almost inevitable.

When he'd gone back to finish law school, they'd been engaged. Frank had wanted to marry immediately, but his father had been opposed, and for once, she'd agreed with the judge. Her mother had needed time to adjust to the loss of her husband before thinking about her daughter's wedding.

They'd had their engagement pictures taken by the falls, and she still remembered the mix of love and tenderness she'd felt at the moment.

Deidre was smiling at the memory when she crossed the street a couple of blocks from her house. Suddenly her mood changed. The hair at the nape of her neck seemed to rise. Someone was watching her.

She glanced around. Foolish. What if someone was watching her? She was out in public, after all.

Telling herself that didn't seem to help. Another quick look around didn't show her anyone moving on the now-quiet street. A half hour ago it had been bustling with kids headed to school and cars pulling out of driveways. Now it was deserted. Empty.

Nonsense. Even if someone was watching her, they wouldn't do anything. Not in broad daylight. But she couldn't stop her feet from moving more quickly. She wouldn't run. But there was nothing wrong with walking fast, was there?

By the time she reached her own yard, the feeling had increased to a conviction. When the branches of the rhododendron in the corner of the yard rustled, she lost it, racing for the door, pulling her keys out as she did.

Two keys to fumble with—the regular door key and the dead bolt that Chief Carmichaels had insisted she lock. But it took too much time, and her fingers were icy in spite of the warmth of the day, and she'd never...

She swung open the door, darted inside, slammed it behind her and flipped the locks. For a few minutes she stood there, leaning against the door, half expecting to hear someone on the porch.

Nothing. Gradually her breathing settled, her pulse slowed and her common sense began to reassert itself. She was being ridiculous. She hadn't seen a soul. Call-

ing the police on no basis at all was out of the question.
She needed to drown these morbid imaginings in work.

As always, there was plenty to do. Deidre started
for the kitchen and froze, her mind scrambling to identify the sound from in front of the house. A swishing
noise, as if something or someone had brushed against
a windowpane.

The wind, she told herself, but a quick glance out the
nearest window showed her that the trees and bushes
were perfectly still. She was letting her imagination…

Something flickered past the living room window,
caught just out of the corner of her eye…a change in the
beam of sunlight streaming onto the carpet.

Grabbing her cell phone, she retreated toward the
back of the house, away from whatever was out front.
Ridiculous to think someone would try to get in during
the day, but it would be worse to ignore it. If someone
was there legitimately, he'd knock or ring.

Deidre listened, straining. Nothing. And then something scraped on the porch. Her overactive brain immediately provided her with an image of someone shoving
the wicker table away from the window in order to
look in.

That decided it. No matter how foolish it seemed,
she'd call the police. But first she'd get farther away.
Cell phone in hand, she hurried to the back door. Once
she was outside, someone would hear her if she had to
call for help. Inside…inside no one would hear, just as
no one had heard Dixie if she'd cried out.

Deidre yanked open the back door and charged out,

colliding with someone and stumbling back, a scream stifled in her throat.

"Billy! Goodness, you scared me."

Poor Billy looked as if she'd frightened him just as badly. He stared at her, the whites of his eyes showing like those of a terrified animal.

"It's all right," she said quickly, fighting to regain her composure and more than a little embarrassed. "I just didn't know you were here. I didn't hear the truck. Were you out front just now?"

He seized on something he understood. "Truck's broke down. I walked."

Her breathing had steadied. "That's too bad. Did you come to the front door?"

Billy shook his head, his eyes shifting from one side to the other as if afraid.

"I thought someone was on the front porch." She gestured with the cell phone, forgotten in her hand. "Will you come around with me and see?"

His face set in the mulish look that meant he'd been asked to do something he didn't want to do. "Best just go inside till they go away."

"If someone's there, I want to know who." Amazing how much courage it gave her just to have another person there. She grasped his wrist firmly. "Come on." Tugging him protesting behind her, Deidre marched around the house.

There was no one there, of course. An army could have come and gone while she was questioning Billy. The wicker table stood exactly where it should on the porch.

She glanced at Billy in apology. "Sorry. I guess I'm just nervous."

His dark eyes met hers and slid away. "You gotta be careful," he muttered.

The advice didn't come as a surprise, but its source did. Or had Billy heard about the break-in?

"Why do you say that?"

Billy didn't like being asked a direct question. She knew that. He backed away until he bumped into the porch railing. He shrugged.

Deidre studied his face. Did he actually have a reason for the warning, or was it just the general fear that seemed to have permeated life here since Dixie's death?

"I'll be careful," she said finally, knowing she wasn't going to get anything resembling a reasonable answer from him. "Are you going to do some work today?"

He seemed to brighten at the change of subject. "Thought I'd do the trimming. Didn't finish yet."

Deidre nodded, walking with Billy back the way they'd come. She shot a sideways glance at Billy as they went. What was he thinking? It was often hard to tell, even though she'd known him all her life.

"Thanks for going with me," she said.

He ducked his head in what might have been a nod, but he still seemed apprehensive. It was there in the way his eyes shifted, trying to take in everything at once, alert for any threat.

"I'm all right," she added.

Billy's face worked. She had the sense that he wanted to tell her something. She waited.

"You gotta be careful," he said again, and turned away.

Deidre looked after him as he headed for the tool shed. What was behind all this? Did Billy know something? But what could he know?

Jason popped into her mind. He wouldn't be content with nonanswers from Billy. He'd insist on answers.

She couldn't. She couldn't possibly start being suspicious of people she'd known all her life. That would turn her into someone she didn't want to be.

BY THE END of the day, Jason still hadn't had an opportunity to speak privately with the judge about Deidre and Kevin. If he'd heard about the break-in, which he undoubtedly would have, he was probably holding it as another black mark against Deidre—not that she could have prevented it.

Jason was still trying to reconcile the judge's obvious bias against his daughter-in-law with his spotless reputation for scrupulous fairness on the bench. If he was as reasonable as everyone believed, surely he'd listen to Jason's arguments.

Unfortunately, he didn't have much in the way of facts. As long as Dixie's death remained a mystery, a cloud would hang over Deidre, irrational as that was. Still, everyone he'd talked to in town had nothing but praise for Deidre. If there were those who spread rumors, he hadn't found them.

Even assuming the police discovered the killer, and it became evident that the death in Deidre's house was as little her fault as a lightning strike would be, there was still the matter of the anonymous letter and the whisper that Frank had suspected her of an affair. If not for that…

What was he thinking? He was sure in his own mind of Deidre's complete innocence, but Judge Morris was hardly likely to be swayed by Jason's opinion. Maybe the time had come for him to have a talk with Adam Bennett. If the young minister realized his attentions to Deidre had caused talk…well, Jason wasn't sure what he could do about it, but bringing it into the open might clear the air.

Adam had been openly welcoming each time Jase had run into him. Maybe he should take Adam up on his invitation to drop in anytime.

With that in mind, when he left the office he headed for the Bennett house instead of going home. At least it was a positive step to take. He didn't like the sensation of sitting back and waiting for the next thing to happen.

The minister's home proved to be a sprawling brick structure next to the church, which looked as if it had been built for the large families of an earlier age. Since it was nearly what Echo Falls considered suppertime, Adam should be at home.

As he approached the house, the sound of a baby crying reached him from an open window. Sounded as if his timing might not be great, but he was here now.

Jason rang the bell and waited. The sound of crying came nearer, and the door was thrown open. The woman who stood there, a crying baby on her hip, was young, disheveled and frazzled-looking. The baby, his small face puckered, took one look at Jason and increased the volume.

"I'm so sorry." She thrust a plastic toy at the child, which he grabbed and threw on the floor. "He's teething. Can I help you?"

She looked as if she needed help herself. "I'm Jason Glassman. I'd like to speak to Pastor Bennett, if he's available."

The young woman's jaw clenched, and he reflected that his would be clenching much worse if he had to listen to that ear-splitting crying much longer.

"He's not home." Her voice was tart. Clearly she had reached the end of her tether. Jason had a brief impulse to offer to hold the baby and shuddered away from it.

"Can you tell me where he is? I really need to talk with him."

"Probably at Deidre Morris's house," she snapped. "He always is."

For a moment they stared at each other. He saw the horror dawn in her face as she realized what she'd said.

"I…I'm sorry. I don't know why I said that." Tears filled her eyes and threatened to spill over. Even the baby seemed to sense her distress and stopped crying. "Please, forget it. I didn't mean it. Please."

He studied her face. "You received an anonymous letter, didn't you?"

She turned nearly as red in the face as the baby was. "I didn't… How did you…?" She seemed to run out of steam.

Now was the moment for the prosecutor to pounce— to bombard her with questions and demand answers. And he couldn't.

"If you did," he said carefully, "the best thing you

could do is to talk this over with your husband. You haven't told him, have you?"

Her averted eyes gave him his answer.

"People who write anonymous letters feed on silence. Show it to Adam. Isn't it better to do that than to wonder?"

She stared at him for a moment. Then she groped for the door. As she closed it, he heard the crying start again.

Jason walked away quickly. Six months ago he'd have been all over the woman with questions, exploiting her obvious vulnerability. Now he seemed to have turned into some kind of marriage counselor. What was this town doing to him?

THE HOUSE WAS quiet after Deidre got Kevin to bed that night. This was when she minded being widowed the most—the evenings stretched long and lonely. Dixie had been the person most likely to pop in to chat around now. Maybe she had recognized Deidre's feelings, although she'd never come right out and said so.

She may as well face the other person who lurked at the back of her mind. She hadn't heard a word from Jason since she'd wept all over him. Hardly surprising. She doubted that there was a man in the world who appreciated being cried on.

Switching off the television she hadn't been paying any attention to, Deidre paced back through the house, ending up in the workroom. But even the sight of the new crib quilt she'd been logging into the system couldn't cheer her. She flipped a corner back, marveling at the intricate twining lines formed by the quilting stitches. Who would believe those tiny, even stitches had been made by hand?

The quilt failed to distract her, as did the wooden toy train her cousin Josiah had made. He'd claimed he'd have to do one for her in a hurry, before it was time to start on Christmas gifts for all the toddlers in the family, but you couldn't tell from the craftsmanship. It was excellent.

This room had been the spot where her mother had sat and sewed in the evenings. Her father had claimed the rocking chair in the corner as his domain, where he'd rock and read the newspaper, a cup of coffee at his elbow. She could almost see herself, a skinny, pigtailed nine-year-old, sitting at the table and wrestling with the complications of long division.

This house had been home for her entire life. Was it ever going to feel as safe as it had been when she was a child? Maybe that was too much to hope for. A better question was could she make it feel that safe for Kevin?

Deidre was reaching for the telephone, thinking to call someone, anyone, just to hear another voice, when the doorbell rang. The sound jolted her nerves, setting them tingling. Stupid. She'd been longing for company, hadn't she? Well, she was about to get some.

Mindful of the precautions Chief Carmichaels and Jason had drilled into her, she peered from the side window. Jason stood there, obviously watching the window to be sure she checked before opening.

Smiling, she unlocked both locks and opened up. "See how careful I'm being?" she said.

"Keep it up." Jason stepped inside, bringing a sense that the house was suddenly full. "I hoped to stop by before Kev went to bed, but something came up. Is everything okay? You look a little strained."

"I'm fine." She wouldn't let herself add the word *now*. "Come on into the kitchen. Judith dropped off a schnitz pie today. She's convinced food is the answer to any form of trouble."

"That's the kind of friend to have." He followed her to the kitchen. "Should I ask what schnitz pie is?"

She actually felt able to laugh, the remaining loneliness dropping away. "Dried apple pie. Drying apples is a way of preserving them." At his doubtful look, she picked up the golden-brown pastry to show him. "Trust me. I wouldn't steer you wrong."

He sat down, a smile lighting his expression. "Seems to me I've heard that line from a used-car salesman."

"Just wait." Deidre cut a wedge of pie, added a scoop of vanilla ice cream and set it in front of him before pouring coffee and cutting a small slice for herself. She sat down and watched as he put the first bite in his mouth.

"Well?" she said.

"Heavenly. My compliments to Judith. If she ever wants to go into business, I'll be her backer."

"Don't suggest that," she said with mock severity. "She already has a business partner, remember?"

He dug into the pie. "How is your business going?"

"We're actually busier than I ever anticipated. I expected it to be a hobby, taking a few hours a week. Instead it's turned into a paying proposition, and best of all it lets me be home with Kevin."

Jason's smile faded, and the gaze he fixed on her was serious. "I'm happy about your business. Now tell me what has you upset. And don't bother telling me there's nothing."

Deidre told herself she ought to show a little restraint, instead of pouring out her troubles. But it wasn't easy to say no to him, not with that dark gaze fixed intently on her face.

"Maybe my imagination was working overtime, but I thought someone was watching me when I walked home from taking Kevin to kindergarten this afternoon. And I'm sure I heard someone on the front porch, but whoever it was didn't knock or ring the bell."

"Did you call the police?" He rapped the words at her, his pie forgotten.

"I started to. I had the phone in my hand, and I thought I'd go out the back to get a safe distance away. When I went out the door, Billy was there."

He frowned. "Billy. Was he the person out front?"

"He couldn't have been. He couldn't have gotten around the house that fast. Anyway, by that time I was starting to feel foolish, but I made him go around the front with me. Of course, there was no one there."

"You still should have called." Jason reached across the table to clasp her hand.

"Why? No one was there. There was no sign anyone had been there." The warmth of his clasp strengthened her. "Half the town already thinks I'm headed for a nervous breakdown."

He seemed to ignore that. Probably because he didn't care what the town thought. "I don't like it. What did Billy want?"

"He said he'd come to finish the trimming." She could hear the hesitation in her own voice. Jason would hear it, too. "He seemed very worried about me. He kept saying I had to be careful."

"Did he say that as a threat?" Jason's grip tightened.

"No, no, not at all. He was worried about me, but he couldn't manage to say why." She went over that conversation again in her mind. "He seemed afraid. That's as close as I can get to it, but I'm not sure what scared him."

"I should talk to him."

"Please don't." How could she make him understand? "He gets so upset and confused at questioning that he just retreats into himself. He knows and trusts me— that's the only reason I got as much as I did from him."

Jason didn't look entirely convinced, but he nodded. He stared down at the remnants of his pie. "I had a rather interesting encounter today, too." He glanced up, as if needing to see her face. "With Adam Bennett's wife."

"Amanda Bennett? Where did you run into her?"

"It wasn't exactly an accident. I went to the house to talk to Adam." He looked as though that should mean something to her.

"What did you want to see Adam about?" She felt a wave of defensiveness, remembering his rather acid comments about the amount of attention the young pastor paid her.

He seemed to pick up on her feelings. "Look, I know you don't want to believe this, but there appears to be some talk going around about you and Adam. If I'm going to help you convince the judge to back off…"

"That's ridiculous. No one could think that." Anger replaced the defensiveness.

"Tell that to Amanda."

The quiet words knocked the wind out of her. "You mean she believes that?"

"Believes?" He considered. "I'm not sure. But she's definitely heard something."

Deidre had felt this way once as a child, when she'd fallen from a swing and had the wind knocked out of her. For an instant she couldn't get her breath.

"But…what did she say? What did you say?" This was bad enough already. If he'd said anything to make it worse… She shoved to her feet, and he grabbed her wrist.

"Where are you going?"

"I'm going to call Amanda right now and straighten this out."

"Don't." His voice was sharp, but then he looked apologetic. "Sorry. But I don't want you to make it worse."

"That's just what I was thinking about you. What did you tell her?" She wasn't ready to let go of her ire just yet.

His fingers encircled her wrist. No doubt he could feel the furious beating of her pulse.

"I told her if she had any doubts, she should talk to her husband."

Deidre sank back into her chair. "Do you think she will?"

"I hope so." Jason caressed her skin, his touch soothing. "It's better if you stay clear of it, at least for the moment. Let them settle it between themselves. Really, that's best."

She nodded, lifting her free hand to rub her forehead. "I'm beginning to think I don't know anything about what goes on around me."

"It's not that bad." He frowned, as if trying to find the right words. "When something like Dixie's death happens, it brings a lot of things to the surface that otherwise might never come up. Sometimes that's good, but—"

The sound that pierced their ears was so loud, so sharp, that for an instant Deidre couldn't move or think. Then she was up, running toward the stairs. Kevin—Kevin was screaming. She'd never heard a sound like that. *Kevin— Dear God, please—*

CHAPTER THIRTEEN

JASON'S FEET POUNDED on the stairs behind her, and he was next to her when they burst into the bedroom. She bolted for Kevin's bed, while he paused to snap the light switch on.

The light revealed Kevin, sitting upright in bed, eyes wide and unfocused, mouth emitting one scream after another. No one else was in the room.

Deidre reached him, pulling him into her arms, heart pounding. He was stiff, rigid, not even bending as she moved him, and still he screamed.

Was this some new complication from his head injury? She tried to thrust the terrifying thought from her mind.

"Kevin, Kevin, it's okay. It's Mommy." She cupped his face in her hands. "Kev, look at me, honey. You're safe. It's Mommy. It's all right."

The screams stopped, as abruptly as if someone had turned off a burglar alarm. Her ears still rang with the echo of the sound.

"Talk to me, sweetheart. Please. Talk to Mommy."

But he stared as if he didn't recognize her.

She hadn't heard Jason move, but he was next to her, his hand strong on her shoulder.

"It's a nightmare, isn't it?"

"I...think so. But worse than any he's ever had. Night terrors, they say. If I call the pediatrician..." But even as she said the words, she felt Kev begin to relax against her.

"He's coming out of it," Jason said quietly. He sat down on the bed next to her, reaching around her to put a comforting hand on Kevin's back.

Relief made tears sting her eyes as her son gave a little sigh and snuggled against her.

"Mommy?" He sounded confused.

"It's all right. You just had a bad dream, that's all." Instinct told her she couldn't just soothe him back to sleep. "Let's go downstairs and get some milk. Okay?"

Kevin nodded, his head bumping her chin.

She started to rise, holding him, but Jason lifted him from her arms. "Let me carry him. That's okay, isn't it, Kev?"

As if in answer, Kevin wrapped his arms around Jason's neck.

The kitchen was an oasis of calm, the overhead light touching the warm glow of honey-colored wooden cabinets and brightening the colors of the pink and white geraniums on the windowsills. A family kitchen spelled home. It was the very definition of normalcy. If any place would reassure Kevin, this would.

While Jason took his seat at the table with Kevin snuggled on his lap, Deidre got out the milk bottle with hands that hadn't quite stopped shaking. On second thought, hot chocolate would be more soothing than cold milk, so she poured it into a mug, added chocolate syrup and popped it into the microwave.

When she turned back to the table, Jason's head was bent over Kevin, and he talked to him so softly she couldn't quite make out the words. She could see Kevin's face, though, and the trust in it as he looked up at Jason twisted her heart.

As soon as the hot chocolate was warm enough, she took it to the table and sat down, pulling her chair close to the other two and giving Jason a look that she hoped expressed her gratitude.

"Here you go, Kev. Try some hot chocolate." She held the mug while he put one hand on it to guide it. She noticed he continued to clutch Jason's hand with the other.

Her heart clenched, and she blinked back tears. Kevin had such need for a strong male presence in his life. She hadn't realized how much he missed that until Jason had started to fill the gap.

Jason glanced up and caught her expression. He lifted an eyebrow in a question. "Missing Frank?" he asked softly.

To her surprise, she realized that wasn't even in her mind. She shook her head. "Just...touched by the way he trusts you."

That seemed to startle him. He didn't speak for a moment. "I hope I won't ever let him down." His voice deepened on the words.

Her smile trembled. She hoped not, too. It was a dangerous thing—letting a stranger into her son's life. But all her instincts told her Jason was one of the good guys, and she longed to trust him.

Kevin's head drooped, his eyes closing. He nestled against Jason's chest as he drank a little more of the hot cocoa. Then, gradually relaxing, he drifted into sleep.

Her heart twisting at the sight, Deidre set the cup back on the table. Now that her panicked reaction had faded, the dull worry had set in. She rubbed her temples. If only she could see more clearly…

"All kids have nightmares, don't they?" Jason spoke softly, obviously not wanting to wake Kev.

"I suppose. But this…this was scary." She let her troubled gaze meet his. "And unlike him. I'm afraid. What if…what if it means he's starting to remember?"

Jason's jaw hardened. "Has he said anything to make you think that?"

She shook her head. "No, but he may not realize it himself."

"Or think it's a dream, I guess." Jason cupped Kev's head in his hand in a protective gesture that stirred her heart. "I don't pretend to know a lot about kids, but…"

"What?" That sounded sharp, and she forced her voice lower. "Please, if you have any ideas, tell me. I'm at a loss."

He studied her face for a moment and then nodded. "I'm a great believer in using a professional when in doubt. Have you talked to his pediatrician recently about the chances of his remembering?"

"No." Deidre rubbed her forehead again. "I guess I've been thinking if I didn't pursue it, I could pretend things were normal. Acting like a stupid ostrich."

Jason's lips twitched, and he put his hand over hers.

"I don't see you hiding from the facts. The trouble now is not knowing what they are."

She was getting entirely too used to relying on him. "I'll give Liz—his doctor—a call tomorrow. Just to see what she thinks about it."

He nodded, then looked down at the sleeping child in his arms. "Want me to carry him back up to bed?"

"I can do it…" she began, but he was already rising, holding Kevin lightly against him. Kev stirred, then pillowed his head on Jason's shoulder and slid back into sleep again.

Deidre followed them up the stairs, trying not to think how natural it all was. She drew the covers back as he deposited Kevin on the bed and then pulled them around him, snuggling his favorite stuffed toys close.

Sighing a little, Kev shifted to the side, hand curled against his cheek, his breathing deep and even.

Deidre bent to kiss his forehead and stood, looking down at him with a mixture of love and concern. She felt Jason move behind her, and his hands on her arms drew her gently back against him. Almost without willing it, she relaxed against him, taking comfort much as her son had in his steady strength. Jason's breath stirred her hair and moved across her skin. She sighed, content to take in the moment.

Jason wrapped his arms snugly around her so that she felt the solid warmth of his body pressing against her. So that she sensed the desire building in him. An answering response built in her. If only she could give in…

She straightened. Not a good idea, especially not

now, when she had to stay focused on what was best for her son.

For an instant Jason's grasp tightened. Then, slowly, he released her. When she turned to face him, he wore a rueful smile.

"Guess it's time to say good-night." He cradled her face in his hands, and then drew her against him again for a long, lingering kiss that set her senses reeling despite its gentleness.

"Dream of me," he whispered against her lips, and was gone.

BY THE NEXT DAY, Jason's frustration had reached a new height. His sense that Deidre was in danger kept increasing, and he seemed to have no way of protecting her from the threat.

What were the cops doing? He hadn't heard one word from Chief Carmichaels in days, and the judge was oddly noncommunicative.

His workload hadn't become that heavy yet, and what there was involved working on situations where Trey had already done the groundwork. His appreciation for the man increased. Anything Trey had done was always meticulous. His manner might be relaxed and easygoing, but when it came to the practice of law, he was a perfectionist.

Funny, that he and the judge didn't seem closer. Since Trey's father and the judge had been partners, he must have known him virtually all his life. But then, the judge didn't seem to find it easy to relate to a different generation.

Stepping from the office into the warm May sunshine, he found himself lifting his gaze to the ridge. He must be turning into a local, automatically checking to see if the falls were visible. Light glinted through the trees, and a faint mist seemed to rise from the falls and hover over the ridge. According to Kevin, the mist was the Native American woman's spirit, watching over the town.

He'd noticed Deidre's slight frown when she'd overheard him say that, and she asked him who'd told him. When she'd learned it was Billy, she'd laughed and assured him that was just a story.

Jason lingered in front of the office for a moment, frowning. Deidre refused to take his questions about Billy seriously because she knew him so well. But someone had killed Dixie, and Billy might have had a motive.

Deidre handed out her trust to everyone, but experience had made him far warier.

And what about Hanlon? If he'd vanished from Echo Falls, that was all to the good, but he'd think the cops would want to know more about him, especially after the episode in the office.

Making an abrupt decision, he wheeled and strode back into the office, surprising Evelyn.

"Mr. Glassman. I thought you'd gone to the courthouse." Her fingers hovered over her keyboard.

"I just realized I'd never heard anything further about the fellow who frightened you the other day. I hope the police caught up with him." Jason always found himself speaking more formally whenever he talked to Evelyn—her very bearing seemed to require it.

She clasped her hands. "Oh, no, I haven't heard, either, and I don't mind saying it troubles me. What if he comes back again?"

"I'm sure he wouldn't make that mistake. But hasn't the judge said anything to you about it?"

Evelyn shook her head. "He's seemed very preoccupied lately, and I haven't wanted to ask." She hesitated. "Do you think you could?"

Somehow he didn't see himself bringing up that conversation with Judge Morris, not with so much unsettled between them.

"I'll do better. I'll go right to Chief Carmichaels and find out what's going on. If it was this man Hanlon, he'll know about it."

He left with her effusive thanks ringing in his ears and strode off down the street toward the police station. Walking was another thing he'd adopted since he'd come to Echo Falls. In such a small town, it didn't make sense to drive. Now, if Chief Carmichaels was in—

He was, and he gestured Jason into his office. "What's up with you today, Counselor? Still worrying about Deidre?"

"Somebody has to." The grimness he felt on that subject crept into his voice. "But I'm here about the character who tried to force his way into the office. Evelyn's still feeling unsettled."

Carmichaels had the grace to look embarrassed. "Sorry. I guess I should have reassured her. She identified Hanlon, all right. But he hasn't been seen in town in the past couple of days. He'd paid for a room at the Town House motel for a week, but the proprietor says it hasn't been slept in the past two nights. His things are still there, though."

"So you assume he's left, apparently without getting whatever it was he came for." Jase wasn't satisfied.

A certain amount of defensiveness appeared on the chief's face. "Look, there's nothing I can do. He's out of our jurisdiction now, and I don't have evidence to charge him with anything. Besides, the judge said he wouldn't press charges about his actions at the office."

"Why not?"

Carmichaels shrugged. "Thinks it would be bad publicity, I guess."

He'd have expected Judge Morris to come down hard on anyone who trespassed on what he considered his. Still, other than disturbing the peace there wasn't much Hanlon could be charged with. The man hadn't actually broken in.

He was silent for so long that Carmichaels gave him a suspicious look. "Do you know something I don't?"

"Nothing susceptible to proof," he admitted. "But I'm still concerned about Deidre and Kevin's safety."

"So am I." For an instant, the professional mask dropped, and Jase was looking at a worried older man who feared making a mistake with someone he cared about. "I agree that Hanlon would normally be a suspect in Dixie's murder, but he wasn't even in town then."

"We don't know he wasn't, unless you've found proof he was elsewhere."

"You think he could have been sneaking around town, watching Dixie?" Carmichaels considered. "It's not that easy for a stranger to lurk around Echo Falls, believe me. He wasn't staying at any hotel or motel within a twenty-mile radius, that I do know."

"You checked?" He shouldn't let himself sound so surprised.

"Sure I checked." Carmichaels sounded affronted. "Listen, you may think we're hicks compared to the city boys you're used to, but we don't do a bad job. At least we know everybody, and that's something a big-city force can never do."

"Sorry. I didn't mean that, exactly. I know you care about Deidre and Kevin." He hesitated, not wanting to give away something Deidre considered private. "There's always the chance Kevin might remember something."

Carmichaels nodded grimly. "That keeps me awake at night, I can tell you. But unless and until he does, we're running out of leads."

Carmichaels probably didn't like saying it any more than he liked hearing it. "It's crazy. Somebody walked right into Deidre's house, knowing Dixie was there, and killed her without leaving a trace of his presence."

"You'd think, with as many busybodies as we have in this town, somebody would have seen something. But no one did."

No one did. And that left Deidre and Kevin as potential targets. To say nothing of the other threat that hung over their happiness.

Something had to be done. But what?

DEIDRE WAS BEGINNING to think she might have to let Jason talk to Billy, not that she could prevent it if Jason were determined. But Billy had been around the house the entire afternoon, going from one trivial thing to another. Sometimes she caught him just standing, watching her as she went about her work.

By the time Kevin got home from kindergarten, she'd decided she'd have to make another attempt at finding out what was on Billy's mind. Leaving Kevin lingering over his after-school snack of peanut butter and apple slices, she tracked Billy down in the backyard.

When he saw her coming, he made a pretense of clipping a lilac bush. She put out a hand to stop him.

"Don't prune that now, please, Billy. You'll cut off the blossoms."

He avoided her eyes. "Sorry."

"I think you've done enough for one day, don't you?"

He shrugged, silent.

Deidre clasped the sleeve of his faded flannel shirt. "Billy, I know you've been watching over us. Won't you tell me why?"

An instant backward step nearly landed him in the middle of the bush. He shook his head violently, lips pressed together.

"You mean no, you haven't been watching, or no, you won't tell me?"

Billy's gaze shifted from side to side, as if looking for a way of escape. She was reminded of the small boy he'd been, seeking escape when some of the bigger boys taunted him on the playground. She'd come to his rescue then, but now she was in the position of pushing him, and she didn't like it. Still, if he knew something...

"Billy, please. Tell me. I can see you're worried about me and Kevin. Tell me why."

His lower lip came out, and he blinked rapidly. "Bad stuff around."

"You mean Dixie?" she asked, keeping her voice gentle.

He didn't answer. After a moment, as if the words were forced out of him, he said the last thing she expected. "Kev says you went to the mill."

Deidre blinked, her mind blank. "You mean the old mill by the falls?"

Billy nodded several times, his head bobbing up and down. "Don't go there. It's not safe."

Puzzled, she studied him. He seemed obsessed with the idea of keeping them safe. "I'm always careful. You know I wouldn't let Kevin do anything that's not safe, don't you? Remember when your brother was daring you to swing on the grapevine up on the hill, and I wouldn't let you? I didn't want you to get hurt."

She hoped that childhood memory might relax him, but it didn't seem to. He nodded, but then he lapsed into his usual silence and started edging away from her.

"Billy, if you know something that will help me keep Kev safe, you have to tell me."

For an instant his flight was arrested. His face contorted, as if he struggled with himself.

Then Jason's car pulled into the driveway next door. Billy turned and broke into a trot, heading off across the lawn in the other direction and leaving the clippers lying in the grass.

Frustrated, Deidre looked after him. Would Billy

have spoken if Jason hadn't happened to pull in just then? She'd never know. But his actions did confirm her opinion that it would be worse than useless for Jason to question him.

Spotting Judith and Benjamin approaching by the path that led along the field, she waved. "Kevin, Benjamin's coming."

Her call was answered by the slamming of the screen door and the thud of Kevin's sneakers on the porch. She shook her head, smiling. If that screen door survived the summer, it would be surprising. At least it might give Billy something to do by fixing it.

Judith reached her, blue eyes amused as she watched the boys greeting each other as if they'd been parted for months. "I thought we'd *komm* for an hour before I start supper," she said.

"You're just in time for a glass of tea. I made the first pitcher of iced tea of the season." Deidre led the way into the house, pausing to pick off a sprig of mint from the bed along the porch.

"Sounds *gut*. But I'll work if there's anything to pack," Judith added.

"I finished it before lunch." She got the pitcher from the refrigerator and added the mint. Judith took glasses from the cabinet with as much assurance as if they were in her kitchen.

Carrying the tray, they went out to the two ladder-back rockers that sat on the back porch—their usual summertime destination.

During the short time they'd been in the kitchen, Jason had appeared in the backyard. He waved briefly and then turned back to the two boys, who were obviously badgering him to play ball again. Good. She really didn't want to interact with Jason in front of Judith's observant eyes, not with the memory of his kiss still on her lips.

"Nice of Jason to spend time with the boys," Judith commented, watching Deidre as if to measure her response.

Deidre took a gulp of her tea. "Yes, it is." She trusted any oddness in her voice would be chalked up to the tea.

"I saw Billy Kline going off. Is he doing some chores for you? You know I'd be happy to send one of the older boys over if you need anything." Judith offered her kids' services as automatically as she did her own.

"I know. I appreciate it. But Billy really needs the money I pay him."

Judith nodded, although she probably couldn't understand fully Billy's situation. In the Amish community, a special child like Billy would be surrounded by the love of a large family who'd take joy in caring for him. Unfortunately, Billy's own family had broken up years earlier, so others had to pick up the slack.

"He does a good job as long as I keep an eye on what he's doing." She glanced at the lilac bush, which fortunately was still holding on to the buds that were about to open. "He's been…a little upset lately."

"He's taking Dixie's death hard, I'd guess. He always was devoted to her, wasn't he?"

Deidre nodded. "He's been hanging around here a lot lately, as if he feels he ought to look out for me and Kevin. Jason thinks it's suspicious," she added, nodding toward Jason, who seemed to be showing Benjamin something about throwing the ball. She'd be interested in hearing Judith's reaction.

"I wouldn't think so. Billy has a *gut* heart, ain't so? He'd never hurt a soul."

"That's what I think, too. But Jason seems to be suspicious of everyone."

Judith studied Jason for a few minutes in that calm, appraising way of hers. "He has the look of a man who's been let down by somebody. Maybe that's why he seems so suspicious."

Deidre watched him, as well. Was that what she sensed about him? That behind the confidence and courage, he was shielding pain? The little he'd told her about his family life sounded so alien to her that she could hardly imagine what it did to a person to grow up that way.

Judith, even with her limited experience of the English world, had very good instincts for people. Deidre was inclined to agree, but it raised a new problem. Those moments when Jason let down his guard with her—were they only momentary aberrations? Or could he really shed that prickly exterior and become someone who could love unreservedly?

Maybe she didn't have the right to be asking that question. A few kisses, especially in an emotionally charged time like this, didn't make a serious romance. She'd come to know Jason when she was shattered by Dixie's death and terrified by Kevin's injury. Was that really a point in life when it was safe to start thinking of forever?

A thwack of the bat announced that Benjamin had hit the ball. Kev went scrambling after it, Jason tried to grab it, and in a moment all three of them were rolling on the grass, laughing and wrestling for the ball.

"They're getting rough…" She started to get up, but Judith caught her hand and urged her back into her chair.

"*Ach*, don't be silly. That's what boys do. It's *gut* for them, and Jason won't let them be hurt."

"You're right," she admitted. "I've been hovering too much, I guess."

"That comes of having just one. If you had six young ones, like me, you wouldn't have time for it." Judith's smile took any sting away.

"No matter how many I had, I'd never be as calm a mother as you are." She watched as Jason rolled to his feet, shedding little boys as he stood. "I hadn't realized how much Kevin has needed a strong man in his life since Frank died. There's his grandfather, of course, but Judge Morris isn't one for roughhousing. Or any kind of play, for that matter."

Judith's expression grew serious. "Has anything else been said about him trying to get Kevin in his house?"

"No, nothing. He's seemed perfectly normal when I've seen him. I'm starting to think Sylvia imagined things. Or maybe I'm just hoping."

"What about that phone message from him? He sounded serious enough in that."

"I know, I know." She'd been trying to tell herself he'd been overreacting, but the judge didn't overreact.

"Have you done anything about getting a lawyer?" Judith pressed, clearly concerned.

"I'd just about decided I'd have to hire someone from out of town, but then…" She hesitated, wondering how much she should say. But Judith could be trusted to keep her secrets. "I hadn't intended to, but I told Jason about it. And he insisted that if that happened, he'd fight for me, even though it would cost his job."

Judith's lips quirked slightly. "That says something about how he feels for you, ain't so?"

That wasn't a question she was ready to answer, but fortunately Judith didn't seem to expect one. Instead she set her empty glass aside and stood, shaking out her full skirt.

"It's time Benjamin and I were heading for home, I think. And I see Jason coming. It's you he wants to see, not me."

With that embarrassing observation, Judith started down the porch steps, pausing long enough to exchange a few words while Deidre gathered glasses and spoons onto the tray. As she started to pick it up, Jason arrived and took it from her.

"I'll carry it in for you." He elbowed his way through the screen door.

"You could probably use a glass of tea yourself after all that wrestling." She took another glass from the cabinet and turned back to find him looking at her with a quizzical expression.

"Was I overdoing it? Being too rough?"

"No. You weren't. I confess, I'm too protective, but Judith gave me a little talking-to, and I'll try to do better."

She handed him the glass of iced tea, and when he took it, his fingers lingered on hers. "It's natural enough, after what happened."

"Probably so, but I shouldn't give in to fear. If I do, I'll make Kevin fearful." She paused, her mind presenting her with a series of images of Frank as a child. "I always thought that was what made Frank doubt himself so much. His mother was afraid of just about everything he wanted to do, and his father...well, the judge wanted him to excel, but only in the things that were important to the judge, not to Frank."

Jason perched on the corner of the table and took a long draught of the tea. "Maybe I was lucky no one cared what I did." He shrugged and went on before she could speak. "Not to change the subject, but I saw Billy taking off when I got home. Did you get anything more out of him?"

"Not exactly." Her frustration showed in her voice, she expected. "He's worried about Kev and me, that's plain. But I'm beginning to think it's just a general fearfulness—knowing that Dixie was killed here and seeing us living in the house."

"Nothing to indicate he was afraid of anyone in particular?"

"No, except..."

"Except what?" He was on that in an instant.

"He knew we'd been to the falls." She tried to remember exactly how he'd put it. "He said to stay away from the mill. He seemed to think it was dangerous."

"Dangerous how? We didn't go inside, so I don't know what kind of shape it's in."

"We went inside last spring, and everything looked fine then. I really can't guess what was in Billy's mind, except that he seems obsessed with safety. Maybe it really is because of Dixie's death. He's afraid of losing another friend."

"Maybe." He frowned at her, his mind clearly elsewhere. Then he gave a short nod. "Okay. I should be able to get away from the office around one o'clock tomorrow. Can you be ready then?"

She stared at him blankly. "Ready? For what?"

His eyebrows lifted. "To go and check out the mill, of course. You don't think we can ignore what he said, do you?"

Jason's energetic approach must be contagious. She felt her spirits lift at the prospect of taking any positive steps. "Okay. I can't imagine that we'll find anything, but okay."

CHAPTER FOURTEEN

JASON MANEUVERED HIS car along the rutted lane through the woods the next day, wincing when he hit a pothole. He glanced at Deidre, but she didn't seem to have noticed the jolt. She was straining ahead, as if anticipating… what? Answers?

He didn't have high hopes of finding anything. Billy might have some reason for fearing danger at the cottage, but he doubted there'd be any indication as to why. Unless, of course, it proved to be so decrepit that just going into it was dangerous.

Any lead at all was worth following, he reminded himself. Besides, checking out the cottage gave him a good excuse for spending time alone with Deidre. Unworthy of him, maybe, but a man had to take what he could get. Much as he liked Kevin, he had to admit that having a small child around was something of a barrier to romance. With Kevin at school and a friend picking him up, they didn't have to hurry.

The tense look on Deidre's face disturbed him, and he sought a distraction. "So tell me about wandering in the woods when you were a kid. Did your parents really think that was all right?"

Deidre blinked, as if trying to refocus. "I guess. They

wouldn't have wanted me to wander off alone, but usually there were several of us. I suppose they figured there was safety in numbers."

"You and Judith, I know. Who else?"

She shrugged. "It differed. Sometimes one or another of Judith's brothers. Often Frank came. And Dixie. And Billy, of course."

"Why 'of course'? Kids can really be unforgiving with someone who is different."

"I was going to say there was more of that now, but I'm not sure that's true. Kids picked on Billy sometimes, I know. But Judith and the other Amish kids are taught to care for people like Billy. And my parents...well, to them, kindness was the most important attribute you could want for your child."

"Billy was lucky, then."

"Maybe we were the lucky ones." Her smile flashed. "You'd be surprised how much we learned from Billy. He might not have been able to read very well, but he could follow the track of a rabbit or identify a bird by its call."

"Your parents did a good job. Raising a kind daughter, I mean."

He loved that her eyes brightened at the compliment. "I hope so."

They were approaching the end of the road, and he slowed. "Sounds like you had a real Norman Rockwell painting of a childhood."

"Maybe so. That's not a bad thing. Sometimes I regret that we've become so cautious in raising our children now. So much organization in their play and sports and lessons can mean little time for just being kids. I'd rather see Kevin running around the farm with Benjamin than playing some organized sport or taking extra classes."

But a faint line had settled between her eyebrows, and he thought he knew what that meant. He parked and turned off the ignition while he tried to find the right words.

"You're a good mother, Deidre. Don't let anyone try to convince you otherwise."

He got out before she could answer, while a skeptical part of his brain suggested that he didn't know a single thing about what constituted good parenting. How could he? Still, he couldn't be deceived about the depth of the bond between Deidre and her son.

A little flushed, Deidre grabbed a small backpack and stuffed a cell phone and water bottle into it. "Okay. Let's go see what we can find."

Deidre set a quick pace along the trail, now that she didn't have to slow down for Kevin's short legs to keep up. Jason stayed at her heels, projecting his mind ahead to the old mill. What was reasonable to expect to find there?

If Billy thought it was dangerous because of a broken stair or a sagging floor, that should be obvious. But he suspected that Billy's fear was rooted in something subtler—maybe something no rational person would ever guess.

"When you were kids, did Billy seem to be afraid of anything up here? The ghosts of long-ago Native Americans, maybe?"

Deidre slowed, glancing over her shoulder. "Not that I can remember. He was impressed by the legends, but then, we all were."

"Legends plural? You mean there's more than the story you told?"

She nodded. "Quite a few. Some unsuitable for a five-year-old, to my way of thinking."

"Like that business of the mist being the Native American woman's ghost?"

The path went from thick woods to the clear space along the banks of the stream abruptly. He'd been hearing the murmur of the waterfall for some time, but now it rushed at them.

Deidre stopped, looking up at the mist rising above the falls, and he moved closer, watching her face. "I wish Billy hadn't told him that story. Maybe it's silly, but I'd rather put off really spooky stories until he's a bit older."

"Then you won't mind?" He eyed her, curious.

Her lips curved as she met his gaze. "I'll probably still mind, but I know better than to try to prevent it. I have vivid memories of the ghost and monster stories we used to tell each other as kids. Especially when we had sleepovers. And of the nightmares I had as a result."

"So Kev comes by his nightmares honestly."

"I never had nightmares like his." Her smile had vanished. "He had another one last night. Not quite as bad, but still scary. I called his pediatrician, and we're going to talk in a day or two if it doesn't get any better."

"Sorry." He touched her hand, wishing he'd been there to help. "I think that's the right thing to do."

"I hope so." She turned and started downstream toward the old mill. "His grandfather stopped by earlier to see how we're doing, so I told him about it."

"What did he think?"

She shrugged. "He didn't seem to take it seriously. Said he thought I ought to just let it run its course." She glanced at him. "Maybe he had a point. He said it wouldn't be good for Kevin to focus attention on it."

"You have to do what feels right to you," he said, putting some iron into his tone. The judge was too fond of making other people second-guess themselves.

They rounded the curve in the path, and the cottage came into view, the mill wheel creaking as the flow of water struck it.

"I have the key." Deidre dug in her pocket. "I remember coming up here once with the other kids, and Frank bragging that we could go into the cottage because his family owned it. But it turned out he didn't have a key, and all we could do was look in the windows."

"I wouldn't let a gang of kids have the run of the place, either," he commented. He caught her wrist as she started up the steps to the porch. "Wait. Let me go first and check it out."

Deidre's eyebrows lifted. "Being macho?"

He grinned. "I'm heavier. If it's going to break under my weight, we'll find out fast."

But the steps seemed perfectly solid. Even the handrail didn't wobble. Deidre followed him onto the porch and put the key in the lock. When she turned it, he reached over her shoulder to push the door open.

Nothing. It was a perfectly ordinary rustic cottage,

the type of place he'd imagine people wanted as a woodsy retreat. A stone fireplace, blackened by years of wood fires, with a deer's head mounted over it. The glass eyes seemed to follow him when he moved. There were a few pieces of soft furniture grouped around the fireplace, and a table and chairs at the other end.

Deidre stepped inside, looking around. "It all seems just as I remember it. I can't imagine what Billy finds to be afraid of here."

Walking over to the gun cabinet on the far wall, Jason tested it. Locked, and no sign of tampering. "Isn't it dangerous to leave guns in an unoccupied building like this?"

"I suppose it is. I'm surprised the judge hasn't removed them. He's certainly aware that there've been break-ins at hunting cabins in recent years."

His lips quirked. "Could it be that he thinks no one would dare steal from him?"

"He does usually put the fear of the law into the people who appear before him," Deidre admitted.

Open steps led up to the second floor. He gestured. "What's upstairs?"

"Two bedrooms. You can have a look if you want."

"Leave no stone unturned, as the cliché goes." He went quickly up the steps and peered into the rooms. A smaller room had a double bed and a dresser, while the larger one was set up with two sets of bunk beds, probably intended for the younger members of the family. It was simple, rustic and perfectly ordinary, posing no danger at all that he could see.

"What exactly did Billy say about the place?" He

asked the question as he rejoined her on the lower floor. "Do you remember his exact words?"

"Not perfectly, I'm sure." She frowned, rubbing her arms as if chilled. "He mentioned the old mill—that's what he always called it. He said we shouldn't go there. That it was bad."

"Bad. Well, that could mean anything."

Deidre shivered, rubbing her arms. "Let's get out of here. It's chilly and musty. And I never did like that deer staring at me."

He had to laugh, but he understood. There was something desolate about the mill, maybe just because it hadn't been used in a long time. "Does the judge ever come up here?"

"Not that I know of. He rarely takes time off, and when he does, he and Sylvia spend a few days in Philadelphia or New York."

"You'll inherit it eventually, I suppose." He held the door for her to go out.

Deidre looked startled. "Me? I doubt it. I'd imagine he'd leave it to Kevin, if anyone. Or possibly donate the rest of the land to the state."

He lingered on the porch while she locked the door, and then they both moved to the steps. He went down first, and just as he reached the bottom, he heard it: the crack of a weapon, followed by the thud of a bullet hitting the wood facing of the cottage.

Jason spun, reaching for Deidre. She stood at the top of the steps, face white, eyes dazed. He grabbed her, pulling her down beside him, then dove with her to the side, searching for shelter—any shelter.

They fell, with him trying to soften her impact. "Are you hurt?"

"No, I... It must be a hunter," she gasped.

"It's not hunting season." And that shot had been too close to be an accident. They were too visible here. He had to get her to safety.

No time to get back into the cabin, not with the door locked. There had to be another place. His gaze caught the paddle wheel, leaning drunkenly against the bank. "Crawl. We can shelter behind the paddle wheel. He can't get a clear shot there."

"Just someone trying a gun..." she began. Another shot hit barely a foot from her.

A rifle, he decided. The shooter had to be at the top of the escarpment, giving him a clear view of the cottage.

"Someone's shooting at us." Deidre sounded stunned. Looked stunned. She needed reassurance, but not now, not until they weren't out in the open.

"Move," he ordered, crawling backward and pulling her along. "When we get to the stream bank, slide down it and grab on to the wheel."

He could see his words penetrate. She nodded and began moving with him. It was slow, too slow, but they couldn't risk getting up and running. Another shot, but this one hit farther away. Maybe the shooter was getting rattled. It was taking too long, every second giving them a chance to call for help.

Not until he had Deidre safe. That first bullet had been intended for her.

He was pushing her now, trying to keep himself between her and where he judged the shooter might be. It seemed an eternity before he felt her slipping back, over the bank. He heard a separate splash of water.

"Okay, I'm down behind the wheel. Now you." Her hand grasped the leg of his jeans, pulling him.

He slid down, felt the shock of cold water up to his knees and grabbed on to the paddle wheel. It held fast even with his weight added. Holding on with one arm, he wrapped the other around Deidre.

"Sure you're not hurt?"

"Just shaky. But my phone… In my backpack, and I must have let go…"

"It's okay. I have mine." He pulled it from his shirt pocket and hit 911. It connected immediately, and he breathed a sigh of relief. He rattled off his name, location, their situation. "Tell Carmichaels I'm here with Mrs. Morris, and there's a shooter on the ridge firing at us."

The dispatcher repeated it back to him. "Help is on the way. Shelter where you are."

"We will." Standard advice that had become too familiar in an era of gun violence. But he didn't think the man on the ridge was a random nutcase.

He slid the phone back in his pocket and focused on Deidre. Her face was white, she was shaking, but she hadn't lost her composure.

"Has he stopped?"

"Hard to say." There hadn't been any fresh shots since they'd made it to the stream. "He may be waiting for us to show ourselves. Or he might be gone." Or he might be trying to get a better angle on them, but he didn't think he'd say that to Deidre. It would take him time to get to the other side of the falls, if so. Time for the cops to get there.

"He was really shooting at us?" she wondered aloud.

He was shooting at you. Maybe that was another thing better not said, not to her. He'd tell Carmichaels his opinion. When the first shot came, he'd already been down at ground level. Deidre had been standing on the porch, and the bullet had slammed into the siding, missing her by inches.

He felt a shudder run through Deidre and tightened his grip on her, pulling her close against him.

"How long will it take?" Her voice was muffled against his shirt.

"Soon." And even as he said it, he heard the wail of a siren.

BY THE TIME the police were there and satisfied it was safe, Deidre didn't have enough strength left to pull herself out of the water. Jason lifted her while Chief Carmichaels grasped her shoulders and pulled. The ground beneath her had never felt so good, and she sank down and watched while Carmichaels helped Jason up the steep bank.

She was vaguely aware of voices, and then Sam Jacobson came running from the patrol car with blankets. He wrapped one around her, and she huddled into it, grateful for its rough warmth.

"I've sent for an ambulance." Ben Carmichaels squatted next to her, patting her shoulder in an attempt at comfort.

"I don't need an ambulance." The words came through chattering teeth, but at least she managed to say them. "In the cottage. There'll be something dry we can put on."

"She's right." Jason half helped, half lifted her to her feet. "We need to warm up, and you need to get moving on identifying the shooter." Jason was obviously too upset to be tactful, but the chief didn't seem to take offense.

"I've sent the township officers up on the ridge to locate the spot and look for evidence. I'm not going to overlook anything, but the shooter's bound to be long gone."

Jason's jaw hardened. "You think the township boys are up to it?"

Carmichaels grinned. "Toby Morgan is retired state police. Took the township office because he figured it'd be a nice little retirement job, but he's capable. If anything's there, he'll find it." He took Deidre's arm. "Let's get you inside and warmed up. Then we can talk."

Sensing a retort building in Jason, she squeezed his hand in warning. Nothing would be gained by alienating Chief Carmichaels. Something she'd thought impossible had happened. Someone had actually shot at them, and they'd need all the help they could get in dealing with it.

The first few steps were a struggle, but once the feeling in her legs returned, she managed to walk with the chief's support on one side and Jason's on the other. Unfortunately, the return of feeling meant pain. She'd never felt such cold. Not even the hardiest soul would go wading in a mountain stream in May.

It was marginally warmer in the cottage, but luckily firewood and tinder were stacked by the fireplace. Leaving the chief to start a blaze, she and Jason stumbled up the stairs. She pointed at the chest in the kids' room. "There should be something in there you can put on. Not guaranteed to fit, but at least it'll be dry."

Jason paused, brushing her hair back from her face with gentle fingers. "You sure you can manage on your own?"

Her face warmed at the thought of having him help her out of the sodden jeans, imagining his touch...

"I'll be fine," she said firmly, and walked as steadily as she could manage into the other room, closing the door.

They were alive and in one piece. Surely it was enough to just be thankful right now. She stumbled to the bed and sat down, staring ruefully at her sneakers. Just getting them off was going to be a job.

Wet shoelaces, she soon found, were impossible to untie. At last she managed to yank the shoes off, then her soaked and muddy socks. The jeans were another challenge, but she peeled them off and left everything in a sodden pile as she rummaged through the dresser, still shivering.

The family usually left a few things here, and eventually she came up with a pair of sweat pants that weren't too bad once she'd doubled the waist over and a heavy sweatshirt that felt good. No shoes, but a heavy pair of hiking socks would do, so she pulled them on.

When she stepped back out into the hall, Jason was leaning against the wall, waiting for her. Like her, he'd settled for thick socks in lieu of shoes, and his jeans, an old pair of Frank's, were only a little too short.

"Better now?" He studied her face, his gaze intent.

"Almost stopped shaking." She tried to produce a smile.

"Good." He put his arm around her. "We'd better go down before Carmichaels decides to come up."

They went down the steep stairs together. Jason's hand at her waist gave her a fleeting sense that there was nothing coming that she couldn't face. But the certainty faded when she saw the grave expression on Chief Carmichaels's face.

"How are you, Deidre?" He came to escort her to a chair near the fire. "You sit here and warm up, and we'll try to make this as quick as possible."

She sat down, relieved when Jason grabbed a chair and pulled it up next to hers. Carmichaels frowned, as if he'd intended to sit there, but then took the chair opposite them.

"Now, let's start with what brought you up here today." He leaned forward, forearms resting on his knees.

"We… I just wanted to check out the cottage. I didn't come inside the last time I was here, so no one had been here since last fall." She was editing the facts a little, but she didn't want the chief to go pouncing on Billy and get him all upset.

"You just came along for the ride, Counselor." He shifted his focus to Jason.

"I didn't think Mrs. Morris ought to go anywhere alone." His jaw hardened. "It looks as if I was right."

Chief Carmichaels gave a noncommittal nod that could have meant anything. "How long were you here?"

"Not long." She glanced at Jason, questioning. "Maybe fifteen minutes or so?"

He nodded. "Just long enough to be sure nothing had been disturbed. Mrs. Morris had mentioned that you sometimes have trouble with thieves or vandals getting into this kind of place."

She had said that, but it hadn't been in quite the way he implied. Still, he seemed willing to go along with keeping Billy out of it.

"Can't be everywhere at once, can we? And properly speaking, that job belongs to the township." Carmichaels glanced around the room. "So you found everything was all right in here, and then you went out. That's when the shooting started?"

A shiver went through Deidre, and she rubbed her arms, nodding.

"I was already down the steps." Jason took over the story. "Mrs. Morris had stopped to lock the door, and she was just about to step down when the first shot was fired. It smacked into the cottage not a foot from where she was standing."

Carmichaels looked from Jason to her, considering. "Could have been someone hunting illegally. Or target shooting."

Jason seemed to hold on to his temper with an effort. "That doesn't account for the other two shots he fired, also too close to be accidental."

Remembered fear swept over her, nearly as strong

as when she'd been living through it. "If it hadn't been for Jason…"

She couldn't finish the sentence. What would happen to Kevin if something happened to her? It had been so close. She hugged herself, suddenly needing to see her son, to touch him, to hold him close.

"I have to go home," she said abruptly. "Kev will be coming home from school. I have to be there."

"I can have an officer meet him," Carmichaels began, but she interrupted him.

"Absolutely not. Do you think I want him scared to death?" She shot to her feet. "I have to go now."

"My questions…" Carmichaels began, but the wave of panic she felt drowned out his words. She had to be home when Kevin was dropped off. She had to put her arms around him and know he was safe.

"Look, I can stay and answer anything you have to ask." Jason stood, putting a steadying hand on her arm. "Let one of your people drive Mrs. Morris home now. She's been through enough lately."

Carmichaels frowned, but he nodded. "All right. Sam will drive you home." He gestured to the young patrolman. "See that Mrs. Morris gets home okay. And check the house for her."

"Yes, sir." He looked gratified at being trusted with the responsibility. "Anything else?"

"No siren. No point in upsetting the neighbors." He turned to Deidre and took her hand. "Now, don't you go worrying yourself about this. We'll find him, whoever it was. If I need anything else, I'll stop by the house later."

She nodded, suppressing the longing to remind him that he hadn't yet found the person who'd killed Dixie.

If it was the same person...

Deidre thrust that thought away. Because if it was, that could only mean he thought she was a threat to him. Didn't he realize that if she knew anything she'd long since have told the police?

Jason put his arm around her shoulders and walked with her toward the door. "I'll come out with you." They crossed the porch and walked down to the waiting police car in silence.

"Stay safe, and don't worry." Jason spoke quietly as they reached the car.

"You'll come by later?" She hated sounding needy, but she couldn't help what she felt.

"I'll come by as soon as I can." He glanced back over his shoulder at Carmichaels. "I want to make sure they're not letting anything slip through their fingers. And when I leave here, I'll check the motel where Hanlon was staying. If he's back in the area, I want to know."

His expression was grim, but it softened when he looked at her, his eyes seeming to darken, his lips to soften. Heedless of the police, he took both her hands in his and lifted them to his lips. The touch warmed her more than any fire could, rippling through her.

"Stay safe," he murmured against her skin, and then slowly let her go.

CHAPTER FIFTEEN

IT WAS LATER than Jason had expected when he reached Deidre's house—nearly five. She'd probably be getting supper for Kevin about now, but maybe they could find enough privacy for him to tell her the latest on the investigation.

But when Deidre opened the door and he stepped inside, he discovered he wasn't the only visitor. Adam Bennett rose from the sofa, nodding to him. Jase's jaw clenched. Hadn't he done enough damage already?

"Bennett." His voice was chill.

"I was just leaving," he said quickly, obviously embarrassed. "I just had to be sure Deidre was all right after what happened." He shifted uneasily and came toward the door. "Be sure to call if you need anything."

"Thank you, Adam." Deidre didn't promise to call, Jase noted with approval. At least she was conscious of the danger of being seen with him.

The door closed behind him, and Jase looked at Deidre, brows lifted.

"I couldn't very well refuse to let him come in." Exasperation threaded her voice. "What else could I do?"

"Nothing, I guess. But I wish he'd exercise a little discretion." He glanced around, realizing the house was too quiet to contain a busy five-year-old. "Where's Kevin?"

"Judith came over and took him home with her." Deidre pushed her hair back with a nervous gesture. "And just in time, because the judge stopped by. He'd heard already, and he insisted that Kevin shouldn't stay here. He wanted to take him back to Ferncliff, so I was glad to say I'd already made other arrangements."

He wasn't surprised that the judge had jumped in so quickly. He wanted his grandson in his house, and this situation had lent him ammunition.

"Are you going to pick him up later?"

Deidre shook her head. "She's going to keep him overnight. I know I shouldn't let him sleep over on a school night, but it seemed like the best solution. I'm so rattled I don't know what's safe and what's not. But Judith and Eli will take good care of him."

He studied her face as she led the way into the living room. "What about you? You're not staying here alone." He made it a statement, not a question.

"Judith wants me to stay over, as well. That's cowardly, I guess, but at this point I don't care." Her smile was rueful. "I think I've run out of courage."

He sat down on the sofa next to her and took her hands in a firm grip. "You've got plenty of that, but you're being sensible. Besides, Chief Carmichaels wants to keep an eye on the house tonight, so he'll be just as pleased if you're safely tucked away elsewhere."

Her blue eyes widened. "He thinks the person who shot at us might make another attempt?"

Jason didn't want to frighten her, but she had to be on her guard. "It's possible."

"But it's crazy!" That was almost a wail. "The only reason he could have would be if I knew something about Dixie's murder, and I don't."

He rubbed her hands, hoping to soothe her. "Apparently he thinks you do."

"If I did, I'd have told the police already. What could I know? The police have already announced Kevin doesn't remember anything. Maybe I should put a sign on the door, saying I don't know anything." Her voice had regained its tartness, relieving him. Better for her to be fighting mad rather than frightened.

"Maybe we should try that," he said lightly. "It would at least confuse the neighbors."

Deidre almost chuckled at that, some of the color coming back into her cheeks. "They're already interested enough in what I do." She leaned back. "Seriously, what would someone think I know that would make me a danger?"

He'd given that considerable thought. "You are the one who sorted through Dixie's belongings. And you were a person she confided in. He might think there was something to give him away in that."

"If there is anything, I haven't recognized it." She rubbed her forehead. "We were friends, but Dixie wasn't one to confide in others about her private life. She'd mention guys she dated or ones that hit on her, but never by name."

"Whether it's true or not, the killer seems to see you as a threat."

She was still for a moment, frowning. "I almost wish I were. Then maybe there'd be an end in sight to this terrible situation. What happened after I left?"

"Not much. I had a heated discussion with Carmichaels over whether it could have been a mistake—someone just out shooting who didn't realize we were there."

"Maybe...maybe he's right."

"I know it's tempting, but it would be dangerous to believe that. I don't really think Carmichaels took it seriously himself." He frowned, trying to find the right words for his impressions. "He's a good guy. Conscientious. But he may be out of his depth in this business. Don't get me wrong—he took all the appropriate steps. Right now he's got every man he can spare checking the hunting cabins in that area, in case the shooter broke into one of them for the gun."

"I hadn't thought of that, but I guess if you're going to shoot at someone, you don't want to use your own gun, do you?"

He shook his head. "They recovered the shell casings, so they know what they're looking for. And it was Carmichaels's idea to keep a watch on your house tonight, just in case." He let go of her hands to pull out his cell phone. "I should let him know what you plan to do, in case he wants to talk to you before you go to Judith's."

But when he called Carmichaels didn't seem to see any need for that. He was too excited about his find—a hunting cabin that had been freshly broken into, and a gun case with one rack empty. He was preoccupied with tracking down the owner to find out exactly what they were looking for.

"So that's that," Jason concluded once he'd clicked off from the call. "He'll stop by tomorrow to check on you. And he has one car cruising around town, trying to spot Mike Hanlon."

"Hanlon?" She straightened. "I thought he left town."

"So did the police," he said, jaw tightening in irritation. "I stopped by the motel where he'd taken a room for the week, and it turns out someone had slept in the room last night. The manager claimed he didn't see Hanlon." No point in telling Deidre he'd slipped the man a fifty to ensure that he called Jason immediately if there was any further sign of him.

"If it was Hanlon…" Deidre considered, a line forming between her brows. "That must mean he didn't find what he wanted when he searched the box I brought from Dixie's. Assuming, of course, that it was Hanlon who broke in here."

"He seems the most likely suspect. There aren't exactly a lot of people who were involved with Dixie, unless there's someone nobody knows about."

She rubbed her forehead, banishing the line. "I guess there could be. I probably didn't know about every guy she went out with. She might have met someone where she worked."

"Wouldn't she have told you? I had the impression you talked a lot."

"We did, but as I said, Dixie had her privacy zone. There were things she didn't discuss. Her marriage was one of them. Aside from saying Mike had been a mean drunk and she was well rid of him, she didn't talk about that. Mostly she joked about the guys she went out with, but without naming them."

"Making fun of them?" That opened up a thought he hadn't considered. If she'd humiliated the wrong person— But then why would she open the door to him? The trouble was, that question applied to almost anyone who'd have a reason to kill her.

Deidre looked troubled. "Dixie had a kind heart. I don't think she'd have done that to them. It was just... you know, girl talk."

"Well, the ex-husband is still the most likely suspect." And he was keeping Billy as a possibility, but he knew better than to say that to Deidre. "That's why Carmichaels has got to find him."

"I can't go on living like this indefinitely—always waiting for something to happen, listening for the other shoe to drop." Her face twisted as she struggled to hold on to her emotions.

He took her hands again, wanting to comfort her but not sure how. "You won't have to. Something is going to break soon, I know it. If he'd left well enough alone and walked away once Dixie was dead, they might never have caught him. But now he's making mistakes."

"Like shooting at us." Deidre grimaced. "It felt a lot worse than a mistake."

"You know what I mean." He put his arm around her, and she turned into his embrace so naturally that he wondered why he hadn't done it sooner. "He's panicking. Yes, that's dangerous, but it means he'll give himself away." He smoothed his hand down the curve of her back. "You have a lot of people trying to look out for you. You know that."

She nodded, and he felt the movement against his shoulder, felt her silky hair brush his cheek. "I know," she murmured. "I trust you. I'm just worried about Kevin. How do I protect him? How do I keep him from being affected by all this?"

"You just go on the way you are." He cradled her cheek in his hand, meeting her troubled gaze. "You're a strong woman. As long as Kevin has you, he'll be fine."

He lowered his face to kiss her, but even as he did, her words kept replaying in his mind. *I trust you.* And when she knew that Judge Morris had used him to investigate her, what then?

He should be honest with her. He was back in the same quandary again. If he told her, she'd be angry. She'd push him away, and then who would be here to protect her? And if he didn't tell her, she'd still find out eventually, and she'd hate him forever.

There wasn't really a choice. For one of the few times in his life, he was putting someone else's needs ahead of his own, no matter the cost.

DESPITE THE FEAR that clung relentlessly, Deidre couldn't help being amused by the way Jason reacted to Judith and Eli's insistence that he stay to supper. He had clearly never had a friendship with an Amish person before, and his usual calm self-assurance was dented.

"Don't worry," she murmured under cover of the clatter as the children trooped to the long table in the middle of the farmhouse kitchen. "Amish eat just like everybody else. And Judith's a great cook."

"I already know that." He leaned over her as he pulled out her chair, and his whisper tickled her ear. "I'd rather not embarrass myself, though."

She gave him a reassuring smile as Kevin claimed his attention.

"Sit next to me, okay?" He tugged on Jason's hand, pulling him to the seat between himself and his mother.

"Sure thing, Kev." Jason's hand rested on her son's shoulder for a moment, and Deidre's heart clenched at the expression on Kev's face as he looked up at Jason.

Once they were all seated, Deidre reached over to touch Jason's hand in silent communication, glancing at Eli. Eli bowed his head for the silent prayer with which the Amish started every meal.

A mystery to outsiders was knowing when to raise their heads again. Long experience had taught Deidre that repeating the Lord's Prayer silently provided just about the proper length of time. When she looked up again, Jason gave her a quick smile.

Serving bowls began to circle the table with bewildering speed, and the usual chatter broke out, but in English rather than Pennsylvania Dutch, in deference to their guests. Eli and Judith's children were alike in their blond hair, blue eyes, ruddy faces and exuberant personalities. Benjamin was the quietest, and Deidre had always thought it was because he couldn't get a word in edgewise with his four older siblings talking so much. At least the baby didn't talk too much yet.

Joining in a lively conversation about whether fifteen-year-old Becky, the eldest, should make a pink dress or a green one for summer, Deidre shot a glance at Jason, to find him watching her with a bemused expression.

Eli leaned toward him, his lean, weathered face creasing in a smile. "*Ach*, how females can get so excited about the color of a dress is beyond understanding, ain't so?"

Jason looked grateful. "I can't say I know much about sewing dresses. I understand you have a dairy herd. Must keep you tied down, doesn't it?"

"*Chust* as well," Eli said. "Keeps the boys occupied, working with me. Farming is the best life for an Amish family, but not everyone can make a living that way."

Did Jason get a glimmer of how the Amish felt about the land? She suspected not. The attitude was familiar to her, having grown up here. To the Amish, tending the land was as close to God as one could get on earth. Eli would be devastated if his boys didn't want to keep working on the farm after him, but she didn't think he needed to worry about that. The three boys took to dairy farming like a duck to water, and they all showed a sense of responsibility beyond their years.

Becky claimed her attention then with a plea for her opinion on the projected dress, and she found herself occupied with the two girls and Judith for the remainder of the meal.

She tried to get up and help clear the table, but Judith waved her back into her chair. "The girls will do that. You relax. You've had a trying day, ain't so?"

Jason leaned over with a smile. "You'll take good care of her tonight, I know."

"We will." Judith's usually serene face grew somber. "All this trouble…it is not what we're used to here in Echo Falls."

Eli, rounding the table, put a hand on her shoulder. "Troubles come in different shapes, that's all. This will pass, like all the rest." His glance took in his sons and included Kevin. "*Komm*, boys. There are chores to be done."

Kevin looked gratified to be included, and he jumped from his seat and scurried to the door with Benjamin. Once they'd gone out, only the clink of dishes and the girls' soft chatter in Pennsylvania Dutch sounded.

Jason rose. "Wonderful meal, Judith. Thank you." He held out his hand to Deidre. "I should get going. Walk out with me?"

Nodding, she took his hand and slipped outside with him. The sun had just dipped below the ridge, and dusk was settling into the valley. Jason had parked the car behind a huge fir tree where it was invisible from the road. He'd seemed confident that no one had been following to see where they went when they left the house.

Still, he stood for a long moment, surveying the surrounding landscape.

"I'm sure no one realizes I'm here. If I didn't believe that, I wouldn't stay. I don't want to bring danger to Judith and Eli's family."

"You're right." He faced her, his palm moving down her arm until he clasped her wrist. "This situation just has me jumpy. I'd like to clap you in an anonymous safe house until it's settled."

"Or a jail cell?" She managed a light tone. "I can't

live my life that way. It's important to keep things as normal as possible for Kevin."

"And as safe as possible for both of you," he added. He frowned, looking down at their clasped hands. "I don't like leaving you."

"We'll be fine here. Really." Odd to find herself reassuring him. Usually it was the other way around. "I just wish I felt this safe in my own house."

"You will." His grasp tightened. "You and Kev deserve that, and you're going to have it. Believe me."

The sudden yearning in his eyes startled her. She'd never seen him look quite like that before.

"I believe you. Don't worry so. I know we can trust you."

Jason seemed to wince at her words. "I'm glad. Especially when there's a whole community of people who think I can't be trusted."

"I...I don't understand." Deidre looked into his face, shaken by the intensity behind the words. "Who thinks that?"

He shrugged, seeming to retreat behind his usual facade. "Never mind. It's a long story."

Deidre glanced around. They had as much privacy here, sheltered by the fir tree and the car, as they would anywhere. "I have time. Tell me." It seemed suddenly to be a measure of their relationship. If they were as close as she thought, he would confide in her.

Jason turned toward the car, letting go of her hands. But before her disappointment could grow, she realized he wasn't opening the door. Instead he braced both hands against it, as if he'd push the whole car over.

"Haven't you ever wondered why I gave up my job in Philadelphia and came here?"

"To the middle of nowhere?" She tried to lighten the moment. "I suppose I thought that you'd become tired of the pressure and wanted a simpler life."

"Not a chance. At least not then." He gave her a wry smile. "Now...well, now I might feel that way. But back then all I wanted was success."

She tried to remember what she'd heard about his life in Philadelphia. "You were with the prosecutor's office, weren't you?"

"Prosecuting white-collar financial crimes—that was my specialty. The last case I worked on was the most important that had ever come my way. We—Leslie and I—thought it was a ticket to the big time. If I'd won that case, I could have walked away from the prosecutor's office and joined any high-profile firm I wanted."

Her mind had gotten stuck on the name. "Leslie?"

"Leslie was my fiancée." His hands tightened into fists.

"Was?"

"Yes." He shot a glance at her. "Whatever I felt for Leslie is as dead as...as yesterday's news. Believe me. After what she did..."

The words trailed off, and she sensed that it was almost impossible for him to go on. But he couldn't stop now—they couldn't stop. Not until she knew the whole story.

She put her hand on his arm, feeling the taut muscles through the fabric of his shirt. *Who was she? How did you meet? What was she like?* She silenced all the questions that pressed at her lips and asked the only important one.

"What did she do?"

"She betrayed me." His voice was harsh. The betrayal still had the power to infuriate him, obviously.

She waited, knowing there was more and sure now that he would tell her.

"Leslie was interested in my case. Natural, I thought. She was an attorney, too. I was stupid. I shared information I shouldn't have with her. Chalk it up to insecurity—I wanted to know if she thought I was on the right track."

"You were engaged. You should have been able to share anything." Deidre could see what was coming, and her heart winced at the thought of hearing it.

"She wanted to encourage me, she said. I was going to win. She kept on saying it right up until the moment I walked into the office and found out the whole case had been shot to blazes. The company in question had learned details of the investigation they never should have known. The people I'd cultivated who were willing to testify were suddenly unavailable or had changed their minds. The DA was furious, knowing the leak had to have come from our office. And I was the person who had access."

Deidre's mind spun. "But...did you realize..."

"That it was Leslie?" His jaw was so hard it was a wonder he could speak. "Oh, yes. She didn't even bother to hide it. She just walked away and stepped into the position they'd obviously promised her, and I was left holding the bag."

Deidre longed to put her arms around him, to hold

him close and comfort him, but nothing about his taut figure suggested that would be welcome. She contented herself with stroking his back, the tendons tight as guitar strings.

"You weren't disbarred." Obviously not, or he wouldn't be practicing now.

"No. I'm not sure anyone believed me, but the DA was decent about it when he'd calmed down. There was enough doubt about who'd done what to keep him from pushing for disbarment. But I lost my job. And my reputation."

Her heart hurt at the picture he'd painted. "But you must have had friends. People who believed in you."

"Funny thing." He clipped off the words. "I thought I had friends right up until everything hit the fan. Then I realized that all of them were people I knew through work. I'd been so busy trying to make a name for myself that I hadn't taken time for anything else. Pitiful, isn't it?"

The bitterness in his voice ran deep. He might think he'd gotten over it, but clearly he hadn't.

"I'm sorry. But that person you're talking about—ambitious, thinking of nothing but success—he doesn't sound like the man I know."

Jason was silent for a moment. And then he smiled, his face relaxing. "I hope that's true. If so, I'm glad."

The warmth of his smile, the strength of his back under her hand, his closeness, all combined to flow around her in a dizzying eddy that drew her ever closer.

She struggled to stay focused. "But I don't understand how you ended up here."

"Judge Morris." His gaze shifted away, and he seemed to close up just a little. "He contacted me. Said he remembered me from when I was in law school with Frank. He must have known how bad things were for me, but he never mentioned that. He just said he had an opening in his firm now that Frank had passed away, and he thought Frank would have been pleased to know he'd offered it to me."

"I'm sure he would have."

"We were never close friends. You probably know that."

"Frank wasn't in touch very much the first couple of years in law school. It was only when he came back that summer that we actually got together."

She smiled, remembering Frank looking at her as if he hadn't ever really looked before. Maybe he hadn't. She'd always been his friend, and then suddenly she'd become someone he loved.

"Yes, well, whatever his reason, I was in no state to turn down the judge's offer. I figured if I came here even for a few years, built up a reputation again, I'd be in a position to start fresh. Not in Philly, but somewhere else." He gave her a crooked smile. "I'm not so eager to get out of Echo Falls now, obviously."

Deidre reached up to touch his face, longing to wipe away any pain that lingered there but needing to hear the answer to one more question. "What happened to Leslie?"

He pressed her palm against his cheek. "Last I heard she was happily enjoying the fruits of her new position as chief counsel to one of the most bent firms I've ever run across. And engaged to the firm's CFO. So if you were hoping to hear she'd come by her just deserts, there's no such luck."

"It will catch up to her one day. You can't prosper living a lie that's based on betrayal and not end up being stung yourself."

"Yes." His face sobered. He looked down at the hand he was holding and pressed a kiss into her palm. "Promise me…"

"What?" She looked at him questioningly.

He seemed to struggle with himself, and then he shook his head. "Promise me you'll take precautions and stay safe. You and Kevin both. No taking risks the minute my back is turned."

Deidre had the strong impression that wasn't what he'd intended to say. But he was looking at her so intently that all she could do was nod in agreement.

"All right. I promise. But I want the same promise from you. Don't go off chasing Mike Hanlon or anyone else alone. Promise."

He nodded, smiling a little, and then took a quick look around. "Any chance I can get a good-night kiss?"

"If you do it quickly. I don't want Eli and the boys to come out of the barn and catch us at it."

He linked his arms around her, holding her easily. "Don't the Amish go in for kissing?"

"They do, but not where kids can see them. That's reserved for the courting buggy."

He grinned. "Since I don't have a courting buggy, I'll have to make do with standing next to the car."

Deidre lifted her face toward his, loving the scent of

him, the warmth of his skin and the slight roughness of his cheek. His lips closed on hers, and she held on tight, longing with all her heart that nothing would happen to tear them apart.

CHAPTER SIXTEEN

BY THE TIME she took Kevin to the pediatrician's office the next afternoon, Deidre felt as if she'd recovered her balance. There was nothing like a good night's sleep and a sunny day to restore her.

Her good spirits had been dented a little by a visit from Chief Carmichaels soon after she'd returned to her own house this morning. She'd been relieved in a way that no one had come near her place the previous night, but a little dismayed, too. If someone had, this might all have been over by now.

But Carmichaels had been pleased on one score. The gun had been recovered. It had been a high-powered hunting rifle that had been taken from one of the hunting cabins. They'd been in touch with the owner, who of course hadn't even known the cabin had been broken into.

His description of the rifle had been enough to make Carmichaels sure that it was the gun his men had recovered from the stream a mile below the falls. Unfortunately, there was nothing to show who had fired it. It was so banged up it probably had gone over the falls.

As good a way as any to get rid of potentially damaging evidence, she supposed. Carmichaels had halfheartedly postulated a teen high on drugs stealing the gun and firing it off at random, but she'd been sure by his expression that even he didn't believe that.

Deidre drew herself up short. She'd better get back her optimism before Kev realized something was wrong with her.

Kevin, however, was pouting on his own account. He didn't see any good reason why he had to go to the doctor's office.

Glancing in the rearview mirror, she saw him sitting in his car seat, his lower lip stuck out and his arms folded. She couldn't help smiling at his expression.

"You know what Grammy always said to me when I had my lip stuck out that way?"

He eyed her cautiously, but the temptation to hear a story about "when Mommy was little" was too strong to be ignored. "What?"

"That my lip stuck out so far a bird was going to come and perch on it. That always made me laugh, and we'd talk about what kind of a bird it was going to be. I wanted it to be a yellow goldfinch."

Kevin's pout had disappeared, and he leaned forward. "I want that. No, I want a crow. A big black crow!"

"That might be too heavy for your lip, don't you think?" She pulled into the small parking lot next to the converted Victorian that housed the pediatrician's office.

"My lip is strong," he announced, pinching it and trying to talk at the same time. "You ask Dr. Liz. I'll bet she'll say so, too."

"We'll see." She opened the door and unbuckled

Kevin's harness. Thank goodness he was easily restored to his usual sunny self.

A few minutes later, Liz was looking seriously at Kevin's lower lip. "I've got to say, it looks pretty sturdy to me."

"See, Mommy?" Kevin was too pleased to have been right to object to a quick physical.

Liz was very deft. Kev probably never even noticed the casual questions she slipped in while she checked his head, his eyes, his ears.

Deidre watched anxiously, wondering what Liz was making of his responses, especially when he started describing a nightmare in vivid detail. Since it involved the bad guy from one of his favorite cartoon movies, she didn't really think it had anything to do with remembering the attack on Dixie. But how did she know?

"You are sound as a bell, Kevin," Liz finally pronounced. "Do you know what that means?"

He shook his head.

"It means you get a whole sheet of stickers and a lollipop." She reached in her desk drawer for the treats she kept there. Deidre was well aware of Liz's conviction that the occasional lollipop never hurt an otherwise well-nourished child, and Kevin certainly was that. Whatever else his injury had done, it hadn't affected his appetite.

"Now, you go out to the office with Connie while your mom and I have a little chat." She ushered him out to the waiting receptionist and then came back to take the chair next to Deidre instead of retreating behind the desk.

Liz was frowning, and Deidre's heart pounded as if she'd been running.

"What is it? What do you think?"

"How often is he having these nightmares you told me about?" Liz answered a question with a question, never a good sign in Deidre's experience.

"Every night," she admitted. "Except last night, when we slept over at Judith and Eli's."

If Liz was curious as to why they'd spent the night away from home, she didn't ask. "That's interesting. Have they all been as bad as the first time?"

Deidre hesitated. "I was going to say no, but I'm not sure that's true. Now that I'm alert to the possibility, I get to the bedroom fast and can sometimes get to him before he has that blind, terrified look."

"That's good, but it's not enough." Liz frowned, clicking her pen against Kevin's records. "The fact that he didn't have a bad dream when he was away from the house may suggest it's related to what happened there. Does he ever say anything coherent while he's actually in the grip of the nightmare?"

"Nothing that really points to...well, to whatever he saw that night. Once he cried out something about the stairs, and about falling. But he never remembers it the next day, and he still runs up and down those steps a dozen times a day." Deidre rubbed her forehead, wishing she didn't feel like crying out herself.

Liz reached across to pat her hand. "I know it's no good telling you not to worry, because you will."

"I'm glad you realize that." She managed a wry smile.

"That's better." Liz nodded approvingly. "Look,

Kevin is strong and healthy. It's true he's been through a couple of traumatic events, but the fact that he's so young is going to help. The thing is, I don't think we can just wait for it to resolve itself."

"You think he's trying to remember what happened." She had to face that possibility if she were to help her son.

"Not consciously, of course. But at some level, the memories of that night are stirring." Liz frowned down at her pen for a moment. "I'm not really qualified to go poking around in Kevin's subconscious. But I think it's time to turn to an expert."

Unbidden, Deidre's thoughts produced Jason saying almost the same thing. "What expert?" Her voice was surprisingly steady.

"There's a child psychologist in Williamsport who is highly recommended by several of my colleagues. I met him once at a medical gathering and was impressed. His name is Harry Whittaker." Liz turned to her desk and began scribbling on a pad. "If you like, I'll call and make the appointment myself. We'll get Kevin in faster that way."

Deidre's fingers felt numb as she took the paper with the name and address from Liz's hand. "You think he can get Kevin to remember, and that will help him. Is that it?"

"I'm not the expert." Liz's tone was gentle. "But I think he'll probably want to help Kevin deal with the memories he's trying not to recognize. With a head injury, the blank spaces can fill in at once, at any time or never. But given what's happening with Kevin, and knowing how scary those memories are, I suspect the sooner they're out in the open, the sooner they can be dealt with."

"And the more dangerous he is to the person who killed Dixie." Her hands twisted in her lap as if they possessed a life of their own.

"I know." Liz paused. "Maybe it's best if no one else knows about this. As far as my office is concerned, you brought Kevin in for a normal post-hospital checkup."

"You're right."

But Jason had to know. He had become too important in their lives to keep this from him. Besides, he was the one person in the world she knew had nothing to do with Dixie's death.

As for what she thought of Liz's idea... "I wish I could be sure that remembering is what's best for Kevin. If only..."

"Never mind 'if only.'" Liz gave her arm a little shake. "You've always been good at facing reality, Deidre. And that's what you have to do now."

Was she? Deidre wished she had Liz's confidence. It was hard to face reality when that reality was so very grim.

DID HE DROP in on Deidre or not? Jason still hadn't made up his mind when he pulled into his driveway. He wanted to see her, no doubt about that. She'd intruded into his thoughts dozens of times in the course of the day, her lips curving, her blue eyes deep with sympathy.

He didn't want sympathy from her. But he'd told her about Leslie, something he hadn't mentioned to another soul. For an instant he saw again Leslie's slim, elegant figure as she'd walked out of his life after smashing it to splinters. Oddly enough, that didn't sting as much as it should.

Deidre's warmth had chased it away. Maybe he'd known it would. Or maybe he'd told her about Leslie because he couldn't tell her the other fact he was hiding from her—the one that would spell betrayal in any language.

Ironic, wasn't it? Leslie had betrayed him. He'd betrayed Deidre. And Deidre wouldn't forgive him any more than he'd forgiven Leslie.

His cell phone put an end to an especially futile line of thought. It was the manager of the motel where Mike Hanlon had stayed.

"He's back." The words spilled out quickly. "I saw him, so I'm calling you like I said I would."

"Is he in his room?" His mind juggled possibilities. Call Carmichaels first to handle it, or go himself? He knew which one he wanted to do.

"Nope. I spotted him just going to his car. Walked right into the housekeeper's cart and started swearing a blue streak. Before I could get out there he'd jumped in his car and pulled out of the lot, spitting gravel all the way."

Not good. "Headed toward town, or toward the highway?"

"Toward town. Listen, I called you like you wanted. You did say there'd be something more in it for me." The voice took on a whine.

"There will be. You said he ran into the housekeeper's cart. Did she see him?"

"What do you think? She was standing right there, wasn't she?"

"Ask her to hang around until I get there. I'm leaving now."

Jason backed out faster than he'd come in. Five minutes to the motel, and in the meantime who knew where Hanlon was headed. Still, he'd recognize the black SUV the man drove, and Echo Falls wasn't that big. If he was coming into town, there was a good chance Jase would spot the car.

But he didn't. He reached the motel without any sign of the vehicle. Driven by a sense that matters were coming to a head, he charged toward the motel office.

The manager he'd spoken to leaned on the counter, deep in conversation with a thin blonde woman whose sharp-featured face turned toward him avidly. He suspected word had spread that he'd pay for information.

"This is June. She's our housekeeper. I had her stay to talk to you." The manager wanted to make sure he wasn't forgotten.

"Thanks, June." He zeroed in on her. "Anything you can tell me about Hanlon will be a help."

The woman shrugged. "Like I said, he barreled out of his room. I didn't even know he was in there. Ran right into my cart and then started swearing at me like it was my fault. I yelled right back at him. I don't have to take that kind of stuff from a guest."

Jase shook his head sympathetically. "He say anything about where he was going?"

She scrunched up her face in thought. It wasn't an attractive expression. "Not exactly. He kept on saying he knew somebody had something he wanted. That it was rightfully his. Muttering, like."

"Sober?" He lifted an eyebrow, and she grinned.

"Drunk as a skunk, more likely. And mean with it. Believe me, I've seen mean, and he was right up there. Kept slamming his fist on the cart so hard I figured he'd break it. But better the cart than me. I backed away in a hurry, but then he jumped in the car and took off."

He didn't like the sound of this at all. If Hanlon was the person who'd rifled through Dixie's possessions, he hadn't gotten what he was looking for. So now he was back for a second round.

He had to get to Deidre.

"Okay, thanks for your help." He pulled out his wallet, dispensing cash quickly. "If he shows up here, call right away. Don't tangle with him yourself."

"No chance." The woman was emphatic, and the manager sidled back behind his counter.

Jason was pulling out his cell phone as he raced back to the car, calling Carmichaels's private line. The chief answered on the first ring.

Quickly Jase filled him in. "I'm headed into town to look for him," he concluded.

"This is a police matter," Carmichaels snapped. "If he's back in town, it's time he answered some questions. And if he's driving around my town drunk, he's headed straight for a cell."

Swinging onto the street that ran parallel to Main, Jason grunted. "Better catch him first."

"We'll do that. Now go home. I'll let you know when we've got him under lock and key."

"I'll let you know when I spot him." Jason clicked off before the chief could utter an ultimatum. The man needed to get busy finding Hanlon, not arguing with Jason. If he hadn't taken the initiative, Carmichaels wouldn't even know Hanlon was in town.

He cruised down the street, keeping an eye out for any sign of Hanlon's vehicle. Echo Falls wasn't that big a town. Hanlon couldn't evade him as well as Echo Falls's admittedly tiny police force for long.

But by the time he'd cruised all the streets in the west end of town, he wasn't so sure. He passed a police car and kept going. If Carmichaels spotted him, he'd just get another order to stay out of it.

A sweep of the east end of town didn't turn up anything, either. Maybe Hanlon had given up. Maybe he was holed up somewhere sleeping it off. Still, his SUV should be visible.

Dusk was drawing in fast. He glanced at the dash clock, startled at the time. He'd fully expected to be ensconced in Deidre's kitchen by now, waiting while she put Kev to bed.

His jaw hardened. Time to stop and think, instead of running around looking for Hanlon. He'd better head back to check on his own building. Hanlon might well be thinking that whatever he wanted had been left there, maybe hidden someplace by Dixie.

What was it? What had Dixie had that Hanlon considered so important to him?

He pulled out his cell phone. He'd let Deidre know

what was going on and just make sure she had her doors locked. He could imagine her response if he reminded her yet again.

He let the phone ring and ring, but she didn't pick up. Given what time it was, she was probably getting Kevin ready for bed. He knew her well enough now to know that that time was devoted to her son. She was essentially unavailable at the moment.

He'd give one more swing up Main and back, and then head for home. If Hanlon intended on breaking into Dixie's apartment, he'd probably wait for it to be darker, assuming he was sober enough to attempt it. And Jase would be ready for him.

DEIDRE STOOD AT the bottom of the stairs for a moment, listening. All was quiet. Kevin had seemed more clingy than usual again tonight. They'd had an extra story before setting up one of his action figures on the nightlight to act as guardian... Although Deidre suspected that he was more comforted by the stuffed dog and teddy bear who snuggled into bed next to him.

She massaged the back of her neck, trying to will away the tension that had gathered there. She was doing the right thing. She needed to believe that. In any event, Liz had called back after office hours to inform her of an appointment with the psychologist for next week. She'd also supplied a pep talk, probably sensing Deidre's doubts.

Walking through to the kitchen, Deidre glanced at the old schoolhouse clock over the stove. She had to admit that she'd expected Jason to show up after work today. Or at least to call.

There was a real possibility that he regretted talking so openly to her the previous night. Or if not regretted, at least felt a little uncertain as to where they went from here. She felt quite sure that he didn't go around telling people about his former fiancée. To be betrayed in that way...

Was it any different than her suspicions of Frank and Dixie? To be honest, it was. Jason *knew* that Leslie had betrayed him, and she'd done it to advance her career.

Deidre only had suspicions, but they seemed to darken every memory of her life with Frank.

The knock on the front door interrupted her thoughts. Her heart leaped. Jason. He might have been late and intentionally waited, not wanting to interrupt while she was putting Kevin to bed.

Deidre hurried to the door as the knocking continued. Her hand was on the knob when all the lectures about safety marched into her mind. Quickly she put the chain in place, hoping she didn't have to explain why it hadn't already been there, and then turned the knob, smiling at the thought of seeing him.

But it wasn't Jason. Mike Hanlon stood there, looking even burlier than she remembered in the half dark. Instinctively she shoved the door closed, but he'd already managed to get his foot in it.

"Wait a minute. Got to talk to you." The words were slurred, and her heart sank. He'd been drinking.

She struggled to sound confident. "You'll have to

come back tomorrow. I'm expecting company any minute."

"No! Now!" He slammed the door with his fist, and she felt it shudder under her hand. "Tell me where it is."

She blinked. "Where what is?"

"You know. I gotta have it." He shook his head as if trying to clear it, but she expected it would take more than a gallon of coffee to do that.

"I don't know what you mean. Come back tomorrow." She pushed futilely at the door.

"It's mine." His voice sank to a grumbling mutter, but his foot remained in the door. "I got rights. Dixie wrote it down for me." He looked at her, leaning his face close to the gap between them. "You know. I was the one who told her to write it all down. Just like insurance, see? It was my idea. Now she's gone, so it belongs to me."

"I'm sorry." For a brief second, something about the way he'd said the words *she's gone* had touched her heart. "I really am. But Dixie never told me about anything she had of yours."

"You must have it!" He was shouting, surely loud enough for someone to hear.

Deidre sent a quick glance toward the end table where she'd left her phone. Not far, but to get it, she'd have to let go of the door. If she did, how long would it hold out against a determined assault? Her heart was pounding so loudly that she could feel it vibrating in her ears.

Jason, where are you?

"I don't have anything." For a second anger seized her. She wouldn't allow him to frighten her. Or to frighten her son. "You should know that. You broke in here and looked through the things I had of Dixie's, didn't you?"

He shook his head, the movement setting his body weaving from side to side. "Musta put it someplace. Where?" His eyes focused, glaring. "Where?" Raising both fists, he slammed them against the door. "Where?"

Deidre braced her back against the door, mind working feverishly. She'd have to risk it. Have to leave the door long enough to grab the phone. If he got in, he'd come after her, wouldn't he? He wouldn't go upstairs to Kevin.

No good answers. She had to move…had to…

The pressure against her back ceased. She turned, prepared for anything.

Hanlon stumbled back away from the door, shaking his head, muttering incomprehensively. Quickly she closed the door, snapped the dead bolt and ran for the phone. Even as she called Jason, she raced to the nearest window. If he tried to get in a window…

She couldn't see him. Where…? There he was. He almost fell down the porch steps, then stumbled onto the grass and dropped to his knees.

"Deidre." Jason's voice in her ear.

"Hanlon's here. He was trying to get in. He's out on the front lawn now." Her stomach clenched. If he tried again…

"I'm on my way. I'll call Carmichaels. He's already out looking for him. Deidre? Are you listening?"

"Yes."

"Go to a room with a door you can lock. Stay there until you know it's me or the cops outside."

"Kevin…" Her ears picked up the smallest sound from upstairs. "I'll be with Kevin."

Clutching the phone, she darted up the stairs and into Kevin's room. He was half asleep, murmuring and tossing from side to side.

She closed the door, then wedged a chair under the knob. None of the old-fashioned doors had locks, or if they did, the keys had long since vanished. There had been no point in telling Jason that. He'd get here as fast as anyone could.

Hurrying to Kevin's bed, she sank down beside him, wrapping her arms around him. She murmured softly, soothing words he didn't need to understand. If only someone were saying those soothing words to her.

Jason, please. We need you.

CHAPTER SEVENTEEN

HEART PUMPING, JASON called Carmichaels again, explaining the situation tersely as he raced toward Deidre's house.

Carmichaels responded with a muttered oath. "We're all clear out on the Greentown road responding to a tipped tractor trailer that never should've been on this road to begin with. I'm on my way. If you get there first…well, don't do anything I'll have to arrest you for."

Jaw clamped, Jason tossed the cell on the seat and took the next corner. If Hanlon had hurt Deidre or Kevin…

He could see Deidre's property now, the house hidden by the heavy shrubbery at the corner of the lot. And there, unless he was mistaken, was Hanlon's SUV, maybe a quarter mile down the road, tilted into a ditch. He clutched the wheel. Go after Hanlon?

No, not until he'd checked on Deidre. He spun into the driveway, grabbing his phone and punching in the number as he ran.

She answered immediately, and relief flooded him at the sound of her voice.

"I'm outside. Are you all right?"

"I'm coming to let you in." Her tone was hushed,

and he guessed she was in Kevin's room. He heard a scraping noise through the phone, and then her feet on the stairs. In another instant she pulled open the door, her gaze darting around the yard.

"Is he gone?"

Jason pulled her against him, succumbing to the need to hold her, even if just for a moment. "His car is in a ditch just down the road. I'll go look for him, but tell me what happened. He didn't get in?"

A shudder went through her, and he tightened his grasp. "No. He was trying, though. And he was too drunk to listen to reason."

"Okay." He forced himself to release her and put his hands on her shoulders instead, focusing on her face, still pale with shock or fear. "We'll go over everything when Carmichaels gets here. I'm going after Hanlon."

"No!" She grasped his arms. "Jason, please. Leave him for the police."

"I'll be careful. But the cops are all on the other side of town. I have to at least check out the car. He could be trapped in there."

She sucked in a shaky breath and nodded.

Jason touched her face and moved a step back onto the porch. "Lock up again. I'll come back as fast as I can."

He stood where he was until he heard the snap of the lock and the rattle of the chain. Then he sped back to the car. If Hanlon was running around unharmed, the police would be better equipped to find him than he would be. But he had to check and see if the man was in the wrecked vehicle.

Jason drove toward the SUV, putting his high beams on. Not much traffic on this road, and he'd guess no one had been past here since it happened, or there'd be flares out. He pulled up, grabbed a flashlight from the glove box and put his flashers on.

Steeling himself, he approached the tilted vehicle and shone his light inside. Nothing. Hanlon wasn't there. He shone the beam around slowly. No blood, so there was no obvious sign that he'd been hurt. So where would he go?

He turned toward his car, intending to get a couple of flares from the emergency kit in the back. His gaze caught a dark shape at the very edge of the range of his headlights. It could have been something thrown from a passing car, but he didn't think it was.

Jason approached, shining his flashlight on what remained of Mike Hanlon. The cops wouldn't have to mount a search for him. He hadn't gotten far.

Pulling out his cell again, he studied the body as he dialed the chief.

"What?" Carmichaels snarled the word, and Jason could hear the wail of sirens through the phone.

"Deidre and Kevin are okay. Hanlon's car is ditched down the road, and he's lying in the middle of the road another fifty feet or so away. Dead. Looks like he's been hit by a car."

"We'll be there in a minute or two. Don't touch anything."

"No." He didn't have the desire to do so. Alive, Hanlon had been a threat. Now he was just an oddly vacant figure huddled on a dark road.

By the time he'd set up the couple of flares he had, he

could hear the sirens without the use of the cell phone. He went back to his car and waited as two police cars shrieked to a stop.

Carmichaels looked grim in the reflection from the flashers. "This is how you found it?"

He nodded, a flash of irritation going through him. He'd been a prosecuting attorney. He knew the ropes.

"The two flares are mine. I spotted the car when I drove up, but went to check on Deidre and Kevin first."

"Sure they're okay?"

"She had a bad scare, but he never got in the house. She said he was drunk and not making much sense."

Carmichaels held up his hand. "Okay, I'll get all that from her. Just tell me what you did after you checked on them."

"I thought I'd better have a look in the SUV, just in case he was trapped or hurt. I didn't touch anything— just looked. Nothing to see. I was going back to my car when I spotted the body." He glanced toward the figure, spotlighted now by the police lights. "I got close enough to be sure he was dead. Called you. Set up the flares and waited."

Jason suspected Carmichaels would want him out of the way while he investigated the scene, and that was okay by him. He'd much rather be with Deidre.

"I'll have questions for you and Deidre once I've gotten things under way here, so don't go anywhere."

"I'll be at Deidre's." Jason turned to his car. Carmichaels would probably prefer to keep them apart until he'd had a chance to talk to each of them, but that wasn't going to happen. For one thing, the chief didn't have enough staff to handle what he had going. And for another, Jason had no intention of leaving Deidre alone.

THANK HEAVEN JASON had come back at last. Deidre flung the door open at his call.

"You're all right? I was worried." He looked fine, except that his face had a grim expression—jaw set, mouth a firm line.

He clasped her hand for a moment before coming through into the living room. "Fine." He glanced up the stairs. "Kevin okay? Did this wake him?"

"He stirred but didn't wake up entirely. Not even when I was moving furniture around." She tried for a smile and didn't quite make it.

"Good." He turned to her and took both her hands in his, and she knew something bad was coming. "Hanlon is dead."

"Dead?" Deidre's mind grappled with it. "How can he... He was okay when he was here. He'd been drinking, but otherwise he seemed all right."

"It looks as if he was hit by a car."

Her gaze sharpened at the way he phrased it. "Do you doubt it?"

Jason's frown deepened. "I'm sure a car hit him—obviously a hit-and-run. I'm just wondering if his death is not a little too neat."

"You mean you think it was deliberate." Her nerves started quivering again.

"I wouldn't go that far. But I'd guess that Carmichaels will seize on Hanlon's actions as proof that he killed Dixie. Everything wrapped up nice and tidy."

For an instant she thought wistfully of a moment when all of this would be behind them. But she didn't want it at the cost of not knowing what really happened to Dixie.

Jason ran his palms down her arms. "You're shaking. I shouldn't be throwing all this at you at once. Let's go into the kitchen, and you can make us some of that mint tea you like so much."

"I don't think mint tea is strong enough to calm me in this situation," she said, but she led the way to the kitchen.

Once she had the kettle on the stove and the teapot warming, she let her thoughts edge back to the problem of the moment. "I heard the sirens when the police cars came by."

"I called the chief back again when I found the body." Jason stared down at the tabletop as if visualizing the scene. "When I stopped by Hanlon's car to check it out, my headlights just picked out something farther down the road. He must have driven the car into the ditch, gotten out and started walking." He frowned. "But it's odd. Why would he be heading away from town?"

She set mugs, spoons and sugar on the table. "Maybe he was disoriented. He'd been drinking, and then with the accident…"

"That seems most likely." He frowned. "Once past your house, it's all fields on either side of the road. A dark stretch to be walking along at night."

Deidre tried to remember what Hanlon had been wearing when she saw him. Jeans and a black T-shirt, she thought. "He was wearing dark clothing. That wouldn't help." She repressed a shiver. "Hard to believe someone would hit a person and just drive off. The driver couldn't help but know he'd hit something, even if he didn't realize it was a person."

"It happens."

Deidre felt his gaze on her and tried not to look as rattled as she felt. Somehow she'd always imagined herself enjoying a little excitement in her life. But not this kind of excitement.

"What will Carmichaels want from me?" She glanced toward the road, half expecting to see the police car approaching. But all she could see from here was the reflected red glow beyond the trees.

"Just tell him what happened. You can't do more. But see if I'm not right. He's going to be sure Hanlon killed Dixie. After all, it would solve all his problems."

There was a bitterness in his voice that Deidre didn't miss. Was he thinking about the business that had ended his career? Maybe that DA had gone for the easy answer that would solve all of his problems, too.

Jason shook his head, as if shaking off his thoughts, whatever they were. "Looks like we'll have a little time before Carmichaels gets here. You feel like telling me what Hanlon said to you?"

Deidre rose to silence the kettle that had started to shriek. She focused on pouring water over the mint tea in her favorite teapot—the blue glazed one she'd picked up at a crafts show.

"I've been trying to get it straight in my mind." She jostled the teapot gently to encourage the brewing. "He insisted I must have something of Dixie's, and he wanted it. But he never said what it was."

"Did you ask?" Jason took the teapot from her hands and poured the tea.

She pushed her hair back, trying to concentrate. "I think so. I was so afraid he was going to break in, and he was so drunk. It wasn't exactly a logical conversation."

"I can imagine." His fingers closed on hers again. "You did the best you could."

"He did seem to imply that what he wanted was something in writing. A paper of some sort. He talked about insurance, but I didn't understand what he meant. Honestly, he was rambling and muttering so much that I'm not sure whatever he did say had any basis in fact."

"Insurance," he repeated. "Is it possible he thinks Dixie had a policy that benefitted him?"

Deidre shook her head helplessly. "If so, she never mentioned it to me. It doesn't seem likely. I didn't find any life insurance paperwork in her belongings. And even if she had taken out insurance benefitting him at some time, she'd have changed the beneficiary when they were divorced."

"If he wanted something he thought you had, we'd better go through the box again. You haven't sent it to her mother yet, have you?"

"No. I suppose I should make a decision about what to send her." Her thoughts flickered to the necklace. But surely that rightfully belonged to Deidre's mother-in-law, didn't it? But if Frank had given it to Dixie... Her head throbbed with the ramifications of that action.

"Don't let anything leave your hands," he said quickly. "Not until all this is settled. We don't know what might be significant."

"I'd like to be rid of it."

That sounded heartless, but the boxes that sat on the worktable in her office were a constant reminder of the unanswered questions about Dixie's death.

"It's got to be over soon."

He answered the feeling rather than the words. How had they reached the point of reading each other so well in such a short time?

A knock on the door heralded the arrival of the chief, and a few minutes later there were three of them sitting around her kitchen table.

Carmichaels had made a face at the offer of mint tea but accepted coffee. Even though it meant extra effort, Deidre welcomed the chance to do something so normal in the face of so much craziness.

"So you don't have any idea what Hanlon wanted with you?" The chief asked the question once she'd told her story. He held his mug between his hands, but his shrewd gray eyes focused on her face.

Deidre shook her head. "He wasn't making much sense. I'm fairly certain there was no insurance policy among Dixie's papers. In fact, she had very little of that sort of thing." Her nerves twitched, remembering.

Always travel light. That way nobody can catch up to you.

Poor Dixie. She'd traveled light, but in the end someone had caught up with her.

"Way I see it, most likely Hanlon was afraid he'd missed something that would tie him to Dixie's murder." The chief shrugged. "Whatever he thought it was probably didn't exist, but I guess you can imagine most anything if you've got a guilty conscience plaguing you."

"So you're assuming Hanlon killed Dixie." She could feel Jason simmering, so she spoke first.

"You ask any cop, and you'll hear the same thing," Carmichaels said, with the air of one repeating a self-evident truth. "The person most likely to have killed someone is a spouse or ex-spouse. If Hanlon had come to your door that night, Dixie would have let him in, even just to see what he wanted. Wouldn't she?"

"I guess she might have." Deidre's answer was reluctant. Dixie hadn't been afraid of anything. She probably would have thought there'd be no harm in talking to her ex here.

"You figure he shows up out of the blue after over a year and suddenly decided to kill her?" Jason's tone made his doubt clear.

Carmichaels's heavy face tightened. "Not just like that. But if the talk got heated, he could have acted impulsively and then panicked when he saw what he'd done."

"So you're going to close the investigation?"

The chief shoved his chair back with an irritated movement. "You know better than that. It's open until we have proof one way or another. But I imagine the DA is going to figure it can go on the back burner unless and until something else turns up."

"So you think it was Hanlon who broke into Deidre's house and went through the box. That makes sense," Jason conceded. "But what about shooting at us up at the old mill? How would he have known where we were going? Or where to get a rifle? Or how to get the best sight line on the mill?"

"I don't know." Carmichaels's irritability increased. "But it could have happened. Or that might have been something separate all together—a kid stealing the rifle and trying it out."

"I can't buy that," Jason said flatly.

She felt as if she were watching a tennis match where each of them was trying to hit the other with the ball. But she didn't know how to stop it.

Carmichaels made a chopping gesture with his hand. "I can't help that." He turned to Deidre. "It's small comfort for losing your friend and having your boy hurt, but at least you can get back to normal life now."

She managed to smile, managed to nod. Jason had been right. The police would seize on Hanlon's actions as a way of wrapping up the case. It seemed logical, she supposed. But she couldn't help feeling that it was all wrong.

And a glance at Jason told her he was thinking exactly the same thing. The chief's explanation was logical, but it was dead wrong.

JASON HADN'T CHANGED his mind by the next day, but he'd had time to consider. The assumption of Hanlon's guilt in Dixie's murder might actually help Deidre, whether it was true or not. If Dixie had let her ex-husband in the door and a subsequent quarrel had led to her death, there was surely no way in which the judge could use that as leverage against her.

He tapped the pen in his hands against the desktop

and found himself wondering what life had been like in the office when Frank was alive. He'd think most fathers would be proud to have a son to succeed them, but he'd never seen Frank and his father together. And he certainly had no experience of his own upon which to base a judgment.

Just now, with the spring term of court in session, he and Trey were handling all the work themselves. Since the judge was rarely present, the two of them had dealt with the caseload together, dividing it according to which of them had more expertise in a given area.

Jason didn't miss the constant competitive spirit that had existed in the DA's office when he was there. He and Trey were more of a team than he'd ever been with another attorney.

But he did miss the challenge of criminal law. He was beginning to think that, given a choice, a small private practice where he could take on defense cases as they came along might be a good fit for him.

Musing about the future led him, inevitably, to Deidre and Kevin. They wouldn't want to leave Echo Falls. If what he had with Deidre proved to be the real thing, he might be here longer than he'd ever anticipated. That should dismay him, but it didn't.

A discreet tap on the door brought him back to the current moment with all its complications. "Come in," he called.

Evelyn glanced in with a look that said she hoped she hadn't disturbed him. Since he'd been daydreaming, he instantly felt guilty. "Pastor Bennett would like a few minutes, if you can spare the time."

"You mean now?"

"He's waiting." Evelyn lifted her eyebrows. "If you're too busy, I can set up an appointment later."

"No, no, that's all right." He closed the file that lay open on his desk. "Ask him to come right in."

Jase stood, extending his hand, as the young minister came in. Bennett seemed ill at ease, and he darted a swift look around the office before his gaze landed on the day's newspaper, which lay folded on the corner of Jason's desk.

"I heard about the hit-and-run accident near the Morris house." Bennett took the client chair Jason indicated. "Terrible thing."

"Yes, it was." He hadn't come here to talk about Mike Hanlon, Jase guessed.

"I understand you found him. Do the police have any idea who the driver was?"

Jason shrugged. "They don't confide in me." In regard to a search for the driver, that was true enough.

"The newspaper says they're looking for a vehicle with damage to the front end. I suppose there will be evidence they can match to the car."

He nodded, waiting. The man was showing all the symptoms of someone who wasn't sure he wanted to bring up the subject that had brought him here.

In the face of Jase's silence, Bennett seemed compelled to speak. "I guess you're wondering why I'm here." His face flushed. "My wife told me what she said to you."

How did anybody respond to a statement like that? He tried for a neutral but receptive expression.

"I thought… I… She also told me what you said to her. About bringing her concerns to me, I mean."

"I guess she did so."

"Yes, well. It was a shock." His face worked, making him look even younger than his years. "I never knew she…well…"

"Suspected?" He finished the sentence, fearing if he didn't, they'd be here all day.

"There wasn't anything to suspect. I mean, I do admire Deidre. Well, anyone would. But there's never been anything between us at all improper." He straightened as he said it, meeting Jase's gaze steadily. "I never said a word to her that the whole congregation couldn't have heard. I swear it."

"It's not me you need to convince. It's your wife."

Despite Bennett's obvious distress, Jase couldn't find it in himself to feel sorry for the man. If he'd been more mindful of Deidre's situation, he'd never have let her in for the kind of gossip that would lead to the anonymous letter the judge had shown him.

"I have… I mean, I think I have." Bennett stared down at his clasped hands, a picture of misery. "I didn't mean anything. I was trying to give her the pastoral care that…"

"Right." Jason leaned forward. It was obvious what he was holding back. "The truth is that you developed feelings for Mrs. Morris, didn't you?"

A moment passed. Another. Finally Bennett raised his head. His eyes were wet.

"Okay. You seem to know everything. I started having feelings for her. But I never said a word, not one

word. What harm did it do? I just liked to be with her.
To feel like she relied on my advice."

"And while you were doing that, people were talking," he said bluntly.

"No!" He looked honestly startled at the thought.
"No, I'm sure nobody had any idea."

"Somebody had an idea. Somebody wrote at least
one anonymous letter. Maybe more."

Bennett seemed incapable of doing anything but
staring.

"You made things difficult for Mrs. Morris. And
came close to ruining your own marriage. That doesn't
sound harmless to me."

"I'm sorry. Really. I didn't have any idea. I thought…"

"No, you didn't think." Jase let his exasperation
show. "Didn't they teach you anything about bound-
aries in that seminary you went to? You crossed the line,
whether you meant to or not, and other people got hurt."

Bennett wiped his face with the back of his hand, like
a child who was guilty and ashamed. "I should apolo-
gize. To Deidre, to the congregation—"

Jase slapped his hand down on the desk. "No, that's
just what you shouldn't do. Don't you have any common sense? If you go to the congregation with this, it
becomes public property. And Deidre has enough on
her plate without dealing with you feeling sorry for
yourself."

The blunt words seemed to have the impact of a dash
of cold water in the face. Bennett gaped for a moment.
Then he seemed to grab hold of some shreds of his self-
respect. His face firmed.

"Of course. That was a stupid and self-indulgent thing to say." He stood. "You're right. I have to do my best to repair things with my wife. Other than normal interactions at church, I'll stay away from Deidre—Mrs. Morris—altogether. I don't want to cause any more trouble."

"I think that would be the best thing you could do." Jason rose, too. It was easy enough for the man to be sorry. But he didn't know exactly how much damage he'd done Deidre with the judge through that anonymous letter.

At least Bennett could be relieved that this awkward interview seemed over.

Bennett reached the door before he glanced back, a rueful smile lighting his face. "Deidre always treated me like a naive little brother, anyway."

Jason exhaled as the door closed behind him, feeling as if he'd skirted a minefield. At least that aspect of the judge's suspicions had been allayed. And if he accepted that Dixie's death had nothing to do with her presence in Deidre's house, his whole case against Deidre's fitness as a mother fell to pieces.

Regardless of the judge's opinion, Jason knew that his own moment of truth had arrived. He had to speak privately with the man, tell him what he'd found and say he was finished with this. If that cost him this position, well, so be it. Then, at least, he could go to Deidre with a clean conscience.

CHAPTER EIGHTEEN

KEVIN HAD WOKEN in the night with another nightmare. While he seemed his usual sunny self this morning, Deidre felt as if she'd been pulled through a knothole backward. The phrase her grandmother used to say brought a wry smile to her face. Sometimes those old expressions caught the feeling perfectly.

At the moment he was busy putting together a complicated structure with his linking blocks, humming to himself as he often did when his mind was engaged. Sometimes she imagined him off at college, still humming while preoccupied with final exams.

She tried to focus on the updates she was making to the business website, but her brain seemed hopelessly fuzzed from lack of sleep. The events of the previous night played themselves over and over in her mind.

That visit from Mike Hanlon had been so frightening at the time that in spite of repeating the story both to the police and to Jason, she still hadn't fully absorbed it. Little details kept resurfacing in her thoughts, like the smell of stale beer that clung to Hanlon's clothes.

He never touches the hard stuff, but he can turn into a mean drunk on four or five beers.

She'd forgotten that conversation with Dixie, but it

came back to her now. Funny, how Dixie had talked about her brief marriage with such detachment, as if it had happened to someone else.

Deidre frowned at a close-up photo of a double wedding ring quilt. In retrospect Dixie's attitude had been odd. She seemed to have no trouble separating her essential self from the things that happened to her.

One thing was certain—Dixie had never expressed any fear of Mike. She'd claimed that the only time he'd tried to get rough with her, she'd hit him with the nearest hard object, which had happened to be an aluminum skillet.

Dented the skillet and didn't even raise a lump on his hard head. I told him next time I'd use a cast-iron one.

No, Dixie wouldn't have been afraid if Mike had come to the door that evening and said he wanted to talk. That part of the chief's reconstruction made sense, but she still wasn't sure of the rest of it.

Granted, Hanlon could have been the person who'd gotten into the house and searched through the boxes of Dixie's belongings. He probably had been, no matter who else had done what. He'd passed by when she and Judith had carried the boxes home, and he'd easily guess they were from Dixie's place.

But that still didn't explain what he'd been looking for. That mention of insurance—she just didn't buy that as an explanation. He couldn't have thought Dixie had insured her life and named him as beneficiary. That was such an un-Dixie-like thing to do.

Deidre pushed her chair back and stared at the single box, now sitting under the table. Once she'd been through both of them, she'd been able to combine the contents in one overstuffed box. It looked perfectly innocent.

Jason had cautioned her not to get rid of anything, and she wouldn't, but that didn't mean she couldn't have yet another look through the contents herself. She'd already searched several times without finding anything that seemed pertinent, but maybe she was missing something.

Unlikely. Presumably Hanlon had known what he'd been looking for, and he hadn't found it. So how could she?

Assuring herself that Kevin was completely occupied, she pulled out the box and began setting the contents out, one by one, on the table. Miscellaneous papers, none of which seemed important now but should probably be kept. A packet of photos, stuffed into a manila envelope. Those she emptied out onto the table.

Most of them were fairly recent—pictures of Dixie with Kevin riding the carousel at last year's fair, a snap of him on the first day of kindergarten, one of the falls, several with the other servers at the restaurant, laughing it up after a long shift probably.

Some went further back, though. Funny that Dixie had never put those in an album, but Dixie had laughed at Deidre's collection of photo albums. Deidre had one for each year, and they lined a bottom shelf in the living room cabinet.

Dixie wasn't a saver, she'd always insisted, but apparently these were important enough that she hadn't wanted to throw them away.

Deidre spread them out and studied each one. Most of them were from Dixie's high school years, after she'd left Echo Falls, showing Dixie clowning with a number of people. Deidre studied the young faces. Had Dixie stayed in touch with any of those high school friends? She'd never seen any indication of it, but here were the photos to prove she'd cared enough to hang on to them.

At the bottom of the stack were a few photos dating back to Dixie's life in Echo Falls, including a class picture when they'd been about nine or ten, standing in a self-conscious row on the steps of the elementary school. There was one of her and Dixie dressed up for their first dance.

That made her smile, because the same picture was in one of her albums. They'd still been little girls then, even though they'd thought themselves so grown-up.

The last of the batch had to have been the summer they were twelve, judging by the fact that while Deidre still looked like a child, Dixie had suddenly blossomed into a young woman. Deidre held it up, looking at it closely. They'd been in the woods, with the stream in the background.

Had it been one of their excursions to the falls? She'd stood tall for the photo, trying to match Dixie's height, while Dixie had her arms across her chest, as if trying to hide her breasts.

Billy had probably taken the picture. He'd usually accompanied them on their hikes, trailing along behind or darting off into the woods in search of something, coming back with a leaf or a blossom for them to admire, much the way Kevin did. The photo had the slightly crooked look that marked his attempts at photography.

And that was it for photographs. She couldn't see that any of them had any relevance to Dixie's murder. Pushing them back into the envelope, she laid it aside. Jason was welcome to look through them, but it wouldn't help.

At the bottom of the box was Dixie's collection of china pigs. For someone who'd insisted on traveling light, Dixie had had a weakness for the useless objects, ranging in size from a small piggy bank to an assortment of six-inch figures with silly expressions and odd hats, all the way up to a large one intended to grace a flower bed.

She picked up a pig wearing a graduation mortarboard. Dixie had won it at the county fair, throwing baseballs at milk bottles, and had been inordinately proud of it, saying it was the only thing she'd ever won.

Memory produced an image of the two of them, wandering from stall to stall at the fair, with Dixie clutching the pig and saying he was her good-luck charm.

Her reverie was cut short by the ringing of the doorbell. Kevin glanced up and then returned to his construction, his humming uninterrupted.

To her astonishment, it was the judge. He wasn't one to drop by, and generally called first, as if an appointment were needed. But here he was, and Deidre decided to take that as an olive branch.

"Please, come in." She turned to Kevin. "Look, Kev, your grandfather stopped by to visit."

Kevin scrambled to his feet, thank goodness, making her feel that her efforts to teach manners hadn't been entirely in vain.

"Hi, Grandfather. Want to see what I'm making? It's going to be a space station."

Franklin's face softened in the indulgent smile he wore just for Kevin. "That sounds great." He squatted next to the stack of blocks. "Your daddy used to make airports and cities when he was your age."

The tension that had seized Deidre's stomach at the sight of the judge eased. She appreciated it when Kevin's grandfather made an effort to interact with him this way, but it happened all too seldom. Usually the judge had some other agenda when he came over, and she suspected that he had little tolerance for the slightly untidy coziness that characterized her home.

Besides, each time they'd talked recently, there had been a barrier between them. He'd reiterated his desire to have them move in each time, and she'd continued to say no. But she hadn't quite been able to bring up Sylvia's idea that he wanted to take Kevin away.

Smiling, she left the two of them alone, retreating to the workroom. She heard their voices from there, but couldn't quite distinguish the words. If only the judge could always be this way, life would be easier for all of them.

He hadn't immediately mentioned his plans for them to move in with him and Sylvia, and she hoped maybe today was the day when he wouldn't press her.

But before she could get comfortable with that thought, the judge joined her. He stood for a moment, surveying the objects from Dixie's collection that still stood on the worktable.

"Collecting things for a yard sale?" he asked.

"Not exactly." She didn't want to bring up Dixie and risk causing a flare-up of his disapproval. "I'm glad you stopped over to see Kevin. There's plenty of time to spend with him. He doesn't have to get ready for kindergarten for another half hour."

"It's always a joy to see my grandson, but he said that he has to see a new doctor next week. Is something wrong?"

Deidre's heart sank. Why hadn't she realized Kevin might mention it? Maybe she shouldn't have told him at all, but she hadn't wanted to spring it on him.

"It's nothing to be alarmed about. But I talked to the doctor about those nightmares I told you about, and she felt I should make an appointment with a child psychologist for Kevin. She thinks it will help him adjust to the trauma of the accident to talk with a professional a time or two."

He was already frowning. "I don't see why. The boy seems perfectly well-adjusted to me. It's not as if he even remembers what happened."

"Not consciously, no." This was a conversation she'd hoped to avoid having with him, but she couldn't dodge it now that it had come up. "But he's been having nightmares nearly every night. The doctor feels that even if he doesn't consciously remember, the memories are there, surfacing and upsetting him when he's asleep."

"Sounds like a lot of psychological babble to me." The frown grew heavier. "What is this child psychologist supposed to do about it? Make him remember? It seems to me that's the worst thing for Kevin."

"The aim isn't to force him to remember, but just to get at the fear that is causing his nightmares. That way he can deal with it instead of having bad dreams every night."

"All children have nightmares," the judge said with authority. "I remember Frank at that age, having night-

mares every time his mother let him watch an unsuitable program. They grow out of them."

"Yes, normally, but this isn't a normal situation."
She tried to hold on to a calmness she didn't feel. "The
nightmares are terrifying, even though he doesn't yet
remember them the next day."

"Yet?" His tone was sharp.

"I don't know for sure, but this might mean the memories of that night are beginning to come back. I feel
strongly that we need to have some expert advice on
how to handle that."

She hoped that "we" would mollify him. She wanted
to include Kevin's grandparents, but not at the cost of
what was best for him.

"Maybe I'm prejudiced, but I've never seen a psychologist do much good. Look at all the counseling
Sylvia has had over the years. If you wait, the situation
may resolve itself."

She wasn't really surprised that the judge didn't think
this was a good idea. Proud, conservative, controlling...
He already considered Sylvia's drinking an embarrassing weakness. He'd hate to have it said that his only
grandchild had psychological problems.

And he cared about Kevin. She'd never doubted that,
which made it harder to disagree with him on this, especially when she wasn't as confident as she'd like to be.

"I understand your concerns. Really. I've worried
about this, too. But I think I should at least keep the
appointment and talk to the psychologist about it. If
I'm not convinced it will help, I won't go on with it."

He nodded, seeming to accept her words. But he'd

planted even more doubts in her mind. This was uncharted territory, and without Frank, she had to decide on her own.

JASON HADN'T YET been able to catch the judge alone, and the office day was nearly over. When questioned, Evelyn seemed to assume His Honor was heading straight home. She clearly intended to do the same since she stood at her desk, bag strap already on her shoulder.

Jason summoned a smile. "That's fine. I'll speak to him later. You'd better get on home."

"If you're sure." Her face cleared, and she was already headed for the door as she spoke.

Trey had left a good half hour ago, citing a dinner date, so he was alone in the office. Well, if the judge wouldn't come to him, he'd go to the judge. With no children in the house, it was safe to assume they didn't have dinner this early. On the one occasion that the judge had invited him to a get-acquainted dinner, it had been at seven. And Jason's itchy conscience wasn't going to leave him alone until this was accomplished.

The drive to the judge's home was uphill. As seemed to be true most places, the wealthy chose to put their residences on an elevation, presumably so they could look down on the rest of creation. Rather than buzzing to have the gate opened to the circular driveway, he parked on the street and walked up to the house.

The house was elegant and classic in style—sort of Greek Revival updated. He crossed the portico and rang the bell. Who knew if they'd even hear a knock, given how large the house was?

He tried to imagine a two-wheeler with training

wheels leaning against a pillar, or a skateboard on the step. Impossible. The house itself would reject any such intrusion, he suspected.

Just as he was about to ring again, the door was opened by the woman he'd seen on his previous visit— Madge Hepple, he recalled. "Evening, Mrs. Hepple. Is Judge Morris at home? Jason Glassman to see him."

"Of course, Mr. Glassman." She didn't look particularly welcoming, but that might be because he'd come unannounced. "Just wait for a moment, until I see if the judge is available to see you now."

Leaving him standing there, she trotted off toward the room he knew was the judge's study. He glanced around. Marble and more marble.

He'd hate to think of Kevin taking a tumble down those stairs. He could understand Deidre's aversion to moving in here. Apart from everything else, the atmosphere seemed to impose quiet on visitors. Impossible to picture a child sliding down the banister or playing hide-and-seek in the hall.

And yet Frank had grown up here. Maybe it had been different when he was a boy. Or perhaps there was some more welcoming part of the house he had yet to see.

Mrs. Hepple emerged from the study, pulling the door partially closed behind her. "Judge Morris will see you now," she announced, in tones that seemed reminiscent of a dentist's office receptionist's.

Jason gave her a deliberate smile, wondering what it would take to pierce that formal manner. "Thank you, Mrs. Hepple."

He entered, and she closed the door noiselessly behind him. He'd give a lot to know if she still stood on the other side, listening.

"Jason. I wasn't expecting you." Judge Morris half rose, nodding toward a chair, and then dropped back heavily into a richly padded leather desk chair. It struck Jason that for the first time since he'd met him, the judge looked his age. Tension highlighted every line of his face, and his eyelids drooped as if he were too tired to keep his eyes open.

"I'm sorry to trouble you at home." He made the routine apology as he took a seat. He'd actually rather stand, given what he had to say, but that would be too pointed.

As it were, this conversation would be short, even if it wasn't sweet. No matter how the judge reacted to his statement, there was nothing he could do or say that would change anything as far as Jason was concerned.

Morris regarded him for a moment before he spoke. "I take it this is a private matter, not something that concerns the firm."

"Yes." *Keep it simple and short*, he reminded himself. Sharing facts, not feelings. "I've done as you asked in regard to your daughter-in-law. I haven't found a shred of evidence that would lead anyone to believe that Deidre is unfit to raise her son."

The heavy-lidded eyes stared at him. "What about the anonymous letter? Are you forgetting that?"

"No, sir. But you know yourself that an anonymous letter is hardly evidence, and I can't imagine trying to present it in a courtroom. I've never seen Pastor Bennett act in anything but a pastoral role toward your daughter-in-law." He sucked in a breath, knowing he needed to say more. "I spoke with Bennett myself. He admitted that he had developed…an admiration, he said, for Deidre. He enjoyed feeling that she relied on him. A feeling that I suspect was largely imaginary."

"If he admits he has improper feelings for my son's widow, haven't you considered that she may return them?" It was an example of the judge's questioning style—quick and incisive.

But he was already shaking his head. "I've observed them together. I would say she treats him as she does everyone else. And he said himself that she acts as if he were a naive little brother."

"He may be lying to protect her." But the judge's decisiveness had drained away, and he leaned his head on his hand. The statement seemed like a halfhearted effort.

Jason shook his head again, mustering a slight smile. "Bennett made himself look foolish with that admission. He's young and very conscious of his dignity. He wouldn't say that if he could possibly pretend anything else."

"A woman still died in her house—a woman she never should have entrusted with my grandson." A flush of anger brightened his face. "Even if she wasn't unfaithful to my son, Deidre certainly exercised poor judgment in her friends and put Kevin in jeopardy."

This was going to require careful handling. He couldn't let any hints of his own doubts show.

"I'm sure you're aware that the police seem convinced that Dixie James was killed by her ex-husband. What happened was between the two of them and could have happened anywhere. It was just bad luck that it happened to be that particular evening, when she was at your daughter-in-law's house. If you're thinking of taking this matter to court, you know yourself how a judge is going to view it."

Judge Morris didn't respond. In fact, he seemed to have stopped paying attention altogether. He watched the pen he held in one hand, making intersecting circles on the pristine blotter on the desk.

Apparently it was up to Jase. "My best advice to you is to drop the entire idea of pressing Deidre and Kevin to move in here. Right now you have a good situation in which you can see your grandson as much as you want. If you persist, you could turn Deidre against you entirely, and she might make it very difficult for you to have access to the boy."

Knowing Deidre, he didn't think she'd do that, but it was just as well to remind the judge that it was a possibility.

When the silence stretched on too long for comfort, he was forced to speak again. "I believe that I've fulfilled the task I agreed to. If my employment in the firm was conditional on resolving it to your satisfaction, I can turn my caseload over to Trey and be gone in a couple of days."

Judge Morris waved that away, but Jason thought his mind was elsewhere. "No, of course not. You're doing a good job, and the firm needs you. Perhaps it was futile to set about this to begin with." He touched the silver-mounted photograph of Frank that sat on his desk. "I hoped to make amends to my son, but it's too late. Too late."

Jason let himself relax, only now realizing how keyed up he'd been since he walked in the door. It was done. Now he had a chance at a fresh start. With Deidre.

DEIDRE WAS SURPRISED to find Sylvia at her door that evening. "Sylvia, how nice." She peered beyond her. Madge Hepple's car sat in the driveway, but Madge was nowhere to be seen. "Did you drive yourself?"

"I had to." Sylvia hurried into the living room, cast a glance at the front windows and spun toward the kitchen.

Bemused, Deidre followed her mother-in-law. She didn't care where they visited, and it was less likely Kevin would hear them talking and pop out of bed if they were away from the stairs. "I don't understand. Doesn't Madge usually drive you when you want to go somewhere?"

Sylvia went into the workroom and drew the shades on the windows. A little shiver slid down Deidre's spine. Was Sylvia on the verge of one of what the judge referred to as her nervous breakdowns?

"I couldn't let her know what I was doing. Nobody must know I came here tonight." She turned to Deidre, her eyes very bright. "Promise me."

That glittering gaze alarmed her. "Yes, all right. I promise."

She took Sylvia's arm and led her to a chair, pulling another up next to it. "Now. Tell me what's wrong."

"I had to see you, and I didn't want Madge spying on me." She giggled, giving Deidre a sidelong look. "I couldn't get my car out because Franklin keeps the garage locked, so I watched for my chance and took Madge's keys. She really shouldn't be so careless with them."

This last bit was said with a righteous air. Deidre decided not to comment on that statement. There would be too many potholes to avoid.

"Well, I'm glad you're here, in any case. Kevin is already in bed, but we can have a good chat." She patted the woman's heavily veined hand. "What's on your mind?"

But Sylvia's gaze was darting around the workroom. It lighted on the desk, and Deidre realized, too late, that the necklace was lying out. Naturally that was the first thing Sylvia zeroed in on.

"My necklace! I wondered where it had gotten to." She scooped it up and held it against the blue sweater she wore, where it looked incongruous. The diamond piece really needed a cocktail dress or a gown to show it off.

"Yes, I...I found it." Her mind scampered through possible explanations and didn't find any. Anything but the truth, it seemed.

But Sylvia didn't even ask the question, instead focusing on the sparkling of the diamonds.

"I never go anywhere suitable to wear it these days. I think the last time I had it on was the bar association's Christmas dinner. Remember, Deidre? I wore my lace dress."

"Yes, I remember." The county bar association had one gala event per year, always during the holiday season. "You looked lovely."

"That was a nice night." She let the necklace drop into her lap. "I wish…" She let that trail off, and tears formed in her eyes.

Deidre took her hand in a warm clasp, trying to communicate calm and comfort. "What do you wish?"

Sylvia shook her head and blotted the tears away carefully. "I'm being foolish. That isn't why I came. I had to come." She grasped their linked hands, her fingers like talons. "I had to tell you. To warn you."

The chill settled in the pit of her stomach. "Warn me about what?"

"About *who*." For a moment Sylvia seemed almost rational. Composed in a way Deidre hadn't seen in years. "You've gotten close, but you mustn't trust him."

She could only stare, trying to understand. "Who are you talking about?"

"Jason Glassman, of course. You can't trust him." Sylvia sounded perfectly sensible even as the outrageous words were spoken. "He's working for Franklin."

Deidre steadied. "He works at the office, Sylvia. He took Frank's place in the firm. You knew that, didn't you?"

But Sylvia was shaking her head. "No, no. That's not what I mean." She closed her eyes, seeming to struggle for control. "You have to listen. I heard them. Franklin and that Glassman. Tonight. They were talking in the study. I wanted to know what was happening, so I slipped into the sitting room. I was clever. I eased the door open so quietly they never knew. Then I could hear perfectly."

The room spun around her before returning to stability. Was this real, or a product of Sylvia's disordered imagination?

"What were they saying?" If she knew what Sylvia thought she'd heard, she'd be able to judge.

"Glassman said he'd done everything Franklin told him. He'd tried to find something against you. I guess he didn't, because he thought Franklin would fire him."

Deidre pressed her fingers against her lips, trying to sort this out. It couldn't be true. The implication was that Jason had been working against her all the time he'd been acting as if he cared. Even worse, he'd let Kevin become fond of him, start to rely on him.

"No." The word burst from her. "It can't be. You must have misunderstood."

Sylvia gave her a pitying look. "You think I've been drinking again. That I imagined it all. But I didn't. It happened just the way I said." Her grip tightened painfully. "That's why I had to come. I had to warn you not to trust him. He'd help Franklin take Kevin away from you."

The pain in her heart was so real that Deidre pressed her hand against her chest. Was this what it felt like when your heart broke?

Betrayal. Jason had talked about how the woman he'd loved had betrayed him. Had that even been real, or just a ploy to touch her emotions?

"Sylvia, you have to help me." She leaned toward the older woman, her eyes intent on her face. "If this is real, if Franklin is trying to take Kevin away from me, you have to help me."

Sylvia's gaze faltered. "I don't… How can I? I can't do anything."

"Of course you can. You'd have to agree if he tried to bring suit to be declared Kevin's guardian." Just saying the words was difficult. "You have to stand up against him. Tell him Kevin belongs with me. That's what you think, isn't it?"

"You're a good mother." Sylvia's eyes filled with tears. "I wasn't a good mother to Frankie. I was too weak. I let Franklin drive him away with all his demands."

It took all the strength she had to remain calm. "Frank loved you. You know that. You have to help me now, for Frankie's sake. For Kevin's sake."

But Sylvia had lost whatever poise she'd mustered. The impetus that had brought her here had spent itself, and she seemed to sag into herself. "I can't. You know I can't. How can I stand up against Franklin?" The words poured out. "He wouldn't let me. He'd have me locked up in that hospital again." Fear flooded her face. "Don't ask me. I can't."

She dissolved in tears. Deidre put her arms around her mother-in-law and faced the truth. Sylvia couldn't help her. Jason… A knife pierced her heart. Jason had betrayed her. There had never been anything real between them. All that was left was misery.

She had to face the judge's plans alone.

CHAPTER NINETEEN

BY THE NEXT AFTERNOON, Jason couldn't possibly wait any longer to see Deidre. He'd been so eager to see her the previous evening without his deception weighing on his mind that at first he hadn't noticed how strained she'd sounded on the phone.

It had been nothing, she'd insisted. A headache, that's all. Too many sleepless nights, and Kevin might well be up in the wee hours again. She was going to bed early.

Now that he thought through that short conversation, he saw what he should have seen immediately. She'd given a few too many excuses for any one of them to be the entire truth. With a client or a witness, he'd have seen that instantly. He didn't seem able to think rationally where Deidre was concerned.

He had to see her, to tell her...what? If he came out with the truth about his deal with the judge at this late date, how could she—how could anyone—forgive?

At least this was a good time to catch her alone. Kevin would be at kindergarten, so he'd have the privacy he needed. Everything was falling into place, so why wasn't he relieved?

Jase's fingers tightened on the steering wheel as he slowed in front of the house. He'd thought getting things straight with the judge would be enough, but it wasn't, and he had to stop kidding himself. He had to tell Deidre what he'd done, or their relationship would be built on a lie.

Parking the car, he walked to the door, formulating opening sentences in his mind. If he could prepare an argument for the court when a man's life and liberty were at stake, he ought to be able to find a way to say he was sorry for what he'd done.

As it turned out, he didn't need any of the possible approaches, because the instant Deidre opened the door and looked at him, reproach and pain filling her clear blue eyes, he understood. She already knew.

"Deidre…"

She clutched the door as if to prevent him from entering. "Just tell me one thing. Is it true? Have you been conspiring with the judge to take my son away?"

The words were a blow straight to his heart. "Deidre, you have to let me explain." He grabbed the door when she would have closed it. "Please. It's not what you think."

"No? Do you deny that you were spying on me for Judge Morris?"

"No." He forced the word out between stiff lips and saw her whiten as if he'd struck her. "But it's not as simple as that makes it sound. At least give me five minutes to explain. That's all. Just five minutes. Then I'll go."

For an instant she held out against him. Then she took a step back and opened the door. "Five minutes."

Jase moved inside, buying time by closing the door carefully behind him. He'd presented arguments with a time limit before. Why should this be any different?

Because it matters, a voice whispered in the back of

his mind. *It matters more than anything you've done before in your life.*

"Five minutes," she reminded him. "The clock is ticking."

"Do we have to stand here in the hallway for this?"

Her face tightened. "You've come too far into our lives already. I don't want you any further. So talk."

Nothing but the truth would do now. He blew out a breath.

"You know what my situation was before the judge offered me a position. I told you about it. I'd begun to think I'd never work again when he appeared. He offered me a lifeline."

"With strings attached," she snapped. "A job in exchange for spying on me, gaining my confidence, making me think…"

She broke off, pressing her lips together, and crossed her arms over her chest in a classic protective posture.

"Not then," he said quickly. "Not when he offered me the position. He said he was doing it because I'd been a law school colleague of Frank's, and I believed him."

She didn't look as if she felt the same about him. "So when? When did he make you an offer you couldn't refuse? Or maybe didn't want to refuse."

No protestations would do any good right now. "After I accepted the job, he called me a few days later. Said he was worried about his grandson's well-being. Said that he suspected you of being an unfit mother."

If possible, she went even paler. "And you believed him."

"I hadn't even met you then. And I wasn't exactly in any shape to believe anything good about any woman."

He spared a brief thought for Leslie, who seemed so unimportant now. "He said that Frank had believed you were being unfaithful to him."

He saw the blow of that land, saw her reel from it and then grab hold of some core of strength.

"Frank can't have thought that. If anything…" She stopped. Shook her head. "In any event, you bought it."

"I didn't have any reason not to believe him. The man's a respected judge. He'd just given me a chance when no one else would. And he made it sound so innocuous. Just keep an eye on you and watch for anything that he could use for leverage to get you and Kevin to move into his house. So he could watch over his grandson."

"And you agreed. You worked your way into my confidence at a time when I was the most vulnerable I've ever been in my life."

That was the crux of it for her, he knew. The idea that he'd used Kevin's injury to further the judge's aims. He wanted to take her hands but sensed her precarious grip on her self-control would explode if he touched her.

"If you don't believe anything else, at least believe this—when I saw Kevin lying there hurt, helping him was the only thing on my mind. Afterward, at the hospital, I talked to the judge. I assumed he'd give the whole thing up then." He shrugged. "But he didn't. He made it sound so logical. You would need someone to run interference with the police. And he had to be assured that Kevin's injury hadn't come about because of some careless action of yours."

"Such as having a friend he didn't approve of." A

spasm of pain crossed her face at the thought of Dixie, but at least she seemed to be listening.

"I guess that's true, but I didn't know that. Believe it or not, I did want to help you. Sensing your pain over Kevin, seeing him lie there so vulnerable and helpless— it touched something in me. I think that's when I started to have doubts. The more I got to know you, the surer I was that he was wrong. You're a good mother."

He dared to move a step closer to her...close enough to catch the faint, elusive scent of her. "Deidre, you have to believe me. My feelings for you are real. If you doubt everything else, at least you have to believe that."

"Do I?" Deidre closed her eyes briefly, and he feared she couldn't stand to look at him. "If what you say is true, why didn't you tell me a long time ago?"

Pain clutched his heart. This was the question he didn't want to answer, even for himself. "I persuaded myself that you needed me, and that if I told you, you'd shut me out. I couldn't let that happen."

She just stared at him, waiting.

"Don't you think I wish I'd told you a dozen times over?" Passion overflowed into his voice. "I just kept lying to myself, when all the time it was me. I couldn't trust. I couldn't let go. I had to protect myself."

He'd been a fool. If he'd told her to begin with, been as honest with her as she was with him, she'd have forgiven him. Now it was too late.

"If you'd told me then..." He saw the muscles of her neck move as she struggled to swallow. "You didn't. You didn't just hurt me. You hurt Kevin by letting him grow to love you." She turned away, as if she didn't want him to see her face. "Go away, Jason. Don't come back."

She couldn't forgive him. Ever. Deidre was the most honest person he'd ever known, and he hadn't trusted her enough to be honest in return. He deserved what he got. Whether he still had a job with the judge's firm or not, it was time he left Echo Falls behind.

DEIDRE WENT THROUGH the rest of the day on autopilot. She continued to smile and talk, fixed supper, helped Kevin figure out the complexities of printing the alphabet and acted as if nothing was wrong.

But that was all on the surface. Inside...inside she was a wreck. Her heart lay in little pieces, and a nameless dread filled her.

Maybe not so nameless. So much had happened that she still hadn't absorbed Sylvia's conviction that the judge intended to get hold of Kevin, no matter what he had to do to achieve that. Each time she tried to think about it, she started to shake.

Enough, she ordered herself. She could be as strong as she had to be where Kevin's happiness was at stake. The judge was never going to get custody of her son, not if she had to fight him in every court in the land.

Tomorrow she'd contact an attorney—one safely removed from the judge's sphere of influence. She'd tell him or her the whole story. She'd been a good mother and a faithful wife. No one could possibly prove otherwise.

Faithful. Something started hurting where her heart used to be before it was shattered. Had Frank really believed that she'd been untrue to him? He couldn't have.

And yet…if he had had an affair with her best friend, who could say what he might have convinced himself of in order to justify his own betrayal?

The questions went around and around in her mind like the horses on a carousel, all while she was putting Kevin to bed, tucking him in, sharing just one more story. It was when she was going back downstairs that something occurred to her.

In all the things Sylvia had said, there'd been one thing so seemingly unimportant that it had slipped to the back of her mind. When she'd reminisced about the necklace, Sylvia had talked about wearing it for the bar association Christmas gala. But she couldn't have—at least not this past event. Frank had been gone by then. He couldn't have given the necklace to Dixie if Sylvia had worn it then.

Sylvia must have meant the previous year. That had to be it. The gala was an annual event, much the same from one year to the next. They seemed to blur together in Deidre's mind…the same people, the same venue, the same decorations, even the same menu for the most part, unless someone very daring had been on the committee.

Deidre walked around the downstairs, unable to settle. She couldn't bear to be on the side of the house that looked out toward Jason's apartment… It was as if she was sensitive even to the building's nearness.

She started to unload the dishwasher, but the dishes were still too hot. Besides, she felt oddly exposed under the kitchen's overhead light. In contrast, the darkness outside pressed against the windows.

If Chief Carmichaels was right, there was nothing to be afraid of now. Hanlon had killed Dixie and then been killed himself by the hit-and-run driver who hadn't yet been identified.

That in itself seemed odd. There wasn't much traffic down that road. She'd think, when the police had checked the possible vehicles, they'd have come up with something. Or someone would have come forward who'd been on the road at the relevant time.

She still couldn't quite buy that explanation. Even assuming Hanlon had been the person who'd broken into her house, what had he been after? And why had she sensed someone watching her that day when she'd walked home from Kevin's school? The same someone who'd been on the porch? Possibly Hanlon, watching for his chance to get in.

It couldn't have been Billy on the front porch. There hadn't been time for him to get around the house. Her imagination? A stray dog? The wind?

She could think of a dozen explanations, but none of them satisfied her.

Giving up in the kitchen, Deidre walked back into the living room, flicking the television to a news channel. She wasn't in the mood for canned laughter, but maybe hearing about the world's woes would keep her mind off her own.

After a few minutes of floods, tornadoes and unrest, she was ready for anything else. Her gaze fell on the row of photo albums that Dixie had laughed at, teasing her about preserving pictures the old-fashioned way. But if she wanted to browse through a year's happenings, she'd rather do it in an album than on the computer. Besides, Kevin loved looking through them, especially at the pictures of himself when he was small.

Smaller, as far as she was concerned. He was still a very little boy, though he'd never admit it.

And he was going to be hurt when he realized that Jason had walked out of his life so abruptly. Yet another hurt that she found impossible to fix… Scraped knees were definitely easier than emotional wounds.

Needing to do something, she pulled out the album for the year before last and settled back in her chair with it on her lap. Just to satisfy that little niggling question in her mind, she flipped through to the photos from December. She'd find that was the year that Sylvia had worn her lace dress with the diamond pendant.

But she didn't. That year, the image of the four of them at the event showed Sylvia in her turquoise silk dress with her pearls. Thoughts roiling, Deidre went back to the shelf and drew out last year's album. She balanced the two books, turning the pages impatiently until she found photos from the Christmas event.

This time there were just the three of them in the photo. Frank had been gone for months, and she'd felt odd about going to the gala without him. But Sylvia had begged her to go along for moral support—and the image clearly showed Sylvia wearing her lace dress with the diamond pendant.

Deidre set the books down carefully on the ottoman, feeling as if the slightest untoward movement might send her off her balance entirely. Sylvia had the necklace in her possession in December. That meant Frank couldn't possibly have given it to Dixie.

Laughter and tears fought for supremacy. She'd been wrong. Frank hadn't been involved with Dixie. She could think of Frank as he had been—a normal, imperfect being who had loved her and loved their son.

She wiped away tears with her fingers. The pain of betrayal was erased from her marriage. Unfortunately, there was no doubt of the betrayal she'd suffered at Jason's hands.

Deidre wrenched her mind away from that memory, forcing herself to concentrate on the necklace. How had it come into Dixie's possession? Dixie had been a lot of things, but not a thief. Besides, she'd never, so far as Deidre knew, been inside the house on the hill.

Her thoughts tumbled over each other. And then they froze. She froze, staring at the door. Hearing the familiar click of the key in the lock. Watching as the knob was turned from the outside.

The door opened. Judge Morris stepped quietly inside and just as quietly closed the door behind him.

Deidre could only stare blankly at him as thoughts and ideas jostled with each other and then fell into an inescapable pattern. Frank hadn't given the necklace to Dixie. The judge had.

JASON GAZED AROUND the small apartment that had become home during his time in Echo Falls. It was nothing like the upscale apartment he'd had in the city, but he'd been comfortable here.

He felt the urge to start packing, but that wasn't really practical. Professional etiquette dictated that he should notify the judge that he was leaving before he did anything else. He'd tell him when—but not why, that was certain.

There would be things to clear up at the office, cases to transfer back to Trey, who wouldn't be happy with this turn of events. Any thoughts of getting in the car and driving as far and as fast as he could would have to be abandoned. He had responsibilities, odd as that seemed.

Would Deidre allow him to say goodbye to Kevin? He doubted it, but at least he could send the boy a card or a note, just to let him know that he'd valued their friendship.

First things first. The judge had to be told, and there was no point in delaying it. He could drive over to the house now and settle the matter. Doing it now had the advantage of allowing him to leave immediately. If he waited to tell him at the office tomorrow, he'd still have to be around most of the day.

He drove through Echo Falls's quiet streets, still amazed at how tranquil it was after dark. With the shops and businesses closed, people were absorbed in their own activities at home.

At least he'd accomplished one positive thing, to combat all the negativity he'd caused here. From what he'd said last night, the judge had given up his plans to either coerce Deidre into moving in with them or sue for custody of Kevin. Deidre could relax on that score. Somehow that wasn't as comforting as it should be.

Was he really that selfish that he couldn't just be happy for her? Or was it a niggling little sense of doubt telling him that Judge Morris would never give up on what he wanted?

Again parking at the curb, Jason strode to the door. He wanted to get this over with, and he could only hope the judge wasn't going to be difficult about it. He rang the doorbell. Waited. Rang again. Waited some more.

What was going on? Surely the housekeeper would

be there, if no one else was. The hall light gleamed through the long, etched glass windows on either side of the double front doors, but he didn't hear any movement.

Determined not to give up, he put his thumb on the bell and kept it there. Finally, he was rewarded by the sound of hesitant steps on the marble floor. The door opened, and Sylvia Morris peered out uncertainly.

"Is the judge…" He stopped when he got a good look at her face. She'd been weeping, her face red and blotchy with the tears.

She grabbed his arm, shaking it. "You have to stop him. Please. Stop him."

He felt her nails digging into his skin and put his hand over hers. "Easy. You're upset. Can you tell me what's wrong? Stop who?"

"Franklin. He has to be stopped. I tried, but I can't. You have to stop him."

Was this the alcohol talking? He wasn't sure, but even if it was, that didn't mean there wasn't cause to be shaken.

He grasped the woman by the shoulders, resisting the impulse to shake her. "Tell me where the judge is. What is he doing that has to be stopped?"

Sylvia let out another choked sob. "Deidre. He's gone to Deidre's. I've never seen him like that. He frightened me. You have to help Deidre. I should have, and I didn't, and now I don't know what he's doing." Her voice rose. "I'm so afraid. Help them."

His heart had started pumping at the urgency in her manner. "I will. I'm going." He spun and ran back toward his car.

"Warn her!" Sylvia cried behind him, her voice high and uncontrolled. "Warn her!"

He had to get to Deidre. He accelerated down the street, taking the corner far too fast. It wouldn't do to be stopped by an accident now. Not when he was filled with a nameless dread for Deidre's safety.

He went through the traffic light on the corner by the police station. If a patrol car started to follow him, that was fine. He'd lead them right to Deidre's.

It didn't make sense. Was he seriously thinking that Deidre was in danger from a pillar of the legal establishment like Judge Franklin Morris? But he was beyond deeming anything impossible at this point. Sylvia's fear had been infectious. It rode along with him, impelling him faster and faster.

He spun into the driveway at the apartment and ran for the gap in the hedge, leaving the car door hanging open. He was halfway through when his outstretched hand touched something.

No. Someone. In another instant he recognized Billy. He yanked him out of the shelter of the hedge, pulling him into the yard.

"What are you doing here? Are you spying on Deidre?"

Billy's face crunched as if he was trying to hold back tears. "I followed him. He's in there. In there with her. You have to help."

CHAPTER TWENTY

SHE MUST BE WRONG. That was all Deidre could think as she stared at the judge. He was so dignified, so distinguished, so essentially self-disciplined that it was impossible to envision him embarking on a sordid affair right in his own backyard.

But if not, how did she explain Dixie's possession of the necklace?

In any event, she couldn't let him know what she was thinking. The album still lay open to the photos from the bar association dinner, but he couldn't have any idea what that meant to her.

"You startled me." Astonishing that her voice sounded so ordinary. "I wasn't expecting you to stop by. I'm afraid Kevin is already in bed."

He moved toward her with what seemed to be his usual assurance. But was it her imagination that some tiny fissures showed in his facade?

"Yes, I realized he'd be asleep. I want to talk to you."

"Please, sit down." She gestured toward the sofa, trying to convince herself that there was nothing odd about this visit.

The judge ignored the suggestion, stopping at the edge of the living room area rug as if he didn't want to come any closer to her. "Are you still determined to take Kevin to the child psychologist?"

Deidre blinked. Whatever she'd expected, it wasn't that.

"I don't like the idea, either." She rubbed her hands along her arms, suddenly chilled. "But I'm sure he's an experienced professional who won't do anything to upset Kevin. We can't go on the way we are, letting him endure terrifying nightmares every night." She hesitated. "I wish I could feel I had your support." It was a plea for support. For understanding.

"Never." His voice was so harsh it startled her. "It would be better for Kevin if he never remembered what happened that night. As for your friend—" his face twisted on the words "—she was nothing but a tramp. She never should have come back to Echo Falls. It's time to forget her."

Deidre's emotions flared, her control faltering. "How can you say that? Dixie was a decent, honest person and a good friend."

"I told Frank he should exercise more control over you, but he wouldn't listen. If I'd had my way, she'd have been sent back where she came from the instant she showed her face here." His face flushed and his hands clutched into fists.

"Why?" She was so angry that the words spilled out. "Because you had an affair with her? Because you gave her Sylvia's diamond pendant?"

"Never!" He was almost shouting. "Your precious friend was a blackmailer. I would never have had a relationship with a woman like that. Never."

Deidre's breath caught in her throat. She suddenly stood at the edge of a precipice, and she had to back away quickly. But what could Dixie have known about the judge that would warrant blackmail? And how far had he been willing to go to protect that secret?

She clutched at her vanishing self-control. "Please, stop. We're both saying things we'll regret. You should leave now, and we'll forget this conversation ever happened."

"I can't do that." His eyes were like ice. How much did it cost him to keep that facade in place? "I can't leave until I have your promise to give up this plan of yours. I won't let you put Kevin in danger by forcing him to remember what happened to Dixie."

He took a step toward her. Her body recognized danger even before her mind did.

A cry ruptured the air. Deidre whirled toward the sound.

Kevin stood on the stairs in his superhero pajamas, the way he must have the night Dixie died. He pointed a shaking finger toward his grandfather.

"Dixie said he took her to the cabin." Kev's voice was high with fear, his eyes dark and unseeing. "Dixie said he hurt her. She said she'd tell. And he hit her."

Deidre ran toward her son, her heart pounding. If he took a step he might fall. Even as the thought formed, Kevin stumbled.

She threw herself forward, grabbing him. Her arms went around him, shielding him as she fell on the stairs.

Get up, run, go upstairs, away from him...

But even as she turned, trying to get her feet under

her, Deidre knew it was too late. The judge stood over them, holding the heavy brass lamp like a club.

"No! You can't do this—not to Kevin!" The cry came from her heart. Not Kevin—not his own grandchild.

"It's too late." His voice sounded normal, but his eyes were the eyes of a stranger. "Once I took care of Dixie I should have been safe, but then that ex-husband of hers came. Ready to take up blackmailing me. I'd have never been free. I had to act." He looked faintly regretful. "And now you."

"I don't understand." Her mind sought frantically for any way to delay the inevitable. "What did Dixie know? How could she be a threat?"

That distracted him for an instant. "What the boy said. She had no right refusing me. I could have sent her to a juvenile facility. I'd have helped her."

Helped her. Revulsion seized her. Dixie had only been thirteen when she left town. Was he saying what she thought…that he'd molested a child?

The revulsion must have shown in her face. He seemed to harden, swinging the lamp up, ready to strike.

"You can't! Not to your own grandchild!" Shuddering, she kept her body between her son and this madman.

Something crashed in the back of the house, distracting him for an instant. Billy stumbled in, white-faced, even as the front door burst open and Jason barreled toward them.

They weren't close enough. Was he mad enough to strike in front of witnesses?

"Not Kevin. You can't!" she cried again.

For an instant that lasted a lifetime, the lamp was poised above them. Then, slowly, he lowered it, letting it drop onto the stairs.

"No. You're right. I can't." He turned, walking steadily toward the door.

Jason moved as if to stop him, but he turned at a cry from Kevin, his face working. He rushed to them. "Is he hurt? I'll call for help…"

Deidre smoothed the hair away from Kevin's face. "Kev, does anything hurt? Tell Mommy."

Kev's eyes lost their unfocused look. His lips trembled. "Mommy? Jase?"

"Are you hurt, sweetheart?"

Kevin shook his head. Tears started to spill over. He threw one arm around her neck and reached for Jason with the other.

Jason put his arm protectively around both of them. "It's okay now. Nothing's going to happen to you."

"We're safe," she murmured, her heart filling with thankfulness.

Jason stiffened. As if reminded, he shot a glance toward the door. It stood open, and the judge was gone. "I should have stopped him."

Deidre clasped his hand. "We needed you. And maybe it's better this way," she said. "He knows it's over now. I don't think he'll go far."

Jason hesitated, but then he pressed his face against hers. "There's only one way out for him now."

IT FELT LIKE the middle of the night, but a glance at the clock told Jason it was only just after eleven. They were sitting around the kitchen table, having tacitly decided that the living room was no place to be just now.

Deidre wrapped her hands around a mug of steaming mint tea, although he hadn't seen her drink any of it. Judith hovered over him with the coffeepot, but he shook his head. He'd had enough caffeine to keep him awake for three or four days as it was.

Judith had arrived in response to the flashing lights and sirens at her friend's house. Her husband had apparently insisted on walking her over, but he'd retired to the back porch as if to give them more privacy.

Jase couldn't seem to take his eyes off Deidre for more than a few seconds at a time. He'd come so close to losing her that it didn't bear thinking about.

As if she felt his gaze, Deidre glanced at him, managing a slight smile, before her eyes returned to dwell on her son.

Kevin actually seemed far better than Jase would have thought possible. He had a cup of cocoa in front of him, but he didn't seem to be paying much attention to it. He was watching Billy, who'd pulled a penknife and a small stick from one of his numerous pockets and was busy shaping it into a snake.

Did the boy realize that his grandfather had intended to kill him? Or did he think it was all part of a nightmare?

Deidre was worried, obviously. He was, as well, but he suspected the five-year-old was more resilient than either of them.

There was a babble of sound at the front door, and

then Sylvia Morris erupted into the room. She'd dressed since he saw her, but that was about all he could say. Her hair stood out as if she'd combed it with her fingers, and her face still bore the traces of tears.

She heaved a sigh when she saw them. "You're safe. Thank the Lord you're safe."

Sylvia seemed ready to burst into tears again, and Deidre got up quickly and went to her. Obviously she didn't want an outburst in front of Kevin, who watched them with a bright, interested gaze.

Jase moved over next to the boy and directed his attention to the figure Billy was carving. "You think Billy could teach us how to do that?"

Kevin considered for a moment, and then shook his head. "Mommy says everyone has a gift. That's Billy's."

"Good thinking." He ruffled the boy's silky hair. "You're a pretty smart kid."

Kevin grinned and leaned against his arm as he switched his attention back to the deft movements of the knife.

It felt ridiculously good to have Kevin leaning against him, relying on him. He'd thought he'd lost the boy altogether, but he'd begun to have confidence they were going to be in each other's lives, no matter what.

The young patrolman the chief had left at the front door had followed Sylvia inside. At the moment he looked relieved that Deidre had taken over responsibility for Sylvia, talking to her quietly, arm around her.

Jase jerked his head, and the Jacobson kid came over to him. "Did you go get her?" Jase asked.

He shook his head. "She just turned up." He grinned.

"She said her garage was locked, so she backed her car right through the door to get here."

"I wouldn't have credited it." Jase suppressed a smile of his own at the idea of the usually immaculate woman crashing through a garage.

"Broke a taillight and left some dents in the trunk," the patrolman said. He sobered. "But there's some damage to the front of the car that I think the chief will be interested in. Might be the hit-and-run vehicle we've been looking for."

Jase wasn't surprised. "That's why he had the car locked up in the garage. Supposedly no one had driven it for months."

"Seems hard to believe. About the judge, I mean." The young man didn't seem able to assimilate the toppling of a pillar of society. "How could he think he'd get away with it?"

"Maybe he'd been in power so long he thought he could do anything." That was as close as he could come to an explanation. And it just might be the truth. How had he never seen how destructive the judge's need to control was? But no one else had, either, except possibly Sylvia. And Billy.

He glanced at Billy. Out there in the dark, stammering to get the words out, Billy had poured out the story. How he'd followed Dixie to the cabin that long-ago day, hopelessly devoted to her and not able to tell her so. He'd seen Judge Morris arrive. He'd heard the sounds and cries from the cabin, had guessed what was happening, but had been too afraid to go and help his friend.

Bitter tears had poured down his face as he confessed his weakness. He'd been afraid... All these years, he'd been afraid. But he couldn't let the judge hurt Kevin and Deidre. He couldn't.

Would he have done anything if Jason hadn't arrived when he did? Jason wasn't sure. Anyway, he had been in time. He'd sent Billy around to the back to create a distraction while he attempted to break in the front. A cold chill went through him at the thought of how close they'd come to not being on time. If he hadn't...

The front door opened, and everyone in the room looked up except for Billy and Kevin. Chief Carmichaels came in, glancing from one to another.

"Did you find him?" Jason stood, voicing the thought that was on all their minds.

"We did. Down along the river by the interstate bridge," he said heavily.

Jason asked the question with a look, and Carmichaels shook his head mutely before crossing to Sylvia and speaking to her in a low voice.

So it was over. Judge Morris had taken the only way out that was left for him. Jason couldn't manage to feel anything but relief that he was gone.

Unfortunately, the rest of them were still here. They'd have to bear that brunt of the unpleasantness that followed. Everyone in town would know what had happened, and why. The judge's reputation was splintered to dust, but how much would the rest of them suffer? Deidre had gone to put her arms around her mother-in-law, but her gaze met his over the woman's bent head.

A lot can be said with just a look. This one said that they were in this together. For now, that was enough.

DEIDRE WAS STILL heavy-lidded at three the next afternoon, but she clung to the thought that a few more nights would see the return of her ability to sleep. At least Kevin hadn't had a nightmare after she'd finally gotten him to sleep. Maybe the reality had been bad enough that he hadn't needed to dream about it.

She'd still keep the appointment with the child psychologist, of course, and follow any schedule he thought necessary for continuing visits. So much that had once been completely unthinkable had occurred in Kevin's young life, too much to let her take anything for granted.

She stood at the sink, looking out the window at Kevin and Benjamin chasing each other around the swing set. She'd been reluctant to leave them alone outside, but as Judith had sensibly reminded her, she would only make Kevin anxious if he felt she couldn't trust them.

"Can't let him out of your sight?" Jason spoke from the doorway. Judith stood behind him, having obviously just let him in.

"Something like that." Deidre felt oddly shy, as if they'd gone so far in their relationship over the past twenty-four hours that she needed to find a new balance.

"I'll go outside with the boys." Judith, smiling, glanced from her to Jason, rather obviously determined to leave them alone together.

When the door had closed behind her, Jason came to stand behind Deidre, looking over her shoulder at the children. "I was thinking that it might be a good idea to get Kevin a dog."

She blinked. "A dog? Why?"

Glancing up, she found he was watching her with a smile lurking in his eyes.

"Seems fitting—a boy and his dog. Part of a typical American childhood."

"We did always have dogs when I was growing up. Two Border collies—Daddy called them Ruff and Ready." She wrinkled her forehead. "Corny, I know, but as a kid I thought it was really clever."

"It'll be a good distraction for him." Jason put his arms warily around her waist, as if half expecting a withdrawal. "Something to love and talk to."

She nodded, pleased that his first thought had been for her son. "Good. We'll start looking for a puppy."

He seemed to relax at her response, coupling them together as he did. He drew her closer, so that she felt his strength.

"Sylvia stayed here the rest of the night," she said. "She just went home a short time ago."

"How is she?" He didn't seem surprised that she hadn't wanted to go back to that chilly mansion alone.

Deidre considered. "She's better than I'd have expected. She insists on taking over the funeral arrangements and dealing with all the things that have to be done. It'll be as quiet as possible, of course."

"Carmichaels is obviously relieved that he was spared arresting the judge. The story is out, but at least you won't have to go through a trial."

She nodded. "We're in for some rough times, but

I think Sylvia will get through it. She said that once it's over, she'll go for whatever treatment the doctors think best."

"I understand she's been in rehab in the past, but maybe this time it will be different."

She didn't blame him if he was skeptical, but with everything out in the open now, Sylvia might have a better chance of making it. "I think it might. She told me that she was determined to get well so she could be the grandmother Kevin deserved. She felt she failed Frank, but she's not going to fail her grandson."

Jason gave her a questioning look. "You still want her to be part of Kevin's life?"

"Of course. What happened wasn't her fault. The judge fooled everyone." She felt a frown beginning and tried to will it away. "I just wish…"

"What?" He studied her face, as if wanting to read her thoughts.

"What he said…about Frank thinking I'd been unfaithful. I just don't see how that could have been true. Wouldn't I have known?" The question needled her, refusing to be willed away no matter how she tried.

Jase was frowning, too, and she suspected he wished he'd never told her that. "He brought it up when he was pushing me to continue investigating. I wouldn't have taken it seriously, if he hadn't shown me the anonymous letter. But you can't blame yourself for what Frank might have imagined."

"Letter?" She caught at the word. "You didn't mention anything about a letter before." If someone had written an anonymous letter, the rumors must have been widespread. How had she not known?

"He showed it to me. A computer-generated letter, with no way of tracing it, citing the minister."

"Why him? And when did he get it?"

Jason shrugged. "I don't know why anyone would send it to him. He said it arrived a couple of months before Frank's death, so…"

"Wait. When?"

"He said he didn't remember exactly, but about then. He assumed maybe Frank had received one, too, and…"

"But that's impossible." Her bewilderment sounded in her voice. "Adam Bennett only took up his position here a few weeks before Frank's death. He didn't even have all his furniture moved in before having to deal with the services."

Jason seemed unable to do anything for a moment. Then his face hardened. "He did it himself."

"What?" Her mind was already reeling.

"The letter. I had shown doubts about the whole idea of investigating you, so he decided to provide me with a little more evidence. That's it. It has to be." His jaw clenched. "And then he sent a letter to Adam's wife, just to muddy the water a bit more."

"I want to say I don't believe it," she said slowly. "But when I think of everything else he did, I suppose that's a small deception. He seemed to feel anything he did was justified, as long as he got what he wanted." She shook her head. "I don't understand why no one started to wonder about him. I guess we were all so used to thinking of him as the respected judge, the pillar of the community, that we were blinded to everything else."

"He hid it well, but I suspect there were those who weren't sold on him. Billy knew the truth. Chief Carmichaels seemed to have some reservations. And Trey... Trey and I have done some talking. He'd begun to move very cautiously where the judge was concerned."

"He manipulated all of us in one way or another." Strange, but she was beginning to see him more clearly now, as if the blinders had been removed from her eyes. "But he wasn't able to hurt Kevin." She met Jason's gaze, hoping he understood. "At least I can remember that."

Jason gave a rueful grin. "You're more generous than I am. I almost wish he'd lived to stand trial so he'd be humiliated the way he deserved."

"No, you don't," she said gently. "You know how much that would have hurt the rest of us."

"I guess." He looked as if he wasn't quite as ready to accept what had happened. "We've still got a lot of cleaning up to do. And a lot of talk to live down."

"You wouldn't say that if you'd heard all the concerned calls I've gotten today, or seen the steady parade of people stopping by with food and offers of help. This will be a nine days' wonder, I know, but people are essentially good-hearted."

"I'm beginning to think Echo Falls is unique, not just for its falls, but for its people."

That was a good thought. She'd try to hold on to that. But in the meantime...

"Have you thought about what you're going to do?"

She'd thought she might have trouble asking the question, but it came out naturally.

"Actually, I had a long talk with Trey Alter today while we were trying to sort out what's left after the explosion." He leaned against the counter, looking more relaxed. "He suggests we team up, the two of us. Retain as many clients as we can save, and maybe add criminal defense to our bag. He thinks we could make a go of it."

She studied his face, not sure how he felt. "Is that what you want?"

Jason didn't answer directly. "I like Trey. He's a good guy. Honest, easy to work with." He met her eyes squarely. "I'd like it, but only if you want me to stay. You have every reason not to trust me, but I promise you that everything between us was real, no matter how it started. I want you and Kevin in my life. Forever."

She didn't doubt him, but still she hesitated. This wasn't a step to take lightly. From here there would be no turning back.

"We'll have to take our time, for Kevin's sake." She looked up at him, finding nothing but caring in his face.

"As much as you want." He touched her face with his fingers. "We can start again from the beginning, if you want."

For an instant she thought about Frank. What she'd had with him had been special. Knowing that he hadn't been unfaithful had been freeing. They'd loved each other as best they could, but that was in the past. Jason... Jason was the future.

She smiled at him, sliding her arms around his neck, and he straightened, drawing her close. "I don't think we need to go back that far. I don't want to forget how you've been there for me. Let's just move forward from where we are now."

There was a steady flame of love in his eyes as he lowered his head for her kiss. The future was theirs, together.

* * * * *

If you enjoyed Jase and Deidre's story,
don't miss the next book in the ECHO FALLS *series*

SOUND OF FEAR

Coming soon from Marta Perry and HQN Books!

STRS17